Praise for Wayn

"A literary giant who has god-given talent."

—Will Ferguson, *The Globe and Mail*

"If St. John's looms large in the Canadian literary psyche, this is due in no small measure to the novels of Wayne Johnston, a native of Newfoundland's capital city and one of its most diligent chroniclers."

—*Quill & Quire*

"A brilliant and accomplished writer."

—Annie Proulx, author of *The Shipping News* and *Barkskins*

"Johnston is a wondrous writer—of rich, irresistibly readable prose. He possesses a deft intelligence and a rare sense of what's truly interesting to tell about life." —Richard Ford, author of *The Sportswriter*

"A natural teller of complex, textured narratives. . . . Johnston writes very well and is unafraid of balancing the harshness of men with their humanity."

—*The Irish Times*

"Johnston spins wonderful stories; he is a gather-you-round-and-I-will-enchant-you raconteur. He has absorbed the world around him—the tall tales, the history, the epic of a place—and adapted it to a narrative style that is clearly his own. His stories charm and beguile. He writes about the ordinary and extraordinary people of Newfoundland with great empathy and without a shred of sentimentality. At the same time his fiction has a mythic quality. . . . [It] is subtle, his passion understated, his humour underpinned by tragedy. All of his work, superbly written, is a powerful combination of insight, talent and revelation. It is made to endure."

—Writers' Trust Engel Findley Award jury citation
(David Bergen, Joan Clark and Miriam Toews)

ALSO BY WAYNE JOHNSTON

The Story of Bobby O'Malley
The Time of Their Lives
The Divine Ryans
Human Amusements
The Colony of Unrequited Dreams
Baltimore's Mansion
The Navigator of New York
The Custodian of Paradise
A World Elsewhere
The Son of a Certain Woman
First Snow, Last Light
Jennie's Boy

WAYNE JOHNSTON

The Mystery of Right and Wrong

VINTAGE CANADA

VINTAGE CANADA EDITION, 2023

Published by Vintage Canada, a division of Penguin Random House Canada Limited, Toronto, 2023. First published in Canada in hardcover by Alfred A. Knopf Canada, a division of Penguin Random House Canada Limited, Toronto, 2021. Distributed in Canada by Penguin Random House Canada Limited.

Vintage Canada and colophon are registered trademarks of Penguin Random House Canada Limited.

www.penguinrandomhouse.ca

LIBRARY AND ARCHIVES CANADA CATALOGUING IN PUBLICATION

Title: The mystery of right and wrong / Wayne Johnston.
Names: Johnston, Wayne, author.
Description: Previously published: Toronto: Knopf Canada, 2021.
Identifiers: Canadiana 20210145455 | ISBN 9780735281653 (softcover)
Classification: LCC PS8569.O3918 M97 2023 | DDC C813/.54—dc23

Cover and interior design by Terri Nimmo
Cover image: Pedro Cunha / Unsplash

Printed in the United States of America

2 4 6 8 9 7 5 3 1

For Angela, untimely torn;
For Carol, who was second born;
For Barbara, third born, like me;
For you, the youngest, Rosemarie.

Before I found the yellow wood,
I fell in with the Sisterhood.
The silent sirens of these coasts
were mortal once but now are ghosts.
They lost their way one winter night
when they misread the Cape Spear light,
the flash of blue that comes and goes
at intervals that no one knows.
Unschooled in what the lost must do,
they sang and lost their voices, too.
Although the sirens could not sing,
they watched and witnessed everything.
They could not sing but they could write—
they wrote their songs night after night
until they solved, in their last song,
the Mystery of Right and Wrong.
The song they wrote no one has heard—
they taught it to me word by word.
I know it well but no one who
can sing the way that sirens do.

—Rachel van Hout, *The Arelliad*

CAPE TOWN

RACHEL

One Saturday, when I was seven, I climbed up onto the roof of our house in Rosebank. I stood on the rail of the back deck, hoisted myself onto the flat roof of the porch, shimmied up the drainage pipe onto the main roof, where, on my hands and in bare feet, I clung to the clay tiles, scrambled to the peak of the house and wrapped my arms around the chimney. The rough bricks warm against my cheek, I nodded off to sleep. I was spotted by a neighbour three houses down and woke to the sound of my father shouting, "Don't move, Rachel. Stay exactly where you are." Still holding the chimney, I threw one leg over the peak of the roof and sat astride it, looking down at all the people who had gathered to look up at me. I waved and some of them waved back. Some looked distraught, some took pictures. Two fire trucks came screaming down the street and parked along the curb. As a fireman was ascending his ladder, I told him I wouldn't let go of the chimney unless he promised to give me two rand once we were on the ground. He promised. I was rescued like a cat from a tree, the crowd applauding when we made it safely down. I saw my father give a two-rand coin to the fireman, who then gave it to me, though my father later took it back, had it framed and hung it on the wall of our front room. The caption read: "Rachel's Ransom." Side by side with the coin was a photograph of me up there on the roof, unconcernedly astride the house as if it was some enormous, well-tempered horse.

Among the many things pasted in the family photo albums was the brief correspondence that took place between me and the president of South Africa, Jim Fouché, in May of 1968. It began when, in school, we were asked to write a letter of appreciation to him. I wrote: "Dear Mr. Fouché, I am very glad to have you as a State President. Lots of Love and Kisses. XXXXX. Rachel van Hout." My father sent my letter with a covering note in which he described me as "a very sincere little girl" and hoped the president could take a moment to reply. Mr. Fouché wrote back, saying that he was "glad to have such a nice little girl as one of my people," and hoped I could visit his swimming pool so that "I can meet you and give you my kisses in return. Best regards and kisses. XXXXXXX Uncle Jim." My father replied to Mr. Fouché, claiming that he had had the letter framed and that it was now hanging on the wall above my bed. My mother explained this lie to me by saying, "Your father likes to remember things as they should have been."

There was a photograph of Dad in the albums, taken when he was a young man in Holland and not yet wearing glasses, though he was already balding. He is looking just to his right, away from the camera, sporting a neckerchief, dashing, intense, unyielding, trying to look modest about his feats in the Dutch Resistance, which all who saw the photograph would know him to be famous for, would admire him for, things he wished had never needed to be done and took no pleasure in remembering.

There was another photo showing Dad, in winter in Cape Town, smiling, sitting on a park bench surrounded by leafless trees and wearing a light coat that seemed to have a fur collar until you looked closer and saw that he was posing with a pet monkey wrapped like a stole around his neck. The monkey's name was Chimp. Dad appeared in many pictures thus adorned by Chimp, whom the rest of us couldn't stand. He was an unhygienic, ubiquitous nuisance, as likely to stretch out on the dinner table as to lie quietly beneath it at Dad's feet.

"The *four* girls," our parents called us, always emphasizing the *four* as if my father, Hans, and my mother, Myra, who always went by "My," were the first parents who had ever had to contend with having that many daughters but no sons. We were, in order of descending age: Gloria, Carmen, Bethany and Rachel. Hans was the lone male among a feminine collective of five. "We gave up trying for a boy," my mother often told people, whether she had just met them or had known them for years. "Hans was worried that, if we had a fifth girl in a row, he would feel like the last of his species." Girls' and women's things were everywhere around the house. Bras, nylons, tampons, knickers, high-heeled shoes, purses, dresses, compacts, tweezers, eyeliner, mascara, lipstick, earrings, necklaces.

The four girls. In the albums, we were often posed in descending order of age from left to right: the four girls riding on an elephant at Cape Town's zoo, facing sideways on a bench just wide enough to hold us all, me at the far right peering out from beneath the brim of the large straw hat that, from the age of four, I couldn't bear to be without; the four girls in front of the family car, or spanning the driveway, or perched like birds in the branches of a jacaranda tree in Pietermaritzburg, where Bethany was born; the four of us acting as flower girls at a wedding, dressed in white, wearing small crucifixes on chains around our necks, though the only thing the van Houts did religiously was go to lunch on Sunday.

We sailed away from South Africa on the *Edinburgh Castle* in late July of 1969—first class from Cape Town to Southampton, courtesy of a new and obscure university, such was its desperation for qualified faculty. The voyage, which followed the western coast of Africa north to England, took two weeks. In the albums, there were many mementos of the journey, including a photograph of my sisters and me taken at a party at which all the children in first class were issued personalized Neptune diplomas, signed by the captain, certifying that we had crossed the equator. Chubby-faced and beaming in the photo, my sisters and I are again wearing white dresses and have wide white hairbands, the four of us posing side by side, our Neptune diplomas at waist level, our resemblance to each other uncanny despite the discrepancies in height, our eyes as alike as those of quadruplets. We swam in the outdoor pool, which stayed open until late at night, and spent the balance of our time in the games room and the massive dining room, never going to our cabin until we were so tired that even thirteen-year-old Gloria had to be carried there by Dad.

There were photos of us bobbing for apples on the ship, me on my knees, head submerged in a plastic tub of water, my frilly white underpants showing; the four of us competing as a team in a tug-of-war with four other girls. But there were no shipboard photos of our parents. My mother had cried for days after my father told her we were leaving South Africa for Canada. Gloria didn't want to go either, because she had a boyfriend. I don't remember how Carmen and Bethany felt about it, but I was young enough to think that we were leaving everything, good and bad, behind.

It seemed to me that the migration of the van Houts, ultimately bound for a remote island in the North Atlantic, was an epic one, especially as we travelled by sea and were therefore so long in transit. Four girls uprooted from their childhood home and taken half a world away. Cultural displacement—a lot of things were attributed to that.

Every night, on the *Edinburgh Castle,* Dad read to us girls from something he'd been writing for years and called *The Ballad of the Clan van Hout*, the first time he read from it when we were not at home. He started with the opening passage because, he said, leaving South Africa reminded him of when he moved there from Amsterdam after the Second World War.

From *The Ballad of the Clan van Hout*, by Hans van Hout

THE PLEDGE (1962)
The guest room is the Ballad Room—
of all the rooms I like it best:
a guest room though we have no guests.
We meet here almost every night,
a banker's lamp the only light;
the four of you upon the bed
where you lie head by head by head by head.
I now begin The Night Salon—
I feel a bit like Lord Byron
reading to a room of women
overcome by adoration,
swooning on the Ballad Bed,
four cherubs on a snow-white cloud,
each one of you so smitten
by the words that I have written,
little angels in pyjamas
considering my every comma,
reflecting on my choice of rhymes,
cherubic critics of my lines.

My girls, this is my pledge to you
that every word I write is true.
I dedicate to all of you
The Ballad of the Clan van Hout
(for I am he, let no one doubt
who took the time to write it out).
Who tells this tale as well as me?
Who knows a life as well as he
who lived the life he writes about?
The Ballad of the Clan van Hout
is yours and will be when I'm gone,
solely, wholly yours alone—

these lines are for the four of you
(but not for Mother, though they're true).

Four muses! May you guide my pen:
(I think of Milton, who had nine—
the four of you inspire rhyme
far more than nine inspired him.)
The *Iliad*, the *Odyssey*:
I call upon your poetry
that I may meet the task ahead—
the Truth will out, as Shakespeare said!

You must read it to each other
(never speak of it to Mother),
the story of our family,
the four of you, your Mom and me,
until you know it word for word—
I mean it, girls, so mind my words—
until you know it word for word,
until you know it inside out,
The Ballad of the Clan van Hout.
This is a task of no great size—
rhymes are a cinch to memorize.
So memorize it line by line
(but never, never write it down . . .)
and page by page, and verse by verse.
(. . . or keep a copy in your purse!).
Say it softly to each other,
say it underneath the covers
(but not at the dinner table),
in your sleep if you are able.
When My van Hout is not about
the four of you can shout it out.
Say it aloud or in your head
when you are in the Sisters Bed,

the big bed that you all sleep in,
the biggest one that's ever been.
I'll read it to you every night
so that you'll get the words just right.
So say the words along with me,
or memorize them secretly.

I love it in the Land of Hout
when all my girls just lie about
the bed at night, eyes wide open
with delight as you listen
to me read to you about *us*,
not Peter Pan or Mother Goose,
not Heidi, or some kangaroos.
I read about the world you know,
things near at hand in our land,
our house, our merry band.
What better thing to read about
than the secret Land of Hout?
I spend my days awash in verse—
I write or mentally rehearse
a verse that I wrote long ago,
a verse that Gloria will know
and faithfully recite with me,
or interrupt, correcting me,
should I quote me unfaithfully.
My other three are mesmerized
by words that you don't recognize.
You hear the sound, you hear the rhymes
and you join in from time to time.
You look from Gloria to me
and chant with us uncertainly,
afraid of making a mistake
that will force Gloria to break
a line, to go back and restart

to prove she knows it all by heart.
Rachel guesses the meaning of words
from what she's seen and what she's heard:
the looks on her sisters' faces
are enough in many cases—
the squeals of laughter, gasps of fright—
the silence when the House by Night
appears, or demons climb the wall
and slide like ghosts into the hall.
You know the words so well it seems
they are the soundtrack of your dreams.

(The room is a tiny chapel,
not lit by flickering candles
but by that single banker's lamp
from which a golden chain hangs limp.
Green, and tilted at an angle,
it casts its light upon the bed—
there isn't light enough to read;
saying the words, I close my eyes
and see what I have memorized;
our voices in this solemn room,
five voices chanting in the gloom.)

Mother Myra must not hear it,
Mother My must not come near it.
She must not know the name of it,
let alone that she is in it.
The years will pass—if you forget
The Ballad of the Clan van Hout,
remember that I have it yet—
so come to me, I'll read again:
to think that you'll be women then!
You'll understand what it's about,
you'll understand the ways of men,

the reason some of them give out
before their time and some do not,
the sacrifices that I made,
the prices that could not be paid
without exaction from my soul
things that time could not make whole,
without the paying of a toll
that left me lesser than before—
you'll know all this and so much more.
Some men have no one but their wives—
they have no girls but only boys.
But Hans van Hout has five of you—
you all know that, I know you do.

I'm not the star that I should be
because so many worker bees
have spent their lives opposing me.
It's been so since the dawn of man,
the great held back by also-rans
who live lives of such fecklessness
they cannot tolerate success.

So promise me you won't forget
The Ballad of the Clan van Hout,
the man who left the Land Without,
which none of you know aught about,
to travel here from far away,
the wounds he suffers to this day.
I have been your loving father,
each of you my loving daughter:
you'll be my daughters all your life—
and She has had to be my Wife.

Things that we see fade like a dream
and what we see we soon forget.

What we forget soon reappears
though none of it is really there.
Girls, get used to contradictions,
truthful lies and false non-fictions.
What isn't there is everywhere;
the things which are, are not, you see,
however much they seem to be—
and what is not is what will be
as long as you and I agree.

ST. JOHN'S

1983

WADE

No one else from my small town went to university. I moved to the city straight out of high school. At university, I made few friends, set apart by my outport accent and my inclination to be a loner. I wanted to make my way into the greater world, on which, I fancied, my island birthplace had yet to make a mark, in part because so few books had been written about it, none of them good enough to earn the attention of my teachers, all of whom were from countries that no one I knew had set foot in. I dreamed that I would put my island on the map by writing about it as no one ever had or ever would. Books were what I most admired. Poets, novelists, philosophers and historians seemed to be pursuing Truth, something that, everywhere but in books, was unrecognized, mocked or forgotten. Only when I read a book did I feel that I was meeting a fellow uncompromising soul. These were not notions that I ever spoke aloud, for I was aware of how young and green they would have made me sound, how foolishly earnest and intense, besotted with ambition that would most likely come to nothing more than the kind of ordinary life to which others my age were sensibly reconciled.

By the end of university, I'd written nothing, because I believed that I was not ready to write. Instead, I'd devised a regimen of reading, a rigorous one that, so far, I had stuck to—five hours a night of making my way through all the big books of Western culture, most of which I hadn't encountered in the four years I'd spent getting my degree in English literature. I was a reporter for a small newspaper, a way station, I believed, on my journey to greater things.

When I wanted to escape my small apartment, I went to the university library to read, and it was there that I met Rachel van Hout. There have been few times when I can look back and say that there, exactly there, my life was changed. The moment I met her was one of them.

I had seen her before in the periodicals section, sitting at the head of a table whose chairs were otherwise empty, writing with her left hand in a paperback, pressing hard with her pen, her lips a tight line. I, too, was left-handed, often with a similar blue smudge on the heel of my hand. This time, she looked up for a moment and our eyes met, but she looked away as if she had known me for years and I was the last person she wanted to see. She was there again the next night, in the exact same place. She sat there, facing the entrance to the section, like a receptionist to whom I was required to state the purpose of my visit.

I wandered about among the stacks for a few minutes and then headed toward the door, but I couldn't resist another glance in her direction. "Hi!" she said when our eyes met, again acting as if she'd known me for years but this time was glad to see me. I walked over to her.

"What are you reading?"

"I am *re*reading—" she raised the book so I could see the cover—"*The Diary of Anne Frank*."

"I read that in grade school, grade eight, I think."

"You outgrew it long ago."

"No, I—"

"Not me, though I also read it in grade five, six, seven, eight, nine and ten. Long story. Mine, not hers. Hers was all too short. She's still my favourite writer. I'll never outgrow this book. It shouldn't be called *The Diary of Anne Frank*. It's called that because that's what the Broadway play and the movie were called. *Het Achterhuis* is what she called it. Dutch. It means 'The Secret Annex.' For a while, the book was called *Anne Frank: The Diary of a Young Girl*."

"You seem to know a lot about it."

"I have a personal connection to it. Through my father. Dad grew up on Elandsstraat, two streets away from the Secret Annex, which is on Prinsengracht in Amsterdam. Mom and Dad go to Holland a lot.

And other places. We're travel poor. Everything I'm wearing is home-made by me or my mother. Only my shoes are store-bought."

She wore a handkerchief-like head scarf, a too-big yellow blouse, a long white skirt that was so heavy and stiff it might have been fashioned from a sail.

"Holland, Switzerland, South Africa. My parents visit acquaintances and distant relatives in all three countries once a year. My sisters and I took turns spending a summer in Switzerland when each of us was fourteen. My sisters went alone but I went with my mother. Long story. We stayed in the Alps at my father's third cousin's house. He died last year and his wife is too old for visitors, but my parents still know plenty of people who are willing to put them up and put up with them when they drop in unannounced."

The torrent of words left her flushed and breathless. She'd spoken as if she'd had to get it all out in a preordained amount of time. I wondered how much of what she had just said was true. I wondered if there might be something wrong with her.

"I've seen that look before," she surprised me by saying. "My name is Rachel van Hout. My father is a professor in the accounting department here. I was born in Cape Town, South Africa. I finished my growing up in Newfoundland. Would you like my rank and serial number?" She had a way of not looking at me while she spoke that made it seem like she was transfixed by someone looking at *her* from behind me. I kept wanting to glance over my shoulder.

"A lot of what I just said is from something I wrote and memorized years ago."

"I have to go," I said. She nodded and went back to her book as if she'd expected me to say those very words.

The next night, I barely recognized her, though she was sitting in the exact same place, jotting down, it might have been, the names of those who came and went. She wore a red cotton dress that fit perfectly. No longer tied up with a scarf, her brown hair hung down her back, almost to her waist, parting over each shoulder so that two long strands of it hung down the front as well, flanking a row of buttons undone in a deep V. Her outfit of the day before had made me overlook her eyes—wide, brown, long-staring eyes, whose effect on me she seemed not to notice. Every inch of her bare skin was deeply tanned. Even her feet were, her Birkenstock sandals kicked off on either side of them.

I paused beside her table. "You're still reading that book."

"I'm still *re*reading it." She didn't look up. Suddenly, and loudly, she snapped the book shut.

"I'm sorry I interrupted—"

She put up her hand to stop me and rose from her chair. "I'm going outside for a while," she said as she slipped her feet into her Birkenstocks. "You may join me if you like." She headed for the exit, walking at the pace of someone storming off in a huff. We were outside by the time I caught up with her. She removed her sandals on the last of the library steps and walked barefoot through the grass and onto the parking lot, which we crossed to get to a handful of picnic tables on the far side. We sat opposite each other. "My name's Wade," I said.

Removing her shoulder bag and placing it on the table, she crossed her legs, reached down and massaged one foot. "The soles of my feet are not as tough as they used to be, Wade," she said. "As kids, in South Africa, we never wore shoes. We climbed trees barefoot, walked everywhere barefoot. We were always getting cuts from thorns and broken glass, and splinters from broken branches, but we didn't care. My calluses became so thick I could have walked on burning coals. I cut my leg once on a rusty nail and fell asleep while my dad drove me to the doctor. Pretty weird. I have three sisters but no brothers. Two of them got married when they were nineteen, but not because they had to. Four daughters born at two-year intervals, almost to the month, aged thirteen, eleven, nine and seven when we left Cape Town. Oh, and let me show you a picture of my unmarried sister, Bethany. She has anorexia."

She rummaged in her shoulder bag and held out a photograph of a girl in a green bikini. Smiling, her arms outstretched, Bethany ran toward the camera, her body like that of the little napalm-burnt Vietnamese girl on the front page of the *New York Times*. Rachel put the photograph back in the bag. "How big is *your* family?" she said.

"I have three brothers and two sisters. Mom had four boys in a row and then two girls."

"It must have been hard for the first girl."

"Cathy? Not really. The four of us raised her. Mom and Dad both worked until a couple of years ago."

"Hmm. My name's Rachel, in case you don't remember."

"I remember."

She nodded. "Someday I might tell you about the ballad," she said. "*The Ballad of the Clan van Hout*. Something Dad wrote for us in rhyme when we were kids. He'd read it to us at bedtime. You must never tell Dad or Mom or my sisters that I mentioned it to you. I mean, you may never meet them, I'm not saying that. It's not as if we're engaged. I'm saying just in case. It's a small town, after all." Then she shook her head slightly, rolled her eyes and sighed. "Look, Wade, if you're still sitting here because I'm so beautiful, you may as well leave now."

Just before that last sentence, I'd thought about leaving.

Eyes downcast, she looked as if she expected me to go, perhaps even wanted me to. "It's okay," she whispered. Those wistfully spoken words, which seemed meant to reassure her, not me, convinced me to stay. I felt like whispering her name.

We met several nights in a row at the picnic table. I spoke of things I had never spoken of before. I had told few people of my plan to be a writer, but enough for it to have become common knowledge. Among the reporters at the paper I worked for and those who worked for other papers in the city, I was known as "Shakespeare." When the nickname was first coined, I had had sense enough to take it good-naturedly, and that was how, for the most part, it was used. At worst, I was regarded as amusingly delusional by my co-workers and rivals, all of whom were older than me.

I didn't talk about writers or books, and probably wouldn't have had there been anyone around to talk about them with, my reticence owing to a near-superstition that my chances of ever doing or becoming *anything* would have lessened in direct proportion to how covetous of success I revealed myself to be.

In my world, the gods rewarded ambition, ostentatious or not, with humiliating failure, which I so wanted to avoid that I numbered myself among those I had to hide my secret from. I didn't keep a diary or a journal. I didn't read about writers who were not among my favourites. I read far more poetry, philosophy and history than fiction, though fiction is what I wanted to write.

Everything Rachel told me about herself seemed exotic. She told me she was the star pupil of her drill-sergeant-like yoga teacher, who belonged to an especially rigorous school of yoga called Iyengar-Hatha, named after the man, Iyengar, who invented it—a man with whom her teacher had had an affair while in India, as had almost all the women he taught, as if women could not fully get the knack of the Iyengar method without sleeping with him. She seemed to think this was not only entirely reasonable, but something she would do if Iyengar was not so far away. "I do three or four hours of yoga a day. It's one of the few perks of still being subsidized by your parents when you're twenty-one. I'm told I'm not quite ready for a job."

"Not ready?"

"Long story."

She *looked* ready for anything. She exuded an air of perfect poise and had the straight-backed posture of a ballet dancer. She was tall, slender but big-breasted, round-eyed and quick to smile, as if the sight of everything delighted her. When I told her that I was a newspaper reporter, she seemed impressed, as if she didn't know my employer was a tabloid that made up the news almost as often as it got it wrong. "It's only until I save up enough money to be able to take time off to write a book," I said.

"What kind of book?"

I said, "A novel."

To which she replied, "Oh, really? Fiction or non-fiction?" She burst out laughing at the look on my face. "I'm kidding," she said. "A lot of novelists were newspaper reporters. Ernest Hemingway was, wasn't he? For the *Toronto Star*?"

I was impressed that she knew of Hemingway's brief stint at the *Star*. I told her I thought that, in order to write about Newfoundland, I would have to leave it.

"Because of things that have happened to you here that you can't bear to be reminded of," she said, nodding. "I took you for a tortured soul the second I laid eyes on you." I must have looked as sheepish as I felt, because she sighed. "Erase all that," she said. "I misplaced my irony. Where did I put it?" She rummaged in her shoulder bag. "I know it's in here somewhere." I laughed. "Thank God," she said, glancing up for a moment. "I thought you missed it altogether." She took out a pack of cigarettes. "Want one?"

"No thanks," I said. I'd quit smoking because I couldn't afford it. She shrugged and lit up a cigarette with a Bic lighter. "I only average one or two a week," she said, "if you count every day since I was born."

I told her that what I'd meant about getting away was that, in order to write, I would need the perspective that only distance and the passage of time would allow—otherwise, the people and things I would write about would be ever-near, ever-present, inhibiting. I said that I would be muted by the immediacy of the landscape to whose desolate beauty my writing would never do justice unless recollected in tranquility.

"Erase that last sentence," she said. She raised her eyebrows and shook her head in mock wonderment. "You sound younger than you look. I think it's sweet. My mother . . ." She threw back her head and laughed as one might at someone else's punchline, her mouth so wide her back teeth showed, then resumed the sentence, thereby stepping on a remark that might have seemed as funny to me as it did to her. "My mother once wrote a sixty-seven-word short story about two goldfish. The male goldfish ate the female goldfish. The story was called 'We Two Are Now One: A Marriage Allegory.'"

"Your mother is a feminist," I said.

She laughed again, her eyes wide with incredulity. "Yes. In the same way that the pope is Jewish."

RACHEL

I told him I was ten when I first read *Het Achterhuis*. I joined the Anne Frank fan club. It cost fifty cents to join and the money went to the upkeep of the Secret Annex. They would send photographs of Anne and some of the others she shared the annex with, Anne in Germany at various ages when there was as yet no need to move to Holland or for hiding out, Anne in a beach chair with a book on her lap, Anne wearing what looked like a new pair of glasses, Anne posing on a beach somewhere with her sister, Margot. Anne before the world went stark raving mad. There were quizzes about her life and her diary, and essay-writing contests about what Anne Frank meant to you or to the world. For a while, I thought of her as a fictional character like Anne of Green Gables. Anne of the Secret Annex. Often, I wished I was her.

Then I read survivors' accounts of her time at Bergen-Belsen concentration camp, and soon I had pictures in my mind of her and Margot shorn of all their hair, unclothed, barefoot, peering through a barbed-wire fence as if they had never seen a camera before and assumed it to have some sinister purpose.

Nothing really bad happened in *Het Achterhuis*, so I tried to concentrate on that. But images of Bergen-Belsen kept interfering. I knew she was dead but I couldn't stand to be reminded of it by my sisters, who did it because they grew so tired of hearing me talk about her that they began calling me the Anne Frank Freak, a nickname that caught on at school.

I often thought of her father, travelling by train from Auschwitz to Amsterdam in 1945, after the war ended. He found out on the train that his wife had died in Auschwitz, but he hoped to be told in Amsterdam that Anne and Margot had survived Bergen-Belsen.

My mother made me promise not to mention *Het Achterhuis* to my father and to keep the book hidden from him lest it remind him of the wartime suffering he endured and witnessed in Amsterdam, and of the Jewish girls of his daughters' ages who, like Anne Frank, were mass murdered in the Holocaust. It was a book he couldn't stand the sight of, she said, because it made him imagine what being helpless to save his own daughters from the Nazis, what being separated from them forever upon arrival at a concentration camp, would have been like. He knew Jewish fathers who had survived the camps but whose children had not—men like Otto Frank, who were heartbroken, haunted by guilt, conscience-stricken—fathers whose sons and daughters were failed by the Resistance, of which, she reminded me, my father was a member. That was how he thought of it, she said: he and his comrades had failed them. For no matter how many you saved, it was the ones you didn't save that you remembered and imagined. She said he was too modest and too haunted by the horrors of the war to talk about it or stand to be publicly acknowledged for his heroism.

I didn't keep my promise to my mother to be discreet with *Het Achterhuis*. I took to reading it in front of my father, the story of two Jewish families and an unmarried Jewish dentist who lived for years in hiding under the very noses of the Nazis, in defiance of them, held together and sustained by the most powerful of bonds, those of family, a shared past, a common origin and purpose, until they were secretly betrayed, possibly by a fellow Jew, the moral being—according to my mother—that unless everyone pulls together, they will be destroyed. "I want you to be proud of your father," she said, "even if he never knows how proud you are."

I read *Het Achterhuis* for hours on end right in front of my father and he didn't seem to notice. I read and wore to pieces so many copies that I wound up wearing Band-Aids on my fingertips because of paper cuts.

Anne Frank had seen an autograph album in a store window and thought it would make a good diary because it had a clasp and it was bigger than most diaries, so it would take a long time to fill up all the pages. Yet she sometimes went for days without writing in it. I could never do that. Her first diary was covered in red and white plaid cloth and had a lock that she opened with a key. My first diary was a black date book that I stole from a stationery store.

WADE

In my world, no one was from anywhere but Newfoundland. Certainly no one was from South Africa. I assumed that everything about her was South African. No one did yoga or was, as she had confided one night, a vegetarian. If I had any image of a vegetarian, it was that of a pasty-faced, skinny, slump-shouldered university professor with an unkempt beard who wore knee-high rubber boots, disapproved of pleasure and tried to turn his students into communists.

Where I came from, no one's father was a university professor or had been a member of the Dutch Resistance. No one had been to Switzerland, let alone claimed to have been bored by it. No one who had a TV set was unsure if it worked. There was no such place where the lone television channel broadcast four hours a day, offering only endlessly repeated episodes of *The Brady Bunch* and *The World at War* and government-censored newscasts.

No one who looked like her claimed to have three better-looking sisters.

We met several more times at the picnic table by the parking lot, which was unlit but for a single street lamp swarmed by moths and mosquitoes.

"I have a bit of a reputation," she said one night. "I'm kind of a loner."

"So am I."

"I'm sure you think you are. Still, I'm much, much better than I used to be."

"What do you mean?" I said.

"Just kidding."

She leaned slightly toward me across the table. "I think you should ask me out," she said. "You don't have to, but I think you should." It sounded as if she was offering advice that, if I followed it, would have no effect on her but would be good for me. "I'm not . . . entirely normal, as I'm sure you can tell," she continued before I could respond, "but I think that you should ask me out."

I did ask her out, not because she advised me to, but because of how I felt every time she smiled when she set eyes on me after we had been apart. Never in my life had the sight of me made anyone seem so happy.

We went to the cinema to see *Hair*. While we were standing in line, she said, "You save my spot. I'll be right back." I thought she was going to the bathroom, but she came back with two dipped-in-chocolate soft ice cream cones and gave me one. "Better to eat them fast," she said after swallowing a great gulp. "We're not allowed to take them inside." During the movie, she took hold of my hand. The ice cream and the hand-holding seemed part of a routine. Was this what a white woman from South Africa customarily did on dates? I liked posing that silly question to myself about almost everything she did. After the movie, we went back to her father's car, a rusting white Malibu Classic in which she had driven us to the movies. It had a hole in the floor through which you could see the road as it went whizzing by.

"You may kiss me now," she said before she started up the car. I did. She declared that I was a very good kisser. "You don't just pucker up and press like most guys do. So we're going to my house but we're not going to bed. I'm unseducible. Don't even bother to try."

She drove across town, up a steep hill, then pulled into the driveway of a somewhat dilapidated two-storey house. "Welcome to 44 Freshwater Road," she said.

When we were inside, she left the lights off but lit the coal fireplace. Standing with her back to the flames so that I could barely make her out, she took off her clothes, lay down on the rug and held out her arms to me.

"I didn't come prepared," I said.

"I did."

"That was my first time," she said, stretching out with her arms above her head. "Don't be fooled. I was scared to death."

"It didn't feel like it was your first time."

"Well, that's thanks to my sister Gloria, who gave me a certain gadget that starts with *d* and ends with *o*. She said that it was important that my first time wouldn't seem like my first time to the boy I was with. I believed her. I wanted to be cool. Gloria said that, although a man would think it was great to take your virginity, he wouldn't want you after that because he would compare you to other girls who, having had experience, were better in bed." She laughed. "My mother is just the opposite—she says no man will want you for his wife if he finds out that you *aren't* a virgin. She says that it's okay to sleep with someone once you're engaged to them, but men will reject you if you let them sleep with you before that."

"Neither of my parents has ever mentioned sex to me. I guess they're pretty old-fashioned."

"Well, don't mistake mine for being progressive. My mother made me promise to tell her if I lost my virginity before I got engaged, so I guess I'll have to do that when she gets back from Switzerland. I think she thought the prospect of having to confess something so embarrassing to her would keep me chaste."

"You're going to *tell* your mother?"

She threw back her head and laughed as if the joke was on her.

From *The Arelliad*, by Rachel van Hout

FIRELIGHT (1983)

I must try not to think in rhyme
lest I be rhyming all the time,
declaiming out loud, in my head,
as Dad did on the Ballad Bed.
To rhyme in dreams and memories,
in reveries and diaries
until I lose my mind in rhyme—
that punishment would fit my crime.

"If you choose love, kiss life goodbye,"
My Shadow She told me today.
"You won't have love for very long,
so, clearly, choosing love is wrong.
Better to be a survivor
than to be a short-lived lover
that your Wade will not remember;
this novelist that you adore
may not be long for 44.
Few things are what you think they are.
Let's not forget, that's why you're here
and why you see what isn't there."

I know he's there, I've tasted him,
I've felt his hands upon my skin—
I know he's there, I took him in—
the smell of summer in his hair
last night when he first touched me where
I've never touched myself before.
There was no yellow sky last night;
the fireplace, the firelight,
the flames that warmed the wooden floor—
of those, at least, I can be sure,
of those, at least, if nothing more.

I've been fooling Wade. I don't think he notices the changes in me from day to day—the smudge of blue ink on my hand that is getting bigger and darker. No amount of scrubbing can wash that ink away. (I may end up like Macbeth's wife, who bore the blame but not the knife. She had no luck with Duncan's blood. What isn't there will drive you mad much faster than what is.) Even if he saw it, Wade wouldn't know it was proof that I've been where I shouldn't be, writing almost constantly in Arellian, as I have been for the past four years.

Arellia. Every time I go there, it's like returning home. I'll never lose the language that I've spoken since the night that I invented it. Arellian. I know the words for everything, the things I see that aren't there, the yellow sky that was overcast the winter night a teenage girl was killed. The only light was the lighthouse light that came and went, out of sync with the muffled blare of the foghorn at Cape Spear.

How real love seems to be in books, where it happens all the time. I've never been in love before. Is it too soon to call this love—I slept with him; what does that prove? Some days, I spend more time in Arellia than I spend in what people like to call the Here and Now. If he knew, Wade would make a quick escape. Doc told me I could trust my heart, if not my mind. Large-hearted me, I fooled Doc well. And if I add a broken heart to a broken mind?

No matter what my Shadow She
predicts is in the cards for me,
another break, something the rhymes
have been withholding all this time,
the fate that once was hers is mine—

How can I deny that something new has begun at last?

WADE

We took to sleeping in her parents' bed, the only full-sized one in the house. "If they only knew," she said one night.

"Won't your neighbours notice that I'm sleeping over?"

Rachel shrugged. "I told Mom and Dad about you on the phone. I said that you might sleep over sometimes, but that we wouldn't sleep together. They either believed me or pretended to."

"They don't care what the neighbours think?"

"Not as long as the neighbours say nothing to them about it. Which they won't, because they never speak to the neighbours other than to say hello."

"If your parents can't wait to get out of here and go travelling, why did your family move to Newfoundland in the first place?" I asked.

"Well, it wasn't because we heard good things about it, because we'd never heard of it at all until Dad told us we were moving here. It was more of a beggars can't be choosers kind of thing. No offence. Actually, it was more of a man who's a failure in a country with a perfect climate reckons his chances of prospering might be better in a country where, because of the climate, no one with a grain of sense would want to live kind of thing. Again, no offence. Not even to Dad, who I don't really think of as a failure. It's just that he says whatever's on his mind without thinking of the consequences. It doesn't matter who he's talking to."

She told me that her father graduated in commerce from the University of Amsterdam and then became a chartered accountant, only to have to retire from accounting in his early thirties because of fast-failing eyesight. He moved to South Africa in the hope that a friend in Cape Town, whom he had known when they were children in Amsterdam, could help him get a job with South African Airways—the company his friend worked for. When he was turned down by South African Airways, he applied for the job of lecturer in accounting at the University of Cape Town. Chartered accountants who were willing to forego the private sector in favour of teaching at any level, let alone that of a lecturer without tenure and benefits, were rare. He got the job and, in a few years, rose to assistant professor, but it became apparent over the next decade that, without an advanced academic degree, he would never again be promoted. He completed a master's at the University of Cape Town but, by this time, had managed to alienate most of his colleagues by repeatedly telling his department head that they were incompetent as teachers and accountants. Given that the tenure committee consisted largely of his colleagues, he was told that he wouldn't get tenure at the University of Cape Town if he had a fistful of advanced degrees.

At age forty-three, he decided to uproot his entire South African–born family to start all over again elsewhere in what was known as the White Commonwealth at some university where he could be both a teacher and a student until he earned his Ph.D., soon after which, he believed or hoped, he would be named a full professor. He applied for non-tenured jobs at every university in Australia and New Zealand but failed to get so much as an interview. He worked his way down the list of possible institutions until there were none left but those of Canada, every one of which, except a fledgling university in Newfoundland, ignored his letters. Memorial University, which had been founded just six years before, sent him an encouraging reply. He was hired after answering in writing a series of examination-type questions that were sent to him. The university, MUN as it was called, agreed to pay all the expenses of moving him and his family to St. John's.

In South Africa they had lived as well-to-do people did in Newfoundland. They had servants, a maid and a gardener. South Africans leaving the country for any length of time were allowed to take only a small amount of money with them, so Rachel's parents sold everything they had, combined the proceeds with their life savings and spent almost every cent on furniture and furnishings far more expensive than they had hitherto been able to afford, the result being that they were house poor before they even got their first glimpse of Newfoundland. Having had a maid and other black servants all her life, Rachel's mother was as disinclined to keep house as she was inept at it, and her father had lost whatever home repair skills he might once have had in Amsterdam.

By the time I first saw it, the furniture still outshone the house to the point of looking absurdly incongruous. In the very expensive buffet, there was very expensive but ill-maintained china—twelve pieces of everything, all white with a gold trim that was chipped in many places or dulled to near-invisibility. It had arrived at the house fourteen years earlier, packed in large wooden crates, every piece of it intact. The six of them broke up the crates and burned them in the fireplace, which they huddled around for warmth, though it was August—the house was drafty and an August night in Newfoundland was cooler than a winter night in Cape Town—and it was a week before they could afford to fill the coal bin.

Now they had never-burnished silverware, a dining table so long and wide it took up nearly all the space in the dining room, making it difficult to squeeze between the chairs and the wall. The green velvet sofas and armchairs in the front room were pocked with burns from cigarettes and marijuana joints, the never-tended-to damage caused, Rachel said, by four precocious girls who, when their parents travelled, were left to fend for themselves and pretty much ran riot, turning the van Hout house into the neighbourhood's most popular party space.

There was a dusty, top-of-the-line Steinway piano that none of them ever learned to play. It stood on hardwood that sagged beneath its legs, splintered hardwood with treacherous up-jutting nails, blackened with dirt where one strip met the other. The walls had not been repainted since the van Houts moved in. The curtain rods drooped, so that the bottoms of the curtains lay crumpled on the floor. But 44 was a summer paradise to me.

—

I lived on the top floor of a five-storey building, in an apartment that had long ago been written off by the owners, who didn't know that the superintendent rented it out on the sly at half price. It had been a one-bedroom apartment, but the walls of the bedroom were gone, no sign of them remaining but a square black stain on the parquet floor. The super had furnished the apartment with a folding card table, an ancient box spring and mattress, and a sofa whose rear legs were missing, so that it tilted backwards like a recliner. In the bathroom there was another square-shaped stain on the wall above the sink where there must once have been a medicine cabinet and mirror. In the kitchenette, there was a two-burner stove and a half-sized fridge with a freezer that was fully crammed with frost. If I tried to thaw it, the super said, the Freon would escape.

But the place suited me. It needed no maintenance and was devoid of all diversions. I didn't have a TV or phone because I was saving for a grubstake that would allow me to quit my job and write my novel. I'd never had a room of my own, one to read in undisturbed by others. On those nights when I didn't see Rachel, I sat at the card table, side on to the window that overlooked the parking lot, the window from which, when I looked up from my book, I watched the slantwise driven rain by the light of a distant street lamp. Rachel called the place my garret, a touch of irony in her voice, I thought, as if she was teasing me, the writer who had yet to write a word. She sometimes spent the night. Given the state of the van Hout house, she was unfazed by the state of mine.

In late July, Rachel and I went to the long, sandy beach at Eastport, about two hours from St. John's. In spite of how fit she was from doing yoga, she was hopeless at running. We ran along the wave-flattened sand at the edge of the water. I ran faster backwards than she could forwards, the two of us facing each other as we ran, she laughing so hard she would stop now and then and put her hands on her knees, out of breath, her sea mist–drenched hair hanging almost to the ground.

In the Malibu, which I always doubted would start but always did, we drove the Irish Loop, a four-hour trip that included a long stretch of the Trepassey barrens, where the car was so hemmed in by fog that we had no hope of seeing, or even hearing, the caribou herd we had come to photograph. But even such futility struck us as hilarious.

From *The Ballad of the Clan van Hout*

THE EARLY DAYS OF HOUT (1962)
Across the veldt HVH roamed.
(His monogram, a palindrome,
was engraved upon his rings,
as well as many other things,
his tie clip and his money clip,
his pocket flask and pillow slips!)
He liked the look of this new Land,
so it was here he made his stand,
and it was here your parents met,
the best part of the story yet.

You can't be a proper family
Unless you number at least three.
Soon, our number rose to six,
which left us in the strangest fix.
We made up names night after night
because, by morning, we forgot
which names were yours and which were not.
But suddenly it came to me:
it might be easier if we
referred to you collectively.
We called you Glormenethalee.
"Now there's a name we won't forget,
the strangest name we've made up yet."
(Glor)ia was almost eight
by the time she got it straight:
"She is daughter number one,
Car(men) is two more than none,
B(etha)ny is number three,
and last is little Rachel (Lee),
and that spells Glormenethalee."
—

When Hans said "sun," the sun came out—
it hid behind what Hans called "clouds."
When Hans said yes, such happiness—
for certain things were now allowed.
Young Hans said this, Young Hans said that—
soon, this and that were everywhere.
When Hans said "hat," a hat appeared;
Of course it wasn't called a hat
until he said, "Let's call it that."

As the family grew and grew
the fame of Hans van Hout did too,
at least among his family,
for there was no one else, you see,
in all the land of Hans van Hout
that he could tell the truth about
what happened in the Netherlands,
no one who'd ever understand
what his family understood—
that Hans was brave and Hans was good
but there were secrets to be kept,
things done to people while they slept,
while others looked the other way
so some at least could get away.
When you are forced to compromise,
to serve the truth by telling lies,
when you must abandon some
or else abandon everyone,
you'll understand why even Hans
could not abide the Netherlands.

We were safe in the House Within—
no one got in, no one got out.
But still there was a constant din
of noises from the Land Without.
Hans sealed the windows, locked the doors,

cemented all the cracks and pores
and thumbed his nose at those Without
who coveted the girls of Hout.
He kept one eye out for the horde
who wanted in, and one eye out—
O, ever-vigilant van Hout—
for those who thought they wanted out.

He barred the house both day and night;
there was no air, there was no light.
You couldn't breathe or see the sun;
it seemed that Death itself had come.
Hans thought of aught to do but think—
you heard him thinking all night long
of someone who was on the brink
of doing something very wrong.
You heard him thinking through the night
about what was and wasn't right.
Just when you thought you heard him say
that Wrong would never go away,
Hans said that Right had won the day.

There was the house by day,
there was the house by night.
By day you couldn't say
what was or wasn't right.
By night you couldn't think a word
for even thinking could be heard
in the silent house by night.

I tell you now, there's nothing worse
than knowing how the universe
is fixed for sheep that cannot sleep
because you count them every night
and always get the number right.
The five of you, each one a ewe—

I might as well be counting you.
A drink of rum might knock me out
but there is never drink about.
I'd never think of sleeping pills—
I haven't yet and never will.
Why do they say, "*If* walls could speak?"
As certainly as floorboards creak,
these walls can speak, they always have—
some things they say are very bad,
but that is not to say untrue:
walls tell the truth, you know they do.
They never say that I am good,
no matter how I wish they would.
From deep inside his inner ear,
Time is the sound that Hans can hear,
the sound it makes as it goes by.
He cannot sleep and that is why
he drowns out Time with other sounds—
the ones he makes while making rounds,
as if I have it in my head
that you don't hear me leave the bed,
open the door, creep down the stairs,
the creaking stairs that no one hears.
I walk about the rooms below,
roaming from window to window—
I never bother with the lights:
I like to stare out at the night,
recalling this, recalling that,
though frankly I would rather not
recall at all the kinds of sounds
the Germans made while making rounds,
their boots upon the cobblestones
of Amsterdam night after night,
a cry for help, someone in flight
that ended when a shot rang out
far from the house of Hans van Hout.

WADE

"I haven't told you how I came to be known as the Anne Frank Freak," Rachel said. We were sitting on the floor in front of the fire in the front room on a weekend night. "I went through a kind of phase that started when I was thirteen. It lasted from the first time I became *very* obsessed with her book to when I was released from hospital, almost two years later. Yes, I am talking about *that* kind of hospital. My sister Carmen was a secretary for a while. She wrote outrageous things in shorthand on pieces of paper and left them all over the house, things about what drugs she was doing and who she got them from and what she did to get them—I think she made up a lot of it. I asked her to teach me shorthand, but she said it had taken her months to learn and she didn't have the time. So, instead, I made up a pretty simple alphabet code I call "Arellian." The first and last letters of my name, Rachel, are *R* and *l*. *R-l-e-n*. Arellian. Get it?"

"How does the code work?"

She frowned. "No one else knows, so there's no need to feel left out. I left my own risqué notes around the house. It was just for fun, kids' stuff. Other girls at school had codes too. When we got around to studying *Het Achterhuis*, I came up with the idea of writing a diary in Arellian. It was the kind of thing that most teenagers would get bored with in a few days, but I didn't get bored. I started out writing about as much per day as Anne Frank did. Then I sort of became addicted to diary writing—*diarizing* is the word for it. I wrote for quite a few hours every day. I also read Anne Frank's book a lot. A *lot*. I became a hypergraphic, hyperlexic bibliomaniac with a major in Anne Frank.

The Triple Crown of Craziness, Bethany called it. Now the hyperlexia is gone and I only read her book when I feel like it. When I was sick I read it so often that I memorized it. I did. I can quote it, chapter and verse. The hypergraphia is gone too. In the library, when I was writing in the book, I was just making a few notes—grad school habit. I don't keep a diary. When I did, I wrote so many pages a day that I wound up having a kind of breakdown. Her book is still like a security blanket, I suppose. I don't go anywhere without a copy."

"That's your big secret?" I said, trying not to look as taken aback as I felt.

"I didn't say it was a secret. Remember that night at the picnic table when you almost walked away? Don't deny it. I should have told you then, but if I had told you, you really would have walked away. It's not too late. I guess it never will be, will it?"

She began to get up, but I grabbed her arm to keep her there. "I'm glad I didn't walk away," I said.

She stared into my eyes, assessing me. "We'll see," she said.

I tenderly brushed her hair back from her forehead. "Really. I'm glad I didn't."

"We'll see," she said again, this time in that whisper she used when she seemed to be talking to herself.

I was partly bluffing, of course. Would I have run a mile if she had been a less attractive woman speaking almost jauntily about having had a breakdown at thirteen? She intrigued me, and I was flattered that she seemed to find *me* intriguing. I didn't spend a lot of time thinking about it. I had seen nothing more beautiful than the way those eyes of hers lit up when she saw me. I had never been in love. I wondered how I'd know if I was.

In her parents' bed, a couple of days later, I asked, "Do you still have that diary you kept?"

"Yes. Every single volume. I might show them to you sometime. When you're ready."

"But not now?"

"I haven't done much more than glance at them in years. I have this notion that it might set me off again. Or something like that. I'd rather not talk about it." She studied my face. "You look like you're trying to think of a nice way to say that, if we ever meet again, it will be by accident."

I shook my head and kissed her. "Why did you become so wrapped up in *that* book? When we first met you said it was your favourite, but—"

"No. I said that Anne Frank was my favourite writer."

I told her I'd never thought of Anne Frank as a writer. It seemed to me that her diary was more historical document than work of literature, its fame owing to the circumstances of its composition, not to the book itself. For that I could think of no kinder word than *ordinary*, even by the standards of the books I imagined other children her age might write.

"It's a very important book," she said, "at least to non-purists like me. But it's not my favourite book."

I told her I saw the point of this distinction. I said that Thomas Wolfe had once been my favourite writer. Each of his books about small-town life in the American South read like an eloquent catalogue of the contents of the universe. I had spent years under the spell of Wolfe and his repeated attempts to get to the heart of *everything* in page-long, highly repetitive sentences. I had yet to read a writer more driven to write something commensurate in scope with life itself, as if the Answer was always one tantalizing step ahead, one level of perception removed. The question of what lay behind the veil goaded all six feet seven inches of him to a tremendous, formless, outpouring of words and a tumultuous, voracious life that, to a young man like me, seemed profound. When I happened on F. Scott Fitzgerald's assessment of Wolfe—that his "awful secret" of having "nothing to say" was evident on every one of the thousands of pages that he wrote—the spell that Wolfe had cast on me was broken, but I had yet to put Wolfe aside, so in awe was I of the sheer pace at which he wrote.

"All right," she said, "all right, I'll show you the damn diary."

On a bookshelf in her bedroom closet were countless diaries of various sizes and colours. Hardcover diaries, writing tablets without covers, some ruled, some not, children's sketchbooks, graph-paper tablets—I felt her watching me as I surveyed them.

"I actually had two breakdowns," she said. "A few years after I recovered from the first, I had a relapse and disappeared into the diaries again. It's been a couple of years since my second recovery." She pulled a notebook off the shelf and handed it to me. "Arellian," she said. "I call the whole thing *The Arelliad*. You know, like *The Iliad*?" We exchanged smiles. "Remember I told you that I don't go anywhere without a copy of her diary? Well, I don't go anywhere without my translation of her diary, either. They're in that bottomless shoulder bag of mine."

"You translated *The Diary of Anne Frank* into Arellian?"

She nodded. "It didn't take very long. You're not allowed to see it, so don't go snooping."

I crossed my heart and flipped open the notebook she had handed to me. Lines and lines of unspaced, unpunctuated clumps of letters. A single, endless sentence. "I can't read a word of it," I said.

"That's the point," she said, taking the notebook from me and replacing it on the shelf. "The astonishing, fascinating truth about me is written in Arellian in these books. The drama of teenage girlhood. Anne Frank coded her own diary, in a way. She made up pseudonyms for the others in the Secret Annex. She addressed her diary entries to an imaginary friend named Kitty, a character from a book she liked. There are three versions of her diary, A, B and C. A is Anne's original version. B is a revision of A, done by her in the hope that, someday, it would be published. And C is a revision of B, done by her father, just before it *was* published. Layers upon layers upon layers." Arms folded, she stared warily at the shelves.

"It's amazing," I said. "All this writing in just a few years."

She sniffed and whispered, "Amazing."

"But you've written so much, Rachel. Millions of words, judging by the number of books. *The Encyclopediary of Rachel van Hout*. You don't write it anymore?"

"Not much. Hardly ever. It's all very juvenile and boring and repetitive." She threw back her head and laughed. A joke was coming. I felt like telling her it was better to laugh after you told a joke. Then she frowned as if she'd forgotten entirely what she'd been about to say.

I took hold of one of her hands. With the other, she pointed to the opposite closet shelf. On the spine of every book was the name Anne Frank. "My other diary," she said. "Hers, I mean, in a lot of languages." She chose and handed me a German paperback edition—*Das Tagebuch der Anne Frank*—and opened it at the middle.

"I can't read a word of that, either. Can you?"

She nodded. "I'm fluent in German and a few other languages. I prefer to read her book in Dutch, the language she wrote it in."

I shook my head in wonder. *A few other languages.*

"You go through a lot of books when you read them like I did back when all this started," she said. "I joined book-of-the-month clubs. Copies of *Het Achterhuis* were delivered to the house, along with other books I was required to buy, which I chose randomly and ignored when they arrived, presenting my mother with book club bills as if they were report cards. I ransacked used bookstores and libraries for copies of *Het Achterhuis*. I stole them. I stole new ones too. I was a real klepto. I got caught at one bookstore. They called my mother. When she came to get me, she told me she was disappointed in me, but never said another word about it. She actually wrote to anyone even remotely likely to send me a present on a special occasion to let them know that my hobby was collecting copies of *The Diary of Anne Frank*. People she had long since lost touch with sent me books. English, Dutch, German, French, Afrikaans and other editions turned up in the mailbox. Pretty strange, right? All of this, I mean."

I shrugged and tried to look as if I'd heard of stranger things.

"With a face that easy to read, you'll never make a living playing poker. What I have is under control but not cured. I'm recovering and I always will be. It's not contagious. It can't hurt you any more than my having diabetes could hurt you. Arellian is not a language, okay? It's a coded form of English that substitutes one letter of the alphabet for another. It's like the cryptogram in the newspaper, only more complicated."

"Can you say something in Arellian? You could teach it to me and we could have conversations."

She sighed in frustration. "I *could* say something in Arellian but I'm not going to, and you're *never* going to. I'm not supposed to talk about it. Doctor's orders. I just wanted you to know about it. I admit I hear it in my head sometimes. It's really not that big a deal. Prison inmates study law to the point that they can advise their lawyers on how to get them out of jail. They have a lot of time on their hands. So did I. You can accomplish a lot when your days are longer than other people's because you have insomnia. Insomnia brought on by my obsession with Anne Frank."

"And what brought *that* on?"

"Some people just get sick, Wade. But then they get better. Please don't get hung up on this. If you do, I'll get *more* hung up on it. I've told you this much so that you know I'm not stark raving mad, not so that you think I *am*."

"I don't," I said. "You're stuck with me."

She nodded, obviously unconvinced. I may have *looked* unconvinced, though I was feeling less and less so. I brushed her cheek with the back of my hand, which she trapped between her cheek and her shoulder as she tilted her head and sighed. She closed her eyes.

"Tired?" I said. She took my hand in hers, opened her eyes and again surveyed the books in her closet.

"She was an insomniac, too. And chronically depressed."

"Anne Frank?"

"Yes."

"I think of her as an eternal optimist."

"You *really* didn't read the book very carefully. Her parents gave her valerian. It's a tranquilizer. They also gave her dextrose, cod liver oil, brewer's yeast and calcium supplements. None of it worked. The girl who wrote 'Think of all the beauty still left around you and be happy' also wrote 'Outside, you don't hear a single bird, and a deathly, oppressive silence hangs over the house and clings to me as if it were going to drag me into the deepest regions of the underworld.'"

"Now that," I said, "is a sentence that *deserves* to be erased."

"She was fourteen when she wrote it, Shakespeare."

From *The Ballad of the Clan van Hout*

VON SNOUT (1964)
You asked me for a scary story—
I told you that you might be sorry,
but you insisted anyway
and still regret it to this day:

The Tale of Claws von Snout
In the place she left behind,
the baby chick was blissful, blind
to everything except her mind,
and even that she couldn't see
because she had no memory
of anything but sound and touch,
which really wasn't very much
to think or dream or fuss about,
so she decided she'd get out
before she knew that Out was there,
the blank blue sky, the blinding glare,
the cold, the night, the Land Without—
and there were other things about
that thought a chick, though no big deal,
was big enough to make a meal.
So she made an application
to reverse her own creation,
to hire a construction crew
much bigger than the four of you,
to build an egg just like the one
she wished she could make whole again.
Her application was denied—
they said she could not live inside
the confines of another shell
where it was warm and all was well
as that would violate Rule Ten

which said that, once it left the hen,
an egg belonged to Claws von Snout,
the Monster of the Land Without,
"whose property you had the gall
to peck to pieces, shell and all.
You live now in the cold, bright world,
and may I say you were not hurled
but came here of your own volition,
compromising your position.
The order of this court is that—
selfish girl, ungrateful brat—
you owe yourself to Claws von Snout,
the Monster of the Land Without.
But since you cry and since you beg,
you may give Claws von Snout one leg.
If your leg is not delectable,
two arms will be acceptable.
If He is still unsatisfied,
the rest of you must go inside.
That's what you wanted, I recall—
von Snout will eat you, head and all!"

Now that von Snout is in your mind,
you cannot leave the Beast behind;
you asked for him and he is yours
(or should I say that you are his?),
the Beast who dines on things with wings
that play their harps while listening,
the Cherubs of the Land Within.
Henceforth, when he appears, von Snout,
the Monster of the Land Without,
will roar with his voice, not with mine—
it will send shivers down your spines,
spine-sliding shivers that make sounds
like those of mice trapped underground.

RACHEL

It's a very simple code—the English alphabet in reverse. *A=Z, B=Y, C=X, D=W* . . . At first I had to consult a chart I made of the English alphabet stacked on top of the Arellian. It took me an hour to write a paragraph. After I got sick, my output increased until I reached the point of not needing the chart. It wasn't long before I was writing at near normal speed, though I found that it was easier to print the letters than to write them cursively, as I was not used to joining them into words. Printing also *felt* better, more intense and secretive. Once I had completely mastered Arellian, I wrote like a stenographer on speed. I preferred writing my diary to reading hers, constantly rushing headlong, never looking back, never rereading what I'd written.

I didn't mind that people knew that I was writing a diary, because to do so seemed normal, purposeful, even at the rate at which I wrote mine.

The Encyclopediary of Rachel van Hout, Wade had called it. I liked the sound of that. But I remembered what it was like to be unable to go a day without writing reams of words, to go from one sleep to the next without reading, or to write without feeling like a medieval monk whose sole purpose in life was to make handwritten copies of philosophical and sacred texts—to be able to read a book, any book, other than hers.

I didn't often visit the book closet. *Millions of words.* Wade was so impressed. I could hardly believe it myself as I looked at the diary. I'd made it look very orderly, managed, controlled, like a set of files organized according to some simple system, files containing mundane information that was easy to access. But it was not, in any sense, an achievement. Just looking at it gave me cold shivers. Inside each volume of the diary was a foment of words cast in a code that no one else could understand. It's possible that, even had they not been coded, no one else could have understood them because my writing was so cramped. I wrote most of the diary in that bedroom, at my desk or, more often, sitting up in bed late at night.

I knew I should stop. I knew the cost of not stopping. Every night, I told myself over and over that I would stop after I had written one more page. Rest, relief, freedom from the clamour of my mind, was always one tantalizing page away. If I wrote one more page, I could put the diary aside for good. I would sleep and, the next day, I wouldn't fall for the tricks my mind had played on me the night before. The key was to not be drawn in by the first trick, to hold out against the first false promise. But I couldn't.

It got to the point, what with reading the book and writing the diary, that I refused to go to school. My parents didn't mind this part so much because I had been promoted two grades ahead of other girls my age. But I refused to leave my room.

Eventually, I got to the point of doing nothing but writing my diary and reading *Het Achterhuis* over and over. I lost the few friends I'd had. Everyone thought there was something morbid about being obsessed with a girl your age who died in a concentration camp. I didn't stay holed up in my room because I thought I was Anne Frank. Those stories about me were blown out of all proportion. I didn't think I was hiding out from the Nazis. But I did spend hours upon hours in my room reading that book and writing. I wasn't sure if the book was making me worse or if it was all that was holding me together. My supposedly secret illness. But it somehow reassured me to think about the ways my sisters coped. Carmen had her drugs. Gloria had her hypersexuality, though not many people called it that at the time. Bethany had her anorexia. I had my diary and *Het Achterhuis*, which I kept reading even after I knew it by heart. The thought that we were all freaks made me feel less like one.

There was a lot missing from Anne's diary by the time her father had it published, things he had removed for family reasons, such as how much she disliked her mother, and things he removed because publishers said they were unfit for young people to read. Things that she somehow found the privacy to do. Portions of the original were quite explicit. She wrote about exploring different parts of her body, discovering them—that must have raised her father's eyebrows. I saw the movie and a production of the play and I hated both of them. They made her and the others seem like characters in a situation comedy based on hiding out for years from Nazis.

A diary is all about secrecy, writing to yourself and no one else. That's why a lot of diaries have locks. There is nothing more isolating than reading constantly about isolation. In the Secret Annex, everyone was forced to keep secrets because there was not enough room for privacy. No one could say what they really thought of someone else. They had to hold it in to keep the peace. The only exception was that, in the bathroom, you had a few seconds to yourself, but visits were kept to an absolute minimum because of the sound made by running or flushing water. If you wanted privacy other than in the bathroom, you had to do what Anne sometimes did, climb under your bed or your blankets. I thought it must have been suffocating and wasn't surprised that she dreamed of going for walks by herself in the woods.

My parents made excuses for me to everyone who noticed how I looked. They said that I was run down from trying too hard in school, that I was a perfectionist where both my body and my mind were concerned, so I stayed in my room, alternating between studying for school and doing yoga.

They said I had mono and there was no telling how much school I'd miss. They said I was travelling abroad, visiting a series of relatives who made sure that, where my studies were concerned, I didn't fall behind.

It seemed that, overnight, I went from thinking it was funny to leave notes written in Arellian lying about the house, or to write my diary in front of my parents, teachers and classmates, to wishing I could do nothing but read Anne's diary and write mine, to resenting anyone and anything that prevented me from doing so.

Eventually, I couldn't sleep at all. My mother found me sitting up in bed, speaking in what I assume was Arellian, for she wasn't able to make out a word.

When I was diagnosed with bibliomania, one doctor told my parents that it wasn't unusual for teenagers to seek sanctuary from the trials and tribulations of coming-of-age in the pages of a book that focused on such things. *The Catcher in the Rye* was such a book, he said, as well as an example of what could happen when the attachment to a book, for whatever reason, becomes a fixation and the teenager doesn't just identify with the hero or heroine, but begins to mimic them, dress like them or, in extreme cases, believe that they *are* them. I told the doctors I didn't see hidden meanings in the book. I didn't think that Anne Frank was writing to me before I had even been born. I wasn't like Mark David Chapman, who thought *The Catcher in the Rye* was telling him to kill John Lennon.

The doctor said that, no matter what I thought, I was using unhealthy coping mechanisms. I wanted to control everything, but I couldn't, so I tried to control *something*, in this case the amount of time per day I spent at my diary and *Het Achterhuis*. He said that I thought something bad would happen to my family and me unless I wrote and read to the point of exhaustion—he didn't know what I thought would happen, he said, because I refused to tell him, but bibliomanic patients were always compelled to hyper-repetition by the fear of *something*.

"This book doesn't ward off evil or misfortune," he told me. I told him I agreed with him, but he wasn't convinced. He reminded me that, by the time of my admission to the hospital, I was buried in the two diaries twenty hours a day.

They tried to wean me off them altogether, but whenever they took the books away from me, I had a panic attack. I wasn't faking. So they let me keep the books but said that it was likely that I would never get to the point that I could ignore them if they were sitting right beside me. The new goal, they said, was to get me to the point where my obsession with the books was under control and had a minimal effect on how I lived. They got me to that point, then released me.

I decided not to tell Wade that it was two years since I'd even tried to read any book but *Het Achterhuis*.

I did tell him that, after my first breakdown, I was able, with the help of medication, to maintain a front of normalcy but that, as time passed, I began to once again write in Arellian in my diary, always on the sly. The truth was that I never completely put the diary aside. But, as I told Wade, it was also true that, for a while, I managed to not let it interfere with my pursuit of a university degree. In my final undergraduate year, my adviser approved my honours paper proposal—I wanted to write about *Het Achterhuis*, of course.

At university no one seemed to care that I had had a breakdown, or why. I was not the only one who was considered eccentric, or the only one who had had some sort of emotional or psychological collapse. There seemed to be a notion that true intellectuals were high-strung by nature and forever on the verge of something. It was almost a badge of honour to have had a breakdown.

When I told my mother of my honours paper topic, she paused for a few seconds before saying, "Well, you seem to have your mind made up and I certainly don't intend to consult a psychiatrist about my family every other day. You're old enough to do as you like, and to judge for yourself." The only one of my sisters who might have tried to intervene was Bethany, but she was in Halifax, at university too, and, for reasons we would later learn, not keeping in touch with anyone back home.

When I finished my paper, I was invited to present it at an Anne Frank conference at Leiden University, but Leiden isn't far from Amsterdam and I would have been closer to Anne Frank's house than I could stand to be, so I didn't go.

The next year, I proposed Anne Frank as the subject of my never-to-be-completed master's thesis. Great things were predicted for me. My professors helped me get grants. I was believed to be on my way to becoming a significant scholar, my specialty the influence of Anne Frank's diary on post-war writers and historians. What my mentors didn't know about their prodigy was that she was cruising for another breakdown. In the periodicals section, Wade had happened upon as classic a case of burnout as could be found in academia. I had been getting so much done so fast because I never paused to rest, sleeping only when I was too tired to read or write. I was supposed to show my professor a draft of a chapter or two once in a while, but I started making excuses for missing my deadlines. I would tell her that things were going so well I didn't want her input just yet lest it interrupt my momentum—or that I didn't write in drafts but revised as I went along and therefore had only a small number of highly polished pages.

Eventually, I was once again no longer able to do anything but write my diary and read Anne's book. I began to think in Arellian—not always, but often and for long stretches of time. I spoke to myself, struggling to pronounce words without vowels, words without consonants, groups of letters that defied syllabizing, such as *znhgviwzn*, which is Arellian for "Amsterdam." When I realized it didn't matter how I pronounced them, since I was never going to say them in front of another human being, I soon became as proficient at speaking Arellian as I was at writing it. I dreamed in a jumble of languages, Arellian included.

From *The Arelliad*

RELAPSE (1979)

Now comes the quickening of time
that happens in Arellia—
the yellow sky was overcast
that winter night; the wind was west—
of all the winds the West is worst,
though some mistake it for the best—
the only light the lighthouse light
that came and went, the foghorn, too.
Remember what she said to you:
"Von Snout approaches from the past.
He always saves the best for last."
He's not the beast he used to be.
I get away—for now I'm free.
I surface from the page again—
I call upon my heroine
to calm my words and guide my pen.

I learned to write by listening to Dad all those years. My diary goes something like *The Ballad*, an answer to it, I suppose, a kind of anti-*Ballad*, which is why I sometimes drift into his rhyme, his metre, no matter how much I resist.

I used his words to ward off fears
so often for so many years
that over time it came to seem
that I alone had written them.
By then I couldn't frame a thought
except in words my father wrote;
nor could I write a decent line—
they sounded more like his than mine.
In part, at least, most lines were prose,
though I admit that even those

were something like prosaic verse.
The rest I cast as poetry:
a hybrid style, unique to me.
But it became my tendency,
as I declined from bad to worse,
to slip more often into verse.
When I was thirteen years of age,
I sank so deep into the page
that poetry was all I wrote—
reams upon reams of it until
I couldn't hide that I was ill.

My father modestly compares himself to Homer, Milton and Shakespeare—my only inspiration, beyond him, is Anne Frank, in part because I like her book, in part because Dad hates it. "It isn't worth a second look," he said one day when, after months of pretending not to notice what I was reading, he grabbed it from my hands and slammed it shut.

There are many ways into Arellia but only one way out. I went there first at age thirteen. The sky was yellow, everything else sepia-tinted, the vegetation wilted like flowers left on graves too long. There were no animals or birds, which didn't strike me as strange.

Everything made perfect sense while I was in there. It seemed that it was always fall, my favourite season of the year. The leaves were forever falling and yet the trees were never bare. There were no clouds, no sun, no daytime moon, no wind or snow, not even rain. Fall did not give way to winter, the fatal season of the four. There was no night, just never-ending yellow light. There was no way to measure time; nothing could end, nothing begin.

A gentle wind, a warm, beguiling breeze, blew from the west.

Arellia was good for me—at least at first, when I had it all to myself, which wasn't for long.

I invented the language of that yellow world so that I wouldn't have to keep these diaries from prying eyes, or hide out while I was writing them. At night I lay awake and spoke Arellian out loud as if to people gathered around my bed who spoke the language as fluently as I did, though every one of them was me. Once, my mother heard me through the door and came in. I shouted at her in Arellian: "How dare you barge into my room?" She ran off but soon came back with Dad. "There must be something wrong with her," he said before he slammed the door.

I read Anne's book ten thousand times, then translated it into Arellian until my wrist was blue with ink. My secret version of her book—I hid it well, behind the back of the mirror on my dresser, held together in a binder. When I looked in the mirror, I thought of it as a portal to Arellia, a world unlike the one I wished would not be there each day when I woke up.

Arellia. Writing about it doesn't mean that I am in it.

> But then again, I could be wrong—
> I reconsider all night long,
> I change my mind, then change it back:
> it's forward thinking that I lack.
> I'm drifting off into the past;
> I wonder if the light will last.
> I won't last long if this lasts long,
> but then again, I could be wrong.
> Has it been too long already?
> How long since my hand was steady?

Gsv hszpvh. That's Arellian for "the shakes." The thing is, I'm *supposed* to write. My thesis supervisor says she needs fifty pages. I've written more than ten times that. I haven't seen her in a while. I think she thinks I'm writing hard. That's what she calls it, "writing hard," writing prose about Anne's influence on those who wrote great books about the war, the kind of book she's hoping for from me. What would she say if she knew that my book will never be?

I emerge from the page that I plunge into every day, the pen still in my hand. I've spent the last three months in bed, working on *The*

Arelliad, which, like Anne's diary, has a beginning but will never end, only be abandoned. When I'm done for the night, I put my notebook atop the shelf in my closet, signed *Izxsvo ezm slfg*, which is Arellian for "Rachel van Hout." Not that I ever remember getting out of bed and putting it there. The book that seems to write itself appears in the closet each morning. I spend the day poring over weird words that I wrote the night before. *Zivoorzm*. That's Arellian for "Arellian." I won't remember writing these words. But the handwriting will be mine, and no one else can write or read Arellian, a fact it would be folly to forget. I read the pages carefully. They read—I can't say exactly—like dreams that I transcribed, then coded in Arellian. I follow each of the instalments with no idea where they lead, though it's often to *Het Achterhuis*, the Secret Annex.

There she is, the other Anne, not the Bard of Amsterdam but the one who calls herself an also-Anne, a girl I met one winter night, stranded on a city street because she missed her bus. I call her now the Shadow She, the one whom I betrayed. But now she is not alone, for Anne Frank is with her. They speak of me, but soundlessly. The first time I saw the Shadow She in Arellia, I was too terrified to move or say a word, for I could think of no reason for her being there except revenge. Although she has done me no harm, the sight of her still startles me.

I would avoid them if I could, but they follow me. They somehow move about without making a sound, scuffing silently through the leaves, walking behind me, hand in hand, the two of them looking at the ground. I stop and turn and try to speak to them, but no words come. I wave but they seem unaware of anything but one another. When they are almost upon me, they stop too, and resume their scrutiny of the ground. I ask if they have sisters and say that I am one of four. They look up at me but nothing more. They don't reply. They never do, like I'm an intruder in their world who'll go away if she's ignored.

Anne Frank is taller, her face familiar from photographs. The other Anne has the greenest eyes I've ever seen. I saw them once through a glaze of wind-bidden tears in the winter of the year that girls went missing everywhere. The two Annes begin to walk away. "If you leave," I say, "beware of Claws von Snout." They release each other's hand and stare at me accusingly, then wander off, taking different paths into the yellow wood. I wonder if I will ever see them again. An eerie silent twilight falls. The sky turns overcast, and I think that darkness is about to come to Arellia for the first time. Then the yellow light returns, but something about Arellia, for which I cannot find the words, has changed.

Already I can smell his lust.
The wind comes up and one great gust
bares the forest of its leaves.
I see the girls among the trees.
I scream, they seem oblivious.
As always when the light withdraws,
I hear him sharpening his claws.
I see the signs I didn't heed.
I am afraid, I am afraid.
There's no way to undo the past—
this winter night may be my last.

Arellia is now a room lit by a banker's lamp and there is no one on the Ballad Bed but Claws von Snout and me.

From *The Ballad of the Clan van Hout*

RACHEL (1979)

My youngest, once the best times two—
I had the highest hopes for you.
You got the highest grades in school;
you used to be so beautiful.
I thought you would turn out to be
a literary prodigy,
as good as Isak Dinesen,
had you become a baroness
with houses in the wilderness
of Africa, adventurous,
a woman ahead of her time,
a woman with the sort of life
not bound by being someone's wife—
the continent of Africa
the setting of your famous books—
a girl with such a mind, such looks.
But you have thrown it all away
to while away your time all day
in bed in the back of beyond,
a minnow in the smallest pond,
a disappointing parody
of literary prodigy,
an imitator of Anne Frank.
The writer of the famous prank
would not have had the slightest chance
but for a fluke of circumstance,
a mere girl who was deified
because of when and how she died.
I wish you worshipped anyone
but *her*. Instead, you write like mad
in this notepad and that notepad.
You scatter them around your bed;

you sleep with one beneath your head.
Beneath the pillow that you hold,
the tale continues to unfold
inside your head unceasingly,
a strange relentless mystery
that you have chosen as your mode:
the diarist who writes in code—
Arellian, I think it's called.
No doctor, yet, has disenthralled
you from the grip of Anne Frank's book.
It's like a drug on which you're hooked—
the more you take, the more you need,
the opposite of Bethany.
You write yourself into a state
that I can't bear to contemplate,
producing reams of gibberish,
becoming sick and feverish.
Throughout the night you hoard your books
atop the shelf where no one looks—
or so you think, for I creep in
when I know that you are sleeping.
I know because I slip a pill
into your food and wait until
that little pill has knocked you out
so I can sit and read about—
I cannot puzzle out one word,
though on some nights I think I've heard
you speak Arellian out loud.
It sounds much stranger than it looks,
the strangest of the strangest books.

My daughter writes the livelong day
though she has nothing much to say
and she has nothing else to do
but imitate a teenage Jew,

the diarist of Amsterdam
whose diary is such a sham,
passed off as hers, I smell a rat—
no adolescent writes like that!
A girl with nothing more to do
than wish she wasn't born a Jew
at such a time in such a place
becomes the writer of her race?
It's no great thing to write a book—
for proof, you only have to look
at the many masterpieces
tossed off by pubescent nieces.
Some things about Anne Frank are true:
she lived and died, she was a Jew
who might have borne the Holocaust
if not for being double-crossed
by someone who has not been named,
a man anonymously shamed.
Anne, the girl whose scam succeeded—
for Anne Frank, no proof was needed:
the Holocaust-redeeming story
of a girl who longed for glory
and wrote, while hiding like a thief,
a book that would outlast her life.
Forgiveness in the face of hate,
a brave defiance of her fate,
a prayer for universal love
unanswered by the sky above,
a wisdom-dripping document
of innocent bewilderment,
a paradox of many kinds—
the work, no doubt, of many minds.
Perhaps there is no need to say
that books like hers, still read today,
will almost always be believed

by those who need to be deceived.
I've been a writer all my life
(a better one than My, my Wife),
more an author than a father,
as good, I think, as many others,
as good as Anne, rank amateur.

RACHEL

When I broke down for the second time, the moment of my absolute burnout came when I fell to the floor and had some kind of seizure. It happened at home in the kitchen, not in any public place, much to my parents' relief and my own. I wound up in a psychiatric hospital in Montreal, far enough from home, my parents hoped, that word of my breakdown wouldn't make its way back to Newfoundland. I had what I was told was a psychotic break, ten days that I didn't remember much of, though I did remember repeatedly claiming that my name was Anne but refusing to say what my last name was. A doctor or nurse who terrified me one day might seem quite nice the next. I assigned to some of them the names of the people in *Het Achterhuis*. They tried to persuade me to tell them what I was writing in my diary.

"You spoke in what you said was Arellian," an old, white-haired doctor named Hackett said. "You told me that Arellian was the language spoken in the kingdom of Arellia, the place you thought you were living in when you were psychotic."

I laughed at the notion. It seemed like such a juvenile, grandiose delusion.

"You do realize that it's just a code," he said, "not the first I've seen, and unlikely to be the last. Other patients of mine have made up languages. A good code-breaker could decipher yours in no time."

"Then send it to your pals at the CIA," I said, extending my diary to him.

He laughed. "There's no key to your illness," he said. "That book is not a key to a cure. It's just a symptom. It's not intriguing to anyone but you. We don't know the cause of what you have, but we do know how to help you. All we need is your co-operation." I said I would co-operate.

"You're not really writing a diary, are you?" Dr. Hackett said. "You said, when you were admitted, that you were writing seventy pages a day. No one's diary entries are that long."

"Mine are," I said. I appeared to be defiant, but I was terrified that he would soon declare me to be a hopeless case. I was almost as afraid of being committed for the rest of my life as I was of having a psychotic break that would never end, living out my days in a place that didn't exist, mind-confined forever.

"I think you've created an imaginary place that you can retreat to and be safe. I think Arellia is a simpler, safer world where nothing ever goes wrong. Is it something like that?"

I nodded and tried to look found out.

"Don't worry," he said. "We've seen this sort of thing many times."

I nodded again and tried to look relieved.

In spite of what he said, which seemed meant to rid me of the notion that I was in any way exceptional, he and the others kept asking me about Arellia as if they *were* worried that I might retreat into it for good. So, except when answering their questions, I made no further mention of Arellia or Arellian. I followed their instructions and took the medications I was given. But I continued to write and read.

From *The Arelliad*

THE HOSPITAL (1979)

I'll say this for the other me—
she has a better memory.
I don't know her but she knows me—
a strange autobiography.

There are no mirrors in the room. You get seven years bad luck for breaking one, unless you use the broken glass . . . my guess is that I wouldn't, but you never know. Only in the window can I see my reflection, which means I have to wait until after dark to brush my hair. I look out through the criss-crossed wire on the window. A girl is out there, peering in. She looks nothing like me, nothing like Anne Frank, more like the other girl named Anne, the also-Anne, my Shadow She.

The doctors ask me simple questions that I think are meant to fool me. "What day is this?" "What's your name?" I told one that my name was Dr. Hackett, which was *his* name, written on the pocket of his coat. He smiled. "You know what my name is," I said. "It's the one I've had since I was born."

"Since you were christened, you mean."

That wasn't what I meant, but I nodded. He doesn't like it when I disagree with him.

Raindrops run down the windowpane. She must be soaked, but every time I look, she's there—the same face and the same brown hair. She was seventeen when we met, as old as she would ever be. It was the winter of the year that girls went missing everywhere. I hear the foghorn. Its message is *Beware, beware*, though, on some nights, the muffled blare seems to say, *Come near, come near.*

I'm rhyming now. I have to catch myself or else I'll sink deeper into the page and join the other wrecks on the ocean floor. Dad said that rhymes are a cinch to memorize. At times, his rhymes take up my entire mind. I'm almost able to forget the worst things that have happened.

Von Snout appears on many nights—
his eyes are full of firelight
that flickers when the sun goes out:
such are the eyes of Claws von Snout.
They move about among the trees—
he's out there now, he's watching me.

My wired window keeps me safe, but I can smell his spite. He may decide to settle for the girl who looks in from out there, just as he did once before. Because of her, he let me go—the night, the snow, the girl, the ghost. I turn away, and there is no one at the window when I look out again.

Doc mentions the bookcase that the Franks' minders used to hide the entrance to the Secret Annex. "It's like something from a children's book. Do you have to open it or can you walk straight through?"

"I'm eighteen, not twelve."

"I've offended you."

"No."

He keeps asking, "What's your name?" I say it in Arellian. He smiles but I can tell he's mad at me. He has to go; it's getting late. He guarantees I'll sleep tonight. The stronger sleeping pills will work. I know they won't but don't say so.

The drops run down the windowpane. I'll close the curtains but I won't sleep, knowing that von Snout and the other girl are out there in the rain, the soaking-wet girl, her face pressed to the glass, who thinks von Snout will leave her be as long as I'm nearby. If the wind comes up, the rain will drum like fingers on the window.

I wake at the slightest sound, my pen and pad upon the bed.

I wish I could put my pen down and never pick it up again. I write "The End" a thousand times, but still my mind won't let me rest. Sometimes I think I know how and when the end will come.

I plunge into the page and wake up in *Het Achterhuis*. I find the secret passageway that's hidden by the big bookcase . . .

"What about that secret passageway?" Doc says when, later, I emerge from the page. "Where does it lead?"

"In her book or mine?"

"In yours."

I tell him that, when I come out, I don't remember what I wrote. It feels as if I'm reading someone else's words, except that the handwriting is mine and the language is Arellian. I wonder what will happen next, as if I'm reading someone else's book—I don't know her, but she knows me. The pages are such a mess. She crosses out more lines than she keeps, crams corrections in the margins, draws arrows everywhere.

I have to write some words in rhyme,
I have to and we both know why.
I'm getting faster all the time
(so I'm allowed a few half-rhymes).
It would be easy, I suppose
to write the whole darn thing in prose—
the easy way is not allowed,
the easy way is for the crowd.
Doc doesn't know I write in verse,
or that I write it in reverse.
I write my way across the page
from the left edge to the right edge
so that it seems I'm writing prose—
I have to make sure no one knows.
I feel that it would break the spell
if someone knew—I mustn't tell.

"Why do you write in code?"

Code. *Xlwv*. Doc knows I won't tell him.

"Because the Sanskrit languages are dead," I say. He smiles as if to say he can decode my every utterance, as if he's seen sicker ones than me and fixed them with his trickery. There's nothing I can say that someone hasn't said before, nothing that can surprise him.

He wants to know about Anne Frank—why hers and not some

other book? He's read it, looking for clues. "Why does she mean so much to you?"

He talks about the characters—he calls them that, as if she made the whole thing up, as if *The Secret Annex* is a work of fiction, nothing more.

"What do you think of Otto Frank? Is he the dad you wish you had?"

"The one I have is not so bad." I can't hide that I *speak* in rhyme.

He smiles as if I've given myself away.

But then he's on to Edith Frank, the mother that Anne didn't like, and soon he asks about my sisters—he wonders if they make me jealous the way Margot did Anne. I nod. He nods and makes a note.

"You like her book because she died. Could that be it? Could that be why? Have you considered suicide? Death seems romantic to the young—is there a boy? Are you in love?"

(The music stops, the night is done; you haven't danced with anyone.)

"No one will ever understand why you did it. So young, so young. It seems so grand to die and be a mystery—they think about you, finally, the you whose specialness only you could see."

I let him think he's onto something. Psychiatry and alchemy seem similar to me.

> No one was there to hold Anne's hand,
> no one to say, "I understand,
> I've seen this kind of thing before:
> it's only death and nothing more."

Two years younger, Anne outlived her sister by nine days.

Death is always a surprise: there are no words for what it is, only words for what it's not. Poems written by men trying to convince themselves they're not afraid of it. *Death, where is thy sting? . . . the soul will spring . . . One short sleep past . . . Death, thou shalt die.*

Death. *Wvgzs.*

But it's a safety net for me,
this nothing that can set me free.
I hope that I will cease to be
or else be me eternally.
To wish for death is not despair—
how else can I get out of here?
The thought of it keeps me alive,
the ultimate alternative.

"You want to be a writer, a girl who writes like Anne Frank. Maybe death will make you famous. But you have what she wanted most. Freedom."

"Not at the moment, I don't."

"I really think she would rather have been the ordinary Rachel van Hout, don't you, than die so young, so famously?"

How important it is to him that I see myself as ordinary. Renounce exceptionality. Your madness is just vanity.

"Your dad worries, which is what dads do when they can't understand why daughters who once adored them grow up one day and turn on them and everyone and everything. Sex and drugs and self-starvation—your mom thought she'd seen it all, but then . . . but then this code, this creation of your gifted mind, this world that you and only you know how to make your way into and out of has them convinced that they're going to lose you . . ."

One day he said Arellia
was just a place inside my head.
I told him he should tell that to
the monster sitting on my bed.

It's been six weeks now and Doc thinks I'm past the worst of it. He's cautiously optimistic—he'd be less sanguine if he knew that I'm feeling much the same. Only I can make me what I was before I put my life on pause in favour of two diaries; the one I read, the one I write.

It's true that he's partly weaned me off the books. He gives me looks when I admit that I'm still sick, so I'm somewhat under-reporting the time I spend diarizing, the hours of reading and writing before I even think of pretending to be asleep when they come by to check on me. And then there are so many things that I withheld from him.

I told him about *The Ballad*, the Ballad Bed, the Night Salon, the Land Within, the Land Without. But not the rumours or von Snout, or anything to make him think that the Land of Hout was not the perfect place Dad makes it out to be. "Your dad made *The Ballad* up for you. It must have taken ages for him to write that much. Some of the greatest children's books began as simple bed-time tales parents wrote and read to their children." The look on his face. So impressed.

"Tell me about Arellia. Is it like South Africa, or is it like the Land of Hout? Is that where the idea came from, the ballad that your father wrote?"

She writes because her father did, but why so much and why in bed? I mustn't speak of Hout again. This man is from the Land Without. I have to throw him off the scent.

"Tell me about Arellia," he asks again.

"I don't remember it at all. Honestly. You told me I went on about the place when I was so strung out I might have told you anything. I might have said you were the king or called you Santa Claus. I'm just a simple case. I worked so hard that I wore out. The prodigy became the class clown, just as I did when I was thirteen. I think I'm prone to it. I don't know why I try so hard, but I'll probably do it all again."

He nods as if he's found the key,
the answer to what's wrong with me.
He nods as if my words confirm
the answer that's in front of him:
he sees it now, he's worked it out,
it leads back to the Land of Hout.
He has the pieces that he needs;

what is it that he doesn't see?
The one piece that just doesn't fit—
what Anne Frank has to do with it.

I'm discharged a week later.

The lighthouse light still comes and goes,
the foghorn muffled by the snow.
It must have been like this for her.
The sun came up; they found her there.

WADE

"I don't write the diary much anymore," Rachel said. "I don't read hers except for one hour a day. Exactly one hour. My grad school recovery was authentic."

I was on my third beer, she her second, the two of us at the dining room table as if we owned the house. She lit a cigarette, placed it in an ashtray, and reached one hand into the pocket of her jeans, from which she withdrew two large pills, white and oval-shaped. "I have to take these every day," she said. "Lithium. Not to be confused with Librium, which is a tranquilizer—very nice. Lithium is usually prescribed for depression or manic depression, but the OCD drugs they tried on me didn't help, so when in doubt, lithium it is."

"Not to sound like a broken record, but why that book?" I asked.

She rolled her eyes. "Why any book? My sister Bethany is anorexic. Why does a girl who is thirty or forty pounds underweight think she's fat? You're right, there probably is more to it than that, but the doctors can't figure it out. There *are* some similarities between the van Houts and the Franks, you know. Dad is the only male of the house. He has a wife and four daughters. Otto Frank had a wife and two daughters. The van Houts left one country to live in another. The Franks left Germany to live in Holland, and that's where my dad was born. I made my first trip to Holland when I was eight, which was Anne Frank's age when she moved there."

"Wouldn't a book about a family that has a happy ending be better?"

"Better or worse doesn't come into it when you're sick. Well, maybe worse does. *Het Achterhuis* has no ending. That might be why I couldn't stop reading it. Can't stop."

"Well, they all die, don't they?"

"No one dies in her diary. Not to beat a dead horse, ha ha, but you really can't have read it very carefully. After they were captured, all of them but Otto died in concentration camps. But you only find out about their deaths in the foreword or introduction, or maybe the afterword, depending on the edition. But I always tear those out when I get a new copy. I only read what Anne Frank wrote." She took a swig of beer. "You have that look in your eye again. I don't like your chances of becoming the poster boy for open-mindedness."

"No. No, it's just the opposite. I've never met anyone who was anything like you."

"Like I am now, or like I was when I was sick? Is that the me you've fallen for?"

"No—just sometimes I worry that I can't keep up with you."

"I couldn't keep up with me either. '*Beeile dich nicht, ruhe dich nicht aus.*' Do not hurry, do not rest, that's my motto now. It's from Goethe."

For an hour some evenings, we sat across from each other in the front room, she reading her daily dose of *Het Achterhuis* while I read whichever book I was immersed in at the time. Every now and then, she looked up and smiled at me. I smiled back, sometimes wondering if she might be as mentally disturbed as she admitted she was widely assumed to be. I didn't often have such thoughts. One day, she told me she had written a poem about me, about how lightly I slept:

> The slightest sound keeps him awake;
> it seems to him all things can make
> some sort of sound, some sort of squeak.
> He wonders why the wind must blow,
> he hates the din of falling snow.
> They say that, were he deaf, he'd hear
> the sound a mouse makes on the stair;

they say he cannot stand the sound
that earthworms make while underground;
they say that, if he had no ears,
he'd hear mosquitoes cleaning theirs.
The ticking of the kitchen clock
is no worse than the sound a sock
makes inside the dresser drawer—
he cannot stand a sock that snores.

I loved it. I laughed, and *she* loved that. "You don't often laugh," she said. "Your whole face changes."

She said she hated wasting one of the few hours we had together reading a book she knew by heart. "But I'm glad you're here to time me."

Whenever I declared that the hour was up, she closed her book without marking her page, ran upstairs and put it in her closet. Once, when she came back down, she said, "I feel as if I'm on the verge of not needing to read that book at all."

I felt envious of her, even after it occurred to me that *The Encyclopediary* might be nothing but gibberish, millions of words made up of randomly chosen letters of the alphabet. That would point to a madness far more prolonged and profound than the one she had confessed to. Still, she didn't seem like someone who had ever been *that* far gone. I decided that, whatever her state of mind when she wrote, she had, by the age of twenty-one, produced what even Thomas Wolfe might consider to be a lifetime of writing. I imagined an exhaustive autobiography teeming with details, digressions, reams of self-reflection. Freed of her mania, her demons, whatever they were, what might she one day write? I felt plodding, methodical, hopelessly uninspired in comparison with her. But my envy always gave way to admiration and the certainty that she had felt, far more profoundly than anyone I would ever know, the inscrutable urge to *write*, to depict the chaos of the world in words. She had almost died trying to complete what I had yet to work up the nerve to begin.

I'd watch her as she read. No one I'd known was compelled to do *anything* to the point of breaking down. Who *cared* so much that it drove them mad? Unlike me, she was *living*, not preparing to. I imagined the thirteen-year-old she had been, diarizing in a frenzy night after night, the eighteen-year-old who, though she knew the risks, dove so deep into her mind that she hit bottom and would have died if not for the voices she heard calling to her from above. Sometimes I went to her and lay my head on her lap, where, eyes closed, I listened as she turned the pages, as if, in her mind, she was reading the diary to me.

From *The Arelliad*

THE SIREN OF DUPLICITY (1983)

The sirens come ashore at night,
their lights unlike the lighthouse light,
the yellow light that comes and goes
at intervals that no one knows.
In coves you cannot find on maps,
they gutter in the wind, perhaps,
or else they go out when the waves
wash deep enough into the caves.
They do not stop until Cape Spear,
for sirens know what happens there.

In any case, they soon come back.
The flickering along the wrack
continues until morning comes.
The sirens, now that night is done,
must go back to the sea and hide—
they lost their voices when they died.
They cannot sing their secret song,
"The Mystery of Right and Wrong";
they know the words but no one who
would sing them truthfully to you.

The sirens make their way along the coast from cave to cave until they reach the lighthouse at Cape Spear. The flickering along the wrack continues long past midnight. When the last of the sirens have gathered on the rocks below the Light, they try to sing as they once did, but cannot make a sound, so they write the words by candlelight, the scratching of their pens the closest thing to music they have managed since the Light lured them ashore.

When they are done, they file back the way they came, retiring to their caves, where they must stay till morning comes. By day they don't do anything but swim about, remembering when they could sing in voices someone stole from them.

The man who came in from the sea might have heeded the warning of the song they couldn't sing if I'd sung it for him properly, for I, you see, still have my voice. I sold my soul; I made my choice. I changed the words of "The Mystery of Right and Wrong" to suit another melody, the siren song of treachery.

Perhaps that's why he doesn't write, unless he does but never shows a word to me, the Anne Frank Freak who wouldn't get the kind of book he thinks is great. Or he may be afraid to show me anything, worried he may not write as well as me.

But then, he's never read a word of what I write, nor has he heard the language that I

brought ashore
the night that I was banished for
the murder of the Shadow She,
a siren now because of me.
When I betrayed the Sisterhood,
they sent me to the yellow wood,
where I must stay till I atone,
landlocked for leaving Anne alone.
Arellia's the place for me,
the siren of duplicity.
But other sirens leave the sea;
Anne, Margot and the Shadow She,
The Frank sisters, the girl in black—
the three of them keep coming back,
sometimes in twos, sometimes in threes,
three sirens only I can see
who roam the yellow wood with me.
They want something, I know they do,
they blame someone—not one, but two.

The rhymes and metre of *The Ballad* creep back into my prose, sometimes swallowing whole paragraphs. Is this a thing that has to be, presentiment or fantasy?

Uzgv. Fate.

WADE

After I got off work one afternoon, we went out for a stroll and a bite to eat. As we were walking back up the street toward her house, Rachel stopped. "Uh-oh," she said. "Shit, shit, shit." There was a large grey van parked in the driveway, behind the Malibu.

"Whose van is that?"

She sighed, pressed the heels of her hands against her forehead and closed her eyes as if she hoped that, when she opened them, the van would be gone.

She began a kind of slow march toward the house, arms swinging, and I followed. She ran the last few steps and opened the door. "WELCOME HOME, RAITCHEE," came a woman's voice from inside, after which a man guffawed and broke into a rasping cough. Rachel entered the house as if she'd forgotten that she had me in tow.

I hurried to catch up and was almost abreast of her in the hallway when a dark-haired young woman came running from the front room. She stopped in her tracks when she saw me. I knew from having scanned the photo albums that she was either Gloria or Carmen. Smiling, she looked back and forth between us, then put her arms around Rachel, who left hers at her sides. "Raitch," she said, her eyes growing ever wider behind the large square lenses of her glasses as she stared at me. "Who might this boy be?"

"This is Wade." Rachel sighed but didn't turn to look at me.

"Waaaaade? And what is Wade to you, I wonder?"

"What are you guys doing here, Carmen?" Rachel said. Carmen was big-breasted like Rachel, but her shoulders were so narrow that she had to hunch, which made her look as if she were cringing in expectation of being sternly lectured for some wrong that she had done.

Carmen stepped back from Rachel, continuing to regard me with astonishment. "Oh my God, Fritz," she shouted. "I think this boy named Wade has plucked our little Rachel." She giggled. "It's written all over her face, and his."

"Well, come on in," the man called from the front room, as if we were unexpected but welcome guests in his house. "I want to see this Wade. He better get all he can now, because he won't be getting any when Mom and Dad get back."

"What are you doing here, Carmen?" Rachel said.

Carmen looked away from me at last and put an arm around Rachel. "We haven't seen you since our wedding in Halifax," Carmen said, still smiling. "We missed you."

The smell of hash, or weed, or *something*, wafted out of the front room.

"You're stoned," Rachel said just as I realized that Carmen was indeed quite stoned.

"Not stoned enough," the man said from within. "Hi, Rachel."

"Hi, Fritz," Rachel responded warily.

"Come in, come in," Fritz insisted.

Rachel turned to me at last and held out her hand. *I'm sorry*, her eyes said. Taking her hand, I attempted a confident, reassuring smile, which must have been a ghastly failure judging by the way she looked. She tugged me into the front room like a child who had been coaxed out of hiding to meet a grown-up.

A slender, dark-haired, lightly bearded young man sat cross-legged on the floor with his back to the fireplace. He was dressed like someone who had been a protester at Berkeley in the '60s and didn't know that his outfit was out of fashion. He wore a white smock with a deep V-neck that showed his hairy chest and was bordered with a pattern that made it seem like he was wearing a necklace of blue flowers. The bell-bottoms of his jeans were more widely flared than any I had seen in a decade. As if in a final tribute to the era of earnest hippies, he wore on his darkly tanned feet a pair of leather sandals with a single thong. How much of his bronze complexion was owing to his ethnicity and how much to a suntan, I couldn't tell. He had a joint in one hand and a bottle of beer in the other.

"Well, Rachel," he said, "introduce me properly to the young man whose beer I'm drinking."

When Rachel said nothing, Carmen giggled again, then said, "Fritz, Rachel tells me this is Wade. Wade, meet my husband, Fritz Boonzaire."

"Just Fritz is enough," Fritz said. "You still can't pronounce my last name." Her smile vanished.

I let go of Rachel's hand and, extending mine, walked across the room to Fritz. He looked up at me with the trace of a grin. He raised the joint and the beer bottle to indicate that his hands were full. I felt ridiculous for having made such an earnest offer of my hand.

"Well, well, Wade, Wade," Fritz said, not to me, but to Carmen, who burst out laughing.

I felt Rachel's hand on my lower back. "Hello, Fritz," she said, as if she was making fun of his name.

"Hello, baby sister," he said. "I do believe that Carmen's right. You have been plucked. Or some word that rhymes with plucked. You're positively glowing."

"Fuck off, Fritz," Rachel said.

"Read any good books lately?" Fritz said. "Look at it this way, Rachel. At least you're not hung up on *War and Peace*. Lugging that thing around everywhere you go wouldn't be much fun."

Carmen laughed yet again and sat cross-legged on one of the green sofa chairs.

"You and Anne Frank are still an item, right?" Fritz said, looking at Rachel. "Anything or anyone that comes between you and Anne—"

"You are such a bastard, Fritz," Rachel said.

"When the going gets tough, Rachel—"

"She told me all about it," I interrupted.

"I very much doubt that you told him *all* about it, baby sister."

"You should have said you were coming," Rachel said. "I would have locked the house. Or burned it down."

Fritz drew on the joint, held in the smoke, then grinned at me.

"Where did you drive from?" I said.

"Where did you *drive* from?" Fritz repeated, looking again at Carmen, who threw back her head and laughed and flopped back against the chair, her hands on her thighs.

"We drove all the way from Halifax," she said. "We didn't even sleep on the ferry. We had to be careful."

"Shut up," Fritz roared. Carmen bowed her head and twirled a loose thread on the hem of her jeans. "You know something, Rachel," he said, "I bet Wade doesn't know as much about you as he thinks he does."

"Fritz," I started, but Rachel grabbed my hand.

"Just joking, baby sister," Fritz said, "although we did have a nickname for you when you stayed with us during the wedding . . ."

"Carmen," Rachel said, "Mom and Dad left me to take care of the house. You should have called first."

Carmen looked at Fritz, who, tossing the last of the joint over his shoulder and into the fireplace, stood up without uncrossing his legs or using his hands, his balance perfect. "A trick I learned in the national service. I used to do it while holding a rifle in my hands. I learned a *lot* of tricks."

A half foot shorter than me, he sized me up. "Wade is a big boy," Fritz said. "You always did like big joints, didn't you, Rachel?"

Rachel squeezed my hand before I could object. I'd never heard an accent like his before. It seemed faintly Australian.

"Come on, Fritz, be nice," Carmen said.

"Shut up," Fritz said.

"He's usually nice, isn't he, Rachel, when he's not so stoned?" Carmen said. "Fritz did all the driving from Halifax so that I could sleep. Wasn't that gallant of him?"

"I didn't trust her to stay awake," Fritz said. "No matter what I give her, nothing works. She falls asleep. Rachel knows why, don't you, Rachel?"

"She's been shooting up ever since she met you," Rachel said.

Placing his beer bottle on the mantel of the fireplace, Fritz stuck his hands in the pockets of his jeans. "I wonder what Wade's story is," he said. "I'm sure it's a nice, ordinary Canadian story. Is he a hockey player, Rachel? Does he get good grades like you?"

"He did," Rachel said. "He graduated from university."

"A university graduate. I think Wade might be a lawyer. He looks like a lawyer. A corporate lawyer."

"I'll be a writer soon," I said.

" 'I'll be a writer soon,'" Fritz mimicked, grinning at Carmen, who flashed him a look that seemed meant to coax him into going easy on me. "A writer to replace Anne Frank, the one that Rachel lost. Is that how he got you into bed, baby sister, by telling you that he kept a diary? When I was his age, I was on border patrol between South Africa and South West Africa. I had rebels shooting at me. I shot back. I think I might have killed a few. I mean, I hope not, though they killed a few of my buddies. I didn't know it then, but I should have been on their side. What business do white men from Europe or anywhere else have in Africa? Some people are going to do something about that. I'm looking forward to going back home." He kept looking at Rachel, talking about me as if I wasn't in the room. "So, Wade will soon be a writer. What's Wade doing now?"

"He's a reporter for a newspaper."

"Only for a while," I butted in. "Until the end of the summer, maybe."

Fritz guffawed. "A summer job. That's what students have, summer jobs. Not the kind that go on and on. The kind that go on and on are the ones that Wade knows he should avoid. I feel the same way about them, but I like my chances of avoiding them much better than his. Wade is very purposeful, isn't he, Rachel? I bet that boys who want to write get laid a lot. He might be two-timing you or worse, baby sister. I knew a lot of guys like Wade when I was in the national service. Artists on border patrol, killing blacks to keep them from killing whites. Martial artists, you might say. A good pun, don't you think? Your writer should be taking notes. But guys like Wade, they don't age very well. Hans was the true hero, risking his own life to save people from the Nazis when he was only seventeen."

"Fritz is a leather worker," Carmen interjected. "His stuff is amazing."

"Shut the fuck up," Fritz said.

"Don't talk to her like that," Rachel said.

"Truce, baby sister. We'll be gone in two days. Back home to South Africa."

Carmen said, "I'm a South African citizen again, thanks to Fritz. And Fritz is a landed immigrant here."

"Sort of like dual citizenship," Fritz said. "Comes in handy in my line of work."

"What *is* your line of work?" I said.

" 'What *is* your line of work,' " Fritz repeated. "Wade is not very fast on the uptake, is he?"

Carmen jumped up from her chair. "Raitch, we have, like, a ton of coke and ten thousand tabs of acid in the van." Fritz had reached her by the time she finished speaking and slapped her hard across the face. "Fritz is Afrikaans," Carmen said with barely a pause and as if he hadn't touched her. "But he's against apartheid. I mean he's *really* against it, not like some people. He marched in the protests when Steve Biko was murdered. He might be part Bantu." As Fritz raised his hand to strike her again, I headed for him, but was brought up short when he drew the first switchblade I had ever seen in my life and flicked it open.

"Stop," Rachel shouted.

"He stopped," Fritz said, "but I think there might be something running down his leg. He should go back and stand beside you, don't you think, Rachel?"

"Come back to me, Wade," Rachel said.

I backed up, keeping my eyes on the knife.

"Put it away, Fritz, please," Rachel said, but he kept it pointed at me.

"He's nice when he's not stoned," Carmen said. "He is, Wade, he really is." She was not looking at me. "Lots of guys who get in trouble are. I write to guys in jail and they write back. They're really nice. Lots of them are Americans who fought in Vietnam. You can find their addresses in the back of *Rolling Stone*. Fritz sends the money we make to South Africa to help get innocent black guys out of jail. It won't be long until the whole place goes up in smoke and all the white people will get what's coming to them, won't they, Fritz? Someday?"

"Someday," Fritz said, his tone almost wistful, his eyes closing and opening again as if some drug he'd taken had just kicked in. "Rachel, you and Wade sit down over there on the loveseat. When you sit down I'll put this knife away."

Though I didn't resist, Rachel all but dragged me to the loveseat.

Carmen went to Fritz, put an arm around his waist and leaned her head on his shoulder as she looked at me. "The most he ever does with that knife is peel apples," she said.

I thought he would hit her again, but he tapped her so lightly on the cheek it might have been a gesture of affection. "Your big mouth," he whispered. "You should never open it when others are around."

Fritz clicked the knife shut and returned it to his pocket. "Sorry, baby sister," he said. "We wouldn't have dropped in if we'd known you had company. I mean, what are the chances that *you* would have company?"

"So just go, then, Fritz," Rachel said.

"But I haven't told Wade yet what you're famous for. Wade, no one can give a brain toke quite like Rachel."

It was the first time he'd addressed me directly.

"I bet you don't even know what that is, do you? I sometimes use it as a euphemism, but you'll never guess for what."

"Shut up, Fritz," Rachel said.

"So," Fritz said, "I know *you* will keep your mouth shut about what's in the van. It's big bad Wade I'm not so sure about. Does Wade understand that it won't be the end of the story if we get caught? Does he understand that other people are involved? I bought what's in that van with borrowed money. I would have to tell—let's call them 'them'—how we got caught. Does Wade understand what might be at stake?"

"I do," I said. "You don't have to keep asking her."

"What about it, Rachel?" Fritz said.

"I think it's safe for you to get lost, Fritz," Rachel said.

"Well, I guess I'll have to take your word for it, won't I? It's not as if I have a choice. It's not as if I'm stupid enough to hurt Wade just to make a point. I mean, how would I explain it if I did?"

"You don't have to hurt anyone," Rachel said.

Fritz nodded.

"You don't have to hurt Carmen again. She didn't mean any harm."

"Okay, Carmen," Fritz said, "looks like we have to find another place to crash."

Carmen left without so much as a glance at Rachel or me, tears streaming down her face. Fritz took the beer bottle from the mantel, drank it dry and brought it down hard on the coffee table. "Thanks for the hospitality, baby sister," he said, and sauntered out of the room.

Rachel followed him out. I heard the van starting up. A few seconds later, Rachel came back. "They're gone," she said. "For now." She sat on the loveseat, elbows on her knees, hands on either side of her face, holding back her hair.

"I shouldn't have provoked him," she said, as if she was thinking out loud. "I wouldn't have if I had known. He was pretty out of it. Almost as bad as Carmen, even if he didn't act like it at first. Carmen was starting to come down from something, I think. Heroin, maybe. I feel so bad for her. I should have seen how bad things were in Halifax. But it was a wedding. You have to pretend that everything is fine. But you don't have to fool yourself into thinking that it is." She shook her head as if to ward off a dizzy spell and looked at me at last.

"What he said about you maybe not knowing as much about me as you think you do? I used to get stoned a lot, and I dropped acid with them sometimes when we went back to Cape Town in '75, when Dad had a sabbatical. I did a bit of coke, too, but I never touched heroin. We all used to do drugs except for Gloria. She doesn't even drink. But I want you to know that I was never like Carmen, and the most I've done for years is have a toke now and then. Have you ever—"

I shook my head.

Rachel smiled. "Once, when I was on acid, I thought Dad was the Planters peanut man."

I sat beside her and took her hands in mine. I could think of nothing to say.

"You know what I like about you," she said. "You don't follow the crowd. I mean, you don't follow any crowd. I've never met someone who wanted to be a writer or wanted to be anything out of the ordinary and was actually doing something about it instead of just wanting to and never doing anything."

"I haven't really tried yet. I might not succeed."

"You will, because you'll never give up. I think Carmen was right. Fritz was bluffing with the knife. He wouldn't have the nerve, even if he knew he could get away with it."

"Rachel, he pulled a knife on me, on *us*."

She shook her head. "It wasn't as bad as it seemed. I bet there aren't ten thousand tabs of acid in that van. I'd be surprised if there are a hundred. When Fritz is stoned, he has delusions of grandeur about being a major drug dealer."

"And Carmen thinks he's Robin Hood."

"She has all sorts of ideas about him. More than he has about himself. There's more to her than you might think. But look at the way they dress. People haven't dressed like that since I was eight." She stood. "I need a drink. Let's have a drink. Do you need a drink? Not beer. Mom and Dad have some cognac, I think."

I was suddenly shaking and doubted that one drink would stop it. Rachel sat again. "Jesus," she said beneath her breath. She put her arms around me and her head against my chest. "Your heart is pounding way faster than mine," she said. Her blouse was damp with sweat.

"What's a brain toke?" I asked.

"What you really want to know," Rachel said, "is what *brain toke* is another name for."

I nodded sheepishly.

She let go of me and got to her feet. "Why did they have to show up here today?" she said, pacing back and forth. "I can't believe we're talking about something just because Fritz brought it up. Brain toke. I haven't heard anybody use that expression since I was in high school."

She went to the dining room table, took a little notepad out of her shoulder bag, tore off a sheet and rolled it into the shape of a joint. She pointed to one end. "Imagine that this is lit. To give someone a brain toke, you put the lit end in your mouth and put your face close to someone else's. They open their mouth and you blow smoke into it while your hands are cupped around the joint. They get high faster. You don't waste smoke."

It sounded absurd, two people on either end of a joint like that, their faces, their lips, almost touching, while one blew smoke into the other's mouth.

"The trick is to keep the joint lit without burning the inside of your mouth. I guess I *was* good at it. At our parties, people would line up for one of my brain tokes, boys and girls, but mostly boys." She sighed as if she was growing impatient with me. "And surely you can guess what *brain toke* is another name for? Rachel gives good brain tokes. Rachel gives good . . . You get it?"

I forced a laugh.

"Yeah, well . . . Look, there were a few guys at one party. I never even knew their names. I was so out of it I hardly knew what I was doing. Just a few, okay? That's all it was. But Carmen told Fritz about it. When I met him at their wedding in Halifax, the first thing he said after hello was, 'Could I get a brain toke, baby sister?' No, actually, the first thing he said was, 'Well, if it isn't Rachellatio.' He and Carmen thought it was hilarious. You have that look on your face again. You think that I'm as bad as Fritz and Carmen."

"No," I said, though I was reeling from the phrase *a few guys*. "I know how easy it is for a girl to get a reputation she doesn't deserve."

"Well, something's wrong. I can see it in your face. What is it? Are you worried that people might laugh at you behind your back because you're going out with me? Some people already are." She was on the verge of tears.

"Rachel—"

"All right, all right, I'm sorry, I'm sorry. I worry that my family will make you think I'm even crazier than I am."

"I've known stranger families," I said.

"I'm sure you think you have," Rachel said, "but I very much doubt it. The drugs were just a phase for Bethany and me. But Carmen . . ." She shook her head as if to say, *There are no words*. "She used to be so sweet. She *is* sweet, once you get to know her."

Still shaken by that knife, I couldn't get *Rachellatio* out of my head. But at the same time I was wondering if I had yet to write a word of my book because I'd led such a small-town, parochial life. Fritz with his switchblade and his heroin-addicted wife, and all that Rachel had confided in me—I had only ever heard of such things.

Standing in front of the fireplace, we shared a glass of cognac. Rachel said, "Carmen was doing drugs long before they met, so I can't blame him for that, not entirely. I'd only met him once before I went to their wedding. Carmen met him in 1975, when we went back to South Africa for Dad's sabbatical. She came home with us but got herself a pad, as she called it, with some other, older kids in St. John's. Not long after that, Fritz sent her the airfare to come back to South Africa to live with him. She ran off without telling anyone at home that she was leaving. Mom and Dad will never forget that. The first we heard that she was getting married was when we got the wedding invitations. I was the only one from the family who went. Mom and Dad kind of sent me. They'd written to her and told her she was too young, at nineteen, to get married to anyone. After Fritz did his national service in South Africa, he didn't go to university. He had no career plans. Mom and Dad hoped that, if she knew they weren't coming, Carmen might not go through with the wedding. Gloria was in South Africa—she's a flight attendant who's based there now—but she wouldn't have gone to the wedding anyway because she and Carmen don't get along. Bethany was in the hospital. I can't believe that, when I saw the van, I was more worried about the impression Carmen would make on you than I was about Fritz. If I'd known, I would have never let you come inside. I wouldn't have gone in, with you or without you. I don't know what you must think of me having a sister and a brother-in-law like that. My family are all so weird. I hope you don't think I am too. I mean, aside from the time I devote to Anne Frank, I'm not hopelessly weird, am I?"

I put my glass on the mantel and took her in my arms. "You know what I think of you," I said.

She nodded, her head against my shoulder. "Well, the surprises just keep coming, don't they? The van Hout hit parade. How many will be one too many for you?"

"Let's stay at my place tonight in case they come back."

"They won't, but okay. We'll *feel* better at least. But let's walk. I don't want them driving by and seeing that the Malibu is gone."

Later, as we sat at my card table, looking out the window of the garret, her eyes welled up.

"She was my favourite sister, you know. I wish you'd known her back then. She said that I was part of her and that she was part of me. She was always saying things like that. I loved it when she smiled at me. I looked up to her, literally, when we held hands on the playground. I remember the feel of her hand. Those big eyes of hers—I loved the way they smiled at me. She used to have such rosy cheeks. I trusted her more than I trusted anyone. She loved me, and I loved her *so* much. She thought she had to protect me from everyone.

"Once, she took me to the bioscope, the movies, at Rondebosch, and we got stoned while watching *Seven Brides for Seven Brothers.* She was twelve and I was eight. I was so stoned I thought the seven brothers looked exactly alike. Carmen thought that was hilarious. She said the word *septuplets* and it sounded so strange we couldn't stop laughing. We got caught, right there in the bioscope, by some narc who was not much older than Carmen and turned out to be our second cousin on my mother's side. A real goody two-shoes. He called Mom, and she came to get us and talked him out of reporting us. On the way home she told us she was disappointed with us but never said another word about it.

"Once, Carmen and I accidentally got on board a train reserved for non-whites. The passengers urged us to go to the white train. 'Please, miss and miss, go to the other train or we will get in trouble.' Carmen was stoned, so she thought it was hilarious. I thought it was strange that the coloureds would be the ones who would get into trouble for our mistake. At the time, I didn't think that much about coloured people, but Carmen did. She pestered Mom and Dad about how unfairly they were treated. Mom would tell her that coloured people couldn't be given responsibilities until they were educated. Until then, we had to protect ourselves from them and protect them from themselves. Even after they were educated, there would still be apartheid, she said, because, if you mixed the races, God would be displeased and send forth a plague of birth defects upon his people, as he did when children were born of incest. 'Where in the Bible does it say that?' Carmen was always asking.

"We were close until she met Fritz. 'You don't get him like I do,' she told me. 'You have to see beneath the surface. Most people think that what they see is real. I don't. You know that Mom and Dad are not what they let on to be. Fritz says that the whole world has to be torn down and built back up the right way. It might be a long time before the revolution starts, but when it does, there'll be no need for people like our parents.'

"But she knew her way around Mom and Dad. She told me that if we acted as if we were doing nothing wrong, *they* would act as if we were doing nothing wrong. After we came back to St. John's from Cape Town in 1976, Carmen and I used to have these huge parties in the basement. Most of our friends slept over because, by midnight, they couldn't make it up the stairs. We had beer and grass and acid, and there was always someone who could afford cocaine. Mom and Dad must have smelled the grass and heard the noise, but they never came down to complain or check on us. And in the morning they cleaned up after us. They saw the punctured beer cans, the butt ends of joints, the matchboxes stuffed with hash or grass, the scorched tinfoil, the hash pipes. If some of our friends were still there passed out on the floor, they just stepped over them. By the time they were done, the basement looked as if the party never happened. In our house, if you acted like something wasn't there, it wasn't. If you acted like something hadn't happened, it hadn't.

"Mom used to go around singing this song:

Now Cocaine Bill and Morphine Sue were walking down the avenue
Honey have a sniff, have a sniff on me
Honey have a sniff on me.
They walked from Broadway down to Main
looking for a store that sold cocaine.
Now in the graveyard on the hill

lies the body of Morphine Bill
and in the graveyard by his side
lies the body of his cocaine bride.

"That's the closest she ever came to telling us she knew what was going on."

"That's not how I grew up" was all that I could think to say.

From *The Ballad of the Clan van Hout*

CARMEN (1979)
(A piece not read to anyone,
a piece I wrote when she was gone,
a piece withheld from the Salon.)

My second one, a quiet child,
was never one for running wild.
For days you never said a word—
I wasn't certain that you knew
a word of what was said to you.
You had to see a specialist—
he said you lagged behind the rest
and you might never be the best
at anything you tried to do.
"But that of course depends on you.
There's nothing wrong with Carmen's ears.
It's that expression that she wears
that gives me reason for concern.
It might be someone else's turn,
another kind of specialist,
perhaps a child psychiatrist:
I know a good man down the street.
I think he's someone you should meet."
I never saw that quack again—
I'd had it up to here with men
who conferred with one another
about my failings as a father.
You had such lovely long black hair—
you would twist it round your finger
as you stared into the fire,
a schoolgirl trying to think through
a problem she was told to do.
You were slow to learn *The Ballad*—

you were ten before you had it
half as well as Baby Sister;
you recited in a whisper,
beneath your breath, like a prayer
that no one else was meant to hear.

The girl that I think of as you
no longer shy, no longer blue,
burst from her room at age thirteen
as spiteful as she was bone mean.
You mocked my every word and move
as if you thought I had to prove
that I was worth the air I breathed,
as if my little girl had seethed
with hate for me since she was born,
her every word adrip with scorn.
You came home with all kinds of boys—
hippies who would proselytize
as if they had rehearsed at school
how best to prove me but a fool,
oblivious to politics,
an easy mark for all the tricks
of men who needed votes from me.
Your Mom and what you called her kind
you mocked as if they'd lost their minds,
the blinking owls, the abject wives
of men like me who toed the line,
and spent their bland, complacent lives
enslaved by the Establishment—
and there could be no argument
that She, like all the other wives,
in thrall to men like Hans van Hout
who, once a month, might take them out,
who bought them their appliances
and doled out their allowances,

was just another doormat hen,
a racist mom who liked to sew,
upholder of the status quo
who stayed at home and raised her kids
and voted as her husband did.
I heard it all from noon to night
and never once put up a fight.
In fact, I never said a word—
I'd act as if I hadn't heard
you when you barged in through the door.
She tidied up the kitchen floor
as you remarked on what She wore,
her "mousy doormat pinafore."
My silence made you that much worse—
you'd stamp and storm about and curse.
You took some drug in front of me;
I still pretended not to see.
The days and years went by this way:
I held my tongue, you had your say.
Each month it was another boy,
another drug, another toy.
"There never was a Land of Hout,"
you said, "just a garden, a house,
a bunch of rooms with furniture—
now someone else is living there.
It isn't ours anymore.
Why don't you knock on their front door,
say 'Land of Hout, proprietors'
and see how fast you land up in
the lockup or the loony bin?"
Irreverence and sacrilege
are born of too much privilege.
What I think sacred is profane,
especially the family name.
You spit it out, the name van Hout,

like something vile shoved in your mouth.
Things haven't changed, though years have passed,
each day a copy of the last—
I ask what you are mad about;
you roll your eyes, throw up your hands
as if I wouldn't understand
the grudge you hold against the Land.
It's one thing for you to blame it,
another thing for you to name it.
I am the very soul of sin—
and They who let the Rumours in?
You never say a word of Them.
I did the best I could for you.
How could anyone stay true
to such a child, a dissident
with nothing to protest against?

You left before you went away,
you found yourself a place to stay,
a "pad" for which I had to pay.
You called Her My, still called me Dad.
I went to visit, not with My—
I knew She couldn't stand that I
would let you gloat as if you'd won.
You knew I'd let you have your fun;
your tantrums passed and you calmed down.
Till after dark, we made small talk,
the two of us, we took those walks
before we drove out to the Cape.
I dropped you off and got home late.
Your mother did not make a fuss,
a woman scorned by both of us.

I still recall you sitting there
as Rachel brushed your long black hair,

enchanted by the roaring blaze,
a child lost in a fog, a daze,
a child remembering the days
before she came into the world,
before she was a little girl,
a child still in the Land of Hout
before They let the Rumours out,
before the Rumours spoiled Within—
van Hout was cast Without again.

WADE

"So when do I get to meet your family?" Rachel said, a week after the encounter with Carmen and Fritz, as we hiked along the base of Signal Hill, the waves echoing in the caves beneath the ground we walked on.

"They're very short," I said.

"Well, I wish you'd told me that before, because I don't date guys who have short parents."

"It's a defining feature of the Jacksons, except for me. My mom is four ten. Dad's about five two; my brothers and sisters range between five three and five six."

"You're what, six four? How did *that* happen?"

I shrugged. "I don't eat vegetables, as you know. They do."

She laughed. "And you think that's why you're taller than them?"

"That's what *they* think. I eat a lot of protein because I like fish. I had to cook it myself because no one else in the family but Dad liked it. I mean, it's all just a joke. Sort of. *You're* taller than all of them and you're a vegetarian."

"You make them sound like gnomes."

"I've given you accurate numbers. Anyway, consider yourself invited. I'll check with Mom about how much time she'll need to lecture the others on how to behave. Not that it will have any effect."

"Thanks for not making me nervous. Don't say anything about Fritz and Carmen, okay?"

I smiled at her. "Believe me," I said, "I wasn't planning to."

"Well, don't say anything about my diary or Anne Frank, either. Not yet."

"Relax," I said. "I'll think up a pseudonym for you."

"And don't tell your mother that I'm a vegetarian. She'll get all flustered if you do."

"But if I don't tell her, there might not be much for you to eat, and then she'll get even more flustered and so will everyone else, and you'll be hungry. You don't know my mom."

"Well, I know that she'll ask you to ask me what I want for dinner, and it wouldn't be polite for me to tell her what I want. Don't worry, I'll be fine." She sounded as if she'd faced exactly this situation a thousand times before.

A few days later, as we drove to my parents' house, I asked Rachel if she'd ever been to Petty Harbour, my hometown.

"I've driven through there," she said. "And it's on a lot of postcards."

"That's because it's the closest outport to St. John's. Tourists can drive five miles and say they've been to an outport."

"It's beautiful," she said as we drove down the hill toward the sea. "It reminds me a bit of Cape Town."

"Really?"

"All the brightly coloured houses—they're like the ones in the Bo-Kaap, the East Indian part of Cape Town."

"I bet you spent a lot of time there when you were growing up."

"Very funny."

"It doesn't look like the setting of a novel, does it?" I said.

"No place does until it is, I guess," she said. "But I think it's beautiful. Besides, aren't novels set in here?" She tapped her forehead. "That's where everything I write is set."

My parents' tiny house was built into the side of a cliff, as were the houses around it, the front supported by wooden beams that looked like stilts. "No flat land," I said. "Hillside soccer was invented here." As she parked I warned her, "Better put on the handbrake or this car will wind up in the harbour."

As soon as we got to the door, I smelled pork chops frying and glanced at Rachel, who seemed unconcerned. Mom came out to the porch and I introduced them.

"Hi, Jennie," Rachel said and stooped to give Mom a hug. Mom was barely able to rest her chin on Rachel's shoulder. When they pulled apart, Mom smiled at me in a way I knew she couldn't fake. My dad was right behind her.

"Hi, Art," Rachel said, as she hugged my father, too.

"So, Jennie," she said, turning back to my mother. "I'm a vegetarian."

My mother looked at me, nonplussed, then back at Rachel. "My love," she said, "I haven't even got a head of lettuce in the house. Pork chops, potatoes and bread is what we're having. I usually boil up some carrots and turnips, but I forgot to get some."

"I eat potatoes and bread," Rachel said, "and I can make an omelette if you have some eggs."

"You'll *have* to make it, my love," Mom said, "because I've never even seen an omelette in my life." None of us had. Eggs were boiled or fried.

"There might be something in the deep-freeze that she'd like," my father said. We considered him to be an adventurous eater.

He went downstairs and came back up with a frost-encrusted bag of Brussels sprouts—infused with Béarnaise sauce, the label said.

"My God, Art," Mom said, "she can't eat those. They've been down there for at least ten years. That sauce will taste like vinegar."

"All the better," I said. "It might disguise the taste of the Brussels sprouts."

"I'll give them a try," Rachel said.

While Mom tended to the pork chops, Rachel warmed up the Brussels sprouts and, just before the chops were done, whipped up two eggs in a bowl with a fork while my mother, looking worried, watched. "Breakfast for dinner?" she said. Rachel smiled at her and nodded.

Two of my brothers had moved out, but my sisters—Cathy, who was sixteen, and Sylvie, who was fourteen—and my twenty-year-old brother, Paul, were still at home and joined us for dinner. Rachel and my father split the Brussels sprouts between them.

"Dig in," Dad said. The rest of us, as we dug in, watched Rachel. As we noisily and self-consciously cut and chewed our pork chops, she virtuously, frugally and silently devoured an entire plateful of things that had not been killed just to please her palate. She did not eat at what I had once imagined was a vegetarian's pace. She finished everything on her plate before the rest of us were halfway done.

"You don't savour your food," my father said. "You're a bolter."

Cathy piped up: "It doesn't take as long to stab a Brussels sprout as it does to cut a pork chop."

Rachel laughed, but my mother scowled at Cathy.

"Does it bother you that we're eating meat?" my father said.

Rachel shook her head.

"So your motto is live and let live?"

"If it was," Rachel said, "then it *would* bother me that you're eating meat."

"She got you there, Dad," Paul said. My father grinned sheepishly.

After dinner, as my mother started to clear the table, Rachel put her hands on her shoulders and gently guided her to a chair. "You sit down, Jennie," she said. She pointed at my sisters. "And the two of you stay put. I'll do the dishes and the men will help me." And we did.

When the dishes were done, we sat around in the living room. We would normally have watched TV, but Mom considered it rude to turn the set on when company was in the house.

"What's yoga like?" asked Sylvie.

Rachel looked at me and I explained: "I've told them a lot about you."

"Well," she said, "my kind of yoga has nothing to do with burning incense or meditating."

"Do some for us?"

"Is that the price of dinner in this house?" Rachel teased.

"Now, Sylvie," Mom said, "Rachel doesn't have to perform for us."

"I'm not exactly dressed for it," Rachel said, "but there's one pose I can do in a dress." She lay on her stomach, put the palms of her hands on the floor just above her hips and, with no apparent effort, rose up on her hands, her feet off the floor, her legs, back and head in a perfect, horizontal plane.

"Holy shit!" Paul said.

"Do you think you can do that, boys?" my father said. Paul and my sisters stared at Rachel in wide-eyed disbelief. My mother looked mystified as to what the point was of practising for years to get the knack of doing such a thing.

When Rachel went to the bathroom, Paul clapped me on the back and, laughing, said that she was pretty much what he thought the first girl I brought home would be like, only better-looking. The family consensus seemed to be that I had fallen for a surprisingly charming, outdated hippie.

"The yoga girl," my father called her ever after.

When Rachel got back, my father asked her what Switzerland was like.

"Switzerland was boring," Rachel said. "My mother went off to see other relatives in London for a while, so I was there alone in this village in the mountains with my aunt and uncle. Six weeks with no one else for miles. I was twelve. All I did all day was hike."

"Yes, but you were in the Swiss Alps," my father said. "I don't think I'd be bored in Switzerland. I was never bored when I was twelve."

"Because you weren't alone," she said, and smiled at him as if to say she knew that, like her, he couldn't stand to be alone.

"Maybe," he said, nodding.

I couldn't help marvelling that my fisherman father and my girlfriend had just bonded over yoga and Switzerland and boil-in-the-bag Béarnaise-infused Brussels sprouts that had been fossilizing in our deep-freeze for ten years.

From *The Arelliad*

WADE (1983)

I sink into the page again;
I'm writing in Arellian.
It still seems strange, despite the years,
and once again I feel the fear
that comes when I give in to hope—
once I give in, it's hard to stop:
a drug I'm not supposed to take
in case it turns out that I like
it more than those that Doc prescribed
when I began to diarize.

I wish I'd known you years ago, the boy next door whom I'd annoy when I pretended not to see you showing off in front of me. What were you like before you dreamed of writing books, your fondest wish to become what I wish I wasn't? You may have been content to be one of the Jackson family that made its living from the sea, the Petty Harbour Jackson clan that chose to stay where it began, or gave no thought to leaving home for much longer than a week or two. I wish I'd been one of the girls who'd never seen the outside world and never really wanted to, or wanted anything but you. I wish it had been understood that you and I would live together happily in a hillside house above the harbour, where I'd keep watch until your boat came into view before last light.

You still taste like the sea to me,
the fisherman you used to be;
the wind, the mist, I know that smell,
for I am from the sea as well.
Perhaps I swam beneath your boat.
You cannot swim or stay afloat—
the water is too cold for you
to swim in as I used to do.

You skim the surface of the sea—
you cannot make your way to me
so I must make my way to you,
an old tale with a turn that's true.

Do your parents wonder if I'm just a symptom of your far-fetched ambition? Maybe they think that you and I are just putting on airs to set ourselves apart from them. You shun the girls you grew up with and bring home the yoga girl, the foreigner. They might be right, your mom and dad, and I'm nothing more than something weird washed up on shore that will soon go back to where it came from.

I love your home, your hillside lair, but I might not if I'd grown up there. Some of the houses are inches from the road that narrows to one lane where the settlement begins. *Hvggonvmg.* Settlement.

You stressed it: "The proper word is *settlement*. I don't know why, I really don't. The townies come to visit from the city, the Sunday tourists who, after they have been to church, come here to gawk."

You're writing when you talk like that. You haven't got it all worked out, the place you love but sometimes hate, how much you'll miss where you were born once you begin to write about it.

On stormy nights as a child you could hear the foghorn blare from the lighthouse at Cape Spear; the smell of the cold, landward wind, the fishing gear, the nets spread on the rocks to dry. You'll remember it all, what it was like to be a boy, to be a boy there, exactly there, a place you'll long for when you move away.

I know that I romanticize the look that comes over you when we arrive at Petty Harbour—more puzzlement than wistfulness, over a riddle you would try to answer if only you knew what the riddle was. What is it that's eluding you? What's there in every inch of home? You say that it will drive you mad. I doubt it very much, I say—well, not aloud but in my mind, for *mad* is more than just a word to me and something you will never be.

Perhaps I should explain to you how far from mad you are, how far from mad you've always been, but then I'd have to tell it all, spill it all out, and I think I know what you would do.

The Encyclopediary. You didn't get it. How could you? If I showed you pictures of me recovering from injuries, on crutches or in bandages, on life support in the ICU, you'd understand what I'd been through. But you missed my message, which was: Here's what writing books can do; I wrote all these and it's a wonder I'm alive. *Those* injuries you couldn't see because you were so jealous and impressed. A blocked writer and his hypergraphic girlfriend. You can't start and I can't stop. A match made in Arellia.

I've lived in a Secret Annex of my own, left the world behind in favour of the confines of Arellia, the sanctuary of my mind. Or so my mind would have me believe.

I've never been to the secret house where Anne Frank and the others hid out for eight hundred days. I've never seen it except in photographs, though I've often been to Amsterdam. I'm afraid to go there. It might only make things worse.

Avoid the windows lest they see
a face where faces shouldn't be.
Like Anne, I left the world behind—
I chose the confines of my mind,
or was it that my mind chose me
to live in it in secrecy?

It was the same for Anne and me:
the two of us wrote silently.
The time for speaking was at night—
I wrote and spoke by candlelight;
the candles flickered in the gloom
and made a chapel of my room.
I whispered every word I wrote,
but even then I spoke in code
and made sure that Their door was closed.
The candles burned down as I rhymed;
by keeping count, I measured time.
By number ten, the night was done,

the curtains framed by morning sun;
the smell of wax, the smell of smoke—
I fell asleep as others woke
until I heard Her at the door
just as I had the day before.
She turned the knob and peered inside,
surveyed till she was satisfied
I hadn't set something ablaze,
then shut the door and went away.

What have I done all night except
the very thing I shouldn't do,
or run the risk of losing you?

WADE

Rachel's parents returned from Amsterdam, something I'd been dreading all summer, both in spite of and because of Rachel's assurances that they acted the same way toward most people whether they liked them or not. "Remember," Rachel said as she drove me to the house to meet them in the afternoon, "Dad's parents died before the war. He was on his own from the age of fourteen, I think. And Mom is an only child and *her* mother died a long time ago. They've left it all very vague."

"Thanks for the family necrology," I said.

"Touchy subjects, I guess," she said. "Dad's mother died after his dad, I think, which is why he was on his own. I can never remember the story. A couple of months later, the Nazis seized the house and the houses of all his relatives. After that, he was pretty much on his own. I should know more, but I don't."

I met them in the kitchen, where they were standing about, waiting for us.

"Hans van Hout," her father said, stepping briskly toward me with his hand held out. I took it and he looked me in the eye in a hail-fellow-well-met sort of way. His eyes seemed pea-sized behind his thick lenses, the pale blue irises not much more than dots. He was a big man, not quite as tall as me, but broader in the shoulders, his legs of a thickness that even his baggy slacks could not disguise. He was bald but for some shortly cropped grey hair at his temples. Everything he wore had the homemade look of the clothes Rachel had worn the night we met: a wrinkled white shirt, the oversized grey slacks whose cuffs bunched about his shoes, which looked like they had been left to dry in the sun after having been submerged in muddy water.

"Wade Jackson," I said, matching the firmness of his grip and the earnestness with which he'd said his name. I had never offered my name like that before and felt ridiculous. I dearly hoped he was not customarily so earnest. I didn't think I could go on pretending to be the forthright, upstanding young man he seemed to hope I was for very long. I needn't have worried. It would be more than a year before he addressed me directly again.

"Nice to meet you, Wade," Myra said, smiling at me. She had a mass of dark freckles on her cheeks, and eyes as round and brown as Rachel's. Her hair was short and going grey. She was much stouter than the rest of her family, her face and her bare arms darkly tanned. Her accent was not like her husband's. It was, Rachel told me later, the accent of the non-Afrikaans South African, whereas Hans's was a blend of several accents, the primary one being Dutch. Myra stood in a kind of recitation posture that I later learned she had been taught at convent school, forearms at waist height, the fingers of one hand gripping the fingers of the other—Rachel said later it was a kind of glee club singer's pose, taught to her by the nuns of the Star of the Sea Convent in Kalk Bay, a way for a girl to keep her hands, arms and torso absolutely still while she was among grown-ups. She looked about the room as public speakers do to engage their entire audience, smiling all the while in the most gracious-seeming, welcoming of ways. This was Myra's public posture, indoors, outdoors, no matter what the setting or the circumstances, but it seemed to me that it was not meant to fool anyone. It was as if she wanted people to see that she was posing so as to keep them at a distance.

Hans said something in another language.

"Afrikaans," Rachel said, looking playfully at her father, "is the language they speak to each other when they don't want people to know what they are saying. When they're keeping deep, dark secrets. You two forget that I can speak it."

"You speak it very badly," Hans said. "You should never translate it."

"I will, though," Rachel said, and kissed him on the cheek.

"I'm dreading the jet lag from that flight," Hans said to Myra. "Sitting in one place for all that time with nothing to do, it's pure torture. I'm exhausted but I feel like I should stretch my legs for three or four hours."

"Hans is very restless," Myra said to me. "He can't stand to stay put, whereas I quite like having nothing to do but read or talk. Even on a plane he's more often on his feet than not. He stands beside his row as if he's waiting for someone to come back from the washroom."

"I have to drink my Horlicks later," he said. "Don't let me go to bed without it."

"Hans has ulcers. If he is going to have any chance of getting to sleep, I'd better not forget the Horlicks," Myra said. "So Rachel tells us you want to be a writer?"

"Yes," I said, "I—"

"And you're a reporter now?"

"Yes—"

"So you're already a writer. Or do newspapers and magazines not count?"

"They do. I'm a writer but not the kind of one I want to be. The kind who writes."

She smiled and tilted her head slightly to one side as if she was both charmed by my youthful idealism and hoped that the inevitable dashing of my dreams wouldn't break my heart.

Hans appraised me for a moment in silence, or seemed to. It was hard, because of his glasses, to read his eyes or even tell what they were focused on. Then he went upstairs without a glance in my direction.

"Well, it was so nice to meet you, Wade," Myra said. "Perhaps we'll meet again." It was the first time anyone had bid me goodbye before I said that I was leaving.

"What's Horlicks?" I asked Rachel on the doorstep. She laughed. "Some sort of malt beverage. Tastes like chalk. Horlicks is usually prepared with hot milk or hot water, but very few houses in Cape Town are air conditioned and ours wasn't, so he got into the habit of drinking Horlicks ice-cold so it would cool him down at bedtime. Even here he drinks it ice-cold. Mom makes him a glass every afternoon and puts it in the fridge with a saucer on top. He drinks it every night at bedtime, which is always ten o'clock, but bedtime is not to be confused with sleep time. I swear he never sleeps. I've heard him up and pacing around downstairs at all hours. Sometimes he goes out driving."

Hans emerged from the house and, without a word to either of us, got into the Malibu and drove away, seeming quite jaunty despite his complaints in the kitchen. Rachel and I sat on the swing in the front yard. "He'll be back soon," Rachel said. About ten minutes later, Hans returned in the Malibu, and Myra came out, looking almost grim, and stood on the steps as she watched Hans get out of the car and open the trunk. She went to the car and got in.

"Come see, Rachel," Hans called. Rachel took my hand and we walked down the driveway to the back of the car. "We're going out, visiting," Hans said. "Would you like to come with us now that Wade is leaving?"

"No, we're going for a walk." Perhaps a dozen dessert boxes were laid out on the floor of the trunk: on two, "black forest cake" was written, on another two, "lemon meringue pie," on another, "pound cake with cherries." Hans, pen in hand, took a small notebook out of his shirt pocket and flipped through the pages, pausing now and then to write names on the boxes—Halliday, Fitzpatrick, Boone. He tapped his lips with his forefinger, consulted the notebook and silently counted the boxes, pointing at each one with the pen. It looked as if he was about to embark on a dessert delivery route for people who were shut in because of age or illness.

"Mom is exhausted," Rachel said. "Don't be gone too long."

Hans closed the trunk, hurried to the driver's side, got in, backed the Malibu out of the driveway and drove off again.

"He's going to drop in unannounced on friends or even people they barely know until all the pies and cakes are gone. It could take hours. They never stay in one place for more than half an hour, but they bring a pie or cake to every house. They won't be welcomed with enthusiasm. Polite tolerance, at best. But that won't put him off. I went with them a few times. I was never more bored in my life. I would just sit there, praying that my father would show some sign that he was ready to move on to the next house. My mother seemed just as bored and just as eager to leave but, as far as I know, she's never complained. To this day I don't know what all these visits are about."

The next evening, Rachel answered the door and, when I followed her inside, I saw Myra at the dining room table, crying. "What's wrong?" I whispered.

"I kept my promise to her. Remember? I promised her that I would tell her when I lost my virginity. I told her that we slept together."

"Jesus," I said. "Should I leave?"

"No—please stay. Mom won't say a word to you. Just pretend not to notice that she's crying."

From *The Arelliad*

SACRIFICE (1983)

That summer seems so long ago—
it only seems that way, I know.
If he's still young, I must be too—
the world is old, but we are new.

Wade says that he is going to be a writer—not that he is planning to be one, or hoping to be one. He is going to publish his first novel before he is thirty. He is going to make a living from writing fiction. He talks as if he can see the future and is merely reporting what he sees, which happily consists of him getting everything he wants. I don't know if this is bravado or if he is fearless because he doesn't see the obstacles, the dangers and the risks. Perhaps he doesn't know that, for everyone, the deck is stacked against success and even survival, doesn't know the cost of failure, doesn't know that even his own mind might turn on him someday. Of course, no one knows that until it happens to them. Some don't know it even then.

I plunge into the page today, but not into Arellia. I think I've sunk into the future. Wade and I are living in some city far from Newfoundland. I have no memory of the house and yet I know my way around it. Time passes as it does in dreams, in jumps and starts, in jarring transitions. We leave the city but the house seems to move about with us.

It isn't clear how old we are. I *feel* older. Wade looks the same as he does now, but I can somehow tell he's changed. It is a sad and silent house. We sit about and read, though I don't so much read *Het Achterhuis* as silently recite it from memory as I turn the pages. Wade is into something new, reading intensely as if this book will prove to be The Book, the one that will release the words pent up in his head.

We sat about the house like that,
my parents' house, when we first met.
We faced each other as we read

after we had been to bed.
From time to time, Wade looked at me—
I felt him look, I didn't see—
and then he went back to his book.
I took my turn and snuck a look;
I raised my eyes but not my head
and yet he smiled as if he'd said,
"I caught that look, you can't fool me"—
and just like that I knew that we
were young, in love and meant to be.

But now something is wrong. *We're home*, Wade says, but not out loud. In the future, if that's what this is, I can read his mind. The house has touched down like a plane and we're back in Newfoundland, in Wade's hometown. He frowned once when I called it *nice*. A tourist word. He couldn't stand to hear it said of Petty Harbour.

Across the way and up the hill, we see his parents' house. He smiles until I say that no one lives there now—the last of the Jacksons left it long ago, just as he did for reasons he cannot spell out. He thinks of the books he has written that have caused a stir among Newfoundlanders who don't know why he moved away. No one knows but me. Whenever we go back, they smirk at me, the woman he left them for, his high and mighty paramour who thinks the island second-rate.

If they spoke to us, they'd say, "You went away, but you come back so we can see how successful you are, to look us in the eye and say, 'I got away but you didn't.'"

"It's not like that," I'd like to say, but I never do.

He had to get away from here to see it as it really is, to write about it. How often has he told that lie? The truth is that he had to choose between the place he loved and me. The truth is that, if not for me, he would have stayed. I was afraid that it would be too much to bear, the ever-present past, the street, the house, the hills, Cape Spear—the city would have been a constant reminder of all that was done to me and all that I did and should not have done.

I was the one who had to leave, and I told him I doubted I'd survive without him.

Is it too late to set him free? This place is so much in his blood, the city that I never loved, the seaside town where he was born.

He will never fit in where we live. "I think of little things," he says wistfully. "How I felt when the weather turned a certain way, the snow changing to hail so small I heard it clicking all night long against the windowpane."

He thinks of better ways to live—the children that we didn't have. We said we would but didn't try. Why didn't we? I am almost overcome by the feeling that we should have parted ways long ago because of things I know that he does not.

Suddenly, it's dark and dungeon deep. I didn't know that I could sink this far down into the page.

The fairy tale has fizzled out,
as it was bound to do, no doubt.
It had the most unlikely plot:
boy meets girl who's out of his league—
adventure, mystery, intrigue—
out of his league, out of her mind,
out of this world, you know the kind.
He bites off more than he can chew
when he finds love with you know who,
the one this tale is all about,
the femme fatale, Rachel van Hout.
The princess fooled the prince, you see—
she wasn't what she claimed to be.
There was no damsel in distress;
the princess was the villainess.
The ending wasn't hard to guess—
I knew that it would come to this;
no poison fruit, no wake-up kiss,
no wistful smiles, no tenderness:

Wade can't save me and we both know
he'll die if he keeps trying to.
Is this the life that has to be—
presentiment or fantasy?

His world is solid and fixed; mine shifts constantly. I love the way he looks at "me," the woman he thinks I am, the one I wish I was. Until Wade, my only wish was to survive, to resist the urge to cease to be. When I convinced the doctors I was cured, it was me I made a fool of. I'm waiting for the downward pull—he'll sink with me, I know he will, all the way to the bottom, the ocean floor from which no mariners return. I knew he would, or should have known. This is the end of the future. Time's time is up.

For him it might be for the best that he lose me now. I can't just simply hope for the best. I did that once before but I can't again; I have to choose or it will be too late. Should I do what's wrong for me this time, so I can spare him and pre-empt the crime?

Is this the life that has to be—presentiment or fantasy? Is this a broken heart I feel? I feel it, so it must be real.

Arellia is any place in any time, the future merely one of its disguises. The two Annes drift about, not far from the yellow wood, unmindful of the failing light. Dark comes on; the things of night are stirring now among the trees. He's watching them. He's watching me, I know he is.

I hear the roar of Claws von Snout—
I must leave now, I must get out.

WADE

A couple of weeks later, as we sat at the card table, the place in my apartment that had come to be the one where matters of importance were discussed, she said, "I have to go away for a little while. Bethany is just out of hospital and can't live on her own just yet. So I'm going to go to Halifax to help her get set up there, maybe help her find a job. Gloria's husband, Max—he's pretty rich—has kicked in some money for us."

"How long will you be gone?"

"A month at the most. And then I'll be back." She came over to my side of the table and put her arms around my shoulders and kissed me.

"I wish you knew exactly how long you'll be gone," I said.

"I'll miss you, too, you know."

"It seems so sudden."

"When you meet Bethany, you'll understand."

When the day she had to leave arrived, I felt heartsick beyond expression, as abandoned as I used to feel when, as a boy, my father's quest for fish made it necessary for him to spend the night away from home. Rachel seemed brisk, sensible and pragmatic, as if she'd departed for the mainland at the end of every summer of her life, leaving boys and men to pine for her return.

"I'll be home before Thanksgiving," she said. "It's too bad you haven't got a phone."

"No, it's not," I said. "If I heard your voice, I'd miss you so much I couldn't stand it."

After we'd gone to bed one last time, she left me so quickly that we parted without tears or drama, just an awkward severance.

From Halifax, she sent me several black-and-white photographs that had been taken in '75 in South Africa by—I was surprised to read in her letter—Fritz. In the photos, she was sitting or reclining on a piece of driftwood on a beach, dressed in a white blouse and a white skirt, her feet bare, her long hair draped across each breast.

Then she wrote that she was knitting me a sweater, which she was going to give me at Thanksgiving if she finished it in time. Otherwise, it would be a Christmas present.

So that I wouldn't be caught Xeroxing at work a copy of what I knew would be mistaken for a love poem, I printed Matthew Arnold's "Dover Beach" by hand and sent it to her. In her subsequent letters, at least one of which arrived every day, she made no mention of the poem. She wrote that Bethany was "making progress." If I hadn't seen photos of Bethany in the albums, I'd have doubted her existence.

A month went by, and then Thanksgiving, but Rachel did not come home. As I was not an official tenant, my mail was delivered to the super, who left it for me in one of the unmarked, unlocked, dented metal mailboxes on the wall of the lobby. In early November, I found a card notifying me that there was a parcel waiting at the post office. I hurried there and knew as soon as I saw it that it was from her because the outer wrapping was fashioned from the pages of magazines, the whole bundle secured with precisely applied Scotch tape, the flaps on each end expertly folded. I all but ran home with the parcel under my arm.

I tore the paper to pieces and found a light-blue cable-knit fisherman's sweater. It was accompanied by a note:

My dearest darling Wade,
We cannot be together anymore. It will only hurt you more if I tell you what has happened. I'm not coming home for Christmas. I'm not spending Christmas in Halifax. I hope you understand what that means. Please don't write back to me, because I'm very sad right now.

Don't go by the house. My parents are mad with me for not coming home. Again, I hope you understand and I hope you like the sweater. I thought about you when I made it.

Love, forever,
Rachel

My first thought was that she had had a breakdown, so strangely written did the letter seem, as if she had to write to me in telegram form using only as many letters as she could afford.

It will only hurt you more if I tell you what has happened. I'm not coming home for Christmas. I'm not spending Christmas in Halifax. I hope you understand what that means. What could it mean, except that she was spending Christmas with someone she had met? *I hope you like the sweater . . . Love, forever, Rachel.* She knits a sweater for me while she's sleeping with someone else? And then she writes a Dear Wade letter to send with the sweater that she knit for me? *It will only hurt you more*? Nothing could hurt me more than her breaking up with me in *any* fashion. Who sends a present to a person on the occasion of breaking up with them? Who goes on knitting a sweater for someone after they have moved on to someone else? I felt her casual dismissal and betrayal of me so keenly that I ran to the bathroom and threw up.

Love, forever, Rachel? "Forever"? Was this how things were done in her world? She might have had it in mind all summer long to break up with me after she went away. She may even have thought that I knew that we would end in some such manner, that we had tacitly agreed to stick to the rules of the game she assumed I knew that we were playing.

Had her parents warned her away from me? Had they told her that, unless she went to Halifax to be the minder of her sister—Halifax, where she would also be beyond my reach—they would cut off her living allowance?

I wondered if, from the distance and perspective of Halifax and our time apart, she had come to think that I would never be a writer, *could* never be one.

I told my parents, siblings, co-workers and friends that Rachel and her sisters had returned to South Africa to be near their parents, who had gone back to be near *their* parents, who were in their eighties and needed looking after. I couldn't bear to admit to anyone that I was in such a state because a girl I had known for four months had thrown me over for someone she had known for, at most, six weeks.

How could I have been so lovingly embraced and so callously disposed of by the same person?

I worked longer hours than I had to, read even more books, no longer going out on weekend nights or on any nights, but sitting at the window that overlooked the parking lot, the light of my reading lamp the only light in the apartment. I devoured massive books of philosophy and history as if they might offer up the answer to the question of how I could have misread her affection for me so completely. But then, my parents, my brother and sisters had been fooled by her as well. I felt like telling them I suspected that I was one in a long line of men who wished Rachel hadn't made such a good impression on their parents, but I stuck to my story that we had broken up because she and her entire family had gone back to South Africa. "She was the one, Wade," my mother said, as if South Africa was just down the street from where I lived and nothing was preventing me from winning Rachel back but my pride.

I drove past her house, hoping she had come home for Christmas anyway and I might catch a glimpse of her. I thought of calling the house and asking to speak to her as I'd done from pay phone booths before she left. "May I speak to Rachel?" I'd asked Myra, who always answered the phone. "You *may* but you *can't* because she isn't in." You *cawn't*. I couldn't stand to think what she would say to me now. I thought of walking up the driveway and knocking on the door. In either case, I might at least find out if Rachel had come home. But I hated the thought of being told not to call or come by again, or to find out that she had instructed her parents not to tell me how to reach her.

A year went by without a word from her. Every day I went to work and I rode the bus home. One afternoon in September, as the bus headed south on Elizabeth Avenue, I was looking out the window at the northbound traffic—and there it was, the white Malibu, Hans behind the wheel and Rachel on his right, her body turned toward him so that I fully saw the sweetly smiling face I hadn't seen except in photographs since she had gone away. She threw back her head and laughed—and then she was gone.

I drew in my breath as if I'd been stabbed. That she and her father should be headed somewhere in the family car was perfectly reasonable, and yet it seemed impossible that it was her. That she should appear for an instant looking just as she always had and then disappear was maddening. That I could be so near without her knowing it, that she had not somehow heard me gasp or *felt* me staring at her, seemed impossible. Everything I'd felt when I read the note that she'd included with the sweater that, even now, I was wearing came rushing back as if no time had passed. Sorrow surged up in me until I thought my throat would burst. I pressed my face against the window and shut my eyes, my heart hammering, tears dripping onto my cheeks. I reached under the sweater, pulled out the tail of my shirt and used it to dry my face.

It had seemed almost bearable to go on without her when she was far away, but now—I pulled the cord above my head and got off the bus many stops short of mine. How happy, how entirely rid of me, of any need of me, she had looked. More tears fell down my face. I walked along Forest Road, past the penitentiary and the nurse's dorm that used to be a hospital, turned left at the entrance to the parking lot of my apartment building, hurried downhill to the door of my block and ran up the stairs. I could barely see the lock as I stabbed at it with my key. At last I managed to insert it, turned it and thrust my shoulder against the door, which opened with a crash.

As I slammed the door shut behind me, an errant piece of paper fluttered up from the floor, almost high enough for me to grab it. It was a file card of the kind I often used for taking notes. I bent over and picked it up. The front was blank. I flipped it over to find a note in pencil on the back: "I came by but you weren't here. I'll come back soon. I'm home for a bit and thought it would be nice to see you. I've been taking bartending lessons, sort of, and I know how to make some fancy milk drinks. We could have some in front of the fire at the house tonight."

I was just about to throw her invitation in the trash when there was a knock on the door. I looked out through the peephole and saw her, grey-caped and smiling. "Who is it?" I said, to buy time to compose myself. And then there came that laugh of hers. I opened the door.

"I missed you," she said as if we'd only been apart for minutes. She grabbed me in a hug and leaned her head on my shoulder. "Did you miss me?"

I was afraid to attempt a word lest it come out as a sob. I hugged her back, hard, and buried my face in her hair, which smelled just as it always had. I knew that if she was here in the hope that I would take her back, I would put aside all my misgivings and what-ifs and do so in an instant, but I wasn't, in spite of her note and the fact and feel of her in my arms and the smell of her hair, certain of *what* she wanted. What fancy drinks in front of the fire might mean to her, or what she might assume it meant to me, I didn't know. Could it be that she was merely proposing a meeting for old time's sake—two one-time lovers who were so completely over each other they could reminisce in front of a fire, reflecting on the time when they were too naive to see that what they thought was love was just a fleeting crush? Or was this yet one more example of me not having a clue about things that to her were second nature? I was ridden with questions that I couldn't bring myself to ask her for fear of sounding so needy and naive that I might provoke her into knitting me another sweater and writing me another inscrutably motivated Dear Wade letter.

When we pulled apart, she could tell that I'd been crying. Her smile wavered, her chin wobbling just a bit. "So, um—"

"I saw you and your dad from the bus on Elizabeth Avenue just now. I saw you in the car."

She nodded rapidly as if to assure me that I'd seen what I thought I had. "We drove home," she said, "and then I drove back by myself. I was planning to wait in the car if you didn't answer and try again."

"That would have been something," I said, "to see you in the Malibu in the parking lot, waiting for me like you used to."

She smiled. "Do you wear that sweater every day?"

"No. This is the first time I've ever worn it," I lied. "I guess I had a premonition." We were still just inside the door. "Come in," I said.

She put her hands on my shoulders and quickly kissed me, then patted my chest with both hands. "You get a bite to eat," she said. "Let me go pick up some liqueurs and stuff and come back for you. Mom and Dad are going out tonight. They need the car by eight o'clock." She left quickly, smiling at me as she closed the door.

"I missed you," she'd said so lightheartedly, as if it was all she would ever say about what she had done. Drinks in front of the coal-fed fire while we had the house to ourselves as we'd had so many nights before. What did she want?

The second we pulled into the driveway, Hans and Myra came out of the house, Hans in an ill-fitting grey suit and Myra in an unmistakably homemade evening dress. Myra raised her hand to me and smiled as I held the car door for her, but never said a word. As usual, Hans seemed oblivious to my presence. "You're late, Rachel," he said as he got in the car. They were gone before we reached the front door.

"Where are they going?"

"I think there's some sort of faculty event at the university," Rachel said, shrugging. "They're always going to them. I don't know why they bother."

"What do you mean?"

"I'll tell you later."

"Bethany has a friend who's a bartender," she said as we stood in the kitchen. "She taught me how to make all sorts of drinks." She placed a large carton of milk, a bowl of ice cubes, two large brandy glasses, a bottle of Rémy Martin cognac and several bottles of variously flavoured liqueurs—orange, strawberry, chocolate, cherry—on the counter. "There's not as much alcohol in these as there is in rum or whiskey. And the milk soaks up what there is, so that should keep us from getting *too* drunk."

"For what?" I said. She only smiled.

She mixed her concoctions and we went to sit on the floor in front of the fire. The drinks went down as smoothly as she predicted. The house was dark but for the light cast by the fire. We talked, but not about anything of consequence. Insisting that I stay put, she got up time after time and brought back more drinks for both of us, switching from one flavour to another.

"We are going to be so hungover," I said, but she laughed and shook her head. "We won't. You'll see."

"So what happened?" I said at last, not sure that it was not still happening.

She took another sip from her glass. "Strawberry is my favourite," she said.

"Come on, Rachel, what happened?"

She looked as startled as if I had shouted. Maybe I had.

"There wasn't someone else," she said. "I implied that there was in my letter, but there wasn't. You were good for me."

"Well, I'm glad I was able to assist in your personal growth."

That laugh.

"You were a hard act to follow," I said. "In terms of impressing my mother." The laugh again. I hadn't been with anyone since, but I guess I hoped she thought I had.

She stared at the fire as if to assure it that what she said was true. "I'm so sorry. You'll never know, never, how sorry I am. There wasn't anybody. You and I . . . we'd become so close so quickly. *Sex*. God. You have no idea what a big step that was for me. I felt like I had drifted into some normal person's life but wouldn't be able to keep up appearances much longer. And then, in Halifax, Bethany got worse, not better as I told you in my letters. In hospital, out of hospital. She tried to kill herself with pills. I didn't tell my parents, or you, or anyone, because she asked me not to. I did nothing but take care of her when she was out of hospital and visit her when she was in hospital."

"You could have told me. I could have come to Halifax—"

"You don't know much about anorexia, do you?"

"No, but so what?"

"You've read Kant's *Critique of Pure Reason* and Hegel's *Phenomenology of Mind*, but you've barely heard of anorexia. Wade, Wade, what am I going to do with you?"

"Rachel," I said, "I'm the one who should be asking that about you."

Nodding, she took hold of my free hand but couldn't meet my eye. "This past year," she whispered, staring at the fire. It might have been the name of a book that, were I to read it, would make sense of everything. After a long silence, she said, "When they weighed Bethany in the hospital the first time I took her back there, the scales said that she weighed less than she had since she was ten, and she thought it was a trick. She thought that all the people who wanted her to eat more and the ones who thought she was too skinny were conspiring against her, including me."

"But why did you do what you did?" I said.

"I don't *know*," Rachel said, tears streaming down her cheeks. "I was so *scared*. And Bethany didn't want to go home and she made me promise not to leave her. I don't know why I kept that to myself. I guess I was worried that you'd think that all of us were crazy. You probably do. Maybe you're right. I can't make any more sense of what I did than you can."

A whisper was the most that I could manage. "I missed you so much," I said.

She leaned forward and kissed me. I put down my glass, took her face in my hands and kissed her back. Eventually, she pulled away. "We can't go upstairs," she said, putting her fingers on my lips to keep me from protesting.

"Then let's go back to my place," I said. "We could walk or take a cab."

She turned to stare into the fire again. "My parents are going back to South Africa. For good, they say, but they once said they were moving to Canada for good—anyway, Dad has finally admitted to himself that he'll never be a full professor here or anywhere else, so he's packing it in. He can't keep himself from going to the dean with complaints about his colleagues, so he's made a lot of enemies. He might even be making things up about them—that's how frustrated he is. I know I shouldn't say that, but anyway, he's made up his mind. They're going to sell the house."

"What are *you* going to do?" I said.

"Well. So." She tapped my chest with her index finger. "That depends on you."

I was relieved but still perplexed.

"They've convinced Bethany to go to South Africa with them. Well, they're more or less forcing her to go. They don't want her living by herself when she's so sick. My parents have convinced Max not to give her any more money unless she goes to South Africa, where they can keep an eye on her and where they think the medical system is better. The thing is, though—this is the *big* thing—Bethany wants me to go with her. My parents do too. They want me to keep her company. Well, to help look after her. Also, they don't like the idea of *me* living alone again, probably because the last time they left me alone, I wound up in bed with you. And I have no money either. So."

I must have looked as disconcerted as I felt, because she kissed me.

"Sooo, I've told them I'm not going unless you go with me."

She may as well have said she was not going to Mars unless I went with her. *South Africa*. "What would I do there? Where would I live?"

"I've got this all worked out. I thought a lot about it, a lot."

"But I have a job. I still haven't saved up enough to take any length of time off."

"I know, I know, Wade, but just please listen. Because of the way they handle money, Mom and Dad have always known they'd have nothing to leave to us, so years ago they took out life insurance policies for each of us. I'm the only one who hasn't cashed hers in yet. It's worth five thousand dollars. Combined with what you've saved, we'd have enough to live on for, I don't know, a year or two? Not all of it in South Africa, necessarily. You wouldn't have to work. You could write your book just like you planned, and I'd be there for Bethany."

"First you say you have no money and then you say you have five thousand dollars—"

"Without Dad's permission, I can't cash in the insurance policy until I'm twenty-five. Dad altered my policy after my sisters squandered every cent of theirs."

"So you *don't* have any money?"

"Dad's agreed to dole out my insurance money month by month."

"Where would we live? With your parents?"

"No. We'd live together, you and me, in our own apartment."

"Your parents won't mind?"

"They'll mind a lot, but I'm twenty-two years old. They'd rather I lived with you where they can keep an eye on me than five thousand miles away. They don't like the thought of me all alone in Newfoundland, the only one of the family, their youngest, who is not without problems of her own, shacking up entirely unsupervised."

"Keep your friends close and your daughter's boyfriend closer."

She managed to laugh.

South Africa. Could I write there? I'd never done any real writing anywhere, so . . . I couldn't imagine what living there would be like.

"I know, I know, it's a lot to think about, but Bethany really doesn't want to go back there without me. I mean, she *really* doesn't. I love her. I'm in love with you. I'll pick you over her if I have to. I know that now."

"You've never told me you love me."

"I should have. I should have told you a thousand times. Especially since you may think I'm just saying it now to get you to say it back."

"I don't think that. I do love you. I didn't know how much I did until I lost you. I'll go to South Africa with you. I'll go anywhere with you."

"Thank God," she whispered. "Thank God it's not too late." It seemed again that she was either talking to herself or to some third person to whom she said things she couldn't bring herself to say to me. "Fritz and Carmen will be there, but they live pretty far from Cape Town. We wouldn't have much to do with them. Fritz won't try anything like he did before. You were a stranger and strangers make him nervous. You won't be a stranger anymore. Gloria and Max live there when they're not at work—did I tell you he's a pilot with South African Airways? But Gloria and Carmen don't get along, and Bethany doesn't get along with either one of them or Fritz, so it's a bit of a mess, except they all get along with me. Bethany says she thinks she won't get better if she has no one for support but Mom and Dad. But you know what will be the best part of it, Wade?"

Dazed, I shook my head.

"I'll be able to show you where I grew up. My city, my country. I've seen yours but you've never seen mine."

"Be honest with me," I said. "If I had said no, would you really stay here? I mean, would I end up with another sweater in six months after you went off to Cape Town?"

She laughed, then shook her head and frowned, then threw her arms around me and stamped my face with kisses. "You'll love it there. South Africa—it's not what people think it is. But you'll see."

"When will we go?"

"Just after Christmas, I hope. Mom and Dad have to sell the house first—it's all they'll have to live on."

We were in mid-kiss when the front door opened and her parents came in, Myra first through the door, looking flushed and upset, Hans behind her, looking . . . was it sheepish? Chastised? Myra ran up the stairs without a glance at us. Hans gaped at Rachel as if he'd forgotten she'd come home from Halifax.

"My ulcers," he muttered, rubbing his stomach. "I have to drink my Horlicks." He hurried past us to the kitchen.

"I'd better go," I whispered to Rachel. I kissed and hugged her. "I'm walking home," I said. "I could use some air. I'm not so sure about those milk drinks."

From *The Ballad of the Clan van Hout*

ANOTHER LIFE (1984)

I hate those faculty events—
I'd like to give them my two cents.
Instead, we go and make small talk,
ignore the knowing looks and walk
about the room, pretending that
the smirking faces of that lot
have aught to do with Hans van Hout.
Yet there are times, I must admit,
I wish She'd loosen up a bit.
If I could have another life,
if I could have another wife . . .
Ours was a short engagement—
it was short for She was pregnant.
Had I put up more resistance,
not slept with her at Her insistence . . .
I look around the room again,
appraising all the other men,
assessing fiancées and brides
and soon I put all doubts aside.
I realize we're all the same,
all playing at the same old game
of matrimony, parenthood,
all wondering if we should
have found another game to play—
there are no others, anyway.
I would not sully with divorce
what matters most—my name, of course.
The truth is fine for privacy
but matters less than what They see.
I must protect the name van Hout—
I must not let the truth get out.
Just like the light of long-dead stars,
it's but the ghost of what we were.

WADE

"What are we going to tell my parents?" I said the night after we met before the fire. We were in the garret, sitting at the little table. "I don't want to lie to them about us living together as if we're ashamed of it."

"Then we'll just tell them," Rachel said.

"Yeah, well, I know we don't need their permission, but they're not like your mom and dad."

"My mom and dad are more old-fashioned than you think. But let's not tell your parents anything about drugs or anorexia, or Anne Frank, for that matter. I guess we tell them everything else."

"So we won't say anything about your sister Bethany being sick? We'll have to give them some reason why we're going to South Africa."

"We could tell them the truth, or part of it, which is that my parents think this might be the last chance for our whole family to live in the same place for a while. And that you and I don't want to risk breaking up again. Your parents can see that we're in love. They're still in love."

"You think so?"

"Can't you tell?"

"I know they love each other, but I've never thought about them being in love."

"Well, you can take my word for it, they are."

We drove out to Petty Harbour the next afternoon. At the door, Mom greeted Rachel as if they had last seen each other the day before. "Hello, puddin'," she said. *Puddin'* was the ultimate of my mother's many terms of endearment for females much younger than her—nieces, their daughters, my sisters, a rare friend and, rarer still, one of her sons' girlfriends.

When I'd phoned her to tell her we were coming, she'd said: "I knew she was the one, Wade. Remember me saying that she was the one?"

We gave them our news after dinner, which had once again, for Rachel, consisted of an omelette. Paul wasn't home and my sisters were hanging out in Cathy's room. "South *Africa*. To *live*?" my mother said, looking shocked.

"To live for a while," I said, glancing at my father, who I knew would not object to any plan of mine regardless of what he thought. "Maybe just for, I don't know, six months?"

"Maybe not even that," Rachel said. "It depends on a lot of things."

"That means it could be longer, then," my mother said, but Rachel took hold of one of her hands.

"It won't be, Jennie. I promise. I just want to show Wade where I came from. My father is retiring from the university, and he and my mother are moving back home. Two of my sisters live there and the other one will be going with them. My parents would love it if the van Houts were all near each other for a while."

My mother smiled as if she sensed it wouldn't be polite to ask Rachel to explain further. "You'll be staying with your parents?"

"No," I said. "We'd have our own place."

My mother gave me a look that was as good as saying, "You're going to live together even though you're not married?" No one she was related to or knew had ever done that.

"Rachel's parents will be there," my father said, as if the fact that a professor and his wife would allow their daughter to set up house with her boyfriend meant that such behaviour was not looked upon as scandalous in South Africa.

Before Rachel could say anything more, we were interrupted by someone pounding on the front door. "Merciful God," my mother said, rising in a panic from her chair. Rachel sighed and dropped her head into her hands. "I bet they rented a car," she said. Before my mother could begin to make her way to the door, we heard it open.

It was them, her parents, who had stopped to ask for directions to the house from our neighbours up the road. Hans and Myra were in the hallway by the time the four of us got there.

"For you," Hans said, handing a white cardboard box with "Jackson" written on it to my mother. "It's a blueberry pie."

"Thank you very much, sir," my mother said, mystified, as she took it from him.

"Hans van Hout," Hans said, extending his hand to Dad. He firmly shook my father's hand and looked him in the eye as if to say, "Good to meet a man who disapproves of his son bedding my daughter out of wedlock as much as I do."

As I completed the introductions, Myra seemed sincerely apologetic for having barged in by surprise, but also faintly amused, as if she wanted my parents to know that she had long ago resigned herself to being a partner to such stunts as the one her husband had just pulled.

"Come in, come in," my mother said. "I'll put on some tea to go with the pie."

"Oh, don't trouble yourself, Jennie," Myra said. "The pie is a present. Rachel so often has our car these days, we decided we might as well rent one to go for a drive. We often come out this way. It's so lovely. Your home is lovely too, but we can only stay a minute. Believe me, Hans can't stay in one place longer than a minute anyway."

My parents nodded solemnly as if this made perfect sense.

There followed an excruciatingly awkward interval of silence as we all sat in the living room. Dad adjusted his glasses repeatedly. Mom, who would never smoke in front of company, which was when she craved a cigarette most, rubbed together the thumb and the index finger of the hand she smoked with.

"So," Myra began, just as my sisters emerged from Cathy's room.

Hans got up and hurried over to greet them. Crouching so that he could wrap his arms beneath Cathy's backside, he lifted her off the floor, held her aloft and looked up at her through his glasses, grinning until she laughed, at which point he set her down. Then he did the same with Sylvie. Mom was trying so hard to smile I had to look away. Rachel's face was a blank.

The girls immediately retreated to Cathy's room, and Hans returned to his chair, where he began to engage in the smallest of small talk, asking my parents the most mundane things, listening to their answers, his index finger pressed against his cheek as if he was sagely appraising the reply of a student to a difficult question he had posed in class. "So, you used to take Jennie to work unless she was going early, in which case she took the bus."

"Yes, sir," Dad said.

"Ah, I see," Hans said, nodding. "And where did you catch the bus, Jennie?"

"I waited beside the road. There was no bus stop, but if you stood beside the road the driver would stop."

"Ah, so he knew, when he saw you, that you wanted him to stop. You didn't have to raise your hand or anything?"

"No, sir. He knew because he knew me."

"He knew because there was no other reason that you'd be standing beside the road."

"Yes, sir."

Rachel, sitting beside me, stared at the floor.

After half an hour of this, Hans abruptly announced that it was time to leave. Forgoing the usual niceties of leave-taking, he and Myra simply left, Hans barging out as loudly as he had barged in, his wife behind him.

When they'd gone, Rachel apologized to my parents for them dropping in unannounced and leaving so abruptly, but my mother assured her there was no need.

There was an awkward silence until my father announced that he was going outside to the trash barrel to burn the cardboard boxes in which a new coffee table had arrived.

"Let's all go out," Rachel said.

Minutes later, we were standing around the barrel, watching the boxes burn. My father had taken his shirt off—he loved to go shirtless, outdoors, indoors, long past the time of year when his boys thought it was warm enough to do the same, but he never wore shorts or jeans, only slacks. He asked Rachel what the weather was like in

South Africa, and when she told him it was almost always warm, he smiled wistfully, as he always did when told about some part of the world he knew that he would never see. "I've never been anywhere but here," he said, "but there's still plenty of time, I guess. You two— don't take time for granted. Don't be fooled. It all goes by so fast. Take care of each other."

"We won't be able to afford to call you very often," Rachel said.

"I've never called long distance in my life," Mom said, with a sheepish smile. "I don't know anyone who lives far enough away for that. No one has ever called *us* long distance. Besides. South Africa. We couldn't *afford* to call *you* very often."

"Well, we'll send you our number as soon as we get it, anyway," Rachel said. "And we can always write to each other."

Mom nodded and burst out laughing. "I've only received half a dozen letters in my life. And that's about how many I've written. I have some aunts who married Americans after the war and moved to the States. Whenever I saw a letter with an American stamp, I knew it was bad news. You must think we're only half-civilized, Rachel."

Rachel shook her head. "We'll send you postcards," she said. "We'll send one every day. That way, you'll know it's not bad news."

As we were driving back to town, Rachel said, "When we were leaving, your mom looked me square in the eye and said, 'You take care of my boy.' She didn't say 'or else' but she might as well have. Your dad's a very sweet man. He loves you."

I suddenly felt as if I had already left. My eyes filled with tears.

"When you followed your mom inside, he told me he hopes that, one day, one of his children will build a house on that vacant lot next door."

"Did he?"

"Yes, but then he said: 'It won't be Wade, will it?' I said I didn't think so, and he said: 'Wade has always gone his own way. He's always done what he wanted to do. I wish *I* had.'"

I reached out and took her hand. "He thinks he should have done more with his life," I said.

"Don't be sad," she said. "We'll see them again before we go."

From *The Ballad of the Clan van Hout*

RETURN TO TIME (1984)

I loved it in the Land of Hout,
before you knew about Without,
before you understood that Time
would undo all things sublime.
Now that all is ash and ember,
it seems a torture to remember
when the van Houts were together,
my girls agog around my bed,
reciting with me as I read
The Ballad of the Clan van Hout,
oblivious to Claws von Snout.
All the while, Time, Fate and Fall
were gathering beyond the wall.

I wish we *could* go back to when
the six of us are six again.
We never have to lock the door,
we never have a visitor.
We never have to leave the house—
there's no one in the world but us.
The house has everything we need.
We even have a book to read
that's getting longer all the time;
the only book Within is mine,
The Ballad of the Clan van Hout—
we don't want other books about,
just the one, the book you study
(written for the student body)
the history and geography
of each of you and My and me,
a family society.

—

The only sounds come from Within,
Carm practising the violin,
the scratching of my fountain pen—
I'm grading papers in the den.
(The girls know that I'm grading *them*,
for I have no one else to teach—
four daughters with one classroom each.)
We have unnecessary things,
such as a phone that never rings,
and other sounds that no one hears,
the footsteps of the girls upstairs.
There is a mail slot in the door—
we never wonder what it's for—
a radio that never plays,
though Rachel looks at it and says,
"I like not knowing what it is."
We even have a TV set
that no one's figured out just yet.
We have a large grandfather clock
that never ticks and never tocks.
The timeless van Hout family—
I love its perfect privacy.
The van Houts' private universe
consists of nothing but the House,
no History, just Memory
of what took place between these walls,
which only some of us recall.

One day, that silent phone will ring
and, ringing, will change everything,
for all of us will run for it,
and one of us will answer it.
The mail will come in through the door
and lie in piles upon the floor.
The silent radio will play,

reminding us of Yesterday,
and books will turn up in the den,
reminding us of Where and When.
The TV set that we've ignored
will come to life when we are bored.
The silent clock will start to chime
and we will be returned to time.

WADE

"Wade the writer," Bethany said, taking my hand lightly in hers in the front room of the van Houts' house. "What writers do you like, Wade?"

"Thomas Wolfe, Jane Austen, F. Scott Fitzgerald—"

"Ah yes, the great Gatsby. The green light at the end of Daisy's dock, whatever that means. I was supposed to read it at Dalhousie, but I was too busy starving myself."

"It's a great book," I said. "And very short, so you should have been able to make time for it no matter how busy you were."

"Oh, I would keep this one, Rachel. If I had a razor blade as sharp as him, I wouldn't be here now." Anorexia, suicide—she spoke of them as wryly as she did of books. Rachel had warned me she would, but I couldn't disguise how taken aback I was.

Like her sisters, Bethany had round, inquisitive eyes that darted about as she spoke to me as if she was trying to detect what made Rachel fall for me. Beneath hers, however, there were black circles that she had not bothered to conceal with makeup. She wore a heavy sweater and loose track pants that I guessed were intended to disguise her thinness, but she still looked thin, engulfed by the clothes. "The writer appraises me," she said. "He is intrigued. Better than disinterested, I suppose."

"Looking forward to South Africa?" I said.

She arched her eyebrows and turned to Rachel as if in the hope that she would translate what I'd said. "Have you told him about Glormenethalee?" The two of them threw back their heads and laughed. I looked expectantly at Rachel, who rolled her eyes.

"It's a name Dad made up. It stands for the four of us. 'Glor' from Gloria, 'men' from Carmen, 'etha' from Bethany, and 'lee' from Rachel Lee, which is my full name. So, Glormenethalee. The four of us collectively. It's kind of sweet, don't you think?"

"Yes," I said. "And clever."

"And have you told him about you-know-who yet?" Bethany asked. Rachel nodded. "She really took it literally when her teacher said that *The Diary of Anne Frank* was compulsory reading," Bethany went on.

"*Het Achterhuis*," Rachel corrected her.

"*Ik ben je gewoon aan het testen*," Bethany said.

"She knows about twenty phrases in Dutch," Rachel said. "She said she was just testing me, which is meaningless, because I always say *Het Achterhuis*."

The atmosphere in the room was tense now, and I was relieved when Bethany laughed. "The amount of time you spent reading one book and writing your diary. Think of all the books you could have read or written. You could be better read than Wade by now. On the other hand, you do write more than he does."

"Knock it off, sister," Rachel said.

"No one in this family is playing with a full deck," Bethany said to me. "But each of us has a different number of cards missing. I'm sure you know all about my attempt."

"I heard about it, yes. I'm sorry."

"No need to be sorry. I'll get better with practice. So, Rachel, are you on the wagon?"

"Yup," Rachel said, turning to me. "When I'm on the wagon, it means I'm not diarizing. If I was off it, well, you get my drift. It's good for me to be on the wagon but bad for Bethany to be on it, because it means that she's sworn off food. So what about it, Bethany? Are you off or on?"

"On it," Bethany said, "but trying to get off, no double entendre intended, Wade."

"Wrist test," Rachel said.

"What's a wrist test?" I said.

"Rachel puts her hand around my wrist. Like this." She demonstrated, wrapping her own fingers around her skinny wrist. "She can guess my weight by how much her thumb and middle finger overlap. No more wrist tests today. The doctor did one this morning because I wouldn't let him weigh me. And it's not an exact science."

That evening, I stayed for dinner with the van Houts. We all had spaghetti except for Bethany, who delivered a ceaseless, self-lacerating but entertaining monologue while watching the four of us eat, then excused herself as we began dessert.

After coffee, I excused myself too and went upstairs to use the bathroom. When I reached the top of the landing, the bathroom door opened and Bethany came out stark naked except for the towel wrapped around her hair. She didn't run back into the bathroom or across the landing to her bedroom, but simply stood there, her hands on her hips, and stared at me. Her clavicle, sternum, ribs and pelvic bones were far too well defined. Her breasts, which might once have been the size and shape of Rachel's, sagged like those of a woman three times her age. "You look so shocked," she said. "Exactly what kind of games did you and Rachel play all summer?"

I could think of nothing to say or do.

"You're what, twenty-five?" she said. "Surely I'm not the first anorexic nudist you've ever seen." She turned and padded to her room while I went into the bathroom and closed and locked the door.

By the time I had composed myself enough to go back downstairs, Bethany was dressed and sitting on the sofa with her mother and Rachel. Hans was in his study. "So, Rachel tells me you're a Catholic prude like Mom," Bethany said.

"It isn't prudish to think that it's wrong to walk around naked in front of your sister's boyfriend," Myra said.

"I think it is," Bethany said. "Rachel, he looked at me as if he thought I should have numbers on my arm."

"That's not funny, Bethany," Rachel said.

Myra earnestly explained to me that, convent raised, she was long past the point where she could be cured of her shame about her body.

But that didn't mean she couldn't see the folly of raising her daughters the way the nuns had raised her. So, though she dressed and undressed and bathed behind closed doors, the rest of the family passed back and forth naked in front of each other through what they called the Bare Area, the landing onto which the bathroom and the bedrooms opened.

"It saves time," Bethany said. "We don't have to put on a towel in the bathroom and then take it off two seconds later in our bedrooms. We each use one less towel that way, too."

"Professor van Hout—" I began.

"Yes," Myra said. "Hans, too."

Bethany laughed at the look on my face and said that Hans bathed without closing the bathroom door. She'd seen him once, standing in the bathtub, bent over and scrubbing away as soap bubbles formed and broke in the crack of his behind. All five of them crossed paths when they were getting ready to go out somewhere, the girls nude but for the towels on their heads, Hans but for his glasses, his penis flopping up and down as he dodged his daughters, who found the sight of him hilarious.

Rachel, crimson-faced, looked at me as if she hoped the Bare Area hadn't put me off but had merely reinforced the view I surely held by now that the van Houts were eccentric. I managed to smile at her.

From *The Ballad of the Clan van Hout*

BETHANY (1976)
(Addressed to her but never read
upon the Ballad Bed to three—
read only to my Rachel Lee.)

What will I do with Bethany?
I used to call you Number Three.
"Please pass the butter, Number Three,"
I'd say when you sat next to me.
One day you called Her Minus One
and said that I was Number None.
Soon, laughing uncontrollably,
you seemed to slither from your chair
beneath the table, disappear.
I raised the tablecloth to see
you looking, baffled, back at me
as if you'd never laughed before
and couldn't laugh a second more
because your belly was so sore.
Hysterical upon the floor,
you suddenly began to cry—
you couldn't stop, I don't know why.
"What's wrong, my little Number Three?"
I said, but you just stared at me
as if you couldn't stand some pain
you didn't know how to explain.
You never seemed the same to me.
I never called you Number Three,
though She was often Minus One
and I was often Number None.
We pretended not to hear you say
the things you said ten times a day.
You used to act so playfully—

now everything was irony.
You wished that you were never born
but said it with such witty scorn
that even doctors didn't know
how much was real, how much was show.
If we had known what was to come—
but what could anyone have done?
If we'd been able to foresee—
but all of it was new to me.
As for the cause, it seems there's none;
as for a cure, there isn't one.
There is much in the Land Without
that no one knows a thing about.
Things the doctors call obsessions
seem a lot more like possession.
Those who think this superstition
haven't been in my position.
To watch a child as things run wild
in her body and her mind
is something only heard about
in this forsaken Land Without.
I swear that some pernicious elf
turned Bethany against herself.
You shed your body bit by bit—
you cannot stand the sight of it.
Psychiatrists will never find
the demon that controls your mind.
To satisfy this evil thing
you must get rid of everything.
The more of Bethany is lost,
the more must go, at any cost.
The more I try to disabuse you,
the more the risk that I will lose you.
The more you think (you can't refuse),
the more you think you need to lose.

It seems to you that up is down
and truth is nowhere to be found.
The doctors think they know what's true:
they think the truth's inside of you.

CAPE TOWN

(1985)

WADE

In the next few weeks, Hans and Myra did the reverse of what they had done when they moved from South Africa to Canada. They sold all the furniture, which, having been so expensive in the first place, might have fetched a good price had it not been so badly maintained. They had a yard sale for the smaller items, including every South African knick-knack in the house. They got five dollars for the black-and-white aerial photograph of Table Mountain and the City Bowl that had hung for years on the wall above the sofa. They were in such a hurry to get rid of the house that they got far less for it than they should have.

"I've arranged for my diaries and my collection of *Het Achterhuis* to be kept in a storage unit until we come back," Rachel said, as I helped her clean out her bedroom. "It costs next to nothing, and I've been assured that the books will be as safe as they would be in a bank vault. When we were standing around the barrel in your parents' backyard, I thought about burning both my collections, every volume of my diary and every copy of Anne Frank's. Obviously, I chickened out."

"Good," I said. "You would have regretted it."

"Well, I'm taking a couple of copies of *Het Achterhuis* to read while we're away."

Fritz and Carmen stayed at the house on Freshwater Road the night before we all left on the midnight plane to London, the first leg of our journey. To my relief, they lay low in their room, from which the smell of hash wafted downstairs. Rachel and I sat about in the front room while her parents and Bethany confined themselves to the kitchen. Rachel told me that the flight to Cape Town would take twenty-five hours, counting stopovers, one hour, Rachel said, for every year of my life. "You never know," she said, "you might have a fear of flying. In that case, each hour might take a year *off* your life."

"Thanks," I said. "But it can't be worse than bobbing up and down in a dory on a stormy day at sea. I spent my childhood doing that."

"Turbulence," she whispered in my ear. "You'll love it. You might get to be a member of the mile-high club if you play your cards right." I looked askance at her. "You've never heard of it?" I shook my head. When she told me what it was, I said, "Really?"

She burst out laughing. "Really. Gloria and Max are members in good standing."

Even as we spoke, a phrase from *The Great Gatsby* kept running through my mind. Nick Carraway, near the end of the book, wrote of being free of his "provincial squeamishness" forever. I wondered if I would ever be sufficiently rid of mine to write about it, but I also couldn't put aside my feelings of apprehension, of being in over my head with a family as odd-seeming as the van Houts. I thought of my encounter with Fritz and Carmen and of Hans and Myra's surprise visit to my parents' house and of all the things Rachel had told me in the first few months after we met. Because of our encounter in the Bare Area, Bethany had called me a prude and Rachel hadn't come to my defence. I was beginning to wonder if my notions of normalcy seemed as odd to the van Houts as theirs did to me. If they were typical of the greater world, I had more to learn about it than I'd suspected, things that I would never find in books of the kind that I had set myself to read, or in any other kind. I thought of the many hours I'd spent alone in my apartment, hunched over the card table and some massive book. Hans had lived through things about which massive books were written, but there was not a book to be seen in his house besides *Het Achterhuis* and the many volumes of *The Encyclopediary of Rachel van Hout*.

We would soon be bound for a continent that figured in none of the big books I had read or had planned to read. I felt unsure of almost everything except that I was in love with one of the van Houts, a family like none I had ever met in life or in books. Was I finally seeing with my own eyes things that were worth writing about? I'd long ago made up my mind that my first book would, like Thomas Wolfe's *Look Homeward, Angel*, be heavily autobiographical, a barely fictionalized account of my life to date, a coming-of-age novel by a person who, I was beginning to suspect, had yet to come of age. Rachel hugged my arm and pressed her forehead hard against my shoulder. I remembered how I'd felt when I read Rachel's Dear Wade letter, when I'd assumed that she had gone on knitting for me even after she had taken up with someone else. I felt something like that now—uncertain, foolish, toyed with, overmatched. For a moment, I had the same, sick, falling feeling, as if everything on which my life was built had been ripped out from beneath me.

Rachel's life insurance policy and my savings were not enough to pay the entire cost of what we'd decided would be a six-month stay, so she had convinced her parents to contribute what they could and Gloria and Max to cover the rest. It felt strange, as if Hans was giving me money to make it possible for me to sleep with his daughter. I felt sheepishly beholden to him, and to Rachel, Max and Gloria, as if Rachel and her father and her sister and her brother-in-law were pooling their resources so that she, at age twenty-three, a young woman still recovering from a breakdown, could share a bed with a sexual freeloader who would spend his days writing, or trying to write, or pretending to write, a novel. Earlier in the evening, Hans and Myra had looked at me as if to say they had higher hopes for their youngest daughter than the sort of provider a would-be writer who was not allowed by law to hold a job in South Africa was ever likely to become. They knew I had been a reporter with a newspaper that, even in St. John's, was looked down upon by all. I was a young Newfoundlander who had quit his low-paying no-status job to write novels full time for no pay at all while on a kind of furlough in my girlfriend's native country. To make matters worse, their daughter believed he would be a huge success someday. I fancied I would not have looked more like a poseur if I had been wearing a cape and a beret and sporting a cigarette holder.

—

We flew to London on Air Canada, where we connected at Heathrow to South African Airways for our flight to Cape Town. The SAA flight attendants wore light-blue tunics over white blouses, the tunics belted and double-breasted. Around their necks were scarves that bore the colours of the South African flag: red, white, black, green and yellow. Slightly aslant on their heads were pillbox hats with a large, round button on top that looked like the head of a spike that kept the hat in place. All of them were darkly tanned, almost all of them blond. They were all fluent in English, Dutch, German, French and Afrikaans. "*You* could be an SAA flight attendant," I said to Rachel, but she seemed unamused. "One in the family is enough," she said.

We landed in Tel Aviv, the last refuelling stop before the long flight down the African continent to Johannesburg. South African Airways had had its landing rights in the rest of Africa revoked years before. Rachel told me that Israel and South Africa saw each other as allies of a kind—renegade nations.

"Well, we're on our own now," Rachel said when we took off again. "No legal place to land from here to Jo'burg."

"What will they do if something goes wrong?" I said.

"I suppose one of the African countries would let us land if it was a matter of life or death. I guess this is why South African Airways is cheaper than all the others. You get a kind of suspense discount. And they make it up to you. They pamper you from start to finish."

She was right about that. From Tel Aviv to Johannesburg, it was like the flight attendants were serving the consecutive courses of one long meal, food and drink coming at us at a rate we couldn't keep up with. Bethany, sitting in front of us, accepted everything she was offered, then handed it back to me without a word.

Every announcement was made in English and Afrikaans. This was not Myra's Afrikaans, but harsher, more guttural, far more emphatic—something like German as it might be spoken by some profoundly exasperated parent. It seemed odd coming out of the mouths of these young, ever smiling, ever indulgent flight attendants, who, when they spoke English, sounded faintly like the Australians I'd heard on TV.

No one objected when Rachel curled up on the floor between our row and the one in front, her hands joined palm to palm beneath her head. Despite the incessant noise of the servers, I managed to get to sleep about three hours after she did.

When I woke, she was reading her daily quotient of *Het Achterhuis*, so I looked out the darkened window, hoping to make out something of the earth below, but there were only occasional lights, the first lights I had ever seen that were not those of Newfoundland. The continent was just six miles below but I couldn't see it. It seemed right that I couldn't, that I not be fooled into thinking I had seen it just because I had flown over it, looking down from thirty thousand feet.

While we waited on the runway in Johannesburg for the other passengers to board the flight to Cape Town, Rachel told me that, in June 1976, she and Carmen and their parents had been on this very runway waiting for a flight to London as smoke from the Soweto uprising rolled like fog across the tarmac. "I was terrified," she said. "We thought a revolution had started. Dad kept glancing over his shoulder and looking out the window. You could actually smell the smoke inside the plane. I thought we'd never get out of here. Dad said the riots were proof that the blacks were uncivilized and impossible to educate, so they should never be allowed to vote or to mix with whites."

"Your parents—"

"It's hard to say what they really believe."

RACHEL

As a child, I didn't think of Cape Town as being part of South Africa, or of South Africa as being part of Africa. There was only Cape Town, every square inch of which existed absolutely independently of the rest of the world, about which I knew nothing except that it was there. This would be my third sojourn in Cape Town. I'd barely survived the second. No one but my doctor in St. John's knew it, but I had a year's worth of lithium in my luggage in case I needed it—though I'd cut back to a pill every other day when Wade agreed to go with me to South Africa. Lithium dulled everything, sex especially, so I hoped I wouldn't need to take it more often. But it helped to know that I wouldn't have to go to some well-meaning doctor in Cape Town who might insist on me seeing a therapist, which, even if I could afford it, would be hard to do without *someone* finding out. "You're taking on a lot all at once," my doctor had said. "Sharing your life with someone else. Not living with your parents. Going back to where, I'm guessing, not all your memories are pleasant ones."

As we began our final approach to Cape Town International Airport, the sky was full of seaward-racing clouds, the sea a mass of white-crested waves. "I've never seen seawater of that colour," Wade said as we vied for space at the window. "What is it, turquoise? It doesn't look like the sea."

I took his hand. "You know, in the shallows, when it's sunny, seawater takes on the colour of the ocean bottom," I said. "A bottle of seawater from here and one from Newfoundland would look pretty much the same."

"Really?" he said in mock surprise.

"Really," I said, and gave him a long kiss.

"Rachel," he whispered, "if I go through customs standing at attention, I'm taking it out on you."

I lightly bit his ear. "Promises, promises," I said.

As the plane banked sharply, I pointed at things in the distance. "That's Paarl Rock," I said. It looked like a single massive boulder, a beige behemoth that seemed incongruous among a grove of trees and shrubs. "Paarl city," I said. "Wine country. Pretty boring unless you like wine more than we do. It's too bad that we came in from the north like this. Look, though, see there." I pointed out the window. "That's the side of Devil's Peak, and I can see the back of Table Mountain." I looked at Wade and realized that he wasn't seeing discrete landmarks but a blur of colours called South Africa. I wondered what he was thinking. I felt a rush of guilt. "Just wait until we get to Cape Town," I said, holding his arm. "It's so beautiful. We'll go see everything, Lion's Head, the Twelve Apostles—they're sort of mountains—Cape Agulhas—that's the southernmost point of Africa, and the Cape of Good Hope, which everyone *thinks* is the southernmost point." He nodded, his eyes fixed on the ground below, lips moving as if he was talking to himself.

"That's Langa, a black township," I said. Hundreds of rows of identical square shacks with roofs and walls of corrugated tin that reflected the morning sunlight were separated by unpaved roads and alleyways deserted but for an occasional white van that moved at a patrolling pace. "Almost everyone's at work in the city," I said. "The ones who have jobs, anyway. The ones at home stay inside all day this time of year because it's so hot. All the children are at school. When everyone's at home, in the evening, they're out on the streets and in the yards until bedtime, crouching for hours, never sitting down, never standing up. See, there's a firepit at the end of every row. It's very close in those houses, especially at night. Fritz says you can hardly breathe, though I'm not sure he's ever been in one."

Wade nodded but looked as if he hadn't heard a word I said.

WADE

There was no bridge from the plane to the terminal. We walked across the tarmac in the morning sunshine toward a squat, temporary-looking white wooden building that, I was surprised to discover, housed all that there was by way of South African customs, at least for those of us who had flown SAA. Two black beret-wearing customs agents in army fatigues and two security guards holding machine guns, muzzles pointed at the floor, were the only officials in sight. The customs area was so small that only about a third of the passengers on our flight could fit in it—the rest of us had to wait on the scorching tarmac. I was dripping sweat by the time we got inside, where anything said above a whisper was audible to everyone.

Hans, Myra, Bethany, Rachel and I approached the customs agent at the same time. "We are all part of one family, except for him," Hans said, pointing at me. "I will explain." Hans handed over two customs forms, one that I had filled out and one that he had filled out, naming Myra, Bethany and Rachel as co-travellers. "I am a South African citizen," Hans said, louder than he needed to. "I am returning to South Africa from Canada, where I lived for fifteen years. I am a university professor, but I have decided to retire and to live out my retirement with my wife, who is also a South African citizen, in the beautiful city of Cape Town."

There was a smattering of applause from those waiting behind us.

"This is my wife, Myra," Hans went on, "and these are the youngest two of my four beautiful daughters, Bethany and Rachel. They are unsure how long they will be staying, as they are Canadian citizens, though they were born here." He pointed again at me. "That is Rachel's boyfriend. He's Canadian. Along with Bethany, he and Rachel will be staying in our house, in separate rooms of course."

There was some laughter from the passengers behind us. Rachel tightened her grip on my arm.

"He will be staying for six months," Hans said. "He is not bringing any money into the country and he will not be taking any with him when he leaves. He will not be looking for work and will not accept any that may be offered to him. Rachel and I are paying his way, a fact by which he has yet to seem embarrassed."

More laughter. Much more. I wondered how much of this I would have to endure in the coming months from Hans, who seemed emboldened by his return to Cape Town.

"Welcome home, Professor van Hout," the agent said, and stamped all our passports.

"He's just teasing," Rachel whispered.

"He never has before," I said.

We waited on the other side for the rest of our party.

Fritz seemed totally relaxed as he presented himself to the customs agent while looking like central casting's notion of a drug dealer and with a woman on his arm who was obviously as high as a kite. I was surprised when the agent let them through without asking them a question.

After customs, we made our way to the terminal. I tried to take note of everything that was new to me, the sizes and shapes and colours of things, the way people dressed. I had met two black people in my life, both professors at the university. Now blacks were everywhere, pushing trolleys, sweeping floors, polishing countertops. I wasn't able to take in a fraction of what lay all around me. Men were leading women, and women children, just as Rachel was leading me, the children unfazed by what seemed to me like bedlam.

In the onrush of the crowd, I lost hold of Rachel's hand and was borne off as if by a riot. By the time I managed to turn about and resist the flow, Rachel had vanished. I was taller than most of those surrounding me. I looked out over their heads in search of Rachel's bright-blue T-shirt—but it was her face I saw first, her expression as she cast about in search of me as anguished as if she thought I couldn't breathe the air of this place she'd brought me to unless she was beside me. I watched her, wonderstruck that concern for me could make her look like that. "Rachel," I shouted, and our eyes met. When I reached her, she was trembling. She clung fiercely to me as I took her in my arms. "Did you think I'd been kidnapped?" I said as she pressed her forehead against my shoulder.

She took a step back and looked up at me. "You should see your face," she said, and kissed me on the cheek. I fancied that my face registered all the things she'd hoped I'd feel—wonder, amusement, confusion, apprehension, perhaps a touch of dismay. We were on her turf now, that kiss seemed to say, in the greater world, whose marvels she'd been unable to describe.

After we collected our luggage, we said goodbye to her family. We'd arranged to stay with Gloria and her husband until the place we'd rented through a travel agent was available. "They won't be home for a few hours," Rachel said. "Just as well. A little decompression time. She means well, but Gloria can be a handful."

More of a handful than Bethany? I thought but didn't say.

We took a taxi from the airport to the City Bowl area of Cape Town, which spread out like rubble from the foot of Table Mountain. We passed—what did we pass? The definitions of every word I knew expanded all at once. We passed what I took to be miniature oil derricks see-sawing up and down, seemingly unsupervised, sand as dry and white as salt, red soil that seemed to have been sifted free of the smallest stones. Palm trees that bowed slowly in the wind. I was barely able to take notice of anything that wasn't within fifty feet of the road on either side. It seemed the sun was not the sun that shone back home. Aside from being much hotter, it felt different in ways I had no words to describe. The smell of the wind, the colour of the sky, for which the word *blue* no longer seemed quite right—all this I assumed to be as unique to South Africa as Rachel was.

The taxi dropped us off downtown, where we rented a beat-up

Citroën for next to nothing. As the steering wheel was on the right side, which had not been the case with any car in which I had even been a passenger, and as the car was a standard stick, unlike Dad's succession of automatics, I agreed when Rachel said that she and only she would do the driving. "Besides, I sort of know the city. Very sort of. Wish me luck. Some things may have changed since the last time I was here. Traffic lights. Stop signs. Guardrails. One-way streets. Unimportant things like that. You know, in '75, I used to drive Fritz and Carmen home to Fritz's place out on the Flats when they were both too stoned."

We drove to the harbour and parked, and Rachel led me on a walk that, for her, turned into a barefoot run along the seawall at Sea Point, an affluent suburb, the ocean on our left, a high, meandering hedge on our right. "It's so nice and warm," she said. "I can't stand wearing sandals when it's so warm." A sandal in each hand, still clad in her blue T-shirt and jeans, she said she'd race me to the next turn in the seawall. Rachel's running had improved to the point that she could keep up with me while I slowly jogged, which was all I felt like doing in the heat.

As we rounded the turn, we all but ran into an obese black woman and a tall, thin black man, both wearing blue jeans and baggy white T-shirts. They were fighting, grappling in a kind of hug, stabbing and slashing each other with what I thought were knives but turned out to be screwdrivers. Neither of them made a sound as they grimly drove their screwdrivers into each other. They seemed to be bleeding from everywhere, their faces, heads, arms, torsos, legs. Their bloodied T-shirts clung to their skin, fast becoming more red than white. Patches of grass darkened by their blood glistened in the sunlight. "Oh my God, stop, stop!" Rachel shouted. I shouted "Stop!" too, but found I couldn't make a move toward them.

They stabbed and stabbed until at last they fell, side by side. I was about to go to them when we heard a vehicle behind us and jumped off the path just in time to avoid being run over by a Jeep on which a manned machine gun was mounted. Several white, khaki-clad soldiers sporting black berets and bearing rifles piled out. One of them pointed his gun at me and Rachel. "Don't move," he said. His tone was not hostile but like that of a doctor telling you to follow his instructions during some tricky procedure. I'd never had a gun pointed at me, but I told myself that, because I was white, I was safe. I was never so happy to be white. In what seemed like seconds, the soldiers threw the bloodied pair into the back of the Jeep, climbed in and sped off. The only evidence of what had happened were the two blood-smeared screwdrivers lying near each other on the ground, and the black beret of one of the soldiers.

As I put my arm around Rachel, a bareheaded soldier with short blond hair, so pink-cheeked he might have been a teenager, returned to the scene on the run, his shin-high, tightly laced black boots thumping on the path. Without a glance at us, he snatched up the beret and made as if to dash off when he spotted the screwdrivers. He grabbed them and threw them over the seawall, donned the beret and broke into a trot, his face one wide, sheepish smile.

"This is bad," Rachel said after he had gone. "This is a bad omen. It is. This is bad. A man and a woman."

"It's bad for *them*," I said.

"I know. I know. I feel so sorry for them, I do. It was horrifying to watch them. And we'll never know if one or both of them are dead. There'll be nothing about it in the news. But we are barely off the plane and we run into *this*. I brought you here to show you where I come from, and this is one of the first things that you *see*. A man and a woman in some sort of death struggle. I can't imagine what you think. *I've* never seen anything like this before. It's not as if it happens every day in South Africa."

"I know that."

"I wonder who called the police. Someone must have, though I bet they didn't give their name. There'll be no taking of statements, not from whoever called, not from us. Nothing more will be made of it than if they were a pair of dogs."

"What do you think they were fighting about?"

"Drugs, maybe? A few rands' worth of drugs. Maybe one of them cheated on the other, informed on the other. Some kind of betrayal. A lovers' quarrel, maybe. I don't know. I don't know how the blacks live. I don't know what our maids did after Mom and Dad drove them to the train station on Friday afternoons. We had a maid named Elsie. I don't know what she saw when she got off the train that took her home. I never rode the bus that goes from the train station to the township. I've never seen the township except from a plane."

"Let's sit on a bench and catch our breath," I said. She nodded, and we walked over to a concrete bench and sat facing the water. I tried to think of something to say but couldn't. When I closed my eyes, I saw the big woman and the thin man, embracing in their strange struggle. Only two people who had known each other for a long time would fight like that. A married couple. A brother and sister. Lifetime friends.

"I've never seen anyone die," Rachel said.

"They might not be dead."

"I think they are. Or will be soon. They won't get prompt medical help. They must work in this neighbourhood. Otherwise, they wouldn't have been allowed to be here. It says on their identity cards where they can be and when they can be there, and why. They might have been servants in some nearby house. The names of their masters and madams would have been on their cards."

I thought of the boy soldier who came back for his beret and wondered if he would wake from bad dreams tonight or if he would even get to sleep, for I doubted that I would.

"Let's go to Gloria's," Rachel said at last. "I don't think I'll ever stop shaking without a drink."

From *The Ballad of the Clan van Hout*

GLORIA (1975)
(Addressed to her but never read
to her upon the Ballad Bed.)

There really wasn't much to say
when Gloria was on the way
except "I do." My said it too
and we were three because of you.
Not that you had anything to do
with what we did when we were two—
I won't start this by blaming you:
it's not as if you told us to
get up to doing what we did
before we even thought of kids.
I try to laugh it all away.
To think two almost died the day
that Gloria van Hout was born
because you were untimely torn
from Her. You left Her with a scar,
a pale reminder that you are,
that you could just as easily
not be, you and My, the other three,
that I could have another life
with other children and a wife
that isn't Her, some other we
that isn't us: a memory
is all you'd be, the other three
undreamed of by a single soul.
The six of us came through that hole,
the six of us came out of My,
our entire family.

Six weeks in that incubator,
six weeks in your second mother,

you fought for every inch of room
in that artificial womb.
Had you shared it with another,
a combative baby brother
who knew there wasn't room for two,
I'd still have placed my bet on you—
a fighter struck by many blows
your face so red, eyes swollen closed.
I felt your every punch and kick
until I was so stomach sick
I couldn't stand it any longer—
though they said, "She's getting stronger."
They said there'd be no second child
because of what they did to My.
(They were also blaming me.)
The one who almost died would be
the first and last, an only child.
Though sad sometimes, I reconciled
myself to having you and having Her—
and being three and nothing more.

We raised you in the Land of Hout
which I began to write about
when you were hushed and She was out.
At first, *The Ballad* was for you—
you looked at me as if you knew
you were what I wrote about,
as if you thought I thought about
the one child in the Land of Hout
throughout the day, throughout the night,
when it was dark or it was light.
The world existed for we two—
all things were newborn just like you.

The second that you came to be
was not Day One of History.

You're nineteen and you still don't see
your world is here because of me.
A girl raised in the proper way
grows more improper every day.
You're all perverse—it's like a curse:
You just keep getting worse and worse.
You don't care what you grow to be
as long as it displeases me.

The night that I first read to you
from the book, you weren't yet two.
Though you couldn't understand it,
you seemed to like it just a bit,
the sounds, I mean, as if they were
the ones that you were hoping for.
I'd never read the book out loud—
my voice surprised me. I was proud
of what I'd done. I also vowed
no one but us must know about
the book, not even my Right Hand,
who'd be the last to understand
the point of writing such things down:
The Ballad of the Clan van Hout
(or what on earth it was about).

They called you Glory Hole van Hout.
Boys going past the house sung out
all sorts of filthy things that you
had done with more than one or two,
or so they said—who knows what's true?
My reputation follows you,
the things that I was forced to do
when Amsterdam was occupied—
if not for me, *more* would have died . . .
Once you have defamed the father,

you may as well defame the daughter.
What sort of girl could he beget
but one that any boy could get?
Are all my girls presumed to be
the apples of a rotten tree?

You call us weekly on the phone;
you barely have a word for Mom
and then you say, "Put Daddy on."
I take you on the phone upstairs,
where I can close and lock the doors.
You write us seven times a week—
you'd rather write to me than speak
to me, so I seldom write you back—
it's perseverance that I lack.
And Carm will be the next to leave.
It won't be long—I will not grieve
the next departure from my house;
she'll leave as quiet as a mouse
some night when everyone's asleep,
the blackest of my four black sheep.
Then Bethany and Rachel, too,
will leave the way that daughters do.

WADE

The road to Gloria and Max's place wound through the rocky hills just inland from the Apostles—twelve headlands with visage-like cliffs that faced the open Atlantic south of Table Mountain. The road was unlit and treacherous, a steep slope on one side and jagged outjutting cliffs on the other. The house, the only one that was occupied of dozens newly built along the coast, was a sea-overlooking mansion of three storeys, almost all of it made of glass. There was a gatehouse with a white sentry inside it with a rifle slung over one arm. When he saw us, he gave us a perfunctory wave and raised a black-and-white-striped horizontal wooden beam.

Gloria's husband, Max Dekker, met us at the door. He was in his mid-fifties, very tall and distinguished-looking, even though he was dressed in a black bathrobe and black slippers. "Baby sister," Max said as they hugged. When Rachel introduced us, he shook my hand firmly and waved us into the kitchen, where we found Gloria, who, as Rachel had told me on the drive along the coast, was the only one of the van Hout sisters who refused to wear homemade clothes as a child. She was fully made up, in a white bathrobe and white slippers, which she'd accessorized with expensive-looking earrings, as well as a gold watch and a necklace of what I guessed were not fake pearls.

"You're Wade," she said as she gave me a hug and a kiss on the cheek. She wore a perfume that smelled faintly of vanilla, and her hair looked as if she had just come from a salon, thick, lustrous, swept back from her forehead and her temples. She was taller than Rachel, bustier, fit but soft.

She stepped back, put her hand on my shirt and, to my amazement, rubbed my chest. "Mmmm, nice pecs," she said.

I shot a glance at Rachel, who frowned and looked away.

"If Gloria sucked a peck of pickled dicks," Max said, looking straight at me, "how many pecks of pickled dicks would Gloria have sucked?"

"The answer," Gloria said, "is one. I'm old-fashioned that way, Wade, and almost every other way, though *some*one may have told you different. You look familiar. I used to work for Air Canada. I may have served you on a flight."

"I'd never been on an airplane until we flew here," I said.

"*Hij moet grappen*," Max said, laughing.

"He says you must be kidding," Gloria said, and laughed too.

"No," I said. "I mean it. The flight to London was my first time on a plane."

"Where have you been living?" Max said without a trace of a smile. "Under a rock?"

"On one, actually. I've never been anywhere but Newfoundland."

"Oh my God, that's so cute," Gloria said. She turned to her sister. "And he's so gorgeous. How did you find him, Rachel?"

"If you follow a turnip truck long enough, something useful is bound to fall off," Max said, winking at me.

"I bet you do whatever Rachel tells you to, don't you, Wade?"

"He's not a dog," Rachel said.

"I know exactly what he is. Never on a plane before. All his life on an island. Bigger than Robben Island, but still. His first time. He'll never forget. *Ik herriner me mijn eerste keer*. I hope you know how to make *proper* use of him, Rachel."

As if it had just occurred to her that she had yet to greet Rachel, Gloria took her in a fervent hug, shutting her eyes as she stamped her neck with kisses the way Rachel often did to me. "Oh my God, it's so good to see you back home. I missed you so much, sweetie."

"I missed you, too," Rachel said.

"Are you, you know—"

"I'm fine."

"You finally have something to distract you from you know what," Gloria said, turning her eyes on me again.

Leaving Rachel, she took hold of my arm with both hands and led me to the counter. "Max bought up all the overripe bananas in the store today and has been busy making banana daiquiris. He's made enough for a hundred people."

"Pay no attention to Gloria," Max said. "She can't count to a hundred. Her brains are in her boobs." He turned away from the kitchen counter and appraised Rachel. "I think you've filled out a bit since you misplaced your virginity. Not knocked up, I hope."

"*No*," Rachel said. "We invented a way of avoiding that."

Max chuckled. "Well, as long as Wade keeps up the vaginal inoculations, you'll be just fine."

"Stop it, Max," Gloria said, laughing and flashing a flirtatious glance at me.

They went on talking like that about us and about each other and about anyone who came up in conversation. I found it more and more difficult to feign amusement, and Rachel did not even go through the motions of pretending to. It felt like Gloria and Max were following a script from which, even when they were alone, they did not depart.

A large bowl of freckled bananas sat beside a blender on the kitchen counter, along with an empty white rum bottle.

We stood about in the kitchen, Rachel and I with our backs to the counter as Max fed us daiquiri after daiquiri. They were very good and quickly went to my head. Gloria, who was teetotal, sipped from what she called a virgin daiquiri. "I'll never see the point of drinking. Max says that women who don't drink don't enjoy sex as much, but I am living proof that Max is wrong. I wore him out this afternoon. The poor dear, doesn't he look tired?"

Trying to change the subject, I told them about what had happened as we were running along the seawall.

"My God, how awful," Gloria said, but Max laughed. "Duelling screwdrivers," he said. "You could make a novel out of that, Wade. There are people who have lived in South Africa all their lives who have never stumbled onto something like that. They must have known a Canadian was coming."

"You poor *things*," Gloria said. "More daiquiris, Max."

He topped us up.

"Want to know a secret?" Gloria said, meeting my change of subject with another. "Max has malaria. He'll have it forever. He gets a fever at the same time every month and he's completely out of it for five days. He has pals at SAA who cover for him. They arrange his schedule so that he's never flying when he has what we call his period. I have to work during my period, but Max gets time off. Mind you, he's delirious, but still . . ."

"The worst you could do is spill a drink on someone," Max said. "Me, I would crash a plane."

Gloria laughed.

"Are you sure this fever won't just pop up some other time of month while you're flying a plane full of passengers?" I said.

Max grinned. "My doctor tells me it won't, and so far he's right."

I could think of no reply.

"We're going out tonight," Rachel suddenly announced.

"Out?" Gloria said. "I can't believe you have the energy to go out after such a long flight. And you've had too much to drink to drive."

"We can take a taxi."

"They're young, they want to go dancing," Max said. "The kind you do standing up."

"Well," Gloria said, "I'm young too, and if it was twenty-four hours since I had sex, I know what my first priority would be."

"It's because of what we saw along the seawall," Rachel said. "We're kind of restless."

"Max will drive you, won't you, Max?" Gloria said.

"Sure," Max said. "I'm drunker than they are but I know the road better. And I know where all the strip clubs are. That's how I met Gloria. Just kidding. I'll drive you, but you have to find your own way back."

"Rachel," Gloria said, "let me give you some money for the return taxi."

"You don't have to," Rachel said, but Gloria was already digging in her purse.

We endured more of Max as he drove us downtown. After he had driven away, Rachel, her arms at her sides, banged her forehead on my chest. I forced a laugh and put my arms around her. "I think we can expect the Kama Sutra for Christmas," she said.

"It's just talk," I said, trying to sound unfazed so she wouldn't be more upset.

When we got back to their place later that night, we found a note from Max on the kitchen counter, telling us that he had opened all the windows because it was so hot outside and asking us to leave our door open so that there would be a cross-breeze.

The next morning, hungover, we woke to the sound of them loudly having sex just down the hall.

"Oh, my frigging family," Rachel said, covering her ears with her pillow.

"So much for the cross-breeze," I said, as Gloria gasped loudly, over and over. The gasping turned to a kind of screeching, interrupted by loud moans.

"My God," Rachel said, "at least I know when to bury my face in a pillow." I laughed, but I found myself aroused and rolled over onto her. As our bedsprings began to creak, we heard Gloria laugh, then begin to moan again. "My God," Rachel whispered, "synchronized screwing?"

A little later, we joined them in the kitchen for breakfast. Gloria, dressed in the white bathrobe from the day before, walked up to Rachel, put her hands on her shoulders and began to examine her face.

"What are you doing?" Rachel said.

"I'm checking for razor rash." Then she came over to me and told me to examine *her* face for razor rash. "What do you think, Wade?" Gloria said. "Which one of us wins, Rachel or me?"

"I'll be the judge of that," Max said. He examined Gloria and Rachel, rubbing their cheeks with his hands. "I think Rachel wins," he said, "but it's pretty close."

"That's because you're an old man," Gloria said. "You can't keep up with Wade." Max laughed.

"Show Wade your tan, Glore."

"I had a four-day layover in Bermuda," Gloria said. "I spent every minute on the beach." I thought she would pull her bathrobe up above her knees, but she untied the belt and pulled the robe wide to show me every inch of her front. Except for the parts that had been protected by her bikini, she was, indeed, deeply tanned. She stood there, facing me, looking down at her body as if to see how her tan was holding up, rubbing her belly with her fingers, her large breasts shaking slightly with every movement she made. She gave me a frank, wanton smile, then covered up as if to say that it had somehow slipped her mind that she was naked.

"That's a very nice suntan," I managed to say.

Max laughed. "Watch this guy, Gloria," he said. "He might make a move on you." As our eyes met, Gloria's smile vanished as if she had seen something in my expression that she didn't like.

"Jesus, Gloria," Rachel said. "Enough, enough, enough. Does it never stop? We tell you we saw two people stab each other to death—never mind. I give up. I do. You win, Gloria. There is nothing worthwhile in the world but sex. Let's hear some more about this never-ending fuck fest you call a marriage, this ongoing orgy you call a *life*."

"*Rachel*," I said, and she looked stricken as Gloria ran from the kitchen, crying.

"I'm sorry, Max," Rachel said. "I shouldn't have lost my temper. I'm sorry."

"She'll forget," Max said. "You know she never holds a grudge."

"We'll stay at a hotel until our apartment is ready," Rachel said.

"You don't have to," Max said, "but I know that you'll insist even though you'd likely be murdered in the kind of place you could afford. Let me chip in something so that you and your sister live to fight another day."

"Thank you," Rachel said before I could decline his offer.

"*She never holds a grudge*," Rachel said when we were in the car. "I'm completely in the right but I go away with those words ringing in my ears."

"We did take his money."

"Yes," Rachel said. "I feel like an extortionist, but we need it. Did I go too far?"

"Maybe a little? She's just putting on a show. They both are."

"I'll tell her I'm sorry."

"I wish—"

"I know," she interrupted. "I know you do. It won't always be like this. When your books make us rich, we'll look back at this and laugh."

Our apartment was the upper storey of a duplex, small but immaculately kept, fully outfitted with furniture and appliances that looked brand-new. "God," I said. "This would cost ten times as much back home." Rachel went about inspecting it, nodding approvingly. There was daily maid service—we simply had to be out of the house every day between two and three in the afternoon when a maid would come by. From the window in our bedroom, we could see the scree of boulders at the foot of Table Mountain.

A middle-aged woman from Norway who was a visiting professor of mathematics at the University of Cape Town lived on the ground floor. "Dr. Angstrom," read a brass nameplate on the door of her apartment. She would be, for us, the ideal neighbour, as quiet as if she was incapable of making noise. She never had guests and almost never was at home except to sleep.

Rachel walked to the window and looked out. "Things will get better. There's more to this place than you've seen so far, more than anyone can find in books and newspapers. Or on walks along the seawall."

RACHEL

Once we were settled in the apartment, I took Wade on a tour of my South African childhood, starting with Sunny Way Preparatory School, then the Rustenburg Junior School for girls. We visited Rustenburg while school was in session, walking about the playground surrounded by girls who ignored us as if grown-up visitors were commonplace. The school uniform hadn't changed since I left in 1969—a cornflower blue tunic and tam, black shoes and white socks. I tried to imagine a foursome of these girls sailing away from home forever on the *Edinburgh Castle* as my sisters and I had, Canada their final destination. I couldn't believe I'd gone to school there. It was as if I was remembering someone else's life. "It makes me feel kind of sad," I said.

"Time sick," Wade said. "It's not quite the same as homesick."

I nodded. But I was really feeling nostalgia for a life I'd never had. I wiped a tear away, but laughed when I saw how concerned he looked. "I'm just being silly," I said.

From Rustenburg, we went to Westerford, where I'd gone to high school in 1975, when we'd been back to Cape Town for Dad's sabbatical. Older, much more subdued girls hung about on the playground in small groups, their expressions ironic, detached, aloof, as if they knew exactly where they were headed after Westerford, which they had already outgrown. The uniform was also the same as the one I had worn—a maroon plaid tunic and a boater hat with ribbons of maroon and gold, just like the one that was on the dresser in our apartment, one of my few school souvenirs. Wade had taken a liking to it in St. John's and suggested that we bring it with us.

"I was not happy here," I said. "I just wanted the year to be over so I could get back to Canada and my boyfriend."

"You had a boyfriend at thirteen?" I said.

"No," I said. "I just thought I did. His name was Jeff and I worshipped him from afar. But he wasn't the reason I was unhappy here. I was the Anne Frank fruitcake and I wasn't sure we'd ever leave. I thought I'd be stuck in South Africa forever. I thought Mom and Dad might have sold the house on Freshwater Road to pay for the trip. I was terrified that Dad would get a job at the University of Cape Town. I was alone a lot. Bethany had stayed in Canada, at Dalhousie. She was fifteen—another grade skipper, like me—and only came to visit at Christmas, and Gloria was in Quebec at Laval. I was stuck with Carmen and Fritz. Carmen had only just met him but she was already spending some nights in his house on the Flats. I woke up in their house a lot of weekend mornings having no idea how I got there."

As we toured, Wade asked me the names of flowers, plants and trees and, almost always, I drew a blank. "I've seen them a thousand times," I said, "but I don't know what they're called. I should know. I'm a terrible guide, aren't I? You know the name of everything that grows in Newfoundland."

"Only because not much grows there," Wade said. I laughed.

"I know one version of South Africa's history," I said. "The Boers who settled the cape before the Bantu even found it, the Great Trek. Most of it's not true. But the true history—well, I only know bits and pieces. The true history of South Africa isn't easy to find in South Africa."

The effects of it were easy to find, though. I wished that I could hide them from him. Everywhere—on benches, the gates of swimming pools and beaches, the doors of public bathrooms, train cars and restaurants—there were signs that read "*Blanke*" or "*Nie-Blanke*," Afrikaans for "White" and "Non-White." Wade said he doubted that he would ever get used to seeing them or having to abide by them.

I told him, "I'm not saying I think it's right, but you might be surprised how fast you get used to it."

We went by cable car to the top of Table Mountain, from which the view in all directions was spectacular—the sea, the city, the harbour, Devil's Peak, Lion's Head, the Twelve Apostles mountain range, with Max and Gloria's house in the shadow of the first Apostle. And the semicircle of black townships in the distance from whose outdoor fires streams of smoke rose straight up in the air. Gopher-like rodents called rock dassies, seeking shade and safety, peered out from under every ledge and bush. A tourist, definitely North American, declared loudly to his wife that he hadn't travelled five thousand miles to photograph cute rats.

It was sunny but somewhat chilly up there because of the onshore wind. Wisps of low-level cloud drifted by like fog. "I like to watch the ships," I said, staring out at the sea. "They always look so purposeful, going somewhere, making progress." Wade stood behind me and wrapped his arms around me. "Snow fell up here when I was three or four," I said. "Enough to collect on the ground and stay all day long. The whole city went nuts. Everybody crammed onto the cable cars and came up here to touch real, natural snow for the first time in their lives. Snowball fights broke out. The snow didn't last until the next day, but I've seen newspaper photographs. Dad didn't think it was any big deal because he had seen snow plenty of times in Holland, but Mom was pretty amazed. Apparently, they took my sisters and me up here so we could play with it, but I don't remember."

For a few days, we went to restaurants and, for next to nothing, dined on steak-like slabs of butterfish, rockfish, kaberle—at least Wade did. I had one Cobb salad after another and never finished one. "This country is not used to vegetarians," I said. "These salads are pretty bad. What I wouldn't give for an omelette and some Brussels sprouts."

Wade laughed but I thought he suddenly looked homesick.

What I didn't tell Wade: When the family went back to South Africa without her in 1975, Bethany came to Cape Town for Christmas and brought with her a book that contained the painstakingly calculated calorie counts of every known food and recipe. A friend of hers had lent it to her, her only friend, a skinny girl named Sarah Barnes. I had never thought of food in terms of calories before.

Bethany regarded herself as neither odd nor ill, and the rest of the world as both. For her, the sole point of living was to rid herself of the fat that seemed to increase the less she ate. She'd eat the white of an egg but be unable to stand the weight of it in her stomach.

The two of us, naked, side by side, looked at ourselves in the bathroom mirror one day. "Methinks I doth ingest too much," Bethany said. The bathroom scales told her she'd lost weight. I told her that she had. But mirrors, photographs and the looks she got from every person she encountered told her otherwise. Almost all of her energy was spent devising ways of avoiding food without being caught doing so, and getting rid of food she had no choice but to eat lest she arouse the suspicion of people who, inexplicably, couldn't see how fat she was. When our parents had people in during Christmas and insisted on showing off their beautiful daughters, Bethany wore light, full-length dresses that bared nothing but her arms, seeming to think she was fooling everyone.

Bethany cried in my arms for hours the night before she went back to Canada. She only spent a short time in Halifax before returning to St. John's to stay with a girlfriend who had a basement apartment in her mother's house. She soon wound up in hospital after taking an overdose of pills. She was found on the kitchen floor by her friend, who had been brought downstairs by the incessant howling of her dog. My parents and I did not go back to Canada. Bethany insisted that we stay put, that she had "learned her lesson" and was intent on recovering, which she thought she'd be better able to do if she had no choice but to fend for herself. I begged Mom and Dad for us all to go home, but Bethany had chosen the words she knew they wanted to hear. "She's hit rock bottom," Dad said, ignoring me when I reminded him that her being smart enough to make it into Dalhousie at fifteen hadn't made her old enough to live on her own. "That was her choice," he said. "She has nowhere to go but up. She's right. We mustn't interfere."

Word came from her that she was getting better, then better still.

"She's recovered," Mom proclaimed one evening at the dinner table as though Bethany had rallied from some form of womanly fatigue. (Her illness was never given a name in our house.) Soon, it was as if she had done nothing that couldn't be explained away or ignored completely, nothing as ostentatious as dropping out of college in mid-term and being hospitalized and hooked up to a feeding tube. Even Bethany and I did not acknowledge between us in our letters that she had had a full-fledged breakdown and a long stay in a hospital.

Nor did anyone openly acknowledge that *I* was in decline, reading Anne Frank's book for hours on end, writing in my diary furiously, as if I was trying to write a message to Anne Frank about the imminent arrival of the Gestapo before someone snatched my pen away. Our parents pointed to my perfect grades as proof that, isolated, introverted, friendless as I was, there was nothing more wrong with me than that I was going through a phase.

In September, when Bethany wrote to say that she was back in college, I felt betrayed—she had got better and I had got worse. She had left me to fend for myself. I began to dodge school. I dodged it for almost three weeks before the principal informed my parents. I spent every school day of those three weeks riding the Southern Line rail route that ran east for several stops from Cape Town station before it turned at a right angle and headed south, eventually hugging the western coast of the cape. A round trip cost less than half a rand, leaving me enough of my lunch money to buy a melktert, a very bland, very light pastry, near the end of the line in Simon's Town at Mrs. Top's Tea House. Some days, one melktert was the only thing I ate till I got home.

Twenty-eight stops from Cape Town to Simon's Town. It got so that I could riddle them off, forwards and backwards, as fast as I could say the alphabet. For three weeks, my days, and my South African childhood, were measured out in station stops: the first and last stop was Cape Town, where the station let you out at Adderley Street, the main street downtown; Rondebosch, from which I walked to the Rustenburg Junior School for Girls; Kenilworth, where a woman named Mrs. Kennedy had taught me how to swim; Muizenberg, five minutes from the beach that we went to almost every weekend of the summer, where row upon row of brightly coloured change huts seemed to sparkle in the sun; Mowbray—there was a horse farm there that we used to visit because my mother had been a good rider as a child and wanted us to be good riders too, but we never took to it; Kalk Bay, where my mother went to the Star of the Sea Convent School and she and Dad first lived together after they were married—Gloria came home to that house after she was born; Newlands was my stop when I went to Westerford in 1975—there was a brewery close by the station that sent forth the sickening smell of barley malt; St. James, the most nondescript of all the stops; Plumstead, my favourite for no reason but its name; Fish Hoek—there was a marina there that Tante, a distant relative of my mother, painted from a postcard. Ptolemy, the 150-year-old tortoise that lived in Tante's backyard, more or less immobile, once snapped at my mother and sent her running to the house as if she thought Ptolemy was chasing her. It was the only time I ever saw Tante laugh. Glencairn. Directly across from the station was what had once been my grandmother's tiny house, and behind the station was the open sea. Mrs. Top's Tea House was a short distance down the road toward Simon's Town. There was a large naval base at Simon's Town, the end of the line.

Because I boarded at Cape Town station, and reboarded for the return from Simon's Town, I was always able to get a window seat, and I often opened my window to feel the breeze and smell the sea. A round trip, fifty-six station stops, took about three and a half hours. I sometimes did two in one day. I read and scribbled in *Het Achterhuis* almost constantly, looking up from it when the conductor came by to punch my ticket, or when he or one of the regular commuters spoke to me, which they did more and more often as the days went by.

So as not to be too obviously skipping school, I changed out of my Westerford uniform in the bathroom at Cape Town station and put on a T-shirt, a pair of jeans and sandals, stuffing my school uniform into my knapsack. Still, the conductor repeatedly asked me how old I was and why I was riding the train day after day for no apparent purpose but to use it as a place to read the same book over and over—I only wrote my diary at home. "It must be a very good book," he said. I answered him by nodding or shaking my head, or shrugging. "Where are all your friends?" he often asked. Shrug. Then he answered my shrug with one of his own and moved on.

Fifteen return trips. During the first half of each, I felt hopeful, as if I was escaping my life, but on the way back, as I drew closer and closer to Cape Town, I felt as desolate as if I was being taken back to prison. More than once, at the southern end of the line, I got off the train and surveyed the sea, wondering if I could stand the cold of it long enough to drown myself. Sometimes I cried, my face pressed flat against the window of the train as if to better examine something that had caught my eye. Men twice or three times my age often sat across from me, blatantly poring over every inch of me as if they were committing me to memory for future use. This often prompted the conductor to say, "You shouldn't be travelling alone," which sent the men scattering to other seats with their briefcases or satchels pressed against their crotches. Sometimes, when the train swayed from side to side, I closed my eyes and wondered what it would be like if it jumped the tracks.

Africa. Africa. Surely it was possible to vanish into a continent the size of *Africa*. Other people leading other lives got on board or left the train; other people leading other lives stared at the train as it went by, or watched it from the windows of their houses, looking like they wished that they were on it, that they could trade places with the solemn-eyed girl who clearly didn't understand how fortunate she was.

When Anne Frank was fourteen, she had already spent a full year in the Secret Annex, pent up with seven others, hiding out from men who meant to kill her. I put myself in her place, pictured myself knocking down the bookcase that hid the secret entrance, climbing over it and running down the stairs just to revel for one second in the freedom of the outdoors before I was arrested for being born a Jew.

Eventually, the principal phoned my mother, who asked me what I'd been doing for the past three weeks. I told her the truth about everything but the book, and assured her that I was getting one hundred in every one of my courses, which was true because the only grade in which they could find room for me was a year behind the last one I'd completed in Newfoundland.

From *The Ballad of the Clan van Hout*

RETURN TO HOUT (1985)
At least we're in one place again,
though one of them has brought a man
who thinks that I'm an also-ran.

For years she doesn't meet a soul
and then she brings a *writer* home
(she'll only settle for the best)
a real one, not some hobbyist.
The poor girl even *lives* in code:
with him she's found the motherlode.
The world's not what it seems to be;
it's something else that only he
can understand, a mystery
that he will solve, or maybe not—
he might not get around to it.
The boy's a message meant for me;
he'll be a genius, wait and see.
So far a master piece of ass,
someday he'll write a masterpiece—
compared to him, I'll seem absurd.
He's waiting for the right first word;
until it comes, from heaven sent,
my charity will pay his rent.
They'll wind up in some basement room,
then she'll get bored and come back home,
or he will find a paying job
but never be like Bill or Bob.
He'll find something ordinary,
permanently temporary.
It won't be what he *really* does;
he'll find some fellow geniuses.
They'll know his worth and he'll know theirs;

they'll each make fun of their careers.
They'll read their work to one another;
"The others write such awful rubbish—
we're not like them, we should be published."
What will be his consolation?
Posthumous appreciation.
He'll tell himself that, when he's gone,
they'll see, at last, that they were wrong.
She fell for him; who must I thank?
Who else but Her, that fraud, Anne Frank.

WADE

Rachel's parents threw a welcome home dinner party for themselves at the house they rented at 55 Liesbeek Road in Rosebank. They seemed to have kept in touch with no one but one other couple, Peter and Theresa DeVries. Peter was the man Rachel had told me about, Hans's childhood friend, who worked for South African Airways and had moved to South Africa after the war.

The night before the party, Rachel told me that Bethany was going to bring a date. "Well, that's good," I said.

"You don't know the whole story yet."

In 1975, when Bethany made her Christmas trip to South Africa, the DeVrieses' only child, a young man named Clive, had developed quite a crush on her. Bethany and Clive went on several dates and sat together at family dinners. Somehow, it became widely believed that Bethany would stay in South Africa and finish her degree at the University of Cape Town while boarding with the DeVrieses, her future in-laws. But in some way that Rachel said was too complicated to explain, Bethany had engineered her return to Halifax. Clive kept writing to her, though, and Bethany didn't have the heart not to answer at least some of his letters, which came at the rate of one or two per day. They kept up their correspondence even during the time that Bethany was in hospital.

"So," I said, "they're going to pick up where they left off?"

Rachel laughed. "Look," she said, "everyone knows that neither one of them has dated anyone else, ever, so . . ."

We arrived at 55 Liesbeek Road, an unprepossessing, narrow, two-storey house all but obscured by a giant tree fern in the front yard with a spray of yellow fronds erupting from the centre bulb like the spouting of a whale. The driveway was so overgrown that we had to navigate it as carefully as if we were back home driving through a snowstorm. Not easy to locate was an area covered with crushed pink granite, where Rachel parked the car.

Bethany met us at the door. "Clive and his clannette are here. When you rang the doorbell, I told him to stay put just to get a few seconds away from him. He is stuck to me like glue. You guys have to run interference, *please*."

"Why don't you just tell him he's not your type or something?" Rachel said.

"Because," Bethany said, "that will only raise the question of who *is* my type. It's hard to discourage a guy who's never kissed a girl when he knows you've never kissed a boy." She looked at me. "I do like men, by the way, Wade," she said, "just in case you were wondering. I just haven't met one yet who thinks that the most attractive quality in a woman is anorexia."

"Why did you keep writing him?" Rachel asked.

"Just to see what happened, I suppose. Mean of me, wasn't it?"

Bethany led us into the house and introduced us to Clive, whose eyes blinked out of sync, which made it hard to maintain eye contact, to say the least. He was about six feet tall but very skinny, with curly black hair, long sideburns and glasses with small, round lenses. He was paler than I would have thought possible for anyone who lived in South Africa.

"So pleased to meet you, Wade," he said. "All the way from Canada. Wow. Amazing."

"He didn't swim here," Bethany said.

"Of course," Clive said, "of course."

"Mom and Dad and Rachel and I have come all the way from Canada too. Don't we deserve a 'wow' as well."

"Oh, you do, you do."

"Throw in a 'wow' and we'll call it square."

Clive looked perplexed.

"She takes some getting used to, Clive," Rachel said.

"Oh, definitely," Clive said, "absolutely, no doubt about it. I mean, I met her years ago, so . . . Did you know that I'm a junior high school math teacher now?"

"No—"

"Let me introduce you to Clive's parents, Wade," Bethany said.

Clive's father, Peter, was the spitting image of Clive, except that he was several inches shorter and didn't have the blinking issue. Peter sipped from what I assumed was a Bloody Mary. "Tomato juice," he said. "Not because I'm driving. I don't drink, ever. It doesn't agree with me. Or rather, when I drink, I disagree with everyone and everything. So I'm on the wagon. Tied up in the back of it in a burlap sack. But I don't mind if everyone around me drinks."

Before I could even nod my head to acknowledge his odd declaration, he added, "Pleased to meet you, Wade. I've heard a lot about you." His accent was so much like Hans's, he seemed to be imitating him.

His wife, Theresa, was thin as well, but much less awkward than her husband or her son. "It's nice to meet you, Wade," she said, lightly shaking my hand. "Though I have to confess," she said, "I have heard absolutely nothing about you but your name. I can't imagine who Peter's informant is." She smiled at me in a gently reassuring way, as if to say she knew how foreign everything must seem to me.

On the way to the bathroom, I saw Bethany talking to Nora, the maid, a short, stout woman of about forty with skin the colour of toffee, who was listening with eyes downcast. I stopped beside her and waited to be introduced. Bethany, seeming not to notice me, said, "Nora, I'm starving. Get it? I'm literally starving. What I mean is, don't hurry up with dinner." Nora continued to stare at the floor.

"She doesn't get it," Bethany said, not looking at me as she set off to the kitchen.

"I'm Wade," I said, nodding to Nora.

She nodded slightly, said, "Yes, mister," and stood, one hand gripping the other, eyes still fixed on the floor.

"You're Nora," I said.

"Yes, mister," she said.

Hans, whom I'd yet to encounter, came out of the kitchen and, ignoring me, said, "Nora, it's time to make the rounds of the front room. Our guests are running low on drinks."

"Yes, master," she said as Hans pushed past me and Rachel and Myra arrived at my side.

Myra kissed me on both cheeks. "Hello, Wade," she said. "Homesick yet?" Before I could answer, she followed Nora to the kitchen.

"*Master*?" I said.

"It's not meant in the sense of master and slave, as it was on American plantations," Rachel said. "*Master* is what English servants called the master of the house. This is a holdover from that, that's all. Master, madam, mister."

Nora moved among us as unobtrusively as if she were invisible. Rachel's parents spoke to her only to pass on instructions or to issue mild complaints. "Nora, there's no ice left in my drink." Nora, head bowed, said "Yes, madam" or "Yes, master," her tone just as perfunctory.

The inside of the house was meticulously well kept, ordered and clean, not my usual experience of a van Hout residence.

"Thank God I'm back in a country where we can afford a maid," Myra said as she showed Rachel and me about.

When Fritz and Carmen arrived, Carmen flashed me a wide smile and gave me a hug. "Oh my God, look at you, in South Africa and everything," she said, stepping back to appraise me as if she didn't remember that we'd flown in on the same plane.

"Well, if it isn't the tourist and the tart," Fritz said. "You absolutely must come out to our place on the Flats sometime. We've been approved for running water. All I have to do is dig down to the water table. Shouldn't take me more than a year. How is the great South African novel coming along? You've been here, what, a week? You should have it down pat by now."

"I'm not writing about South Africa," I said. "Just about you, Fritz."

"Legs have been broken for less," he said.

"Rachel's Wade is in South Africa, Rachel's Wade is in South Africa," Carmen more or less sang. She was stoned but not like she had been on the plane, staring at me in apparent disbelief that I could exist outside of Canada.

As we stood about the front room while Nora made dinner, Myra told the story of the conversation she'd once had with Tom the gardener, who had worked for them when the girls were very young. She'd asked him, "Tom, if something were to happen, you wouldn't kill us, would you?"

"No, madam," Tom said. "I would get one of my friends to kill you, and I would kill *his* master and his madam and their children."

The DeVrieses laughed. Myra, her hand on her chest, said, "I was so relieved, because I sometimes wondered how safe we were around him, or around Elsie, for that matter."

If something were to happen. That was the euphemism for the uprising that everyone of whatever colour seemed to think was inevitable but never imminent, always vaguely fated to happen during the lifetimes of people not yet born.

"I'll tell you what I'm looking forward to," Myra said. "The Star of the Sea Convent annual reunion and fundraiser. It's not far off. A chance to see so many old friends. Theresa's a graduate too." Theresa nodded and smiled.

"A weekend-long hen party," Hans said. "Thank God husbands are not invited or, worse, required to go."

"When I was in the mental hospital," Bethany said loudly, "I used to have my bed examined. Really. They used to search my bed for hidden food."

"We should all have our beds examined," Fritz said.

Bethany extracted something from the pocket of her blouse. "I have to take my happy pills," she said. She popped two capsules, each one half green, half black, into her mouth and washed them down with a mouthful of water. "Ahhhh," she said. "Now I'm all normal again. I also have some just like Rachel's—higher dosage, of course. They're the ones I stop taking now and then. I hate them. They make me feel like I'm underwater. But I have better drugs than Fritz does, and I'm not risking arrest. What do you think of that, Fritz?"

"Drugs?" Fritz said. "In South Africa? You could get twenty years for smoking a joint, if that's the right word."

Bethany cackled.

When Gloria and Max turned up, Gloria acted as if she had no memory of our short stay in their house or of Rachel's outburst.

After the reintroductions, with everyone settled again in the living room, Max said, "I used to go out with a woman from the Pacific Northwest. She called my penis a scrotum pole." Thinking that, if nothing else, it was an okay pun, I laughed, but no one else did. Gloria shot a glance at Rachel, who affected fascination with the ice cubes in her drink.

Hans, raising his glass of Perrier, stood and announced that he wished to propose a toast. "To South Africa," he said. "Let us live and strive for freedom in South Africa, our land."

"To South Africa," said Bethany, smirking at Fritz, who smirked back.

"To South Africa," everyone but me said in chorus, sipping from their glasses.

"The little verse Dad recited," Rachel told me, "is from the national anthem."

"It sounds better in Afrikaans," Hans said. "It rhymes. The whole anthem does, especially when sung. I try to get Myra to sing it like she used to, but she won't."

"I'm doing you all a favour," Myra said. "I wouldn't want to desecrate the anthem of my homeland."

"We're home again," Hans said. "That dreary place of ice and snow will soon be a distant memory, thank God."

"It's been a long time since all your daughters were together, which means it's been a long time since your last harem, Dad," Gloria said.

"Oh, Gloria," Myra said, smiling, "your father doesn't need a harem anymore. He's let himself go ever since he went completely bald."

"I can tell," Max said. "He has more hair in his ears than I have on my balls."

"And just as grey, I'll bet," Hans said.

Myra surprised me by shrieking with laughter.

"Why a harem?" I said to Rachel. As if my question had set them off, the four girls sprang out of their chairs and fled the room. I heard them in the kitchen and the bathroom, rifling through drawers and cupboards, then running up the stairs. One by one, they returned to the front room. Bethany cleared various knick-knacks and ashtrays from the coffee table, leaving only a white doily. "Everyone but Dad get off the couch," she said. Max and Fritz stood, crossed the room to the loveseat and sat on either side of me. Bethany knelt at the coffee table, where the sisters unloaded Q-tips, tweezers, scissors, nail clippers and a nail file. Gloria plunked down an electric razor and a bottle of aftershave. Hans, removing his glasses, spread his arms and legs wide on the couch in a gesture of helpless abandon.

As the rest of us watched, his four daughters went to work on him, Rachel on his left, Gloria on his right, Carmen in front of him, Bethany handing instruments to the others like a surgical nurse. Rachel and Gloria each swabbed one of Hans's ears with a Q-tip. Then, with small pairs of scissors, they snipped the hair from the insides of his ears. Carmen and Bethany worked on one nostril each, clipping and plucking his nose hairs. Hans, his head tilted back, eyes closed and mouth partway open, obeyed their every command. "Tilt your head back more." "Flare your nostrils." "Don't move. Don't sneeze."

I got it now: his girls were a "hairem." I looked back and forth between them and Myra, who wore a smile of amusement until she noticed I was watching her, at which her face went blank. The girls pored over their father, sometimes holding his head in their hands to get proper leverage, peering into his ears and nostrils as if into his very brain. Rachel and Gloria clipped his eyebrows while Carmen and Bethany shaved him with the electric razor, which they passed back and forth between them. When they were done, Rachel poured aftershave onto her hands and patted his cheeks.

"Ta-dah," Bethany said, throwing up her arms. The four girls backed away from him to survey their handiwork. Hans let forth a tremendous sneeze, after which he slipped his glasses back on.

"Bless you," Myra said.

Fritz and Max applauded, and I joined in half-heartedly, appraising Rachel, who, with her sisters, was staring at their father.

"You seem quite astonished," Myra said, pointedly, to me. "The girls used to do this all the time when they were younger. Self-grooming has never been Hans's forte."

"Come here, Rachel," Hans said, his arms held wide. She went to him and sat sideways on his lap, throwing her arms around his neck and kissing his cheek. He slapped her on the backside several times, then smoothed one thigh, all the while staring at me through his glasses, his smile as wide as it had been when he'd hugged my sisters. After a few minutes, she scrambled off his lap and came back to climb onto mine. I wrapped her in my arms, hoping I didn't look as unsettled as I felt.

Nora served dinner, then retired to the kitchen, where she quickly ate and departed for her shed in the backyard. We had barbecued boerewors, concentric circles of beef sausage that looked like a coiled whip, and cheddar scalloped potatoes. For Bethany, Rachel, Carmen and Fritz, Nora had halved pepper squashes and stuffed them with all manner of chopped vegetables. Bethany never touched her meal, merely sipping water from time to time.

"I can drink as much as I like," Max said as he filled his glass, "because I don't have to drive. It's one of the lifetime perks of being married to a teetotaller."

Fritz laughed. "*Life*time perks? Glore doesn't believe in the 'till death do us part' part of the wedding ceremony, do you, Glore."

"Don't call me Glore," she said.

"That's right," Fritz said, "only Max is allowed to call you that. Was that the pet name your other husbands used?"

I thought someone—certainly Gloria or Max—would object, but no one did.

"Did I ever tell you," Bethany said to no one in particular, "that when I was in hospital, I tried to kill myself so often, they used to call me Deathany?"

Again, no one spoke or gave the slightest indication that *she* had.

I glanced at Rachel, who was sitting beside me, playing with her squash, moving it about with her fork. I gave her leg a reassuring rub beneath the table. She extracted a pea and lifted it to her mouth.

Bethany tried again to get a rise. "I could drink," she said, "but I would have had to skip my pills forty-eight hours in advance, which my doctor advised me against doing. I shouldn't have listened to him. I'd love to get hammered."

"There are other ways, Bethany," Fritz said. "In case you're interested, I've come prepared."

Again, it was as if I'd only imagined that he'd spoken. I looked at Hans, who was cutting his sausage vigorously into identically-sized pieces but seemed not to have eaten any yet.

"I don't know how you're able to stand Canada, Rachel," Gloria said. "It's like the place is starting from scratch. I mean, there's nothing there. Are you really intending to go back?"

"There are places you can go in Canada without endangering your life," I said.

"Screwdrivers at dawn," Max said, pointing his knife at me.

"Canada is a big place," I said. "You all talk about it as if every square inch of it is the same as every other square inch."

"You've never set foot on the mainland of Canada," Fritz said. "Most of us have seen more of it than you have."

"Touché," I said, feeling more foolish than usual.

"Hans," Peter said, "do you still recite that verse when you have dinner guests?"

"Now that I'm back home, why not?" Hans lowered his head and closed his eyes as if to say grace, then launched in:

"In this enlightened century
We're better than we used to be
except when some who've come so far
forget how fortunate they are.
I mean those who have it better
but want it better to the letter.

They know they have improved their lot
but want exactly what we've got!"

Fritz snorted in derision and Carmen rolled her eyes, but most of the others applauded. I joined in out of politeness but stopped when I saw that Rachel's lips were a thin, straight line.

"So, writer," Bethany said, "what are you reading these days?"

"A biography of Albert Einstein," I said.

"Hah," Hans said so loudly that everyone jumped. He put down his knife and fork, placed his elbows on the table and leaned his chin on his clasped hands as if he was pondering what to say. But he said nothing.

"How is this Einstein book, theoretically and relatively speaking?" Bethany said.

I laughed, as did Rachel and Clive.

"Theoretically and relatively speaking," I said, "it's very good."

"A patent clerk is what he was," Hans said. "Once a patent clerk, always a patent clerk. Once a Jew, always a Jew. If not for the Jews, there would have been no war, no reason for Peter and me to risk our lives when we were just young men—boys, really."

Rachel pressed her leg against mine. Peter and Theresa were as blank-faced as Myra.

"Peter went to England and fought against the Germans, didn't you, Peter?" Hans said.

Peter nodded.

"You should have fought against the Allies."

"Hans!" Myra said, laughing in a way that seemed to say that he often said such outrageous things to Peter.

"Daddy, you're awful," Gloria said. Bethany stood up, pushed back her chair and left the room. Rachel and Gloria exchanged a look.

"Hans is just pulling your leg," Myra said to me. "He's been saying the same thing about Einstein since we were married."

"So you're the one person in the world who doesn't admire Einstein," Max said.

"One of millions," Hans said.

"He's having us all on," Myra said, tilting her head and smiling at me. "He never talks about how many Jews he saved. Nor does Peter. It's not bigotry but modesty. Those were hard times. It's his way of dealing with it."

"Let's move on to something else," Rachel said.

"I was passed over time and time again for professorships," Hans said. "Here and in Canada. I was told I'd be made a professor if I earned an M.A., so I did, and then they chose a younger man instead, a man who, like me, didn't have a Ph.D. 'You need to publish a book, Hans,' they said. I did that, a textbook that sold two thousand copies. 'But you published it yourself,' they said, 'so it doesn't count.' Another man was hired, one who'd never read a book, let alone written one. It was all pretense, all politics. I complained to the dean about the conduct of others in the faculty and came to be seen as some sort of informant or bootlicker. I was blacklisted. I am now regarded as someone who came back home because he couldn't make the grade in the least-esteemed province of a second-rate country, an assistant professor who will never be anything more. There's no such thing as an assistant professor emeritus. This is the reward I get for risking my life to help rich Jews get themselves and their fortunes out of Europe. In Amsterdam they stand in line for hours to see the place where Anne Frank and her family hid out from the Germans. There are no plaques on the childhood homes of men like me."

"Dad," Rachel said, her voice barely audible, "please, please don't talk about *her*."

"Yes, Daddy," Gloria said. "You know you shouldn't."

"The Jews whose relatives died in concentration camps, the Jews who survived the camps, they think of me and my fellow Resistance fighters as having failed them," Hans said. "What about the thousands of Dutch who died, or the ones who had to eat tulip bulbs for months to stay alive? Do the Jews stand in line to worship at *their* graves?" He pointed at Rachel. "No one in Canada ever had to live every minute of every day with death one step behind them. What did the Jews do when they had no one to help them? Nothing. They didn't lift a finger for themselves. They marched into the gas chambers like little children marching into school."

"Professor van Hout," I said, as Rachel pressed her leg even harder against mine, "how can you, a member of the Dutch Resistance, talk like this?"

"I could tell you stories," Hans said, though he didn't look at me. "Some of them might not be true. Some of them might. The old farmer I worked for recruited me. He took a chance when he asked me if I'd help him. I took a chance when I said yes. I delivered messages that were written in code that I couldn't have deciphered if I tried. A far better code, I'll bet, than the one that *she* made up." He pointed at Rachel. "It was not a game. I took risks, bigger ones than most. I never met the people who left the messages. It was best to know as few of your fellows as possible in case you were caught and forced to give up their names. I tucked the messages between two cobblestones in the street while I was pretending to tie my shoe. I don't know who collected them. I never knew. How many times did I stop on that very spot and pretend to tie my shoelace while I was wedging a piece of paper between two cobblestones? But no one ever noticed, no one ever recognized me, the young man who so often chose the same place to go down on one knee and retie his shoe.

"What do any of you except Peter know about unbearable memories? What does this boyfriend of yours know, Rachel? Based on what I've said, could you tell what side I chose after the German tanks rolled unopposed into Amsterdam? I may have been a member of the Resistance. I may have believed in it. But the Nazis believed that *they* were right. And they convinced thousands of Dutch to infiltrate the Resistance. Men, women and children were shot right in front of me because the Nazis suspected them of helping Jews, or merely wanted to make an example of them. You don't know how it feels to be always afraid, always hungry. That's how the Nazis infiltrated the Resistance. The people who helped them weren't Nazi sympathizers to begin with. Most of them weren't.

"You think you want to know the truth? Very well. The Nazis put a gun to my mother's head and told me to co-operate or they would shoot her. If I still didn't co-operate, they would put a gun to my brother's head. So I agreed. What was I supposed to do, let my family die, watch them being shot one after the other, just to save the lives of some Jews? Jews I'd never met, rich, money-grubbing old men or women? There you have it. But what do you have? A story of what might have happened or the story of what did happen?

"It may be that I hate the Jews because they brought the wrath of Germany down upon our heads. Why should I feel anything but hatred for the people so many of us died trying to protect? If not for the Jews, there would never have been a war. Is that how I really feel? Who knows? No one knew anything for certain. That's what it was like. Resistance fighters or Nazi collaborators who gave the names and addresses of resisters to the Nazis? You were just as likely to wind up being one as the other. I chose the Resistance. My neighbours, my friends chose to be collaborators. I hated them then, but I don't hate them now. Is *that* true? Here is the only truth: not even Peter knows whose side I was on."

I glanced at Peter, who was staring at his plate.

"And all my youngest daughter thinks about is *Anne Frank*?"

Rachel's eyes were blurred with tears. I wanted to put an arm around her, but I was worried about inciting Hans even further.

Gloria reached out and took her father's hand. "Calm down, Daddy, please." Hans pulled away. The silence stretched and stretched some more.

Could Hans have collaborated with the Nazis? Might others, not only Jews, have died because of him? *A story that might or might not be true.* In the absence of any proof to the contrary, it seemed possible, given how convincing his tirade against the Jews had been. The Nazis had posed him a moral dilemma and he had put family ahead of everything else. Had he? Who knows how many girls like Anne Frank died because of men like him? None, perhaps. Why had he told such a story and then seemingly retracted it?

"Imagine," Hans said. "South Africa's one friend in the world is Israel, a place crawling with Jews. They're our friends because they treat the Arabs the way we treat the kaffirs. Did they repay the children whose fathers died to save the Jews? The wives whose husbands died?

They have their own country now, and anyone who doesn't help them defend it is an anti-Semite."

"Vicious stuff, Hans, vicious," Max said. "You're in fine form tonight."

"South Africa learned a lot from the defeat of the Nazis," Hans said. "It learned even more from the failure of the Final Solution. Once it had nothing to lose by intervening, the rest of the world intervened. It wouldn't have if Germany had won the war, which brings me to the third thing South Africa learned: don't bite off more than you can chew. Look to your own house. Perfect your own country, the rest of the world be damned. If the Germans had simply redrawn their border to include Western Europe, that border would be the same today. There would be no Western Europe, just Germany from Ireland to Poland. If they had let the Jews live and put them to work for next to nothing, Germany would be the richest, most powerful country in the world. It could have achieved all that in six months. Over, done with. In my opinion, South Africa is the closest thing on earth to a perfect country."

Hans pushed back his chair abruptly, rose and strode into the front room. He reversed a reclining chair so that it faced away from us, then sat in it, the back of his neck crimson. He snatched a newspaper from the coffee table and began to read, or pretended to, seemingly unaware that that crimson neck of his was giving him away.

"Hans gets upset whenever someone talks about the Jews," Myra said, frowning at me.

"I didn't," I said. "*He* did."

Rachel, even as tears continued to pour down her cheeks, kept her leg pressed against mine. I tried to take her hand, but she wouldn't let me.

Myra tilted her head as if she was about to impart bad news to me as gently as possible. "Any mention of Anne Frank gets Rachel upset," she said. "She admires her very much."

"It's true," Clive said. "It was Hans who brought up the Jews. All Wade did was answer Bethany's question about what he was reading."

"It's a touchy subject, that's what Myra means," Peter said. "It is for me, too, Clive, as you well know."

Clive, looking chastened, nodded.

"No harm done," Theresa said.

"Except to the Jews and Albert Einstein," Fritz said.

"Not to mention Wade," Rachel said, wiping her eyes with the handkerchief Max passed to her.

"And you and poor old Anne Frank," Fritz said.

"I'm sure there are more pleasant things than the war to talk about," Theresa said.

"Here, here," Myra said. The table fell silent. As bewildered as I was, it occurred to me to wonder who would *not* have felt bewildered in such circumstances, and among such people as I had fallen in with. These were not the people of the greater world into which I had belatedly made my way. These were people of a micro-world of their own exclusive and, thus far, inscrutable design. Fritz's eyes said as much to me every time we exchanged a look. In this way, if in no other, we were kindred souls—that had been the message of that grin of his since the moment we met.

"Let's start clearing up," Rachel said to her sisters.

"I don't know why I have to pitch in," Bethany said, from the doorway. "All I did was drink a glass of water."

I headed for the kitchen as the other men, along with Myra and Theresa, filed into the front room. "What was that all about?" I whispered to Rachel as she moved back and forth between the table and the kitchen counter. "There would have been no war if not for the Jews? That's a strange thing for a war hero to say. Why did he make up a story about being a collaborator?"

"Please drop it for now," Rachel whispered.

"I didn't say a word about the Jews," I said.

"We'll talk about it *later*. Unless you want to march into the front room and, in front of everyone, ask Dad to explain himself."

"We're an acquired taste, Wade," Bethany said. "That's why I gave up eating. Dad was joking. In poor taste, I'll admit. But there is nothing he likes more than getting someone's goat, and he certainly seems to have got yours."

"And Rachel's," I said. "And yours, Bethany. I seem to remember that, when the going got rough, you went upstairs."

"Only because I know his speech by heart and I can't stand to be bored."

"He insulted you, Rachel," I said that night as we were driving home. "He knows how you feel about Anne Frank and her book."

"Really? Do *you* know how I feel about Anne Frank and her book? Here's how I feel about them: I wish I could put both her and that book out of my mind forever. I wish I could work up the nerve to burn every last volume of my diary and every last copy of hers that exists on earth."

"So you keep saying."

"It was when we came back here in 1975 that Dad first started in about the Jews. It was just a few words at first, only in front of the family. 'Another goddamn Jew.' 'Filthy Jew.' My mother told us it was just Dad's way of mocking those who meant it when they said such things, his way of dealing with one of the horrors of the war."

"That's absurd."

"Yes, well, he's gotten worse, but her explanation has stayed the same."

"That makes it more absurd. It makes me wonder if your fixation with that book is . . ." I stopped.

"Is what?" she said, sounding more fearful than annoyed.

"I don't know," I said. I had been going to say I wondered if it was her way of countering his bewildering anti-Semitism. For a minute, neither of us spoke.

"When I was sick, really sick, Mom used to say, 'Your father must have walked past the Secret Annex one hundred times without knowing it. Imagine that.' I did. I imagined him walking past the Secret Annex that many times, not knowing it was there, not knowing that two families of Jews were hiding out there from the Nazis just a few feet away, not knowing that one of those Jews, a mere girl, was keeping a diary that, like her, would go on to be world-famous. Mom said that some of the members of the Dutch Resistance were decorated by the Allies, but most of them remained anonymous because a lot of people in Holland sided with the Nazis, and Dad didn't want to put himself and the people he worked with in danger. Medals didn't matter to him. By 1955, that danger had passed, and that was the reason he was able to say on his resumé that he had been a member of the Dutch Resistance. I have a copy of that resumé. I brought it with me from St. John's. I'll show it to you when we get home. I'd meant to show it to you under different circumstances. For ages, the original was a cherished family souvenir. The closest thing Dad had to a Resistance membership card. Mom gave us all copies and got us to swear not to tell him we had one."

As I sat at the kitchen table, nursing a beer, Rachel rummaged in the bedroom closet and emerged with a single faded mimeographed sheet, which she placed on the table in front of me. "He sent it to Peter DeVries and told him to include it with his letter of application to South African Airways."

The address on the resumé was: "Oegstgeest-Holland/38 Sumatrastraat." Rachel read the first entry aloud: "1942–1945—went into hiding to evade the German compulsory work in factories. Worked for the Dutch during that time under a feigned name as a farmhand and manservant and succeeded in eluding the German suppressors." She looked at me, eyebrows raised. "All the resumé says is that he escaped the Germans by working on a farm outside the city, in which case, by the way, how did he walk past the Secret Annex a hundred times during the war? I don't know, Wade, I don't know. I sometimes wonder if I should believe a word he has ever said about anything."

"Maybe the notion of him being a war hero was just some sort of family myth that caught on over the years."

"Maybe. Maybe *she* made it up. She's always painted him as a hero who is content to keep his heroism a secret, a man so modest, but also so traumatized by the war, that, thirty-five years later, he doesn't want his own daughters to know of his bravery, a man who exacted from his wife a vow that she would never tell them whatever in God's name it was that he told her. Until I became obsessed with the diary, we never brought books about the war into the house. When we came back here in '75, I read *Het Achterhuis* everywhere except at home. I grew terrified that one of my sisters or I would bring everything down around us with one slip of the tongue, one moment of forgetfulness. Then I became terrified that we would provoke him into ranting against the Jews. I still don't know if he was a member of the Resistance or a collaborator with the Nazis."

"Judging by that resumé, I'd say he was neither," I said. "Maybe he was just making things up to impress South African Airways. He mentioned that the Nazis threatened his brother. You never told me he had one."

"He doesn't, not anymore. He died during the war. I don't know how. Another forbidden topic."

"Maybe that explains—"

"Don't bother. Really. There's no point. Maybe, maybe, a million maybes. What you hinted at on the way home? Pretty far-fetched. Driving yourself crazy is a very extreme way of protesting your father's choice of words."

"If that's all it is."

"When you know nothing for certain, you have to assume that's all it is. You know, I used to think it would be fun to hide out in an attic with your family, fun for everyone to always be together and safe, unknown to the outside world, which was a dangerous place where no one could be trusted." She looked at me as if she had confessed to something she knew I didn't understand.

"I'll show you something else: the first copy of *Het Achterhuis* I ever owned." She got up, and once again I heard her rummaging through the closet in the bedroom. She came back to the kitchen and gingerly handed me the "book" with both hands. It didn't look like a book, but like a tangled mass of various kinds of tape—masking tape, duct tape, black electrical tape. Inside it, she said, was a stationery box, and inside that, a paperback edition of the diary. "We can't open it," she said. "It would fall apart. The glue in the binding along the spine dried up years ago. There's just a bunch of loose pages. But I'd freak if you saw it anyway. I wrote notes on every square inch of it, even the inside of the covers, in the margins, in between the lines. I doubt that even I would be able to make out the notes now. Promise you won't ever open it?"

"I promise," I said.

"I'll know if you did," she said. "It's not something you can take a sneak peek at. You'd have to cut it open with a knife and you'd never be able to put it back the way it was."

"I won't *touch* it, Rachel."

"Okay. I'm sorry. It's just that it's pretty precious to me." She went back to the bedroom and replaced the book in the closet, then came out and sat on my lap. She ran her fingers through my hair and whispered, "It's okay. Whatever happens, it's okay."

"I love you," I said. "Nothing's going to happen."

From *The Ballad of the Clan van Hout*

THE MAN WHO ALMOST SAVED ANNE FRANK (1966)

The tanks rolled into Amsterdam,
though many died opposing them.
The Nazis played their Nazi games:
they registered the Jewish names,
they made the Jews wear yellow stars,
they drove about in fancy cars
and rounded up the richest Jews—
they told them that they had to choose
between starvation and a ruse
(they didn't call it that, of course).
They staged the famous "Jewish race":
they made them run on cobblestones
while wearing clogs, the wooden shoes
that no one wore by 'forty-two.
(Remember, now, the four of you,
that every word I say is true.
The naughty get much naughtier
when they have nothing else to do.
They do, it's true, I'm telling you,
the nicest of nice children, too.)
The young, the old, the meek, the bold
(this story is not often told),
the funny-looking naked Jews,
while wearing only wooden shoes,
were chased by dogs across the square
(but for those shoes the Jews were bare:
I want to make that crystal clear).

They slipped, they slid, the poor Jews did.
(The bodies that their clothing hid
were not the kind you often see
at Muizenberg, believe you me.)

They skated on the cobblestones—
you never heard such moans and groans.
There was never such a sorry sight
nor such a pair of sorry sounds:
the clacking of the clacking clogs,
the barking of the barking dogs
were heard that day for miles around.
The Germans, drinking beer and wine,
stood just behind the finish line
where the prizes were displayed,
the wheels of cheese and loaves of bread—
for those who crossed still on their feet
could take home what they didn't eat
to feed their starving families.
Some crossed the line but most did not;
regardless of how far they got,
when they were done, the Jews were shot.
Do not forget about the Dutch—
five hundred of us, forced to watch,
stood silent, frozen to the spot.
The colonel looked from face to face:
"And so it ends, the Jewish race.
How swiftly won the war would be
could it be done so easily."
Among the Dutch, a certain man
whom you all know, your father, Hans,
was sickened by the blood that ran
throughout the streets of Amsterdam.
The Germans laughed, but Hans did not.
"Laugh," they said, "or you'll be shot."
He couldn't but pretended to.
So did the rest—what could they do
but mock the dead and dying Jews?

Not much older than you children,
and much younger than most men,

Hans joined the secret underground
and left the life he knew behind.
You will not find his name in books—
young Hans was not the kind who looks
for accolades or decorations,
yet the fates of many nations
rest on the deeds of unknown men.
No statues have been built for him,
no public buildings bear his name;
no one but you accord him glory—
I tell no one else his story.
The man who almost saved Anne Frank
was mocked by men of lesser rank.
(Yes, it's true, I almost saved Her;
I must save that part for later.)
The man I mean is Hans van Hout—
I speak the truth beyond all doubt.

Historians do not record
what no one saw and no one heard.
Hans, a boy of great persistence,
too young for the Dutch Resistance,
convinced men who were twice as old
that he was brave and he was bold.
They guessed that he was but fourteen,
the right age for a go-between,
so small and thin the German men
would think that he was nine or ten.
For years he moved about the streets,
the very picture of defeat,
the laughing stock of Amsterdam.
"They don't know who or what I am.
The Information Underground
would turn its back if I was found."
Nazis, vicious brutalizers,
sycophantic sympathizers,

he was the mascot of them all,
amused the Nazis with his gall.
He wanted to be one of them,
the master race of master men—
or so they thought; this was the plan.
The Underground instructed Hans
to infiltrate the Nazi ranks:
go-between and infiltrator,
he became "the Nazi waiter,"
despised by starving patriots.
They sent young Hans to penetrate
a café where the Germans ate—
a new place that was called Van Dobben,
where the men of the Luftwaffe
went to find the best Dutch women.
Once popular among the Dutch,
who worked there now for nothing much—
the scraps the Germans left behind,
oddments of most any kind,
bits of grizzle, lumps of rind—
it was the perfect place for Hans,
looked down upon by also-rans,
a skinny runt with spectacles,
a malnutrition miracle,
a bag of bones in stolen clothes.
He had a way of charming those
who held themselves in high regard.
He always played the same trump card:
you best brown-nose brown-shirted men
by wishing you were one of them.
He served their food and poured their wine,
pretended that he didn't mind
that he stood starving while they dined,
lit their cigars and buffed their boots
and imitated their salute
until they said he got it right.

So it went night after night—
they had him goose-step round the room
while shouldering a kitchen broom.
They dubbed him the Nazi waiter
(Hans the master imitator),
Hans the clown, the step and fetcher.
When he was done, dead on his feet,
they ordered things for him to eat,
gave him a table and a chair
and let him put them anywhere,
though never side by side with theirs.
A man they called the *Dutch* waiter,
who considered Hans a traitor,
waited on the Nazi waiter,
who ate just what the Nazis ate
and no longer had to wait.
Each night before Van Dobben closed,
while some still drank and others dozed,
the officers gave him his wages.
Men and women of all ages
were given less than half as much.
Word soon spread among the Dutch
of Amsterdam and far beyond
that Hans, the fawning vagabond,
was growing fat while children died
for lack of anything to eat,
ignoring beggars on the street
where he conducted his affairs.
They said that Hans, the profiteer,
bartered bread for silverware
and marzipan for chandeliers.
Rumours and exaggeration
spread throughout the starving nation.
The profiteer of Amsterdam
was getting rich—they hated him.
A Nazi he would be unless

he turned his back on their largesse.
But the side he was fighting for
could not afford to lose one more.
The Nazis thought they knew for sure
that Hans was really nothing more
than Hans the lackey seemed to be,
so Hans the lackey easily
did what he had to do by night—
by day did what he knew was right.
The man who almost saved Anne Frank
was mocked by men of lesser rank.
Saluting, from the Nazi bars,
the Nazi flags on Nazi cars,
he saved the lives of many Jews,
while loose-lipped Nazis drank Dutch booze.
The Germans, drunk on beer and wine,
each half half-crazy half the time,
swilled sauerkraut and sausages
while Hans wrote coded messages.

By August 1st of 'forty-four,
the master race had lost the war,
but could not say the war was lost
until they hid the Holocaust,
disposed of all the evidence
of history's most vile offence:
the gas, the ovens and the graves,
the remnants of six million slaves,
the Jews that they had yet to kill,
the ones who were in hiding still,
the ones in camps but still alive,
witnesses who might survive.

Hans overheard some drunken Klaus
discussing plans to raid a house

where someone who withheld his name,
who may have thought he'd take the blame,
said that eight Jews had, helped by friends,
been waiting for the war to end.
Hans relayed the information—
he deserved a commendation—
and never thought of it again
until the war was long since won.

RACHEL

In the days after the disastrous dinner party, I thought a lot about Elsie, the last black maid we had before we moved to Canada. The sky was blue, the sand between my toes was warm, and our coloured maid, Elsie, lived in the concrete shed at the end of the garden. It never occurred to me to wonder how things had come to be that way or to ask anyone about it. Elsie's shed had a corrugated tin roof like those of the houses in Langa township, where Elsie lived on weekends. (There was also Tom, the gardener—I didn't know where he lived. He was always just *there*, in the yard, trimming the hedge, raking up leaves, pruning the bushes, anything he could do to look busy. I don't think I ever talked to him, and I don't think he ever came into the house.) Elsie went home on weekends because Elsie went home on weekends—that's just the way it was.

I didn't say goodbye to Elsie when we left for Canada. I was excited that we were going somewhere far away, and I didn't understand what my mother meant when, as she sat crying at the kitchen table, she said that we were never coming back. But that's not why I didn't say goodbye to Elsie. I'm sure that Elsie was more concerned about losing her job than she was about saying goodbye to me, or never seeing me or the rest of us again, but that's not why we didn't say goodbye.

It's hard to imagine that, every morning when she got up, she looked forward to spending time with four spoiled white girls who turned up their noses at the food I'm sure she wished she could afford to feed *her* kids, four white girls who complained about things her kids could never dream of having. She may have seen me as nothing more than a little brat whom she only allowed inside her shed and read books to because I would complain to master if she didn't. How charmed could she have been by the chubby little blond white girl she was paid next to nothing to spend more time with than she spent with her own children?

"I have two little boys and a little girl," she said to me one day. "They are older than you, but not as old as Gloria." I couldn't picture them at all.

I was young enough to think that a woman my parents all but owned was more fond of me than *they* were, that she loved me as if I was her child, cared for me as much as she did for her own children, bore me no ill will for the circumstances of my birth, the manner of my upbringing, for coming into the world on the guilty side of a profound injustice of which she, her husband, her children, her friends and what should have been their country were the victims.

Elsie was allowed to scold us mildly and often did, though she more often invoked the wrath of our parents to try to keep us in line. She was given to hyperbole that we found hilarious: "You mustn't do that. If you do that again, master will smack your bottom one hundred thousand times." Using pen and paper, Gloria calculated that, if done non-stop, this would take about ten days. "Do not talk back to Elsie," Elsie said. "I say goodbye to my three little ones on Monday morning and do not see them again until Friday night. They are always so glad to see me. They do not talk back to me or to my sister, who takes care of them when I am gone. They are like angels, but the four of you are little devils." Yet she punished me only once, by forbidding me to lick the bowl after she made frosting for a cake.

It was because of a thing that happened before we left for Canada that Elsie and I didn't say goodbye. I went out to the shed early one evening to visit her. As usual, she seemed to be glad to see me, even though I was intruding on what little private time she had. I fancied that I made her feel less lonely, that all thought of her own children vanished the second she saw me. Elsie had a stack of Torkar comic books. Written in Afrikaans, the Torkar series was based on the character of Tarzan, the books illustrated not with drawings but with panels of photographs of white actors or models in various action poses. There were rangers of the veldt who, in their pursuit of criminals, were forever throwing or receiving a punch, or pointing a gun while in mid-stride, driving cars, kissing women. Their every altercation was with some city-dwelling villain. The police were assisted by the Tarzan-like character Torkar, a white, tall, handsome, muscular, loin-cloth-wearing veldt dweller without whom they would never have managed to maintain law and order, let alone stop the encroachment of city-born wickedness.

I sat on Elsie's lap while she translated the dialogue balloons and captions from Afrikaans to English. I was never as transfixed by the stories as Elsie was—she covered her face in fright sometimes, or screamed and looked away. I'm not sure how good her translations were. And she may have toned down the violence and skipped ahead when women fell in love with Torkar, as they were always doing. There were Bantu characters in the series, gun-toting assistants to the rangers of the veldt, all happily supportive of the Afrikaans, whose right to own and police the veldt they implicitly acknowledged. When I was older, I wondered if Elsie read Torkar because that was all she was allowed to read when she wasn't in Langa, or because it was all she was able to read or all she could afford. I didn't know.

On that evening, a few days before we left for Canada, Elsie took me on her lap as always. She had no sooner begun reading to me than my father appeared in the doorway of the shed. Elsie froze. "It's time for bed, Rachel," he said, extending his hand to me. I slid down from Elsie's lap, ran to the door and took his hand. I looked over my shoulder, intending to say good night to Elsie, and saw her staring at the floor on which the photo book lay face up, its pages splayed apart. She looked so desolate I didn't say a word.

Hours later, I woke to the sound of someone soft-stepping across the landing, then slowly descending the stairs. I sat up in bed. There was no light beneath the door. I wondered if Dad had gone down to the kitchen for some Horlicks. I lay down and closed my eyes, only to open them again when I heard the creaking of the back door. I got out of bed as quietly as I could, went to the window and parted the curtains. The lamp above the back steps was on and Dad stood barefoot on the steps in his pyjamas, looking up at the sky, adjusting his glasses as if the better to make out a constellation. It occurred to me that he might be sleepwalking.

He took his glasses off and rubbed them on the hem of his pyjamas, put them back on, tiptoed down the steps and made his way over the sun-scorched yellow grass toward the back of the garden, walking out of the light cast by the lamp above the steps into the darkness. I thought he would soon reappear, but he didn't. One, two, five, ten minutes went by. It was as if he had gone off into the night for a barefoot stroll in his pyjamas. Only in the wake of that thought did the obvious truth occur to me. He had gone to Elsie's shed. Dad, who almost never spoke to her when she was in the house, leaving that to Mom, had gone to visit Elsie in her shed. Why? It was for no possible reason but the one I guessed when I was older. But at the time I was stymied. For him to leave the house alone at night, to go out walking, to drive around for hours in his car, was not uncommon, but I had never known him to go out walking in his pyjamas.

I stayed there at the window, ready to scramble back into bed at the sound of Mom opening my bedroom door. At last, after about an hour, when I was just short of falling asleep with my forehead pressed to the window, Dad re-emerged into the light, looking exactly as he had before. He walked slowly to the steps, which he climbed with his arms at his sides, his body as erect as that of a soldier. It again occurred to me that he might be sleepwalking.

I got back into bed and listened to him make his way upstairs to his room. I lay awake for quite some time, wondering why, if Dad had gone to visit her, Elsie had not turned on the light. Why had he gone to visit Elsie, the maid that he and Mom drove to the train station every Friday when she made her way back to Langa township?

The next evening, when I went out to Elsie's shed, she was lying on her cot, her shoes still on, staring at the ceiling. "Hi, Elsie," I said.

"Go away now, child," she said. "I am very tired. Too tired to read Torkar."

"What about tomorrow?"

She moved her head from side to side on the pillow. "No more Torkar. No more. Go back to the house."

"Why are you being so mean?" I said, but she made no sign of having heard me.

"*Please*," I said.

She sat up on the bed, then, her hands supporting her, swung her legs onto the floor and stood. "*Hamba suka wena*," she shouted at me.

Shocked to hear her use an expression that was forbidden at school, only in part because it was Zulu, I ran back up the garden to the house.

Now, in the wake of the dinner party, I thought of Dad standing on the steps, staring up at the sky before he walked across the grass and disappeared into the darkness. Perhaps he had many times thought about visiting the shed but had only worked up the nerve that one night because we were soon to leave for another country. Or had there been other nights?

I doubted it, given Elsie's demeanour those last few days. I doubted it but didn't, couldn't, stop considering it. Soon, my mind was jumping about between seemingly unconnected ideas, something it had also done before each of my breakdowns. I told myself that a third was not imminent even as I began to think of how odd it would be if Wade wrote a book and became as caught up in it as I was in Anne Frank's, read his own book hundreds of times, became consumed by it to the point of nearly losing his mind, read it to the point of excluding all other books and never wrote another one. What if Wade were to come down with what *I* had?

Madness is not contagious. You are nowhere near as sick as you were years ago. A series of such mantras ran through my mind. I began to see myself as I fancied others did, as a figure of scorn and amusement. I felt, more so than I had in years, worthless, hopeless, useless.

I wrote in my diary on the sly, at the nearest public library. I skipped yoga class to do it or, when Wade was working at his desk, told him I was going for a walk or taking the car out on some invented errand. Sometimes, I wrote in the diary while he was out on a run, often having to stop in mid-sentence when I heard him coming up the stairs. I told myself that I was merely having a setback, not regressing, but I wondered how much worse I'd be if I had the privacy I'd had when I wrote in my room back home. I doubled my daily dose of lithium, restored it to its doctor-prescribed level, but it made no difference that I could detect.

I had gone into hiding at the same age Anne Frank did, when I was thirteen. I went into hiding in her diary and mine.

The day I showed Wade my first copy of the book, I'd felt like telling him that there was another version of the book in my mind, one that goaded me on irresistibly toward destruction, a book that was the child of the mating of her book and my life.

From *The Arelliad*

THE SECRET ANNEX (1985)

Resigned to imminent defeat,
the German side will soon retreat.
The Nazi bully boys are done—
their reign was brief, the war is won.

I've sunk into the page and I am in the Secret Annex, where, an invisible voyeur, I move about among the Franks, the three van Pels, the dentist Anne calls Dussel. All of them are fluent in Arellian, though they rarely speak above a whisper for fear of being heard by someone other than their minders, whose tantalizing voices *they* can hear.

If they could see me, I'd warn them that the Nazis will find them soon unless their minders find another place for them to hide. Anne looks as if she senses me when I stand beside her as she writes. She looks up from time to time and smiles as if she knows I share her sense of humour. She seems to sink into the page like me, bears down on her pen as she slowly carves the words, her lips a thin straight line. She sees more than the others see, goes where none of them can go, knows things they will never understand.

She's gone for good, it seems, but then she surfaces and writes again, this time in Arellian. *R drhs r pmvd dsvm dv'oo yv uivv.* "I wish I knew when we'll be free." She doesn't know that they will never be. I was wrong. She doesn't know the things I know. I'm standing on the shore of their stream of time, watching them as they go by. I know all too well where this current carries them, having seen them lose the fight against it a thousand times before.

I wander once again into what might have been. What if they had never been betrayed, the eight of them never caught? Her diary is never published. She goes on keeping it forever in the heaven of what might have been. Or what if the war had lasted far longer than it did? She grows to womanhood in this place, unable to escape, stays on in the secret house in despair of ever being free again.

For a while she fell for Peter van Pels, who did not even have a room shared with others, just a space beneath the stairwell between the first and second floors. It wasn't meant to be for them. For two long years, he was the only boy in her life. Her sister, Margot, three years older, thought Peter hopelessly immature, but what if two years of confinement had become ten and the Frank sisters had become romantic rivals, vying for him?

Anne couldn't stand him at first but eventually decided that his capacity to annoy was less than that of other boys who had annoyed her all the time. One of her greatest fears was that she would die without ever having been in love, or having had the chance to overlook the imperfections of a man long enough to sleep with him.

What might have become of the crush she had on him? They are stranded together forever; it comes down to him and her in that strange, hermetic place, the last two Jews on earth, nothing changing but their ages until their minders stop coming to the bookcase. She panics when she thinks of their confinement going on until they starve to death or simply give up to get it over with.

What if word comes of a settlement, a truce that rests on the abandonment of all Jews to the master race? The war is called a draw but no allowances are made for Jews; better to sacrifice the Jews than destroy the human race. She wonders:

> Is this how minds go back and forth
> when people weigh the cost of truth,
> the ones that could have helped the Jews
> but told themselves they had to choose
> to save their own—why take the chance?
> Besides, there was no evidence.
> The talk of concentration camps
> might just be talk, for all they knew—
> why risk it all to save a few?

I sink deeper into the page, into the yellow wood. Arellia is overcast. Night comes on and, with it, a great storm of snow and wind that blows so hard it shakes the ground.

The snow stops, but the wind gets worse, the cold west wind that blew the night the Shadow She fell into His hands because of me.

I hide behind the only shelter I can find, an old rock wall that someone built, the remnants of a monument in honour of someone who perished here so long ago their names have faded from the stones and nothing but the dates remain.

Now comes the quickening of time that happens in Arellia. I'll fly off into outer space if I let go. Arellia spins the world into winter. My face has never been so cold—I should have worn some warmer clothes. I have to find my way but I don't know which way to go, or how I got to where I am, or even where I came here from. At least, because of the wind, I know which way is west, I think, just as the wind dies down, and once again I spin about.

I stop at last and there she is, the same black coat, the same green eyes. They never found her clothes or books that winter morning. There is not a sound but for the foghorn in the lighthouse on the Cape, the other Cape, not the one they call Good Hope.

"I'd be alive if not for you
and many others would be too;
you could have stayed, you knew, you knew."
I tell myself the words are mine—
I've written them a thousand times:
no one accuses me but me,
but I accuse me endlessly.

She's standing there, I should explain; she looks at me with such disdain.

"What do you want?" I manage to say. I've never asked her that before, though I know the answer. "I wish you'd never given me that book," I say. "I didn't ask you for it. You planted in my mind a word that colours all the other words. Soon, there'll be nothing in my mind but that one word, nothing in the pages of my diary but your name written over and over in reverse."

Zmmu. Anne.

When I reversed the alphabet, I turned the whole world inside out.

Again the horrible vertigo, the spins that come when you lie down and close your eyes after having had too much to drink. By the time the world winds down, I am just able to get my balance and make my way to bed. I think about the things she said to me, the things her green eyes seemed to see when I forgot that she was me. Soon, I am clinging to a corner of the mattress, my knees drawn up to my chest, tears dripping onto the sheets. It hasn't been this bad in years.

Wade must be pretending he doesn't hear the rocking of the kitchen chair when I write at night. He doesn't ask if I'm okay.

From *The Ballad of the Clan van Hout*

THE RECKONING (1966)

Rounding up collaborators,
they dismissed the Nazi waiter.
He hadn't really been a traitor,
for pouring drinks and serving food
was "misdemeanour turpitude."
He'd served no cause except his own
and might as well be left alone.
They laughed at this fool's insistence
that he'd served with the Resistance.
"You worked with a cell so secret
only you knew it existed.
Can you provide us with some proof
of this cell we know nothing of?"
"I can't prove anything," Hans said.
"The men who brought me in are dead.
I left notes in public places,
never saw my comrades' faces.
The record of events is lost
and I am left to pay the cost.
I'll never try to clear my name
by condescending to your game.
I need but say, 'Yes, you are right,
I played the fool night after night
so that I didn't have to choose
between the Germans and the Jews.
No matter which side won the war,
they'd know the uniform I wore
was just a costume, nothing more.
I did not want to starve to death
or slave away to my last breath.
If I could make it to the end,
the winning side would be my friend.

What some did to survive the war
and never had to answer for
makes my crime a misdemeanour:
the prostitutes and other whores
who gave themselves away and more;
the men who offered up their wives
(or anyone to save their lives)
to sate the lust of brutal men
who made them watch till they were done;
wives with children who were crying
stole from others who were dying.
We all did what we had to do—
we could not all be heroes, too.
At least my family survived—
if not for me they would have died.'
I could make this false confession.
It seems such a small concession:
admit that I was ordinary,
just another functionary
who wasn't charged with anything,
that I was just some nothing
who took no credit, bore no blame,
who never earned himself a name,
just a nickname, one of the pack
who was too gutless to fight back,
who, put to the ultimate test,
turned out to be like all the rest,
just the sort that you'd expect
to find a way to save his neck."

Anne Frank returns—I said she would,
but my good name is gone for good.
Eight years since the Liberation,
branded by my reputation,
I was still the Nazi waiter,

still regarded as a traitor,
but I was just a busboy now,
the only job they would allow
the man who waited on the kind
who murdered just to pass the time.

I heard about a certain book,
decided I would take a look.
The book was called *Het Achterhuis*,
something like *The Secret Annex*.
The strangest thing I'd ever read—
the writer of the book was dead,
the father of the writer said
in the prologue he had written
to introduce a girl named Anne
who died when she was just fifteen.
The book was—I was so amazed—
about the Jews I thought I'd saved,
the ones I'd heard of from young Klaus,
the very street, the very house.
Things had not gone as expected.
Perhaps my note was intercepted,
perhaps some comrade had been caught—
perhaps, perhaps, it mattered not.
Two years eight Jews had stayed alive,
but only Otto Frank survived.
Among the dead was the author,
Anne Frank, Otto's teenage daughter.
I felt I was vindicated
by this proof for which I'd waited.
I knew the house, I knew the street—
it wasn't far from Elandsstraat,
my childhood home till I was eight.
That little bridge on Prinsengracht,
not far from where the Jews were caught—

my friends and I had played on it!
To think a girl, a Jew, hid where
we skylarked in the open air,
a girl for whom I'd done my part
but now was gone—it broke my heart.
Yet by her book I was redeemed,
my name was saved—or so it seemed.
The famous book, *Het Achterhuis*,
the famous girl, the famous house—
but then it struck me all at once:
in spite of all the "evidence,"
my name was nowhere in the book;
I couldn't tell them where to look
for proof that the Nazi waiter
was a cunning infiltrator,
the unknown hero of the war
who would have saved Anne Frank but for
the negligence of lesser men
whom I had never met, but then
none of us had met each other—
all of us were undercover.
Had the Franks made a getaway
or found another hideaway
because my warning was relayed
and reached them long before the raid,
Het Achterhuis, the famous book,
would not have earned a second look.
Many Jews, secretly confined,
left something similar behind—
diaries, journals, things they penned
to pass the time until war's end,
commemorations of a war
spent hiding out while waiting for
the midnight knock upon the door.
Such things had to be recorded

in case the Nazis were rewarded
with success, every Jew located,
every Jew exterminated.
The Nazis lost, but Anne Frank died;
the whole world read, the whole world cried.
Her book had put a human face
on the entire Jewish race—
the millions of Jews who were lost
in what they called the Holocaust,
the ones who suffered just like her,
her father, mother and sister,
four more souls whom few remember,
the ones for whom help came too late,
the ones who would not stoop to hate.
Anne Frank became a household name—
she longed for freedom and for fame,
saw neither one before she died
a death that I will not describe.
Her fame grew as the years went by,
as did her book's, and that was why
I could not help but wonder why,
though heaven had ensured her fame,
it had not thought to clear my name.
The Nazi waiter I would be—
at least I would be locally.
The man who almost saved Anne Frank
was mocked by men of lesser rank.
The time had come for me to bear
my burden somewhere far from there.
That's how your father, Hans van Hout,
came to found the Land of Hout.

WADE

Myra and I were in the kitchen at Liesbeek Road—she had retrieved me from the living room, where I'd been sitting with Rachel and her father. She stood with her back to the kitchen counter, arms folded, pressing to her breasts a bulky-looking manila envelope, which she soon held out to me, smiling as if she were giving back to me something she had borrowed long ago.

"My oeuvre," Myra said. "As you know, I'm a published writer. Everything I've published is in there. Magazine pieces. Seven of them. I haven't torn them out, which is why the envelope is so heavy. I wonder, Wade, if you would mind reading them and giving me your opinion as a fellow writer. I know you plan to be a different kind of writer than I am, but I believe that, in some ways, all writers are alike, don't you?"

"I've never met a writer," I said. "But I'm sure you're right."

"Oh, please don't say you're sure until you really are. One of the pieces was published in *Fair Lady*, which is the leading magazine for women in South Africa. Another was published in *Living and Loving*, another South African women's magazine—intended for young women of the kind I fear you think of as old-fashioned. Women very much unlike my daughters." She laughed in a way that seemed lighthearted, as if she was fondly amused by the newfangled notions of her daughters, but there was no mirth in those dark eyes of hers. "But I shouldn't be saying anything that might influence you. Will you read them?"

"Of course. I'd be glad to," I lied.

As we drove home, I told Rachel what her mother had asked me to do.

"Good luck," she said. "I've read everything she's published. You're on your own."

That night, sitting at my desk in the bedroom, I opened the envelope and inspected the contents. On the cover of *Fair Lady* was a photograph of a smiling Elizabeth Taylor and a smirking Richard Burton. On the cover of *Living and Loving* was a pretty, wholesome-looking, bare-shouldered, bare-armed, possibly naked young woman with a bare-backed baby in her arms. In another magazine, there was an article by Myra about the similarities between Cape Town and St. John's: both were port cities on the extreme edges of continents; both had a tower-topped, sea-overlooking hill called Signal Hill from which noonday guns were fired; both were known for their famous Capes, South Africa for the Cape of Good Hope, and St. John's for Cape Spear, the most easterly point of North America. There were two pieces of non-fiction and five short stories.

The short story that appeared in *Fair Lady* was called "Laughter and the Darkening Sky." I read that first and discovered that Myra had taken Henry James's *Turn of the Screw* and boiled it down to a tale of the ghosts of two children who had drowned. The ghosts left wet footprints wherever they went in the house in which they'd once lived. The debt to Henry James was unacknowledged. Another story, called "The Dress," was about a woman who, after being jilted in romance, wore the same dress for the rest of her life. The debt to Dickens's Miss Havisham, from *Great Expectations*, was also unacknowledged.

Two more short stories also borrowed heavily from famous sources. "Your mother is a shameless plagiarist," I shouted to Rachel, who soon appeared in the doorway. "All but one of her stories is a rip-off of a famous short story or plot line from a novel."

"I know," Rachel said. "As I told you, I've read her stories. But you're *still* on your own."

"You knew she had plagiarized them and didn't tell me?"

"What good would it have done? You'd already promised to read them. And I wouldn't say they were plagiarized, exactly—maybe variations on themes?"

"Not very varied."

"Just be nice to her."

The only original story was "We Two Are Now One," the story Rachel had told me about not long after we met, set in a fishbowl in which two goldfish lived, a large male and a very small female. The male fish ate the female fish, then swam about to the end of his life in his lonely world. The feminist slant was heavy-handed, but I thought that Myra was at least trying to say something that was of importance to her.

When Myra and I were next alone—once again in the kitchen of the house on Liesbeek Road, while Hans and Rachel sat in the living room—I lost my nerve and said that I thought all the pieces were good. She looked dismayed. "You're patronizing me," she said, faintly smiling. "I know I'm not a good writer. I base everything I write on what other, far better writers have written. Sometimes people notice, sometimes not. I don't care either way. I'm sorry that you feel you can't be honest with me."

"Sometimes it's hard to be honest."

"So your real opinion is . . . so harsh you thought it best to keep it to yourself?"

"No," I said. "I just . . . I don't read those kinds of magazines. I don't know what their editors are looking for."

"Why do you assume that I base what I write on what editors are looking for?"

"All right. I thought the best story was 'We Two Are Now One.'"

She laughed, fingering her necklace. "That one? I was, for a short time, a member of a women writers' group in St. John's. That's the kind of thing they were all writing, complaints about having had their hopes and dreams swallowed up by their husbands. I found an obscure American short story I thought they would have liked and used it as a model. They loved it. They admired a story based on one that some nobody had written, but they didn't like the ones based on the work of famous writers, because those famous writers were men. That told me something.

"Oh, I'm so disappointed with you, Wade. I think there is something in my writing, something worthwhile. It's been published, after all. I think it would be best if, from now on, we didn't talk about writing. You may think that this, all of this, will make it hard for us to get along. It won't, I assure you. You have your imperfections and I have mine. That's where we shall leave it."

I left that day feeling bewildered and not convinced that I had not been cast into outer darkness.

When I told Rachel what had passed between me and her mother, she flopped down on the sofa with a copy of *Het Achterhuis*, which she'd taken to reading for far longer each day than she ever had in St. John's. "You just got what Gloria, Carmen, Bethany and I call the disappointment treatment. People disappoint her all the time, but they never make her angry with them. She gets more mileage out of disappointment."

I was about to say I might have been more forthright with her mother if I had been forewarned, but Rachel sounded so weary of all mention of her mother that I decided not to.

From *The Arelliad*

MYRA (1984)

Memory makes its way into Arellia. I hear my mother's voice from within the yellow wood that I dare not venture into. It is Christmas night, late and long ago. Everyone has gone to bed but for the two of us. I am reading what she calls "that Anne Frank book," and she has had too much to drink. Her usual limit is two, but there are times . . .

"Someday, my little Rachel Lee, you'll think that you have found true love, a young man you will never leave and who wouldn't think of leaving you. A danger to the family is all that he will ever be.

"True love. I've never had it or wanted it. It's better to marry sensibly than to sacrifice yourself to some idea from a book. In school I knew so many lovesick girls who wound up jilted and alone and miserable ever after, pining for the man who got away.

"Myra Weaver, I used to be. I could have done much worse than Him, not that I had much to pick from, the girl who grew up far too soon on the Cape of Hope and Grope. You've never heard my story, so listen well and don't repeat a word of it to your sisters.

"My father left my mother and me when I was ten. He ran off and we never heard from him again. Left us with nothing but a wad of unpaid bills. My mother nearly lost her mind. She said he left because of me—well, she said he never wanted children and she tricked him into it. From then on, I was nothing but a trick that my mother played on my father. Boo hoo.

"We moved in with my uncle, my father's brother, Dr. Uncle Michael Weaver, who had a wife but loved another. He was well-to-do, a surgeon who took us in because of how it would look if he left us on our own. He sent me away as soon as he found a place for me at convent school, the Star of the Sea Convent School for Girls, where I was brought up in a nun-run Roman Catholic world.

"I was a convent girl who made no friends. Boo hoo. The best Uncle's money could do was make the nuns put up with me. The other girls were from the upper crust, not meant to mix with the riff or the raff, but Uncle paid a premium to get me in and keep me there. So I became a Protestant in Catholic clothes who stuck out like a certain thumb, the school outcast, the heretic-in-residence.

"I was an easy mark for Sister Gail, the principal, who beat me with the strap she carried like a six-gun on her hip.

"While I was away at school, Uncle divorced his wife, kept his lover and also took up with Mother. Dr. Uncle Michael Weaver, Mother's husband, my stepfather, wasn't fond of his stepdaughter, whose father was his brother, Jim, with whom he'd never got along.

"Stepfather eventually abandoned Mother. Twice abandoned she was, and twice she put the blame on me. He bamboozled her in their divorce and left us penniless. In my last year at convent school, Mother was committed to a hospital, where she found a way to end it all.

"By eighteen, I was on my own, a poor shopgirl.

"As you know, boo hoo's not how the story ends. My education was first-rate. At school, I'd learned to scheme and calculate in order to survive. I did some things I had to do, and I would again. But the nuns polished my exterior. I looked and sounded and comported myself like the stars of the Star of the Sea. I got to where I am today by learning how to play the game.

"I saw what life would be like if I held out for love. It would have been like my mother's, except *my* Romeo would not have been a surgeon—a truck driver, maybe, or an office clerk.

"So I chose your father. To be his wife was my one choice, but I let him think the choice was his.

"He was a chartered accountant when I told him I was pregnant. I saw that he'd do right by me because he knew the world would say he was a coward and a cad if he ran off like my father did.

"He had no one to point out my deficiencies, and I had no one to point out his, so I guess that made us even.

"He didn't have a way with the ladies, so he was fortunate that I wasn't one. I never saw him talk to another woman, never saw one look at him, though (as if he thought they wouldn't notice) he stared at them appraisingly. He stared so hard, it was like he didn't know what they were for.

"I sized him up well. This man would never break my heart. Neither handsome nor well spoken, the only heart he'd ever broken was his own. I saw it in his eyes—that sort of thing you can't disguise.

"He did just what I told him to. He seemed relieved, as if he knew he'd never find his own way unless someone took him in hand, someone who seemed to believe that there was more to him than met the eye, that, given time, he would succeed.

"He's all that I have ever had or wanted. I have no time for second-guessing. His wife is all I've ever been or ever will be."

Without me, He would cease to be;
without Him there would be no me.
So I will be my Husband's keeper;
that's all I have, a piece of paper
that certifies that He is mine,
that He and I are intertwined,
by God and man forever joined.

WADE

I was at my desk in the bedroom, trying to coax out a few words about the impossibly distant place of my childhood. The desk had the look of a stage prop in a play about a writer, my old Olivetti in the middle of it, resting on a brown-bordered green blotter, a sheet of blank paper in the carriage, a notebook beside it and, on the notebook, perfectly positioned at a forty-five degree angle, a newly sharpened, never-used yellow pencil. I'd felt foolish just sitting there since my run-in with Myra, who, no matter how you looked at it, was a published writer, a writer who, when she sat at a typewriter, typed words onto the page instead of just staring at it.

"Maybe I could get started if I wrote in code," I shouted to Rachel. "Or I could pretend to write in code. Just hit the keys randomly. Either way, who would know?"

I immediately wished I hadn't said it, but was rescued by the ringing of the phone. Rachel answered it and soon after shouted, "WHAT? YOU'RE *KIDDING*."

"Is something wrong?" I called, but, hearing her laugh, I went back to staring at the page. Minutes later, she burst into the room, both hands on top of her head. "Bethany and Clive just got engaged," she said. It was almost a question.

"That cannot be true," I said.

"Oh, it is," Rachel said. "Mom is absolutely over the moon. That was her on the phone. I think she's calling all of Cape Town. Bethany and Clive. Three weeks ago, Bethany was rolling her eyes at the mention of his name. And one hour ago, she asked him to marry her."

"*She* asked *him*?"

Rachel nodded. "How else could it possibly have happened? There's a get-together at Mom and Dad's tonight to celebrate. The DeVrieses will be there, of course. Gloria and Max are in Amsterdam, and Mom says she couldn't reach Carmen and Fritz."

"What on earth is Bethany thinking?"

"Let's not be like that," Rachel said. "I mean, I feel the same way, but it's not as if Bethany is the most normal person in the world, either. And she's not as hard-nosed as she pretends. Really. Growing up, she fell in love all the time. I'll wear my best dress, the one with the spaghetti straps, if you'll wear a tie. We can buy one on the way. They'll all be dressed to the nines. Or my parents' version of it, anyway. Let's say to the fives."

I nodded. She'd been subdued since the night of her father's rant against the Jews and Anne Frank, and it was nice to see a hint of buoyancy.

At Liesbeek Road, Rachel rang the doorbell. As before, Bethany came to the door, this time holding a martini palm up in one hand and a cigarette in the other.

"Do come in, dahlings," she said.

"I can't believe you're engaged," Rachel said. "I'd hug you if you weren't armed to the teeth."

"You finally popped the question," I said.

Bethany raised her glass in mock tribute. "I'm off my happy pills tonight, so I'm allowed to drink. In fact, I think it's mandatory or else I might get all depressed. The two of you are required to drink as well—a lot. You can always get a cab later or spend the night here. Do come in and give your best to my betrothed."

We followed her into the front room, where Hans and Myra, the DeVrieses and Clive were standing about, all of them but Hans holding martini glasses, though Peter's was filled with what looked like cranberry juice. "Here they are," Bethany said. Myra was beaming; Hans, his hands behind his back, seemed lost in thought. The DeVrieses flanked Clive, whose face was as flushed as if he'd just sprinted a mile.

"Isn't it wonderful?" Myra said to Rachel as she hugged her with one arm.

"It is," Rachel said. "It's absolutely wonderful."

"What's this, now, what's this?" Hans said as Rachel kissed him on the cheek. "Making a move on the old man, are you?" Everyone laughed.

I extended my hand to him and he took it, but not firmly. "Congratulations," I said.

"Bethany proposed to Clive, you know," he said to Rachel, smiling broadly, showing more of his dentures than he ever had in my presence.

"Yes, I know," she said. "Don't draw any conclusions about *me* from that."

"Well, she has always been unorthodox," he said.

"I think it's very charming," Myra said. "And these are modern times. Why shouldn't the woman propose?"

"In that case," Hans said, "I assume that, in spite of what she just said, Rachel will be proposing soon."

More laughter. I glanced at Rachel, who looked away when our eyes met.

Rachel and I congratulated Clive and his parents in a jumble of hugs, handshakes and kisses. "Martinis for Rachel and Wade," Bethany said to Clive, putting her hand gently on his back. Clive made for the kitchen and came back with two glasses. "Ready, made and waiting for you," Bethany said. As we took the drinks from Clive, Bethany stepped into the middle of the room. "Quiet, please," she said. "I would like to propose a toast."

Clive lurched forward as if pushed by his parents. Dropping to one knee in front of her, he pulled a ring box from the pocket of his jacket and opened it. "Will you marry me?" he said, his voice breaking on "marry." Myra gasped as if marriage had not been mentioned until now.

"You stole my line, buddy," Bethany said as if to herself. "But I guess I stole your thunder, so we're even. Yes, I will marry the man who's already agreed to marry me."

"The ring makes it official," Theresa said. Clive stayed there, on one knee, looking up at Bethany with a stricken expression as if she had said no.

"Well, put it on her finger, Clive," Peter said. As Clive stood, Bethany hurriedly handed her drink to Rachel, her cigarette to me, and thrust her left hand out to Clive, her other on her hip, which she cocked in the manner of some movie star she seemed to be imitating. Clive took the ring from the box and, shaking badly, tried to slip it onto Bethany's finger. "It goes on the one to the right of my pinky," Bethany said to a chorus of nervous laughter, using her right hand to steady his. Together, they managed to slide the ring into place.

"Ta-dah," Bethany said, raising her hand so that all could see the ring—the diamond was sizable. Everyone applauded.

"Clive picked it out when we went for the vodka and vermouth," Theresa said.

Bethany lowered her hand to waist height and splayed her fingers as we all gathered around to admire the ring we all knew had been paid for by Clive's parents. Bethany gazed at it as if the sight of it on her hand seemed as unlikely to her as it did to me.

"You were going to propose a toast," I said to Bethany, thinking to rescue her from an awkward moment.

"Yes, I was," Bethany said, "but nothing I could say could top this. Nothing at all."

A few minutes later, Rachel and I found ourselves alone in the kitchen with Bethany. "They wanted to get champagne but I insisted on martinis," she said. "I get no kick from champagne, but mere alcohol drives me insane. I have to blame something." She locked eyes with Rachel. "Out with it," she said. "You look like you think I've gone all the way around the bend and back again."

"I *am* surprised," Rachel said.

"Well," Bethany said, "if I had waited for him to ask first—but he did get down on one knee just now."

"You know that's not what I mean," Rachel said.

If I had waited for him to ask first. I remembered Rachel telling me she thought I should ask her out. *You don't have to, but I think you should.*

Bethany put her martini on the counter and lit up a cigarette. "I know, I know," she said. "I was just kidding. Wade, would you rather have a beer? You're not nursing that martini, you're doctoring it."

"No changing the subject," Rachel said. "I want to know what's up."

"What's up is that I got engaged today. For most of the usual reasons. I swept him off his feet. I guess he loves me or something. So what if I don't love him. He is smitten and no one else is beating down the door. He may not be a knight in shining armour, but he's a nice guy, and most guys are not so nice. His father and mine grew up together. My mom likes his mom. He wants a quiet, normal life. He has a job he hates so much that it may make him love his wife and kids all the more. You know, Rachel, not every woman finds a man who loves her just as much as she loves him. The odds are heavily against it. Even fewer meet one who plans to be a writer, but I have to say, I don't like Wade's chances of becoming one unless you get down on one knee and beg him to."

"That's just the martini talking," I said, grabbing Rachel as her index finger came within a few inches of Bethany's face. She took a deep breath and lowered her hand.

Bethany plucked the olive out of her martini and put both on the counter. "Wade," she said, "what you are witnessing is a standoff between two sisters. Rachel is wondering when I last had a bite to eat and kept it down, and I'm wondering why the underside of her left hand is so smudged with ink. My version of her wrist test."

Rachel glanced down at her hand, which was, indeed, smudged with blue ink, more so than I had ever seen it. How had I not noticed? Rachel shook her head. "I haven't been writing my diary. I can't help it that I'm left-handed and therefore write *everything* left-handed."

"What have you been writing, Wade's novel?"

"Knock it off," Rachel said, but Bethany persisted.

"We're on to each other, Wade. She knows why I'm wearing this loose-fitting dress, and I know why her hand is blue. We know each other's tricks. She worships a book written by a dead teenager and is diarizing day and night. Take my word for it, she is. And people think *I'm* nuts."

Bethany and Rachel looked at each other as if both of them were shocked by what Bethany had said. As Rachel's eyes welled up, Bethany pulled Rachel close and buried her face in her hair, whispering something. Rachel whispered something back. When they let go of each other, they were both smiling and crying at the same time. "Let me get that beer, buddy," Bethany said to me, rubbing tears away with both hands, then patting my chest.

For the rest of the evening, Bethany and Clive sat side by side on the loveseat, holding hands. I felt certain they had never held hands before, let alone kissed. Rachel and I sat side by side on separate chairs, not holding hands, the flagrant opposite of Bethany and Clive, a couple with no plans to get engaged, let alone married, with no plans period except to go on living in disgrace.

On the way home, I said, "So you're diarizing. I don't know why I didn't notice the ink on your hand, but I can't say I'm surprised, given your mood lately."

"I haven't relapsed," Rachel snapped. "A few pages here and there does not a relapse make."

"When have you been doing it? Where? I haven't seen you."

"Sweetie, it doesn't matter. It's maybe a few pages at most."

"A few more than I've written."

"You know—"

"I know," I said. "It's just that, judging by what Bethany said, my being stuck at the starting line is the talk of your family. I don't like to think of Bethany and Clive, *Clive*, exchanging smirks about me."

Rachel took my hand. I raised hers to my mouth and kissed it.

From *The Ballad of the Clan van Hout*

HET PAROOL (1967)

(In which I tell the girls of pieces published about me in *Het Parool*, the official paper of the Dutch Resistance during and after the war.)

At Cape Town University,
I told them of my history.
I told those men of lesser rank
that I had almost saved Anne Frank.
Word somehow spread to Amsterdam,
where my undoing soon began.
My name appeared in *Het Parool*:
"'The Case of Hans van Hout,' the fool
who claims he would have saved Anne Frank
if not for men of lesser rank.
He persists in the travesty
of falsifying history,
dishonours those who gave their lives
or somehow managed to survive,
the heroes of the underground,
some of whom were never found,
but sent to camps and perished there—
no records say exactly where.
Comrades, witnesses testify
that they were brave and that they died.
Who would cheapen the sacrifice
of those who paid the greatest price
so that a man like Hans van Hout
could strut and boast and brag about
such feats as serving sauerkraut?
A craven clown of false renown
impersonates the Underground

and libels the defenceless dead:
'It's their fault that Anne Frank is dead.'"

I admit some of their facts were right—
I'd made them up—not out of spite—
to make my story seem more true.
Details do that, you know they do.
I told them that a German said,
"Tell us the truth or Mam is dead,"
and put a gun against her head
and said that, after he shot her,
he'd hang my brother in the square.

The next file *Het Parool* compiled
read, "Hans van Hout, the only child
of Jan and Cornelia van Hout . . ."
The profs asked why I lied about
"a younger brother, one named Dittmer,
who almost died defying Hitler.
Dittmer must have been *very* young
the day that he was almost hung."
Another of their stupid jokes
that "proved" my story was a hoax.
"Tell us about Cornelia,
the imaginary character,
the one you said was almost shot
the day that Dittmer faced the Knot.
The mother that you haven't got
was dead before the war began.
Het Parool learned this from the man
who told them that your father ran
after the fall of Amsterdam
and never came to light again.
You were alone by age fourteen

but never were a go-between—
the member of the Underground
of whom no evidence was found."
I *did* serve with the Underground
but proof of this cannot be found.
I lost my mother, then my father,
who left me to an empty house—
he ran off like a frightened mouse.
No trace of him was ever found.
Fourteen, I joined the Underground—
the Germans thought me one of theirs,
the Underground *knew* this, my dears.
Het Parool had exposed only
the fraud your dad was *thought* to be.

The truth: to be or not to be
was always, always haunting me,
which ones should live, which ones should die—
none would have lived had I not lied,
agreed I would collaborate.
I *had* to be what I was not
or else more Jews would have been caught.
How could professors understand
the chaos of the Netherlands
when defeat seemed a certainty?
Years of lying from necessity
make habit of duplicity.

It did seem like a game sometimes:
we made up passwords and false names.
Some men were masters of disguise;
my specialty was telling lies.
Deception, misinformation,
codes with multiple translations

depending on the time of day:
you *must* not give yourself away,
you must not know who you work for
lest it come out under torture.
The lone wolves of the Underground
were written off if they were found.
By war's end, few men knew for sure
which uniform their comrades wore.
If truth be told, most still don't know
the traitors from the true heroes.
So much confusion and mistrust,
the worst mistaken for the best—
so, too, the other way around:
the maze we called the Underground.
Whichever way it all worked out
was never good for Hans van Hout:
Hans the deferential waiter,
Hans, inconsequential traitor.

I told them again and again
how close I came to saving Anne:
"They fouled it up, they failed Anne Frank,
those nameless men of lesser rank.
I did my job, they bungled theirs;
I almost saved her—no one cares.
My so-called comrades may have been
traitors, mercenaries, Germans
who duped me all throughout the war—
who knows who I was working for?
I knew the mission only once:
I tried to give the Franks a chance
to get away from Prinsengracht.
I wrote a note and left it where
I found my notes on Henke Square—

when I returned, it wasn't there.
No one is willing to admit
the lie and what lies under it.
The possibilities are clear.
What might have been if not for their
incompetence or apathy,
their avarice or treachery,
will always be a mystery.
The famous bookcase that concealed
eight should, when opened, have revealed
nothing at all, some empty rooms
that would not be the sad heirlooms
they are today. Anne Frank should be
a woman living happily,
untroubled in obscurity."

The truth is I may not live down
the mockery from town to town:
"Henceforth, you'll be the Almost Man,
the almost had a brother man,
a brother who was almost hung
when Hans van Hout was almost young;
a mother who was almost shot
when Dittmer almost faced the Knot:
a gun put to your mother's head
long after she was good and dead.
The man who almost saved Anne Frank
is nothing but a mountebank."

My girls, I don't know what I'd do
without the Special Love that you
hold in your hearts for Hans van Hout—
the Love I could not live without.
I hope that you will always be

what you have so far been for me:
the loyal few, the loving four—
no man could ever ask for more.

It isn't easy to push on
when you alone know right from wrong,
when you alone know truth from lies,
when evil lives and virtue dies,
when you alone know what you've done
but no one else beneath the sun
can see what you are truly worth
because some "secret" was unearthed.
To live in secret and exult—
is anything more difficult?

Anne Frank, Anne Frank won fame, no doubt—
through all the world her name rings out.
She dreamed that hers would one day be
among the names of History.

Hans van Hout, Hans van Hout,
all the world should know his name,
but he prefers to live without
the blandishments of fame.

WADE

A week later, on a Saturday afternoon, Rachel's mother invited us to lunch. Afterward, we sat around the front room with Bethany, who'd stayed put for once while we were eating.

"It's such a beautiful, hot day and so warm in this house," Hans said. "We should go to Clifton." He rubbed his hands together and raised his eyebrows as he looked at Myra, who opened her mouth in a silent laugh. "Yes," he said. "The girls are far too old for Muizenberg. It's not as if you and I have never been there, Myra. What red-blooded man doesn't like to lie in the sun among half-naked girls and women."

"And boys and men," Myra said.

"What's Clifton?" I said.

"Clifton is a topless beach," Rachel said, rolling her eyes. "Bethany and I went there in 1975. We weren't old enough, but I guess we looked old enough."

"*You* looked old enough," Bethany said. "As in two bra sizes bigger than your older scarecrow of a sister. I kept my T-shirt on."

"Naughty, naughty, Rachel," Myra said. "You didn't tell us you went to Clifton. How did you get there?"

"We hitchhiked," Bethany said. "We held up a cardboard sign that I made. I wrote 'Clifton' on it in big letters. We got a ride very quickly."

"There you go," Hans said. "The girls have already been. Besides, they won't be baring anything the rest of us haven't seen before."

"I won't be baring anything at all," Myra said, "but I don't mind going. One beach is as good as another as far as I'm concerned."

"Well, I'm not going," Bethany said.

"Sweetheart, you can always leave your top on if you want to," Myra said. "So can Rachel, for that matter."

"I'm sure Wade has never been to a topless beach," Hans said. I was startled. He'd never said my name in front of me before. "We could broaden his horizons."

Rachel looked dubious.

"I think Rachel doesn't want Wade to see the sights of Clifton," Hans said. "I think she's worried about the competition."

"Don't be silly," Myra said. "It's just people sunbathing. It's perfectly natural. Wade, don't worry. Women my age and size don't go topless there."

"It's decided, then," Hans said, clapping his hands together. "We're off to Clifton and Rachel can wear whatever she likes. She can wear a parka if she wants to."

As we drove to Clifton in our car, Hans and Myra following in theirs, a clunky Ford Cortina, Rachel pointed out to sea. "That's Robben Island out there. That's where they keep Mandela and the others doing hard labour. Half the day pulling cables of kelp from the water and the other half on their hands and knees in some mine that's making them go blind."

"*God*. It isn't very far out."

"No, it's not."

"Why is he in prison? I mean, what did he supposedly do?"

"I should know," Rachel said. "But I don't. Protesting in the streets or something."

"You'd think they'd put political prisoners someplace less conspicuous."

"The point is to *keep* them conspicuous, as object lessons."

Clifton Beach. I had never seen breasts outdoors before. Acres of topless women. It was as if nipples were a kind of berry and breasts the mounds of earth from which they grew—in all sizes, shapes and shades of tan. The sunbathers, male and female, either feigned nonchalance or were regulars, some of them gazing at the sea, propped up on their forearms, or lying on their backs, sunglasses reflecting the sky, others splayed face down, backs glistening with suntan oil.

Myra, her sandals removed but otherwise dressed in a straw sun hat, blouse and slacks as though the beach were her backyard, sat in a folding chair beneath an umbrella, contentedly, incessantly knitting, the needles clicking loudly. She looked up from time to time to stare out across the sea, at Robben Island, it might have been, hazy in the distance. That placid smile never left her face, and eventually, she'd turn back to her project, looping the wool over the ends of the needles as if she was caught up in the obsessive, mesmerizing repetition of a task that had no purpose. She was working on a golliwog—a rag doll with a black face, curly hair, black hands and black feet. The clothing consisted of a hat that could be any colour and a jumper that was always red and buttoned up the middle.

"It would be unthinkable to knit a golliwog in public in Canada," she said, looking up at me as I stood beside her beach chair, "but now that I'm back home, I can knit all the golliwogs I want." She laughed, turning her head from left to right as if addressing a large, sympathetic audience. "Such things are looked down upon in Canada by the same people who have black jockeys holding lanterns on their lawns. Canadians are very selective about what they disapprove of."

Rachel unselfconsciously peeled off her T-shirt, unhooked her bikini top, spread two blankets on the sand, lay down on one and patted the other to indicate that I should join her. Hans, wearing a wide-brimmed straw hat like Myra's, took off his shirt, dabbed white suntan lotion on various parts of his face and shoulders, kicked off his sandals, angled his chair to face the sea, reached into Myra's beach bag and drew out several Tupperware containers filled with food: hard-boiled eggs, cold fried chicken, sandwiches and pieces of watermelon, which he dispensed to us on small paper plates. After he poured us some ginger ale, he sat back to eat. Soon, he put his plate down, mumbled about having eaten too much at lunch, reached again into Myra's bag, withdrew a folded newspaper tied in an elastic band and tapped the paper rapidly against his thigh as if to be thus used was the sole purpose of newspapers.

As I well remembered the Bare Area in the van Hout household, it didn't surprise me that Rachel didn't mind being topless in front of her father, let alone in front of a beach full of strangers, who all seemed more intent on the incoming waves than on their fellow sunbathers. I again wondered if it was all a pretense, and the men especially were appraising the women on the sly. But everyone looked so matter of fact, I tried to look that way too.

I stripped to my trunks and, at Rachel's urging, ran to the shore and dove straight in—and came up gasping for breath, whelping like a seal. The water was frigid. I looked around. There was no one in the water but me. To the amusement of the sunbathers, I waded back to shore and lay down beside Rachel. "It's ice-cold," I said, my hands in my armpits.

"What did you expect? It's the Atlantic Ocean."

"We're in *Africa*."

She nodded and smiled. "But it's still the Atlantic Ocean."

"Yes," I said, "the south, the very south, Atlantic Ocean. You might have warned me."

"What would be the fun in that? Did you know that Cape Town was the starting point for many South Pole expeditions?"

Myra chuckled. She said that there were often jackass penguins at Clifton, though it seemed there were none in evidence today.

"Only one jackass so far," Hans said, and a few people nearby laughed.

Just a few miles away, Rachel said, around the tip of the cape, was the bathwater-warm Indian Ocean. "The water there is so salty, it buoys you up. You don't really need to know how to swim."

"So what are we doing here?" I said, looking at Hans, who pretended not to hear me, still tapping the paper against his thigh.

A slender, small-breasted young woman got up from her place on the beach, walked to the water, waded out a bit, then turned around and toppled backward, the waves washing over her as she held her nose. Then she stood and, nipples erect, waded out of the water, her long black hair hanging in a tail to her bikini bottom. She went back to lie on her towel beside her boyfriend.

"Not polite to stare," Rachel said, playfully punching my arm, "unless you want to stare at me."

Young, skinny black men, barefoot, shirtless, some wearing reversed baseball caps, went up and down the beach in pairs, lugging large orange coolers bearing pictures of their contents: soda pop, ice cream drumsticks and sandwiches, tricoloured Popsicles, Fudgesicles, Dixie cups and even beer. Sunbathers hailed the young men by raising a finger in the air, a gesture that sent pairs of vendors into a race through the sand, the young men glistening with sweat, their chests heaving. They looked as frantic as if they were paid according to how much they sold—a notion Rachel disabused me of. "They're being watched," she said, "supervised, whatever, by the people they work for. See the older guys strolling around with their hands in their pockets?"

I hadn't noticed them until now, white men in short-sleeved shirts and long Bermuda shorts, moving among the bathers, watching the young blacks from behind their sunglasses. "The ones who lose the races could get fired," Rachel said. "The ones who lose a lot of races, I mean."

The supervisors clapped their hands and shouted, "*Vas*, *vas*," urging their employees to outrun the others, shaking their heads and muttering "*Luiheid*" when someone else's workers got to a customer first. "It means 'lazy,'" Rachel explained.

"Would you like something?" I said.

"Sure. I wouldn't mind a Popsicle." Before I had a chance, she raised her finger in the air and several pairs of vendors raced toward us. Two tall young men, one in blue shorts, the other in red, outran the others easily, taunting them in what I thought might be Zulu.

They set the cooler on the sand to Rachel's left. "What would you like, miss?" the fellow in the blue shorts said. Rachel rolled onto her side as, dropping to one knee, he unhooked the handles of the cooler. Propped on her elbow, she peered into the cooler, reached inside and moved the various treats about in search of the pineapple Popsicle she said she wanted. Her large, white breasts dangled over the side of the cooler, from which frost billowed out like smoke. Her nipples quickly stiffened.

"What would you like, Wade?" she said.

The young man in the blue shorts stared at her breasts, then looked at me and grinned. I grinned back just as Hans appeared beside the young man and struck him across the face with his folded newspaper. "What are you looking at, boy?" he said. He glared at me as if he expected an answer from both of us. The young man's face went blank as he gazed at the sand. He didn't flinch, didn't move.

"Dad!" Rachel shouted.

I got to my feet, intending to tell Hans that the young man had merely smiled at me. Before I could utter a word, however, a tall, blond, heavy-set supervisor in a lime-green shirt stepped between Hans and the young man and shouted in Afrikaans; the young man mumbled something under his breath.

"Dad!" Rachel said again, hastily donning her T-shirt as she stood up. She gripped her father's arm with both hands. The supervisor shouted again, and again the young man muttered something, at which the supervisor slapped him so hard across the face that he fell down. The other young man tried to help him to his feet, but the supervisor struck him again, bringing his massive hand down so hard that the sound of it hitting the young man's cheek set my ears to ringing. The young man, still on one knee in the sand, face as blankly defiant as that of someone who, while being interrogated, refused to say a word, looked furtively at me. I looked away. Everyone on the beach was staring in our direction.

"He was leering at my daughter," Hans shouted at the supervisor, tapping the newspaper against his hip. "He was *leering* at her."

"No," I said. "He was looking at *me*, that's all. He smiled at me and I smiled at him and that's all there was to it."

"He had no business smiling at you," Hans said, "and you had no business smiling back. The two of you exchanging smirks about my daughter, my youngest daughter who is only twenty-three."

"But—" I began.

"Please," the young man in the red shorts said to me, looking nervously around. He joined his hands palm to palm. "Please. My friend has been punished. We will go now."

He reached down and helped the other young man to his feet, speaking urgently to him in Zulu. He kept looking about as if he expected the police to show up any minute. "He has been punished, master," he said to the man in the lime-green shirt. "He is very sorry."

"Give me my money," the supervisor said. "All of it, don't keep any for yourself. I will lose money today because of this." The young man spoke to the other in Zulu. "My money," the supervisor said. The young man dug a fistful of bills and coins out of his pockets and handed them to the supervisor. But the one who had been slapped, his expression still implacable, shook his head slightly—and then turned and ran. The supervisor shouted something after him, but, winding his way among a gauntlet of sunbathers and umbrellas, he didn't stop.

"I know where he lives," the supervisor said to Hans, who nodded, still tapping the newspaper against his hip.

"I'm going to lodge a police complaint," Hans said.

"Of course," the supervisor said, folding his massive arms. "I don't blame you, I don't. I am very sorry about your daughter. The boy will be found and sent to jail. I will see to it." The young man in the red shorts hung his head. "You, go," the supervisor said. "Go on, get out of my sight. I have other boys who will work for me without causing trouble."

"Did he *touch* you, Rachel?" asked Myra, still sitting beneath her umbrella with her knitting on her lap.

"No, Mom," Rachel said. "He didn't touch me."

"That boy who touched your daughter," the supervisor said, "he won't get far." He shaded his eyes with one hand as he watched the young man in the red shorts walk away from us. "Neither will that one," he said. "They're not allowed to go anywhere outside Langa without me. I drive them here and drive them back. They'll be picked up as soon as they leave the beach."

"What happened, Rachel?" Myra said.

"Nothing happened," I shouted. "He smiled at me and I smiled back—that's all that happened."

"No," Hans said. "He looked at Rachel and then he smiled at you and you smiled back. What do you think his smile meant? What did yours mean? What do you think that was all about?"

"Now, now," Myra said, "I'm sure Wade didn't mean anything."

"You're blaming Wade?" Rachel said.

"There is nothing to blame him or me for," I said. I turned to Hans. "You struck him with that newspaper, and you"—I pointed to the supervisor—"you slapped him twice, and you're blaming this on *him*?"

The man sniffed. "I've slapped him before. So have other men. He's a troublemaker. I told him to apologize to the young lady. He ran off with my money instead. But I'll get it back. And the two of them will go to jail. That's all there is to it."

"You didn't tell him to apologize," I said.

"Yes, I did. In Afrikaans." He shrugged.

"Dad, don't file a complaint," Rachel said. "He didn't do anything to me."

Hans adjusted his glasses and, hands on his hips, looked out to sea. "Very well," he said. "No complaint. No charges. But, as this man said, the boy stole from him, and the police will pick him up someplace he's not allowed to be, so it doesn't really matter if I complain or not."

"I can't have these boys stealing from me," the supervisor said. "I should have fired their black arses long ago. But they're all like that. Always up to something. *Luiheid*. I have eight working for me and there's not a good one in the bunch." He ran his hand through his thick blond hair. "He's a thief and the other one is not much better."

Hans extended his hand to him and they shook. "Not your fault," Hans said. "Well done. Well handled."

"Are you kidding me?" I said. "The two of you assaulted him."

"This is not Canada," Hans said. "You're in a different, better country now, enjoying a holiday that I'm paying for." He looked at Rachel as if to say it was her he was paying me to enjoy.

"Everyone *stop*," Rachel said. "Just stop." She glared at the supervisor, who nodded at her and lowered his eyes. He closed and picked up the cooler and turned away, trudging off through the sand in the opposite direction from the way the young men had gone.

"We're leaving," Rachel said to me. "Mom and Dad, you stay put."

"*Rachel*," Myra said.

"I'll call you tonight, Mom," Rachel said. "I'm too upset right now."

We drove back toward our apartment in silence, Rachel wrenching the gearshift about as if she meant to tear it from the floor and toss it out the window. When we stopped at a red light, I took her hand, but she pulled away. "They did nothing wrong," I said.

"You don't . . . ," she said, just as the light turned green.

"Don't what?" I said.

"You don't . . . I don't know what the word is. *Engage.* You don't engage them like that. You don't exchange smiles with them. About anything. You don't talk to them except to tell them what to do. You don't introduce yourself to them the way you introduced yourself to Nora at the party."

"*Them*?" I said.

"Look, just forget it," she said.

"You don't *what*?" I said.

"You heard me," she said. "You don't engage them."

"So you agree with your father?"

"No. I don't. I don't know why . . . I guess he overreacted. He's very protective of his girls."

"Protective?" I said. "What was he protecting you from?"

"You don't understand, Wade."

"Explain it to me, then. I'm all ears."

"There is a history here, a terrible history, but you can't undo it in one day at the beach."

"Sorry. You should have loaned me your manual of interracial interaction in South Africa."

"Look, let's drop it, okay?"

"That ice cream vendor smiled at me and I smiled back. That's all that happened."

"No, that's not what happened. First of all, he's not the vendor. Even the supervisor works for someone else. God knows who what you call the vendor is. The two of you, you and the boy, shared a smile about my tits."

"He wasn't a boy."

"It's just a *word*, one I'm used to using. You gave me to him."

"*What?*"

"You did. Just for a second. Maybe you didn't know it, maybe you didn't mean it, but you gave me to him. I'm not saying this because of the colour of his skin."

"You're overreacting."

"No. It was like he was saying, 'Lucky you, banging that piece of ass every night.'"

"What? *No*, it was just a joke. The steam from the cooler made your—"

"Yes, it made my nipples hard."

"Yes," I said. "It was kind of funny, so we shared a smile about it."

We stopped at another light.

"Look," Rachel said, "it doesn't matter why he smiled. It was you smiling back that set my father off. And if you're so concerned about those two black boys, you might want to consider how much trouble they're in now."

"Because of me, is that what you're saying?"

"I'm not saying Dad was right. He should not have done what he did. That supervisor shouldn't have done what he did. But neither of them would have done anything if you hadn't smiled at that boy when he smiled at you, which he shouldn't have done."

"Boy? I think he was older than me."

"I told you, it's just a word," Rachel said. "I grew up calling them that. Whether he's a boy or a man, he's somebody's son or brother or maybe even husband, and he won't be home tonight."

I said nothing, so infuriated that I was worried about what I might say if I opened my mouth.

I *thought* of pointing out that I hadn't "banged that piece of ass" in quite a while. She'd been putting me off with excuses and hadn't seemed to care how transparent they were.

"Look," Rachel said. "He should have known better than to smile at you. He should have known better than to run off like that."

"Maybe he thought it was better to stand up for himself no matter what the consequences. I'm sure he knew that he'd get caught. Maybe what he saw in my smile was that I'm not from here."

"Yes," Rachel sighed. "Yes, maybe. He shared a special moment with a non-racist Canadian. It happens all the time. Sorry. Erase that last sentence. Look, I feel partly to blame too, you know. I should have said no when my father said that we should go to Clifton Beach. But I have—I still have—this stupid notion that you and he will be able to tolerate each other someday."

"The way that he and Fritz tolerate each other? They mostly ignore each other. Look, I know that not every white person in South Africa is a racist. There are plenty who speak out against apartheid. But I guess that's the thing, isn't it? When you're white, you can do that and get away with it. If someone gets rid of apartheid, it won't be the whites. It will be the coloureds and the blacks and the outside world. The liberal whites who stay in the country, the writers who win prizes, what price are they paying? They're not offering to take Nelson Mandela's place on Robben Island. Even if they did offer, they'd be ignored. In South Africa, to be white is to be wealthy by comparison with the coloureds and the blacks. And white liberals are not as liberal as they like to think they are. You see how liberal most of them are when something is at stake for them."

"It's so much more complicated than that, Wade. In university, I read a book by William Faulkner called *The Sound and the Fury*. I'm sure you've read it. There was a character named Dilsey, remember. The way Faulkner told it, her love was so limitless that she transcended vengefulness and raised the children of her enslavers as if they were her own, 'without stint of recompense.' He said that the book was in part a loving tribute to the blacks who, as he put it, endured—the book ends with the words 'they endured.'"

"Yes. So?"

"So Nobel Prize–winning Faulkner romanticized those blacks. They brought him up better than his parents did, not because they loved him or even liked him, but because they had to. As Nora does, and the other maids we had did."

"So Faulkner was a *racist*?"

"I don't know. Then there's your one-time favourite writer, Thomas Wolfe, who Faulkner named the greatest novelist of their generation. He was revered by the Nazis of pre-war Germany because of his portrait of the blacks of the U.S. South. Wolfe was regarded by *many* scholars and others as a racist."

"Thomas Wolfe wasn't a racist. He loved everyone and everything he wrote about."

"My point is that these things are more complicated than you think. You've never lived among blacks."

"Not my fault."

"Wade—look, I'm tired. We're not going to talk about it for a while, okay?"

"Okay," I said. "It's fine with me if we declare a moratorium on trashing my favourite writers."

"Moratorium declared," she said. "Starting now."

We drove the rest of the way home in silence.

Two days later—we'd said no more to each other since the beach than we had to—she poked her head into the bedroom while I sat at my desk.

"I have a confession to make," she said, not meeting my eyes. "Bethany was right. I have had a few pretty bad lapses since we got here. After we saw that couple fighting along the seawall, I wrote about it in my diary. A lot. I've had a couple of other lapses, too. You see, sometimes, since I got better, I've given in to the urge to write in the diary, but only rarely and only for exactly an hour at a time. That's how the doctors told me to handle it. I time myself to the minute. Just like when I *read* the book. I need two hours to myself, period, consecutive or not. It doesn't have to be in private as long as no one interrupts me, which means it's better for everyone if it *is* in private, but I trust you not to interrupt me. I have to have her diary beside mine while I write."

"Or else?"

"Or else I don't feel right. Don't ask me to explain, because I can't. So, every so often, I'm a little bit cuckoo for one hour a day, from eight to nine in the evening, and a little bit less cuckoo when I'm reading for another hour—maybe I'll read when you're asleep. A lot of people are cuckoo twenty-four seven. I used to be. So I think one hour now and then isn't asking very much, do you?"

"No," I said, trying to sound unconcerned. "There are worse things to do with an hour than spend it writing. At least, I think there are. How would *I* know?"

"Don't encourage me. I mean, thanks for the vote of confidence, but don't encourage me. I wasn't a load of laughs back in the bad old days. Also, stop being so down on yourself. Did you know that the average age of first novelists is thirty-eight?"

"What's the average age of writers when they admit to themselves that they'll never be writers?"

"I have *faith* in you."

"You told me, that day in St. John's when you showed me the diary, that you were recovering and always would be. Is that smudge on your wrist what you meant?"

"Yes, but please don't worry. If you worry, I'll worry."

"I'm not worried," I said, all too aware of how unconvincing I sounded.

From *The Arelliad* (1985)

I dreamed I burned Arellia. I burned the whole thing to the ground.

I dreamed I burned *The Arelliad*, including my translation of her book. There was nothing to the pages and to those dry and yellow leaves but dust. A single spark and up they went.

I dreamed I built a bonfire, feeding volume after volume into the roaring yellow flame, all my copies of *Het Achterhuis*, my very first, the mummified one I'd shown to Wade, hundreds of others, her picture on every one, the ever-smiling, cheerful Anne. So many times I burned her likeness and her name.

I wished I could forget that look,
I wished I could forget that book
that I had read ten thousand times,
forget the house, forget the names,
throw them on the yellow flames,
erase *The Ballad* from my brain,
douse the roaring flames with rhymes
collected from the Night Salon
to help the roaring flame along.
The diaries and memories
turned into flame that scorched the trees,
from which flankers flew like leaves
blown by the flame-borne yellow breeze.

From my pyre of burning books
flew a swarm of flaming sparks;
each one began another blaze—
the sky became a yellow haze
till a single conflagration
swept through my imagination
and rid it of Arellia
and all that I've been telling you
and all that I have yet to tell:

the future burned, the past as well.
From deep within the yellow flames
I heard von Snout recite the names
of those purged by the Holocaust,
the souls that were forever lost,
the roll call of the innocent,
the when and where and how they went—
their souls, at last, were heaven sent.
And by that list of those who died,
Arellia was purified.

Or so it seemed within the dream from which I woke, trying to breathe, gasping, crying, wishing I could rest before I plunged into the page again.

It will take all night to undo what I have done. The sky is still yellow, but the trees that never lose their leaves are black and bare. Wisps of smoke rise from the ashes on the ground. I gave no thought to the girls: Anne Frank, now joined by her sister, Margot, and the Shadow She. There is no sign of them. How could there be? I fled the fire that I set and left them as I did before. Did we get away again, the two of us, Claws von Snout and me, and leave three girls to die?

The Frank sisters, the Shadow She—
Was He to blame, or was it me?

From *The Ballad of the Clan van Hout*

THE INFILTRATION (1967)
Brave Hans is sleeping like a log
when, like a sneak attack of fog,
the Rumours spread by Claws von Snout
advance upon the Land of Hout.
They wrap themselves around the House,
they seep in through the cracks and pores,
they drift like mist beneath the doors
and cat-like creep across the floors
and cat-like make their way upstairs
and cat-like trouble no one's ears
and slip into the little room,
the one as quiet as a tomb,
where four girls who have never dreamed
peacefully undreaming seem,
the four of them all in one bed,
one big four-sister poster bed,
head by head by head by head.
The Rumours swirl about the bed
and make their way into their heads
until their once undreaming minds
are vexed by dreams of many kinds.

The Rumours leave the way they came,
up the chimney and down the drain,
across the floors, beneath the doors,
they seep out through the cracks and pores—
the wall that couldn't keep them out
is of no use to keep them in.
No sooner have they come to Hout
than, like that, they are gone again.
They leave but leave their lies behind:
each one of your undreaming minds

becomes a factory of dreams.
There is weaving, there is sewing,
there is the stitching of the seams.
There is Language, there is Knowing,
and Ideas overflowing
that make you toss and turn about.
You think about the Land of Hout—
you go so far as to surmise
your father has been telling lies.
You used to fall asleep at sunset,
you used to wake up at sunrise.
You haven't seen the darkness yet
but now you wake and cannot see—
you think that you are dreaming
though you have never dreamed before.
You hear a sound outside the door;
the door swings open, Light comes in—
you girls can see the room again.
Though this is not the light of day,
though it is but the smallest spark,
whatever chased the night away
is so much better than the dark.
Hans van Hout stands in the doorway,
a pair of candles in his hands.
Myra stands behind her husband
and says, "From now on, they'll be bad."

WADE

Her writing for one hour as I read for one hour soon became an evening routine, she on one side of the room, me on the other. I often found it hard to concentrate on my book because I couldn't help but be distracted by her strange ritual. She said that she wanted to keep the diary in front of me—no secrets. But if she was going to keep the diary in front of me, I couldn't interrupt her and I couldn't ask her any questions about what she'd written. She sat with her notepad at a little desk, a copy of *Het Achterhuis* on her right as she faced in my direction. She pressed down hard on the paper, printing in blue ink slowly but never deliberating, raising her pen after forming each letter as if she was writing a mathematical equation on a blackboard. The scratching of the pen was an incessant irritant, but I thought better of protesting.

As the hour progressed, her writing gathered speed and urgency, getting louder every minute as she dotted *i*'s and crossed *t*'s with more and more emphasis. It was as if she was carving the letters into the page. When I announced, "Time's up," she continued to the completion of a sentence and ended the session with a final flourish of punctuation—a period, question mark or exclamation mark—and a loud sigh such as runners give when they cross the finish line. "Free," she'd say, or "Done," or "Time to play," dropping her pen and raising her hands, a student aiming to satisfy an exam invigilator that she had obeyed his instruction to stop writing.

When reading *Het Achterhuis*, she put the book on the desk, folded her arms in front of it and hunched over as if she had bad eyesight and was examining the text with a magnifying glass. She read slowly, or, at least, lingered a long time before turning a page—a page she had read a thousand times before. I wondered how a page she knew by heart could absorb her so completely, but I never asked.

One evening, I gave in to my curiosity about her writing, though. "Do you write about her diary in yours?"

"Classified information," she replied.

"Who do you address your diary to?"

"That, too, is classified."

I nodded. She smiled and, as if to mollify me by divulging *something*, she said, "The last words in her diary are 'if only there were no other people in the world.' It's just by chance that those were her last words. She was arrested by the Gestapo before she could start another entry. But it goes to show, doesn't it, how much she craved privacy, cooped up with the others for two years in those little rooms. All right, I'll tell you this much: I address my diary to her, to Anne. Books have endings. Lives end. Diaries don't. On the last page of a diary, the next entry is endlessly deferred, as mine will be when I put the diary aside for good."

"How are you able to write so steadily?"

"During the day, I often think about what I'm going to write. I make a mental list."

"Still."

"Jealous?"

"If it's any good, I am."

"It's a private diary that I never reread and wouldn't write a word of if I could help it. It doesn't matter if it's, as you put it, any good."

Before I could say I was sorry, she stormed off to the bedroom.

RACHEL

When my preoccupation with the diaries had just begun, when I thought it may have seemed to others like nothing more than a typical thirteen-year-old's infatuation with a celebrity, a superstar of history, Mom read the book, or seemed to, shadowing me to keep me company, she said, even though I told her that I preferred to read alone. Sometimes, when I stayed home from school on the pretense of not feeling well, we sat around for hours, each of us reading the same book, the house silent but for the turning of the pages.

One day in January, when there was a snowstorm and school was cancelled, she followed me about the house, ignoring my protests that I didn't need to be supervised. We settled in the front room. After a time, I looked up from my book and, as if she'd been waiting for me to do just that, she looked up from hers and smiled at me.

"Are you actually reading that book or just turning the pages?" I asked.

"I'm reading it," she said.

"You don't have to."

"Something's wrong, Rachel," she said. "Each of your sisters began to act up when they were your age."

"Anorexia isn't acting up," I said.

"I don't know what it is," she said. "One of the doctors said that Bethany is punishing herself for something she knows she didn't do."

"Like what?"

"He had no idea. She hasn't said. Or if she has, he wouldn't tell me."

I began to write in my diary.

"What *are* you writing in there?" she said.

I stood, crossed the floor to her and turned my notepad around. "See for yourself," I said. She leaned forward, her face just inches from the page, squinting. "I can't make out a thing," she said. "I never could read your handwriting."

"It's Arellian. You *know* that."

"Why would you want to hide anything from me?"

I left the room and, this time, she didn't follow me.

Another day, I pretended to be so ill I needed to stay in bed, but she came to my room to read with me. I sat up against the headboard with my diary and a copy of *Het Achterhuis* open on the blankets on my lap, a pen in one hand. She drew a chair up beside the bed and began to read her copy of the book. "Rachel," she said, after about half an hour, "I think it's admirable that you've taken such an interest in Anne Frank instead of some rock and roll maniac of the sort that other girls your age adore. What was that book about a teenage drug addict called, the one that Carmen worshipped?"

"*Go Ask Alice*."

"That's it. I think I know why you're so fascinated with this book. You've noticed that there are a lot of similarities between the Franks and the van Houts. The two families had to go to a foreign country because they were being unfairly treated in their home country. There were no sons in either family, only daughters. Like Otto Frank, Hans van Hout is the only male of his household. Otto probably complained about it sometimes, just as Hans does. Otto and Hans are both businessmen. Hans runs his own publishing company. The fact that he only publishes and sells his own books doesn't make him less of a businessman. It's a shame that they rejected his application to the Rotary Club. It hurt his feelings. At any rate, Anne used pseudonyms in her diary for everyone in the Secret Annex who was not a family member. All of the carefully chosen pseudonyms consisted of a German word that she thought best described each person, and almost all of them were uncomplimentary, which just goes to show that you can never tell what someone else really thinks of you, or is writing about you. The only person Anne was consistently fond of was her father."

"I'm not reading the book or writing my diary because the Franks remind me of the van Houts," I said.

"Then why are you?"

"I have no idea."

"Well, I'm glad you don't worship them," she said, "because the Frank family had their flaws. Do you know what they were?"

I sighed and shook my head. "I have to read and write," I said. "I'm falling behind."

"I'm worried about this language you've created. What's wrong with English?"

"Nothing. I speak it all the time. You can't speak Arellian. You can only write it. I can, that is."

"Could you teach it to me?"

"No."

"Well, I was talking about the flaws of the Frank family. So. Their worst flaw, a tragic flaw, was that they trusted other people to take care of them."

I rolled my eyes and slammed my book shut. "They had no choice," I said. "That's the whole point of the book. Or one of them."

She smiled as if indulging a simpleton. "But it brought about their downfall, you see. Surely you see that?"

"Yes, but they had no choice. If they hadn't trusted other people, they would have died long before they did. At least they gave themselves a chance."

She was silent for a while, staring at our reflections in the oval mirror on the wall beside the bed. "That's one way of looking at it," she said. "But I can tell you from experience that there's no telling when someone you think of as your closest friend will turn on you. This happened to your father and me many times until we changed our ways. You should never tell anyone outside your family anything that could be misunderstood and used against you—personal things, private things, family things, the kind of things that make perfect sense when they are said or done behind the closed doors of your house. You see, Rachel, a family is like a diary. In a diary, you are absolutely honest the way you are with your parents and your sisters, but you never show the diary to anyone else. The point of a diary is secrecy."

"Yes, I know."

"Anne Frank kept a diary because of the constant presence of outsiders in the Secret Annex. In the diary, she wrote things about the outsiders that she didn't want them to see. Without her diary, she would have had no privacy at all. She was brave but she was also so naive. She wrote that she believed that, deep down, people were basically good, an idea that her parents probably put in her head, for they, too, were naive in believing that outsiders could be trusted. Sad to say, most people are not basically good. I don't mean that whoever betrayed the Franks was necessarily bad. It may have been one of the people who helped them. They may have realized one day that, for the sake of their own family, whose food rations they'd been sharing with the Franks, they had to turn the Franks in or else be left with not enough to eat. For them, it wasn't a betrayal, except that it backfired on them, because they should never have been hiding the Franks in the first place. Look at what happened to them when they got caught. Some of them were sent away to prison."

"No one knows who betrayed the Franks and the others," I said, "but it wasn't the handful of people who risked their lives for them." I opened my diary and jotted something down in the hope that she'd see that I wanted her to leave.

"That's right. No one knows. But if some family managed to survive by doing so, I don't blame them. I would do worse to protect our family. The Franks put themselves in their own predicament. They were naive enough to think that Amsterdam was a safe distance from Germany. They should have gone at least as far as England or even North America. It would have meant going very far from home, but we, the van Houts, we did that when we had no other choice and, although not everything has worked out, we're getting by, aren't we?" She smiled again as she waited for my answer.

"I suppose so," I said. "But I don't think Carmen or Bethany would agree with you."

"Well, I'm so glad that you brought them up. Carmen spends all her time with the wrong sort of people. Bethany hasn't made another attempt but, as you know, she's in hospital again. Every time she sees a different doctor, she changes her story. This time, she says that it's because of your father and me that she won't eat, but she refuses to explain what she means. It is the height of ingratitude, after all that we have done for her. I left my homeland for my children." Her eyes filled with tears. "In this world, it is every family for itself, so there is no point in starving yourself just because you and your family aren't perfect. She demands perfection from everyone except herself. She will excuse no flaw, no matter how insignificant. A more cold-hearted child has never walked the earth."

"She's sick," I said.

"She's selfish," my mother said. "So is Gloria and don't even mention Carmen. We've given the four of you all the leeway in the world, and what thanks do we get for it? It's my hope, Rachel, that you will prove to be the one daughter who truly appreciates the importance of family."

"I have to read my book," I said. "I have to read it twice today, and after that I have to write for God knows how long or I'll *never* get to sleep. That's how unlike my sisters I am. I'm the normal one."

She wiped at her eyes with the heel of one hand. "You once said that what you love about the Franks is that, in the book, they are always together. No one leaves for school. No one leaves for work. No one goes out at night. It was crucial that they never be apart. I thought it was sweet of you to say that. But now it reminds me of their second fatal flaw. Before they went into hiding, the Franks kept to themselves and didn't interfere in other people's lives, and other people didn't interfere in their lives. But, when they went into hiding, they tried to merge two families, and made matters worse by allowing a stranger, Fritz Pfeffer, to join them. I know that the Franks were not betrayed by Fritz Pfeffer, but they were betrayed *because* of him. Many Jews hid out during the war and many of them were still alive and well when Amsterdam was liberated. The Franks and the van Pels would have made it through the war undiscovered had Otto Frank not allowed a mere acquaintance of his, this dentist named Fritz Pfeffer, to join them in the Secret Annex. Before Pfeffer's arrival, each family had separate sleeping quarters. Mr. and Mrs. Frank slept in one of the downstairs rooms, Margot and Anne in another. It wasn't perfect but it might have worked. But when Pfeffer arrived, Margot and Anne were separated. Pfeffer moved into their room with Anne, and Margot slept in her parents' room in a separate bed.

"Imagine sending your thirteen-year-old daughter to sleep in the same room as a grown man who was divorced and who had nothing but contempt for anything but his own appetites. Pfeffer's arrival literally broke up the Frank family. It also limited their privacy and made life in the Secret Annex harder to endure because there was no longer the same family solidarity or togetherness. On top of that, Pfeffer was a large man who ate far more than his share of the food. He was also loud, boorish and opinionated.

"How *stupid*. Dussel the dentist. *Dussel*. No wonder she chose that word for him—the German word for "dullard," "dunce" or "fool." The Franks and the van Pels didn't become careless about leaving the windows open and raising their voices loud enough to be heard. They did those things because of Dussel. They argued with him and they opened the windows because he made them feel so claustrophobic."

"Anne doesn't say that in *Het Achterhuis*."

"What's going to become of you, Rachel? So much writing and reading. Inventing *languages*?"

"One language."

"You're sad, aren't you?"

I nodded, hoping to speed her departure by agreeing with her.

"I blame Carmen for this. Those shorthand notes she left lying about the house—it would never have occurred to you to write in code if not for her. You're not like my other girls, Rachel. Not yet, anyway. But the way you've taken to this book—I don't understand why you're putting two families of misguided Jews ahead of your own. Why do you spend day after day reading about them and writing who knows what about them when you could be talking to me?"

"I told you I don't *know*. Besides, I don't write about *them*."

"Is that what you tell others when they ask you why that book fascinates you so much?"

"I would if they asked. But no one asks."

"Not even your teachers?"

"Not anymore. When they asked, I told them I didn't know."

"Your father is very concerned. He doesn't say so but I can tell. His insomnia is worse than ever. His ulcers. Is there something you want to tell us? Is there something we can clarify for you? You can always come to us."

"No."

"Did something happen? Have you been with a boy?"

"*No.* Boys avoid me like the plague."

"Because they know you're a good girl." Tears were now flowing freely down her face. "I want you to promise me something, Rachel. If you have intercourse before you're engaged to be married, I want you to tell me."

"*What?*"

"I want you to promise me that you'll tell me. I won't judge you, but I would like to know. Will you promise?"

"Alright," I said, "I *promise.*"

She got up slowly from her chair and, sniffling, left the room, easing the door shut behind her.

Later, sitting in front of the mirror of my dresser, I cut my hair with a pair of scissors, trying to make it look like Anne's did in the black-and-white photographs, the ones in which she was smiling for the camera, her pen in hand and her diary in front of her, one arm curled protectively around it. I lopped off great chunks of hair, which fell onto the hardwood floor. Soon, I had gone past the point where I could make it look like hers. I went on cutting until I had almost no hair left.

Mom came into the room and, when she saw me, put her hand over her mouth. She retreated, and came back with a dustpan and a broom and swept up every last strand of hair. She didn't say a word, but she took the scissors with her when she left.

WADE

One afternoon, while Rachel was out shopping for groceries and I was at my desk in the bedroom, still trying without success to fashion a story from the ever more mundane-seeming chaos of my childhood, our doorbell rang. No one had ever rung it before and I wasn't expecting anyone. I got up, went downstairs and opened the door to find Clive standing there, holding his glasses in one hand as tears streamed down his face.

"Clive?" I said. "What's wrong?"

"Can I come in?" he managed to say, his mouth quivering.

"Of course," I said.

He followed me up the stairs and, when we reached the top, brushed past me and made for the front room as if he had been in the apartment many times. He sat in one of our two leather chairs and lit a cigarette—I'd never seen him smoke before. I handed him an ashtray and sat in the other chair. He could have put the ashtray on the coffee table, but he cradled it on his lap, more or less hunched over it.

"What's wrong, Clive?" I said.

"Bethany is in hospital," he said, and began to cry again.

Before I could ask him what had happened, he said, "She took an overdose of pills."

"Oh no," I said. "Is—"

"It was a few days ago." He put his glasses back on. The hand that held the cigarette shook as he raised it to his mouth. "They, the police or someone, I don't know, someone, they found her early in the morning near Greenmarket Square, sitting beneath a tree. They thought she was dead. There were empty pill bottles all around her. They took her to the hospital. She's fine now, physically."

"That's good," I said.

He shook his head and wiped his nose with the back of his hand. "No," he said. "I didn't know—I mean, no one told me about what happened to her back in Canada. Did you know that she had some sort of breakdown and was in hospital for months?"

"Yes," I said. "I assumed you knew. She talks pretty openly about herself."

"I know she has anorexia," he said, "but I didn't know she attempted suicide. She never mentioned that before we got engaged. She should have, but she didn't. I'm not saying I wouldn't have agreed to marry her; I'm just saying she should have told me."

"But how is she?" I said.

He shook his head again in frustration, as if I was missing the point. "We're no longer engaged. She broke it off. She said she thought it was the best thing for both of us."

"I'm so sorry, Clive."

"I'm going to look like a fool in front of everyone, engaged for a few weeks and then dumped. She said I could have my engagement ring back."

"No one will think you're a fool," I said.

"You're in for quite a shock," he said. "Quite a shock, I can tell you."

"What do you mean?" I said.

"Bethany told the doctor something, and the doctor told me even though Bethany told him not to. He said he thought I ought to know because we were engaged." Clive stabbed out his cigarette in the ashtray and, closing his legs tightly together to hold the ashtray in place, took a pack of cigarettes from his jacket pocket and lit another.

"What did Bethany tell him?"

"She's sedated most of the time," he said. "She talks about everything else but not about what she told the doctor."

"Well, what did the doctor tell you she said?" I was fast losing patience with him.

"Prepare yourself," Clive said, as if he was about to inform me of a death in the family. He drew in a chest full of air and said, "She said that Hans has been abusing her for years. Ever since she can remember and right up until she was taken to hospital."

"What?"

"Ever since she can remember," he said, shaking his head slightly. "And right up until—"

I stopped him. "What exactly did the doctor say? Bethany says a lot of things she doesn't mean. She can be very ironic, and someone who isn't used to her might get the wrong idea."

Clive shook his head. "He said he asked her several times if she was telling the truth. He has no idea what really happened, but he said that Bethany *believes* that what she said is true."

"Well, that's a far cry from saying that it really happened," I said.

"Yes, but Bethany said more to the doctor, much more. She said that Hans has been abusing all of his daughters for years, *all* of them." He looked at me.

"That's ridiculous," I said. "It can't be true. Bethany's been unstable for quite some time. Maybe the pressure of getting engaged, the prospect of so much change—"

He shook his head. "You're acting like I did when I first heard," he said. "Don't you understand what I'm saying? Do you think Hans would do that to one daughter and not lay a hand on the others?"

"Maybe Hans didn't do anything to Bethany is what I'm saying. Maybe that's what the doctor meant."

"It doesn't matter to *me*, now, does it? We're not engaged anymore."

My heart hammered. Sweat had broken out on my forehead and now trickled into my eyes. "Rachel would have said something to me."

"When I told my parents what the doctor said," Clive said, "my father just laughed and left the room. But my mother said she thought she knew what Bethany was talking about. She said that Hans was once accused, years ago, before the van Houts left South Africa, of having done something to a student. The student's mother made the accusation, but she eventually withdrew it and that was the end of it. My mom said that Bethany must have got it into her head while she was on too many drugs that Hans had done something to *her.* My mother said that she was sure it wasn't true."

"Well, there you are," I said. "Your mother might be right."

"*Might* be right. That's the whole thing. All Bethany said to me was 'Don't tell anyone what I told the doctor.' Don't you think it's strange that Bethany has been in hospital for days and you're only finding out about it now, from me?"

"Yes," I said. "I do, but—"

"She asked me not to tell any of her sisters that she's in hospital or why. Hans and Myra know, but they don't know what Bethany has accused him of. I'm not supposed to be talking to anyone about that either, but I had to talk to someone. What are you supposed to do when your fiancée tries to commit suicide and breaks off your engagement—keep it to yourself? When they found her near the square, she had no ID. When she woke up, she refused to tell them who she was until they let her make a phone call. I have my own phone line at home, so she called me. It was in the middle of the afternoon, and Mom and Dad were out. She told me where she was and asked me to come see her. When I got there, she broke it off, and then the doctor told me what she'd said. When I asked her whether it was true, she told me to tell her parents she was in hospital, but not about her accusations against Hans. She also asked me not to tell her sisters where she was, because she wanted to tell them herself. And not to tell *my* parents either, but I did. I didn't speak to Myra or Hans. I couldn't work up the nerve. Mom and Dad did."

"Well," I said, "Bethany didn't tell Rachel."

"Not that you know of," Clive said. He was hurt and maybe thought it would make him feel better if he knew that he was not alone in his affliction.

"Rachel is not Bethany," I said. "She'd tell me about something like this."

"I wanted you to know," he said. "You have a right to know that accusations have been made against Hans by one of his daughters. You have a right to know because you're living with one of his daughters. Unlike me, you didn't have to hear it from some stranger."

"Clive," I said, "I think you're getting too far ahead of yourself. Bethany is sick and medicated. There's no telling yet how this will all play out."

He shook his head, stabbed out another cigarette, stood and, without a word, went to the door and hurried down the stairs.

One minute, you're sitting at your desk as you do every day. You think you know who you are, where you are in your life and how you got there. You have a rough idea of what the future holds. And then the doorbell rings and a man you barely know barges in and upends everything. You wonder if, from now on, you will think of the past as having happened on one side of this moment or the other, before and after.

I considered calling my parents but didn't know how to even describe what was happening. Mom and Dad would fret and attribute everything to our being in a place so far away that no one in their world knew anything about it.

Instead, I waited for Rachel to come home, wondering what it would mean to *us* if Bethany's accusations were true. The Rachel who walked in the door would not be the Rachel who had left an hour ago. She would be a new Rachel, one who had known for years what I had just found out, one who had been dealing with it for years. Her obsession with Anne Frank—was she trying to escape her father by hiding in *Het Achterhuis*? Was this, at last, the explanation for her breakdowns and her illnesses? If Bethany was telling the truth, nothing, absolutely nothing, would ever again be as it had been—as I thought it had been. That was what most galled Clive, it seemed, that Bethany had fooled him, that she'd known all along and hadn't told him—and even asked him to marry her. To Clive, Bethany's deceptiveness seemed to be a greater crime than what she'd accused Hans of. He hadn't said a word against Hans, even though he was more than half convinced that Bethany was telling the truth. He hadn't uttered a word of concern for her, either.

Perhaps Rachel would say something that would explain it all away. Perhaps Bethany had made this accusation before and Rachel would know just how to deal with it. Her father was the man who thought that self-publishing a book would get him his full professorship. He was hapless at best.

When I heard Rachel coming up the stairs, I opened the door before she reached the top. "Bethany is going to be just fine," I said. Rachel stopped and looked up at me. "She made another attempt. But she's in hospital and she's okay."

She followed me into the kitchen, where she sat at one end of the table. I sat at the other. As I told her what Clive had said, she listened with her arms folded as if I was merely relating more instances of the oddness of her family. She showed no sign of surprise or incredulity, even faintly nodded. My first impulse, after I was certain that my sister was in good hands, would have been to defend my father, to wonder what could possibly have motivated my sister to make such accusations against him. Not even when I told her how Clive's mother had explained everything away did Rachel's expression change.

I pulled my chair close to hers. "Rachel?" I said. "Are you all right?" I worried that she was in shock and that I had been in something like shock since Clive had left.

At last, in a tone as flat as if she had been hypnotized, she said, "You're absolutely sure that Bethany is all right?"

"I told you that."

"Yes," she said, "but are you sure? You also made it sound like Clive is more concerned about himself."

"I'm pretty sure he is."

I watched in silence as she got up and made a cup of tea. She sat down again, cradling the cup in both hands, her eyes averted from mine. "I feel ashamed," she said. I began to stand, intending to hold out my arms to her, but she put a hand firmly on my shoulder and pushed me back into my chair.

I said, "Why should you be ashamed? Do you mean you're ashamed of what your father did to you?"

She shook her head. Her colour rose and her eyes filled with tears—at last, I thought, a reaction of some kind.

"I'm ashamed that I am one of them. One of us. The van Houts. All of us. We were taught that, above all else, you must protect the family. Our mother taught us that, sometimes without saying a word. Do as I do. Ignore what you've seen, what you've heard, ignore what happens right in front of you, ignore what happens *to* you. Pretend that nonsense makes perfect sense. The more often you do it, the easier it gets. The abnormal becomes normal, in time, as your notion of normal is endlessly revised. On and on it goes until nothing is abnormal as long as the van Houts keep it to themselves."

"I don't understand, Rachel. Are you saying that Bethany—"

"I don't know. It makes sense."

"It makes sense?"

"You think you want to know what he did because that will prove to you that he did *something*. You think it will take all the uncertainty away and then everything will be just the way it used to be. Believe me, it will only make things worse for us. It will put back in my head pictures that it took me a long time to replace with words."

"So you are saying that what Bethany said about Hans is true and that he did those things to you, too?"

"He never laid a hand on me. Never. But I'm saying it makes sense that he might have done something to Bethany, maybe even to Carmen or Gloria. I once helped him cover something up. One of my friends, a pretty girl named Nancy, slept over one night in my room. We were dressed in lacy nighties, pretending to be twice our age. We were goofing around, kneeling on the bed, bouncing up and down, laughing and singing songs. The door opened and Dad came in in his pyjamas. He had an erection that was so conspicuous it looked fake. Nancy let loose a squeal that sent me into hysterics.

"Dad got on the bed and began bouncing up and down with us. Then he kind of knocked us over and he fell on top of Nancy, trying to make it seem like it was just a game. I was so embarrassed, I acted all grown-up. 'Well then,' I said,' I guess I better give you two your privacy.' Nancy scrambled out from under Dad. She was laughing, but she also looked on the verge of tears. Dad got off the bed, said something about having dropped in just to say good night and left, closing the door behind him. Nancy and I never said a word about it. She was gone when I woke up in the morning. She may have left the house in the middle of the night for all I know.

"The next evening, just after dinner, the doorbell rang. I answered it and there was Nancy's sixteen-year-old boyfriend. He said he wanted to speak with Dad. I told him Dad was out, which was true, but I would have said that anyway because I knew what he was there for. When he told me that Nancy had told him what had happened the night before, I told him he shouldn't be going around making accusations he couldn't prove. I told him that Nancy was not welcome at our house anymore and that he better not show up at our house again. And then I slammed the door in his face and locked it. I looked out the window to make sure that he went away, that he drove off and wouldn't be waiting for Dad when he came home.

"When I turned around, my mother was standing in the front hall. I can't describe the expression on her face. 'You did exactly the right thing, Rachel,' she said, putting her hands on my shoulders. 'You handled that just right. I'm so proud of you. There's no need to tell your sisters or your father about it. They would only get upset with Nancy.' Father's little helper. That's what I was that day."

"You shouldn't blame yourself for that. You were a child. And if that's the worst that Hans did—"

"I knew what I was doing."

"But he didn't actually do anything to you or Nancy."

"No. But you sound as if you wouldn't stick around long if I said he did. I'm sorry, I'm sorry. Erase that last sentence. I wouldn't blame you if you walked away this second, all things considered."

"Rachel, I'm not *going* anywhere."

"You see, we were raised to believe that, whatever happened, we were all to blame for it. My sisters and I, we circled the wagons, not just for him, or her, but for ourselves. I'm thinking about some things now that never did make sense. Dad took Bethany away one summer when he went to the mainland to teach a course to make extra money, as Mom explained it. Why didn't he just teach a summer course in St. John's? There were more extra courses available in the summer than at other times of year. He could have taught two or three courses if he wanted to. But my mother pretended that it made perfect sense. He had Bethany all to himself for the summer in a house that he rented, thousands of miles away from home. When Bethany came back, she told me she'd been bored to death. She said she went visiting with him on Sunday afternoons and played the charming daughter to the hilt. Another summer, he took Gloria away with him to Montreal, and once, he took Carmen to Vancouver. He told Mom that he wanted them to see the world—his daughters who were born in South Africa, had been to other parts of Africa and to various cities in Europe and to England—he wanted *them* to see the world. My mother said it was a good idea for one of us to go with him to keep him from getting lonely. It's so absurd, all of it, but we acted as if it made perfect sense. My turn to spend a summer with him never came. I don't remember why."

"It does sound odd," I said, "but none of it proves anything. The Bare Area strikes me as odd, but it doesn't prove anything."

She went on as if she hadn't heard me. "And look at us, the four of us girls: we're all so screwed up. One with anorexia and suicidal; one a drug addict; one a nymphomaniac or something; one the Anne Frank Freak. That doesn't prove anything—yeah, *right*. It might all just be owing to cultural displacement? That's what my parents put it all down to. An eternity of Sunday afternoons spent visiting near-total strangers. What in God's name was *that* all about?"

She had been so measured, controlled, assertive. But that seemed to have been a disguise that she was shedding piece by piece.

As if she had abruptly realized the effect on me, she stopped speaking, darted a glance at me, looked away, glanced at me again. "Jesus," she said. "You must think I'm a fruitcake. Forget everything I said. I can't remember most of it myself. I'm just . . . so upset about Bethany. Don't worry about me. Please don't worry about me. Dad never laid a hand on me, never. It's not the kind of thing that I'd forget, especially if he was still doing it. And please don't tell your parents that anything is wrong. They would only worry, being so far away. Especially don't say anything about Dad."

"I won't say anything to Mom and Dad, at least until I know what's going on."

Tears began to stream down her face. "I don't mean to sound so vague, so full of riddles. All I meant was that, *if* Dad was ever caught red-handed doing something, Mom would expect us to pretend it never happened. I'm doing the best I can, Wade."

We hugged for a long time, but even as I was holding her, I remembered the way Hans acted when he'd dropped in on my parents unannounced and saw my sisters. Had there even been a minute when, as Myra engaged us in conversation, he had slipped away? I felt a flash of panic, but then assured myself that he had *not* been out of my sight for a second.

That night, Rachel wrote in her diary and read *Het Achterhuis* as usual, and I read the *Cape Times*. When the phone rang, Rachel rushed to answer it. "Hi," she said. I could tell by her tone and the look on her face that it was Bethany. A couple of minutes later, without having said another word, she said, "Okay, we'll—" She looked at me. "She hung up. She said Clive called her after he left here this afternoon and told her that he spoke with you. She wants us to visit her tomorrow."

"Us?"

"You and me," she said.

"Well, that's good, isn't it?" I said.

She crossed the room and pulled me to her as if I was all that was keeping her from falling off a cliff.

RACHEL

The next day, we drove partway up the slope of Devil's Peak to the hospital, a sprawling, white Cape Dutch building with a central observatory tower. Above the hospital, the peak was shrouded in fog that sometimes parted to allow a glimpse of sky that was even more intensely blue than the sky above St. John's.

"The hospital is called Groote Schuur," I said. "That's Dutch for 'Great Barn.' It used to *be* a barn, back when the cape was first settled by the Dutch."

Wade nodded, though he was crouching to get a better look at Devil's Peak, which, as we drew closer to it, seemed to grow steeper, the slope scattered with massive boulders that looked as if they might at any moment continue their long-stalled tumble down the mountain. "This must be a spooky place at twilight," he said.

Neither of us could bear to talk about the reason for our trip.

Bethany's ward looked even more like a psychiatric ward than the one that I'd been in: windows reinforced with thick wire mesh; chairs and tables, their edges rounded, bolted to the floor; the walls bare and painted the same green as the male nurse's uniform. Fluorescent lights buzzed overhead. Bethany, also clad in green, her stick-like arms bare almost to her shoulders, was sitting alone at one of the tables and noticed my look of dismay as I surveyed the visiting room. "It's better than the padded cell just down the hall," she said. "I look quite fetching in a straitjacket, I must say, though it took them a while to find one in my size." She held up her left hand. "See, no engagement ring.

I'm not sure where it is. I might have swallowed it. Just kidding. I left it in my chest of drawers."

But for us and the nurse, the visiting room was empty. The nurse, a blond, burly fellow, stood with his hands joined in front of him, his back against the wall, staring off into space.

"Wade and Rachel," Bethany said, drum-rolling her hands on the table. "Meet Terse the Nurse. Terse, Wade and Rachel." The blond man nodded and smiled at us as if he was well accustomed to Bethany by now.

"How are you, Bethany?" I said.

"Well, I'm dying for a cigarette but I'm not allowed to have one. Apparently, they're bad for your health, especially if you poke one in your eye, which they seem to think I would do. I've been suicide-proofed. They won't even let me have a plastic spoon. And how are you, Rachel, my ever-effervescent sister?"

I sat in the chair nearest her, Wade directly opposite her.

"I'm worried about you," I said.

"You look like you haven't slept in quite some time, Rachel," she said. She took hold of my left hand and turned it over. "Ah. You've been writing your diary. A lot. Living in Arellia? Pay attention, Wade. I told you the signs. See, she has a very dark ink stain on the underside of her left hand. *Very dark*."

"I always forget to wash it off."

"It gives you away. At least to people who don't pretend not to notice it. And you don't forget to wash it off. If you washed it off every day, you'd have no skin left on your hand. Remember the glove you used to wear—"

"I've been open with Wade about writing in the diary," I said as he stared at the evidence of my worsening obsession.

Bethany shook her head slowly. "You can't fool me, Raitch."

"I do know about the diarizing," Wade said.

"My sister is a pro like me, Wade," Bethany said. "You're being played. Haven't you noticed that she hasn't been in bed for most of the past few nights?"

Wade stared at me. I could tell by the look in his eyes that he saw the truth in mine.

"Uh-oh," Bethany said. "Is there no joy in Bedville anymore?"

"Look, Bethany," I said, pulling my hand from hers and smacking it on the table. "I didn't try to kill myself. I don't have the advantage of being on God knows how many kinds of drugs. I should be the one interrogating you."

"Well, I just hope you're not visiting Arellia because of me."

"You know it doesn't work like that." I felt Wade's eyes on me, but I looked at her as I spoke. "Arellia's this place I made up when I first got sick. You know, from Arellian. When I was unplugged, so to speak, I thought I lived in a place called Arellia. Or so the doctors said. I don't remember it. And apparently, I shouldn't have told my sister about it, since she clearly can't keep a secret."

Wade reached across the table and put his hand on my arm. "Let's concentrate on why we're here."

"Yes," Bethany said, "let's do that. I've been rude. Let's have a chat."

When Wade withdrew his hand, I folded mine on the tabletop so as to hide the smudge of ink. Bethany's eyes were sunken and darkly shadowed. She looked at Wade, raising her eyebrows. "So, buddy boy, how are you holding up? This is not what you signed on for, is it? People killing each other with screwdrivers. A night at the Porn Palace of the Twelve Apostles. Hans van Hout's discourse on the awfulness of Jews. The racial and sexual politics of the beach at Clifton. And now this. Deathany returns."

I could think of nothing to say, so I smiled.

"Just trying to lighten the mood," Bethany said. "I *am* sedated, as my sister pointed out." Then she lowered her head and began to cry. "I'm sorry, sweetie," she said. She drew a deep breath and slowly exhaled. "I phoned Mom and Dad this morning. Sedation gives you courage. I told Dad what I told Clive. He didn't deny anything. He didn't admit to anything. In fact, he didn't say anything. He just handed the phone to Mom. 'You've had a bit of a setback, dear,' Mom said. 'Too much excitement all at once, getting engaged and everything.' It seems that setbacks are rampant among the van Houts. I told her that Clive and I were no longer engaged, and she said, 'Perhaps, when you're feeling better, you'll change your mind.' She said I shouldn't try so hard at everything. She actually asked me to give her love to Clive. She put Dad back on the phone, and Dad asked me if I would help him with the new accounting textbook that he's writing. He said he's going to need someone to put the books in boxes and send them off to universities."

"That's all he said?" I almost shouted.

"That's all he said. Nothing else. I was crying, but his voice never changed a bit."

"Well, they were forewarned about your accusations by the DeVrieses," I said. "They had time to prepare themselves."

"Jesus," Wade said. He stood, put his hands in the pockets of his jeans and walked a few steps away from the table, then stood with his back to us.

"Are you all right?" I said. He nodded but didn't turn around. "None of this surprises me," I said to Bethany. "It makes sense."

"Well," Bethany said, "it surprised the shit out of me, let me tell you. Maybe if I hadn't cried, maybe if I'd just stayed calm, Dad wouldn't have thought the time was right to ask me to do some work for him. As far as they're concerned, nothing I said is on the record. I mean, as far as they're concerned, I didn't say it." Tears continued to stream down her face.

Wade turned around. "None of this is your fault, Bethany. It's not Rachel's fault, or Carmen's or Gloria's."

"Wade, you are in uncharted territory, and I am not talking about South Africa. You are in way over your head."

He came back to the table and sat down. He looked close to tears.

"I don't remember him doing anything to me," I said. "He never laid a hand on me and that's the truth."

Bethany nodded but rolled her eyes.

"I mean, I believe *you,*" I said. "It seems like he must have done something to you, but I don't remember him doing anything to me. Maybe I repressed it or something?"

"You said yesterday that he didn't do anything to you, period," Wade said. "You didn't say anything about repression."

"It's the same thing, if you think about it," I said. "If you completely forget something, you're sure it never happened. I wasn't trying to mislead you."

"How could you *forget* something like that?"

"Over here, you two, over here," Bethany said, tapping her sternum with her index finger. "When you leave, all I'll have is Terse the Nurse, so please speak to me."

I leaned to stroke her cheek and brushed a strand of hair back from her forehead. "I love you, sweetie," I said, and began to cry. "I'm so sorry. So sorry you're here and that Dad reacted the way he did and that you made another attempt and—"

"Wade," Bethany said, "I think my sister could use your arm around her right now."

I couldn't help resenting Bethany for telling him I needed to be held, so, when he came to me, I shook him off. He backed away and began to pace.

"Four girls," he said, stopping behind Bethany. "Four sisters, and none of you have ever talked to each other about your father before?"

"Out of the mouth of a babe," Bethany said. "But what would you expect? I mean, if Gloria had spoken out—well, at what age should she have spoken out? When she was five? Ten? The longer it goes on, the more ashamed you feel, because you think it's your fault, that you did something to make him do what he did. You think there's something wrong with *you*, not him. And he knows that, so he blames you to make you keep your mouth shut. What kind of girl would make her daddy do such things? Heaven help *you*, not him, if your mother finds out. So you wind up alone. You're worthless but you pretend you're not. You become very good at hiding and pretending. So no, Wade, we didn't talk to each other, or tell our mother, or our friends."

"Don't speak for me," I said. "And you might want to cut Wade some slack."

Bethany folded her arms and nodded. "I'm sorry. It's just—" Her lips quivered. "I'm told I'm going to be sick for a long time before I get better. You don't just try to kill yourself one day and go back to being normal the next. It's hard to give up everything and then change your mind, you know? It *is*. It's hard to cross that line and then come back. Once you convince yourself you'd be better off dead, it's hard to get going again. Everything seems different when you cross that line. This is my fourth attempt now, not my second. There were two others that no one in the family knows about. Every time I decide to do it, I feel so relieved. It's like this great weight has been lifted off my shoulders. I used to think—I still think—that people who off themselves die in despair. But they don't—you feel hopeful for the first time in a long while. Because you're escaping. The pain will soon be gone, and maybe there *is* another world that's nicer than this one, an afterlife where you can start again. I'm still on the afterlife side of the line. You guys seem very far away, over there. Or maybe it's just the drugs."

She put her hands over her face, then dropped them to the table. "Packing boxes with *textbooks*." She stood and leaned on the table toward us.

The nurse made a step in our direction, but I held up my hand. "She's fine, we're fine," I said.

"Sit down, Bethany," the nurse said.

She shot him a look of scorn. "A world in which your father answers your accusation of abuse by asking for your help with his next textbook is the one I'm supposed to go back to? The one the doctors are preparing me for? Well, I don't think so. I don't want what this doctor of mine keeps calling a second chance, as if I screwed up the first one."

"Sit *down*," the nurse said.

Bethany sat and folded her arms, her chin on her chest, eyes downcast, but she kept talking. "When I asked the doctor if he believed me about Dad, he said, 'I believe that you believe it,' which is his way of saying I'm delusional. He said that, as far as Dad is concerned, no one has any evidence on which to prove it one way or the other. 'All that matters to us, right now,' he said, 'is that you believe it and it made you try to hurt yourself.' Maybe they assume you're nuts if you try to kill yourself. I mean, why, if you weren't nuts, would you try to kill yourself?"

She met my eyes. "Do you think that's the way they look at it? Some doctors see anorexia as a slow kind of suicide. I hope you don't run into one of them while you're here. We might wind up sharing a room if you tell them you believe Dad never laid a hand on you. How could anyone think he did to you what he did to me when you're perfect in every way except for that smudge of ink you're hiding? Don't you think she's perfect, Wade? I've never been in love, but I'm told that love is blind."

"I love you and I see you just fine," I said.

Bethany shrugged and breathed in as if to stave off another burst of tears. "I've thought about filing a charge against Dad. But I won't get very far if you or Carmen or Gloria say he never laid a hand on you."

"I didn't say that. I said I don't remember anything. I don't. But I also said that it made sense to me that he laid a hand on you."

"So it would be his word against mine. Thanks, sis."

"Let's not argue anymore," I said. "It's pointless."

Bethany nodded. "All I'm saying, Rachel, is that I don't think he'll be arrested just because you say you have a hunch about him."

"I know you feel like shit," Wade said. "But don't take it out on Rachel."

"Fine," she said. "Fine. Sorry. I'm a bit out of sorts. Going mad and overdosing in the park has that effect on me. Jesus, of all the places we could be in the world, we have to be in South Africa. Not exactly the world capital of open-mindedness. I suppose I should have spoken up when we were still in Canada. Bad timing on my part. Not that Rachel's memory would have been better there."

"That's not fair, Bethany," Wade said. "If she doesn't remember, she doesn't remember. Is it possible that you're the only one? Or is it more likely that you made it all up?"

"*Wade*," I said.

"It's okay, Rachel," Bethany said. "I don't blame him for wishful thinking. Besides, I think Wade's pissed because you guys wouldn't be here if not for me, in South Africa, I mean. I did ask you to come along. For moral support, remember?"

"Have the DeVrieses been in touch with you?" I asked.

"Hell will freeze over before Peter DeVries speaks to me again. Theresa, too. I've broken the heart of their only child. Some parents tend not to take that kind of thing very well. But they'll stay friends with Mom and Dad. All four of them will just pretend the engagement never took place. And they'll definitely ignore what I said Dad did."

The three of us were silent for a while. Then Bethany said, "You know, sooner or later, they're going to let me out. Mom and Dad will take me back, I know they will. You see, on the one hand, I have to behave myself in here or I'll never get out, but on the other, if I behave myself, who do you think they'll entrust me to? I'll have to live with him again. I have no money, not a cent. Clive and the DeVrieses won't have anything to do with me. Gloria will side with them, so she and Max won't take me in, not that I'd want to go there. Don't even mention Carmen and Fritz. And you guys can't even support yourselves and haven't got an inch of extra space."

"Do you think we should all go back home to Newfoundland?" Wade asked.

"Do you want to?" I said.

"Bethany could live with us there. I could get my old job back, or maybe get a better one. I can't imagine her going back to live with your parents, or us visiting them and being civil under these circumstances."

"Actually," Bethany said, "it's not hard to imagine at all, not if you're one of the van Houts, which you practically are. And no more talk about going home, where all three of us would be miserable. I'd be a handful to live with, Wade. And there's no telling how long I'll be in here. It's not called an asylum for nothing."

"You'll feel better soon, Bethany," Wade said.

Bethany wiped her eyes with the back of her hand and nodded. "I will," she said. "Wade says it, so it must be so. It *will* be so. Or it won't. He lost Rachel once because of me. He lost Rachel *to* me. And here he is, he may think, on the verge of losing her again because of me. Well, thanks for coming, you two, but now you should go before you catch what I have. You know what hospitals are like." She got up and padded out of the room in her slippers, followed slowly by the nurse.

From *The Ballad of the Clan van Hout*

THE LAST NIGHT (1982)
(A piece I wrote for Rachel Lee,
who had not yet abandoned me.)

The last verse of the Night Salon?
The other three have long since gone,
so it's just me and Rachel Lee.
You like to sit across from me;
you look at me, as if to say
you wish that you could get away.
I feel like saying that you could
do as your older sisters did,
abandon me, abandon Dad—
take up with some jock, some hippie,
some boy or man instead of me,
but Rachel Lee is not like them.
Gloria kept coming to my room
but stopped reciting very soon
after she declined the bed
and chose a kitchen chair instead,
a chair in which she sat up straight
and stared as if she couldn't wait
for me to start so she could leave
to go out with her boyfriend, Steve,
I think it was, or was it Dale?
She was a teen before she failed
to show up in my room one night.
The Night Salon was one long fight
with Carmen, who, night after night,
sat in her older sister's chair
and called her younger sisters weird
and laughed at things that they still feared.
The youngest sprawled face down in bed,

as if pretending she was dead,
while Bethany, head in her hands,
recited to the ceiling fan.

Rachel will be the last no-show,
the last to come, the last to go.
I'll wait until it's after nine,
but you'll be gone, no longer mine.
The last night in the Ballad Room?
My sweet, I wrote this just for you.
I'm not sure what is on your mind—
the thought of leaving me behind?
But also something more than that;
I lack the nerve to ask you what.
For weeks, you've watched me on this bed,
remembering, I would have said,
the early days of the Salon,
or something else, for what goes on
inside your head, behind those eyes,
you know too well how to disguise.
Your three sisters were open books—
at least to me, I knew those looks—
but Rachel, you're illegible,
expressionless, inscrutable,
unnerving in your reticence—
what might that blank look mean for Us?

And soon you'll shun the balladry
and turn that hollow look on My.
The only one of four at home,
you all but live in your bedroom.
I stay in mine, across from yours
or go out driving in the car
(my footsteps on the creaking stairs,
the creaking stairs that no one hears).

You keep on with your diary,
you read and write obsessively.
That adamantine will of yours
may break as if a dam has burst—
it did before; this would be worse.
(What might that breakdown mean for Us?)
It bothers me, I must confess,
but not so much as that blank stare.
I'm not alone, yet you're not there.

But I've done things that few can do,
far greater things than any Jew.
So let them jeer and let them laugh
and let them read my epitaph:
"He lived his life as he saw fit,
the man who got away with it.
It doesn't matter what They know:
He lived Above, They lived Below."

You know I had high hopes for you—
the truth is, Rachel, I still do.
If nothing else, the diary
you think you must withhold from me
will serve as your apprenticeship.
You write and I cannot keep up,
you write because you cannot stop.
Did you begin because of me,
because I shared my poetry
with you each night for years on end?
You're sick, my love, but you will mend
and when you do, I hope that you
write even better than I do.
The time that you've spent practising,
the reams you've written with your pen
may vindicate your Mom and me

and you, of course, my Rachel Lee—
it may be this was *meant* to be;
the crucible of misery
that we have burned in all these years
may have refined that mind of yours.
Van Hout the Poet may be you.
If fate dictates that it be so,
I won't be sad to see you go,
for I have taught you all you know.

I loved it in the Land of Hout
when no one thought of getting out,
before the Rumours scaled the wall—
at times it seems beyond recall.
The four girls made me feel so young,
back then before the song was sung,
the siren song's seductive rhymes
that wrecked us on the rocks of time.
We came by love so honestly,
we talked about it openly,
accepted it so gratefully.
The love that we have long since lost
came to us without a cost,
before the girls broke faith with Us,
before the failing of their trust.
They give love so begrudgingly
it hardly seems like love to me,
a hug, perhaps, perhaps a kiss—
how could their love have come to this?
It's something I must bargain for.
The girls keep count, not like before,
when no one ever closed their doors.
I blame the girls for playing games,
for finding men whose very names
preoccupy me through the night:

I cannot sleep, I cannot write.
I must admit they madden me,
the men who gaze so longingly
(as girls their age once gazed at me).
They madden me unspeakably,
the boys and men they left me for.
I must pretend that I adore
the Woman who so loudly snores,
the aging face, the greying head
I cannot bear to touch in bed.

I'll be the van Hout balladeer,
though no one ever comes to hear
the words that I set down by day.
I'll go out in the car alone;
She'll wait up till van Hout comes home.
Each night, before I leave, I'll say
the verse that I wrote yesterday.
I never needed any praise,
just my audience of four,
and I don't need you anymore.
You turned your backs on the Salon—
one day you're there, the next you're gone.
But it goes on, the words still rhyme;
I read them out from time to time.
I put aside some time each day—
I still have things I want to say.
I read aloud when I'm alone;
the house is dark, though My is home.
I'll read it to your children too—
perhaps you'll join us when I do
and say the words along with us
or merely listen to the opus,
the lines you've never heard before.
I go on writing more and more,

though I've no one to read them to,
for I have nothing else to do.
I still go to the Ballad Room
and lie upon the Ballad Bed
and hear *The Ballad* in my head,
my eyes closed as I say the words
I wrote for you, my little girls.

The Ballad of the Clan van Hout
will not end here or in Without,
for you'll be mine despite the years—
forever mine, my little dears.
You'll crave the balm of Daddy's love
as if it comes from God above.
You'll still crave it when I'm gone—
it can't be had from other men.
You'll go without what you once had,
what none could give you but your dad.
It has to do with family,
it has to do with memory,
it has to do with history—
it has to do with you and me.

This piece was composed and read
by me upon the Ballad Bed.
I think of when you were all ears,
when you were in your early years.

This piece was composed and read
by me upon the Ballad Bed.
When Gloria abandoned me,
my audience was down to three.

This piece was composed and read
by me upon the Ballad Bed.

My audience was down to two
when Carmen said, "I'm through with you."

This piece was composed and read
By me upon the Ballad Bed.
My audience was next to none—
just her, the last and smallest one.
When Bethany abandoned me,
I still had little Rachel Lee.

This piece was composed and read
By me upon the Ballad Bed.
For years it was just her and me.
I read to little Rachel Lee
until, one night, she didn't show—
I knew she'd be the last to go.
There was no one left to witness
the first night of my loneliness.

From *The Arelliad*

THE LAST NIGHT (1985)

My father's ballad was in iambic tetrameter, a rhythm that has been branded on my brain. Perhaps he thinks in tetrametric rhyme. Perhaps that fate will soon be mine. He read to me till I was twenty-one, when Bethany, calling from Halifax, said, "Save yourself. He'll read for your entire life unless you say you've had enough. Stop going to the Night Salon. He won't complain or say a word or let on that he feels absurd without an audience. He'll get the message, you know him—he'll think of it as martyrdom."

She rhymes in his metre sometimes too, just like me. But it was easier for her to leave the Night Salon, to walk out on the balladeer, because he still had me, an audience of one. An audience of none?

To be the last to turn my back? It wasn't easy to leave him there with no one to hear *The Ballad*. It should have been but it wasn't.

It turned out Bethany was right; he never said a word the night that I renounced the Ballad Room but fell short of renouncing him. Eight thousand readings in a row but, at last, the balladry was done. Though I had written more than him by then, having taken the torch he offered me.

The four girls. We never spoke of *The Ballad* except when we were memorizing, reciting as he taught us to. I don't know why he bothered to tell us to keep it a secret. The four of us, we simply knew what daughters must and mustn't do. We each, in turn, stopped going to the Night Salon, but still we didn't talk about it.

When Gloria first failed to show—she was sixteen—the rest of us pretended not to notice, him included. Though we were four, no longer five, the Night Salon would still survive. The numbers shrank, *The Ballad* grew until we numbered only two, which means there are five versions of it. No one but him knows more of it than me.

The Ballad of the Clan van Hout means this to Carmen, and that to me, and something else to Bethany, and Gloria may remember parts that I was too young to memorize. Five versions of the gospel truth.

Six if you count *The Arelliad,* though it's getting harder to say how much of that is true. The backwards English alphabet, the simple code, the plain password, the way into another world . . . I'm writing more than ever now. I must get out of here somehow, before I sink into the page—

Gloria: For two years we were only three;
my sister Carmen made us four.
We sisters, love, yes—you and me—
will sisters be forevermore.

Carmen: At first there were the four of us,
but then there was one more of Us.
One more made five, though We were three—
the third one was sweet Bethany.

Bethany: They called me daughter number three
till they no longer spoke to me.
They never called you number four—
my darling, you were just one more.

Rachel: There will be Her, there will be Him—
we never will be free of them:
four sisters We are bound to be
their daughters for eternity.

WADE

As we drove home from the hospital, I wasn't sure what to make of what Bethany had said. For so long, nothing, and now, suddenly, everything. How trustworthy was a woman who had tried for years to starve herself to death and attempted suicide four times? It seemed possible that her behaviour had been brought on by abuse, but it seemed even more likely that her anorexia had driven her to accuse her father of causing all her problems. How could you distinguish one anguish from the other?

"You don't believe her, do you?" Rachel said.

"I wouldn't vote guilty if I was on a jury," I said, "but this is not a courtroom."

"You're wondering why she never said anything before this."

"I am. But you didn't say anything either. And you're still not saying anything, not really. There's more than a semantic difference between 'He never laid a hand on me, never' and 'I don't remember him doing anything to me—maybe I repressed it or something.'"

"I just wanted Bethany to know that I think what she's saying is, I don't know, plausible?"

"Based on her word alone."

"This is not a courtroom, remember. Your words. Besides, it's not just based on what she said. It's based on how I feel."

"If you think it's so plausible, how will you let her go back to that house?"

"I don't know."

"Are you going to speak to Gloria and Carmen about all this?"

Rachel shook her head. "Bethany will speak to them about it when she wants to."

"If she ever wants to. I can't believe your parents haven't called us. I mean, they know that Bethany's made another attempt, that she's been in hospital for days and—"

"This is what I have been trying to explain to you," Rachel said. "This is how they've always done things. If they called us, it would make it seem like they were worried that we believed Bethany. Their silence is meant to say that, like them, we just think this is Bethany being Bethany again."

"But she tried to kill herself."

"Only to cause trouble for them, to upset them, and they won't stoop to doing anything to make it seem like she should be taken seriously."

"I don't understand," I said. "You didn't say a word against them until we came to South Africa, not really. You just acted as if you thought the way they carried on was, I don't know, eccentric?"

"You sound as if you think I tricked you into coming here."

"That's not what I meant at all," I said. "I'm just trying to understand what you mean when you say that you think it makes sense."

She nodded but was silent until she brought up the matter of my parents again. "If you tell them, they'll think I'm not the Rachel that I seemed to be. I know they will. They're so sweet, both of them. They'll think I've fooled them and you. Maybe you really do think I did."

"I told you I don't," I said. "But I feel left out. And you have fooled me about how much you've been writing in your diary."

"I won't hide it from you anymore."

"How will I know if you do? Van Hout this and van Hout that and all these languages that I can't speak a word of. I hate to think of you buried in your diary alone somewhere—"

"I don't speak Arellian. I just write it."

"I wasn't *talking* about that."

We pulled into the driveway of the duplex.

"You go in," she said. "I'm going to drive around for a bit to clear my head."

"We could go for a walk."

"If we did, we'd argue. I won't be long. I just need some time to myself, okay?" She managed a smile. I'll be back soon. Promise."

I couldn't even *think* about writing. Sitting at my desk in front of a typewriter made me feel like some delusional no-hoper. I had always known I would be a writer. I had always assumed it, but now I couldn't account for that assumption or even say for certain when it had begun, let alone what its origin was. I suspected that, were I in the middle of writing a book, I would likely put it aside now and never return to it, so upended by Bethany's accusations did I feel, even as, casting back to when I met Rachel, I began to discern what sometimes seemed like unmistakable signs that Bethany was telling the truth—Rachel's oddly forthright manner when we met, the maniacal smile with which her father greeted the sight of my sisters, *Rachel's* sisters, the relentlessly off-colour banter between Gloria and Max, the Hairem, the way, after the Hairem, Hans had smirked at me while he rubbed Rachel's backside. What *writer* would have failed to see all these things as signs of what now seemed to be obvious?

I paced the apartment, waiting for Rachel to return. I felt ridiculous for wondering if it was possible that she alone of the four girls had escaped untouched, but I wondered anyway. Perhaps whatever Hans had by way of a conscience had lent him just enough restraint to spare his youngest daughter for no reason but that she was his youngest daughter. Perhaps one or more of her sisters had shielded her from him by threatening to tell unless he left her alone, or by some other impossible-to-imagine strategy. I concocted outlandish scenarios in which she avoided the fate that might or might not have befallen her sisters. Perhaps Rachel, by sheer smarts such as the other three did not possess, had evaded him for years, avoided situations of opportunity, such as spending the summer alone with him in some Canadian city. Perhaps her being spared had happened by sheer fluke. *If* what Bethany was saying was true, and if Gloria and Carmen had suffered the same fate, there had to be some explanation for the fact, if it was one, that Rachel remembered nothing. I once again tried to convince myself that Bethany had invented everything and that Rachel, when she said "It makes sense" and talked about not remembering and repression, had merely been responding out of love, panic and confusion.

I went back and forth like that, trying to explain it all away, until I realized that I was doing exactly what Rachel said she and her family had been doing for years.

We argued when she came home, the two of us moving about the apartment, barely avoiding collisions with each other, rehashing and rehashing my questions, Bethany's accusations, Rachel's uncertainty.

"Maybe you should go see a therapist."

"I've seen plenty of doctors. I was in hospital for months. They didn't uncover anything like this. Why do I suddenly need another therapist?"

"Because your sister suddenly attempted suicide and suddenly blamed it on your father. Because you're writing in that diary for far longer than you're admitting to me. Things have changed."

"Have they? For whom? If you're disgusted by me, or ashamed of me, if you think I'm tainted or defiled, that's not my fault."

"I never said that."

"Look, I know I'm not undamaged, so it makes sense that I was damaged by something. But Bethany said it's been going on since she can remember, and is *still* going on. Going on since we came back to Cape Town. You said yourself that surely I'd remember if he did anything recently. Jesus, Wade. What do you think, that he's been coming here when you've been out? *Jesus*. Look, the answer to all of this might be Bethany. She's got you thinking that, if it comes down to a choice between her and you, I'll choose her."

"Like you did before."

In the days that followed, in order to avoid such arguments, we had to avoid not only each other's company, but even the sight of each other. I stayed in the bedroom, my elbows on the desk, my hands cupping my face, my eyes closed, my mind racing. She lay on the couch in the adjoining room or sat at the table. I heard the pen scratching, stabbing, slashing the pages of her notebook. We spent mealtimes in more or less complete silence, sitting opposite each other, as immobile and intensely adversarial as a pair of chess champions.

We still slept in the same bed. But we didn't touch. We didn't talk except to say good night. She stayed on her side and I stayed on mine.

One night, I woke to find myself alone. It was dark, so I assumed Rachel was in the bathroom and waited for her to come back. After ten minutes, I got up, checked the bathroom and found it empty. I called her name but got no answer. I went to the front room and saw that the door that opened onto the stairs was ajar, but she wasn't on the landing. It was too dark to see the bottom of the stairs, but I heard a noise down there, perhaps a door opening. "Rachel," I whispered, fearful of waking Miss Norway. The downstairs door opened and I saw Rachel standing on the lower landing, beneath the light of a single bulb, looking out across the parking lot. She was bare-legged and barefoot, dressed in nothing but her nightshirt. "*Rachel*," I said, but she kept staring out as if at something in the parking lot.

I tiptoed down the stairs and was about to put my hand on her shoulder when she half turned my way. "Wade," she said, "I don't remember coming down the stairs. I must have come down in my sleep."

"For Christ's sake, Rachel, let's stop playing van Hout games." She turned the rest of the way toward me and I saw that she held her diary in her left hand, the underside of which was intensely blue. "It looks like you came down to write for a while," I said.

She looked at the notebook. "I'm scared," she said. She sat down, the book on her bare knees. "I've never walked in my sleep. But I must have. What if I had tripped and fallen?"

"I'm sorry I snapped at you," I said.

"I couldn't get to sleep, so I went out to the couch to write. I remember that. And then I woke up. Here."

I sat beside her on the stair. "Come back to bed," I said, but she shook her head. "I'll never get to sleep now. I'm afraid to go to sleep. After I've written for a while longer, I'll take a sleeping pill. I have some in my drawer."

"You can write in bed with the lights on or under the covers with a flashlight, just as long as you don't come down the stairs in the middle of the night. I don't want you to think that you have to hide things from me."

"I might be writing for quite some time," she said. "I feel like I might have to write for three or four hours before I can even try to get to sleep. The longer I write, the faster I write and the more worked up I get. I know you feel like maybe I'm cracking up again."

"I hope you're not cracking up, but what should I do?" I said. "I'd be happy to sit beside you while you write. I'll read, you write, like we used to do."

She shook her head. "I don't want you to see me," she said. "I'm not doing this to upset you. I just can't help it. Just go back to bed. I'll be as quick as I can."

"Wouldn't it be better in the long run if you didn't give in so much?"

"You may have noticed that there are no photos of me in the family albums from my extreme Anne Frank phase. I was not a pretty sight. I dressed as dowdily as I could to ward people off. I didn't want friends. Spending time with others only made it harder for me to meet my daily reading and writing quotas. I avoided anyone who came from outside, the anti–van Houts, the non–van Houts, for there was no telling where the enemy, the stranger whose purpose was to do us in, might come from. I read and wrote day and night. It was like searching for the answer to a riddle without ever having heard the riddle. Oh, *Jesus*, the more I talk about it, the more worked up I get and the more upset you get. I can see it in your face. You're scared."

"Come upstairs," I said. "Let's open a bottle of wine—"

"Reading was as bad as writing. I would run my forefinger down the left page, line by line, then the right, then turn the page so fast I sometimes ripped it in half."

"Fine. Sit here and write for as long as you like. Don't worry about what I'm thinking. It's not as if you have to get up early in the morning. Don't worry. Bethany will be better soon and so will you, and everything will work out and there really is a Santa Claus."

"Don't compare me to Bethany."

"I was joking. Or trying to."

I threw up my hands in frustration and went back up the stairs, leaving her there with her notepad on her lap.

A few days later, Rachel came into the bedroom while I was sitting idle at the desk. She stood in front of me, put her hands on her hips and said: "If you want to go on being with me, you have to start believing me and you have to stop asking me questions. You have to stop insisting that I give you an explanation of my behaviour when no explanation exists. You have to stop keeping track of how long I write in the diary. You have to stop guessing to yourself about it. You have to stop staring at the smudge on my hand. It's not the Scarlet Letter. You have to stop it—all of it."

I would have been surprised if she had delivered such an ultimatum after any length of time, but that it had come so soon from someone whose love for me I didn't doubt made me realize that she had just set out the only terms by which she could carry on from day to day, that I had been obstructing her bid for survival, that she was on the verge of seeing me as someone she might have to live without if she was going to survive. I knew what losing her was like. I doubted that I could go through it a second, final time, except at the cost of abandoning the balance of my dreams. I had long believed that, if you tried hard enough, you could find the truth. But nothing I had experienced or read seemed of any use in getting at the truth of this one family, let alone the ultimate truth that I had fancied philosophy and history were inching toward.

I promised her I would never again challenge her about her past, or insist that she somehow find the root cause of her obsession with *Het Achterhuis*, or doubt her love for me or mine for her. She climbed onto my lap and kissed me. "Let's go to bed," she said.

That night, she sat at the kitchen table for two hours, pen in hand, a copy of *Het Achterhuis* and a notebook in front of her. She sat there for all that time and never wrote a word. A couple of days later, she wrote frantically in the notebook for almost three hours, barely pausing to think, filling line after line, page after page. And then she ripped out the pages, methodically tore them into pieces smaller than postage stamps and threw them in the garbage can. Why she bothered to do this with pages crammed with notes written in a language that no one but she could read, I didn't dare ask.

RACHEL

Everything seemed important. Everything seemed as important as everything else. My hand couldn't keep up with my mind. I jumped from one thing to the next, rarely finishing a sentence, never finishing a paragraph. I regained my fluency in Arellian to the point of dreaming in it more often than I dreamed in the other languages I knew. I woke in the middle of the night to find myself speaking it. Wade slept so soundly that he didn't hear me, though I was always convinced that he had and checked to make sure that he really was asleep.

By day, especially when I was alone, Arellian crept into my mind more and more. It began to seem that it was not just my language but everyone else's as well. In grocery stores, I saw it written on the labels of the items on the shelves and on the signs above each aisle, displacing English and Afrikaans. I was terrified that I would forget myself and speak it aloud in public, address perfect strangers in this language that they would take to be gibberish, proof that I had lost my mind. One afternoon, I held a can of tomato sauce in my hand and stared at it for minutes as the words on the label changed from English to Arellian, Arellian to English, back and forth until I was so dizzy that I nearly fainted. Only when I absolutely had to, when I was conversing with or listening to others, was I able to ward off what I feared would be a complete retreat into an imaginary world from which no doctor or medication could bring me back. Only in the evenings, in Wade's company, the two of us having a drink in the kitchen after I had written in my diary and read *Het Achterhuis* for hours, was I able to relax for a while and put from my mind the language that I had invented, taught myself to speak and read and write when I was just a girl.

From *The Arelliad*

DEAR ALSO-ANNE (1985)

I read the Diary she kept
by day, by night while others slept,
when she was all she'd ever be,
a girl named Anne, like you and me,
a girl who grew up happily
until the world, struck by a curse,
turned good to bad and bad to worse.
How could a girl who braved the odds
go unacknowledged by the gods?
If gods there are, strange gods they be
who match a child with history
in history's worst century.

If only I could pace myself, or read something other than her diary, or nothing. Write nothing. Sit back and rest until my pulse slows down enough for me to sleep. But I'm driven to keep up with something that forever pulls away from me. Some nights, fragmented sentences are all that I can manage, and even those disintegrate and I'm reduced to syllables that race like mice across the table. It can't be done, it can't be done, put down your pen, don't start again. I'm not looking for pity from you, Anne. You must think that this is just what I deserve, or that it's not nearly enough.

Arellia is treacherous. There are no maps. The signs are unreliable. It's dark now, but there is light enough to see you watching me, the Shadow She, the small girl in the black peacoat, too thin a coat for such a night.

It seems the wind will never rest. This is not the kind of west wind to which English odes are written, but a wind as brutal and lethal as the barrel of a gun. The sun comes up; the wind dies down. The sky is clear; there are no sounds on days when girls like you are found.

I must avoid the yellow wood. If I go in, I won't come out. Your fellow Anne is nowhere to be seen. You follow me, silently, stopping when I stop lest you get too close. You might be my reflection except for your eyes, which are nothing like mine, so green they don't seem real. I'm not the age that I was then, but you're the same, still seventeen, as old as you will ever be, as old as Margot Frank was when she and her sister died. It's ten years since you and I first met here in Arellia. Ten years you've been pursuing me, accusing me with silence or with words.

I've had enough but can't say so, for you are right: I know. You know.

Wade must be thinking that, if what Bethany has accused Dad of is true, there is much that I've been keeping from him, wondering how much of Rachel van Hout is real and how much is not, such as the things I say he makes me feel. If Bethany's accusations are true, how much of me is false? He may no longer believe that, before him, there was no one else.

If I endured what Bethany says she did, how could I not be forever changed by it? Perhaps he thinks of Dad when he's with me and thinks that I do too. How could I not have thoughts of Dad running through my mind when he and I are in bed, when I only *seem* to lose myself? I told Wade once that it felt "like God" when we made love. It did, but I doubt that he believes it now. He may think it was all an act, and that's all it ever was.

My breakdowns and my illnesses, my mania, these diaries—he thinks it's my dad who makes me scribble in my notepad right in front of him night after night. Dad is what that's all about, me thinking I can rid myself of him if I get it all down on paper. Or else he thinks the diary is purposeless, a mounting obsession that will put an end to me.

I wonder if Wade used to think that it was him I was writing about. *Does she ever think of me when she's recording history?* Or is it by Her that he believes I'm possessed, by Anne Frank, the dead diarist whose diary, he may think, I'm somehow trying to complete. *Small wonder that she's going mad, the ingenue of such a dad, the tutelage she must have had.* He may think me Dad's protegé in denial, but every time I see Dad smile it sickens me, as the sight of me may sicken Wade.

I'm putting thoughts into Wade's head, words into his mouth that may be nothing like the truth. Perhaps he thinks of me even more tenderly than before, just as he would if some disease was slowly stealing me away but leaving him behind, untouched, more in love with me than ever, to ask why fate or God had let someone so young, who bore no blame for anything, suffer so unspeakably? His darling Rachel. The disproportionality, the pitiless disparity of it, a mere child pitted against a man like Him, a mismatch that Wade could not have conceived of until now.

I hope he prays that I don't bear those scars, not just for his sake but for mine. Surely he does. But if he suspects that these things, or worse, are true, I hope he believes that I am still and always will be *me*, my body just as beautiful, my soul inviolable, as sweet as when we met—that nothing can change that.

But then there is the Shadow She, who roamed the yellow wood before Wade met me. I was already lost in Arellia to expiate another crime of little Rachel Lee. Wade would not be so sure of me if he knew why the Shadow She keeps coming back. Arellia and Claws von Snout, the girl who wears the black peacoat, the things I think and dream about. Do I want my diary as much or more than I want Wade? I don't know where such thoughts come from. I left him but went back to him. He took me back; I took him here. He looks at me resentfully sometimes, as if I am greedily using up all the words allotted to us by the gods, taking his share as well as mine, hoarding them in my notebooks.

Wade wants to know what makes me write. He wants to catch what I've got, hopes that he'll come down with it, the van Hout family disease. It doesn't occur to him that he might be my Muse, because he's always thought I would be his. I don't need his inspiration, but it's starting to seem that, without mine, he'll never write a single word. The irony will drive him mad—I'll write and write, and all he'll ever do is read, the novelist he thought he'd be stifled by a wife who, if she had her way, would never write again. I never show a word to him, or anyone.

Two books elude him, day and night:
the one I will not let him read,
the one I will not let him write.
He looks at me resentfully,
as if he could, if not for me,
write something good, or even great—
write anything instead of wait
for inspiration from above
to free him from the one he loves.

He sits for hours in that room and tries to write, or thinks of trying, anyway. As he sits and stares at his typewriter, it's hard to say if anything about his homeland goes through his mind, so preoccupied is he with my strange family, the strangest one of whom is me. He thought he had to get away to see things in perspective. I wonder if, someday, he'll think he should have got away from me. I hate to hear him sigh in there, the silence of his typewriter—I know he's come to doubt that he can write.

"All those hundreds, *hundreds* of books I read—better to have *written one*. I'd take one line for every night I spent reading Shakespeare. Perhaps it's time that I owned up to being whatever in God's name it is that I'm supposed to be."

I chose him, not his vocation, but don't dare tell him that in case he thinks I am agreeing with his self-assessment.

It's been five months since I re-chose him, and I'm writing in Arellian more often than not. If I'm the impediment I suspect I am, what if, one of these days or nights, Wade puts me aside and that book of his comes pouring out at last?

I hope I never see Wade in Arellia, staring at me accusingly, alone among the yellow leaves. I might end up writing of no one but him while burning candles in my room. For me, he puts aside his dream. He follows me, he lives for me and, in the end, he dies for me, the mad autobiographer who writes the books he planned to write while he watches over her, his blood drained of its ambition. I become his one vocation. To be my minder becomes the main work of his life.

The book I take such pains to hide I leave to him when my mind and body fail, but he isn't able to decode one word of *The Arelliad.*

They're drawn to me, the mad, the dead, but Wade is not yet one of them—

But now I sink deeper into the page and see that Wade *is* in here with me. I've invited him in to show him where I live—Arellia, the yellow leaves forever falling from the trees. I take his hand and lead him about. "See that one in the peacoat, the one in black, the Shadow She—she always stares like that. And look, the Frank sisters are over there, Anne and Margot . . ."

The very worst has come to pass—Wade is now among the lost. He leaves me and he goes to them, the Frank sisters, who take him by the hands.

His eyes tell me and them that he's never known unbearable, abiding pain. He'll speak of me when I can't hear, tell them about the things I did to lure him in.

The blue sweater I gave him should have been a goodbye kiss. My reappearance at his door was a sad mistake. How could unlucky Wade say no? Arellia—he mustn't stay. I have to make him leave or find a path to lead him out before von Snout appears.

How strange it is to see him here among the girls who died when they were young. How tall he is compared to them. Their loyal minder he might be, their guide through Time, through History, a man, at last, among three girls, the only one left in this world.

Now comes the quickening of time that happens when I start to rhyme, the vertigo . . . the wind picks up in one great gust, a churning vortex from the west in which the beast conceals himself, the Monster known as Claws von Snout.

They scream and strike out through the trees, the Frank sisters, the Shadow She. I try to grab Wade's hand, but he runs away from them and me. I can't keep up, I never could—I lose him in the yellow wood. I hear him shout, "Where have you gone? Why did you leave? Remember what the sirens said? The sun will rise; they'll find me dead."

—

I hurry into the woods. There's no sign of Wade, no sign of the Frank sisters or the green-eyed Anne.

Arellia, before the dawn. The smell of Snout is in the air. He's still out there, waiting for me and the others. The darkest hour of the night—no light but for the eyes of Snout, two coals of red that flit about like fireflies between the trees. He's blustered in like this before. He's unsure of me, though he's been tracking my decline, waiting for the perfect moment. If I weaken further, he'll strike. He growls as if to say, "Not yet. Ten *years* without a taste of you, so what's another day or two? It won't be long; I'll come for you. I'll come for you another night."

He'll slink off before the sun comes up, smouldering in spite as he retraces his advance.

Head bowed, he'll keep a cold eye out for witnesses of his defeat.

WADE

Five days after we'd seen Bethany in the hospital, I went out for an early-morning run. When I got back, Rachel was sitting, slumped, at the kitchen table. She didn't turn toward me when I reached the top of the stairs.

"Bethany called," she said. "She says none of it was true. All of it was a product of what she says was a psychotic break."

"She retracted everything?"

Rachel wore the same look as she had when I told her about Clive's visit.

"What did you say to her?" I said.

Rachel didn't answer. She looked as if she was weary of trying to think it through, weary, perhaps, of trying to think.

"Did the doctors really say that it was a psychotic break?" I said.

"I don't know what the doctors said," Rachel said, not looking at me as I sat beside her. "Psychotic breaks are not uncommon among people who are severely depressed."

"You had one; now she has one?"

"I think she believed what she said about Dad. Even if she made it up, I wouldn't blame her. Considering all that she's been through and all the drugs that she's been on over the years." At last she looked at me and I saw that her eyes were red-rimmed from crying. "She told me that she called Mom and Dad and apologized to them, and they came to the hospital and took her back home, against the advice of her doctor. Home is where she is now."

"With him?" I said.

Rachel shrugged, pushed her chair back on two legs and put her hands behind her head. "That would seem to be the case," she said, a full stop between each word. "When we spoke, she was in tears the whole time. She kept saying over and over how sorry she was."

"Do you really believe that she made it all up?"

Rachel rocked backward and forward on the kitchen chair. "I didn't want to press her about it. I just told her I was glad that she was out of hospital. She's a mess. She may change her story again. Who knows? Maybe she just lost her nerve. I didn't want to upset her. She doesn't want any visitors for now. Except for Clive and the DeVrieses." I looked at her, even more startled.

"The engagement is on again. She apparently apologized."

"And they're fine with it? Their future daughter-in-law tells their son that her father has abused her since as far back as she can remember. She comes this close to destroying her father's life and her mother's and all your lives. And then she changes her mind, retracts everything, just like that. She's ill, Rachel. That's the only explanation."

Rachel stood. "I'm well aware of how this sounds."

"I'm sorry. It's just that I don't know what to think. Do you still think that the accusations against your father make sense?"

"I'd suggest that you and I go back home if I hadn't promised Bethany that I'd be here for her. I can't leave her."

"There's just so much pretending, so much looking the other way. I can't imagine what it will be like from now on, except that it will be worse."

"Then you go home and wait for me," she said. Her tone was flat, as if she didn't care if I went home or not.

"I'd *never* go back home without you, Rachel," I insisted. "You know that, don't you?" She gave no sign of having heard me, but she began to cry. I took her in my arms and kissed the top of her head.

"Please don't think that I'm like them, my parents and my sisters," she said. "I'm not. I don't know why, but I'm not. Maybe it's because of you that I'm not. Please don't lose faith in me."

—

As it turned out, Bethany had told Gloria, Max, Carmen and Fritz about her suicide attempt and her brief breakup with Clive, but not about the accusations she had made against her father. All this Rachel revealed to me as we were driving to a gathering at Liesbeek Road. I didn't think that we should go, but Rachel felt there was no point in staying in Cape Town if she avoided the sister she had come here to support.

Bethany answered the door when we rang the bell. In jeans and a loose-fitting black sweater, she didn't look much different than she had at the last such gathering. "I can still do wonders with makeup," she said to Rachel, "whereas the heel of your left hand is still smudged with ink. Don't worry. I couldn't say for sure that anyone but Wade and I even know that you're left-handed."

We were the last to arrive. Without a martini and a cigarette, Bethany seemed not to know what to do with her hands. She didn't wait for us to come inside so she could close the door behind us, but merely turned her back and walked off.

Everyone was seated in the front room. "One beer and one wine coming up," Bethany said. "Grab a chair and I'll be right back."

Everyone but Hans acknowledged our arrival, though no one stood. It was the most tense-looking group of people I had ever seen. Rachel and I sat on separate chairs across the room from her parents, near Gloria and Max. Fritz and Carmen sat cross-legged on the floor just to the left of the loveseat where Clive was sitting, his parents flanking him like Swiss guards. So there we were, two factions in the room, one that knew of the accusations against Hans, and one that didn't. I assumed that conversation would be even more than the usual minefield.

I was proven wrong. When Bethany returned with our drinks, she sat on the floor in front of the loveseat, at Clive's feet, and announced, "No booze for me. I think we all know what that might lead to." Everyone tried to laugh. I stared at the DeVrieses, who seemed entirely unfazed by our presence or by my prolonged scrutiny of them.

"I bet they have you on the good stuff now, Bethany," Fritz said. "They should have had you on it from the start. Those Canadian doctors haven't got a clue about drugs."

"Mom is now the keeper of the pills," Bethany said. "My personal pusher. She doles them out and makes sure that I take them, and all I have to do in return is eat a handful of raisins for breakfast, a banana for lunch, and a bowl of Special K with skimmed milk for dinner. Makes sense. We mustn't have Bethany stockpiling pills. And we can't have a drama queen starving herself to death when there are so many more decorous ways to end it all."

"None of this would have happened," Hans said, "if not for those incompetents in Newfoundland. I never thought I'd say this, but Fritz is right."

Bethany stared straight ahead, an odd smile on her face. She raised her hand in the air as if she wanted to ask a question. "I apologize for being so dramatic," she said, dropping her hand. "But I was never at risk for anything more than a really bad hangover. I have always known my limits. So it wasn't a real attempt."

"Just a cry for help?" Fritz said.

"Help me, help me," Carmen said, high on something as usual, her eyes barely open.

I wanted to blurt out the truth, and I might have, but Myra, as if prompted by my expression, said, "Wade, how is your book coming along?"

"I don't think I've adjusted to my new surroundings yet," I said, wishing I'd been able to come up with something more ironic.

"Well," Myra said, smiling, "now you know why I found it so hard to write in Newfoundland."

I nodded, though she had never said a word to me about finding it hard to write in Newfoundland.

"You'll never become adjusted to South Africa," Fritz said. "I haven't and I was born here."

"We were all born here except for Dad and Wade and Max and Peter," Carmen said. "The only men in the room who were born here are Fritz and Clive. And Fritz is the only Afrikaner."

"The guest of honour," Fritz said, looking at me as if at the man he had deposed.

"You will get used to it, Wade," Myra said. I thought she meant her family. "It's a distractingly beautiful country, but, after a while, you'll stop noticing the scenery and be better able to concentrate."

"I wish I could use the beauty of the scenery as my excuse."

"The only beauty Wade is distracted by is Rachel," Fritz said. "He's not distracted by other things like bigotry, exploitation, slavery and censorship."

"So endeth the sermon," I said.

"A woman who is always available, that's what he's distracted by," Fritz said. "And they're not even married."

Carmen laughed, dropping her head so that her hair hid her face, her shoulders shaking. I glanced at Rachel, who had turned crimson.

"I'm glad to see that marriage is working out so well for you and Carmen," I said to Fritz.

Bethany got to her feet, walked to the middle of the room and raised both arms over her head. "Announcement. Announcement." She lowered her arms. "Clive and I have set a date."

"Oh, isn't that *marvellous*," Myra said.

"Absolutely marvellous," Hans said, moving forward onto the edge of his chair. "I can't think of better news. So when is the big day? A year or so from now, I suppose."

"Well, actually," Bethany said, "it's May 17."

"Well, that's about a year," Myra said.

"No, I mean May 17 of *this* year," Bethany said.

"But, Bethany," Hans said, "Myra and I are going to give at least one of our daughters a proper wedding. We have to make plans."

"We had a proper wedding in Halifax," Carmen said, "but you missed it."

"Well," Bethany said, "you'll have to put together the world's fastest perfect wedding, because May 17 is the big day."

"*Bethany*," Myra said. She turned and smiled at Clive as if asking him for support, but he looked at the floor.

"Now, now," Hans said. "May 17 *next* year it is, then."

Everyone looked at Bethany. She rubbed the front of her sweater in slow circles. "Well," she said, "by May 17 of next year, it will be too late to have a proper wedding."

"What?" Myra said to Bethany, who smiled.

"Yup," she said. "I'm pregnant. For those of you who might not be inclined to take my word for it, Clive was with me when the doctor at Groote Schuur confirmed it."

Peter and Theresa stared at their son. "Is this true?" Theresa said. Clive nodded as if, even so, he wasn't sure if it was true. *I* wasn't sure, given what Bethany had done, and said and unsaid, in the past few weeks. I looked at Rachel. Her mouth was partway open, her eyes darting about.

"The two of you haven't been alone together long enough to *kiss*," Rachel said at last.

"Oh yes we have," Bethany said. "Clive came by when Mom and Dad went out without me."

"Clive, you dirty dog," Fritz said.

"Oh, but you see, but you see, it's perfectly all right," Hans said. "There's nothing wrong with it as long as you're engaged."

"But they may not have been engaged when they did the deed that did the deed," Fritz said.

As if he hadn't spoken, Myra said, "Peter and Theresa, isn't this wonderful—a double surprise!"

Peter, Theresa and Hans all but leapt to their feet. Clive managed to hoist himself off the sofa and take the hand Bethany held out to him. I felt a flash of panic. *Right up until she was taken to hospital.* If what she'd said about Hans was true . . . I reached for Rachel's hand, but she pulled it away, her eyes fixed on her father, whom, I feared, she was about to confront. I grabbed her hand then and held tight.

"The baby might be his," I said as we were driving home. "That's what you were thinking."

"He wouldn't be that stupid," she said.

"Accidents happen."

"I wasn't thinking that the baby might be his, all right? I have to write tonight. A lot. Just giving you the heads-up."

RACHEL

I tried to make sense of what Bethany had said. Clive had been dropping by when Mom and Dad were out—starting when? Since the first party, when she said she was eager to avoid him, so eager that she asked us to run interference between him and her? Before that? If they had been having secret assignations at our parents' house, it could only have been because she asked him to or, Clive being Clive, told him to, perhaps in the *hope* of getting pregnant so that the question of what she should do with her life would be irrevocably answered—she would marry Clive and have a baby. Had she changed her mind and hoped that an overdose would abort the baby if it didn't kill her? Possibly. More likely, she didn't know she was pregnant when she took the pills, which she did because she hadn't, as she hoped she would, felt relieved, unburdened or purposeful when she decided to marry a man she didn't love. Giving in to our parents' notion of an ideal life did not make her feel better. Life with Clive made life seem unendurable. Until she found out she was pregnant. Why else had she accused Dad of those things and Mom of turning a blind eye to them, and then said she'd been mistaken, if not for the sake of the baby?

She recanted all of it when she found out she was pregnant. And one of the few unassailably true things in her life—the *fact* of a child that was *hers*—restored her conviction that the best thing to do was start a family with the only man who would have her. She was still pregnant, despite her overdose, and the wedding was not only back in play but needed to be soon. I thought of how, according to her, Mom and Dad had reacted to being accused. I thought of how they acted when she announced that she was pregnant. Half the people in that room knew what she had accused Dad of and yet acted as if she had never said a word against him.

I really wouldn't have blamed Wade if he had walked away. Most men would have done so already. I knew that if he wanted to leave, he would. He would work up the nerve, because he was not like Clive. He didn't need my permission to break my heart as I had once broken his. He wasn't a lamb that I was leading to the slaughter.

WADE

"I think we should tell Gloria and Max about Bethany's accusations," Rachel said a couple of days later. "I'd like to see how Gloria reacts."

"You said she'd take your parents' side."

"She probably will, but it's possible she won't. She might not be able to help herself if I confront her out of the blue."

They were out by the pool, Gloria topless in a deck chair and Max fussing over something on the barbecue.

Rachel wasted no time getting down to business. She walked over to Gloria and said, "When Bethany was in the hospital, she told us that Dad has been doing things to her for years, ever since she can remember and right up till the present."

"Well, well," Max said in a kind of what-else-is-new tone.

"Yes," Gloria said, "well, well."

"I must have known you were coming," Max said. "I put on too many burgers. How do you like yours?"

"Jesus," Rachel said, "did either one of you hear what I just said?"

Gloria stood, removed her sunglasses and tugged on her bikini bottom, snapping it into place.

"I'm going for a swim," she said. She turned around, dropped her glasses on the chair, walked to the edge of the pool and dove in. She swam near the bottom, her body a blur, and surfaced at the other end; facing away from us, she put her forearms on the edge of the pool and stayed that way for several minutes, her chin resting on her arms.

"Gloria," Rachel shouted. Gloria pushed away from the edge of the pool and swam back toward us, again underwater, then climbed the ladder, emerging inch by inch, eyes closed, hair matted to her head, water dripping from every part of her. She dried herself with the towel that Max tossed at her, smoothed her hair back from her forehead, her breasts rising and falling. It was as if she was presenting her body to us as proof that Bethany's accusations were untrue.

She put her hands on her hips, water pooling around her feet, and addressed Rachel. "Over the years, Bethany has accused Dad of a lot of things. Not to his face. Not to anyone but me, as far as I know."

"What things?" Rachel said.

"Well, let's see. Where to begin. She said he plagiarized parts of his master's thesis. Told lies about other professors to the deans at the University of Cape Town and in Newfoundland. She said he left Cape Town, we all left Cape Town, because he had no other choice. That's what she said. *No other choice.* She wouldn't explain what she meant. Then, two weeks after she said that, she told me she'd been joking. Joking. She's been telling lies for years about just about everything. She told me Dad wasn't really a member of the Dutch Resistance. Two weeks later, she told me she was kidding, that she had made it up. She's the pathological liar, not him. I used to get upset with her for making up lies about Dad, even if it was just for fun. All she ever said was never mind. 'Never mind, Gloria, it doesn't matter.' I knew she was nuts long before any doctor said she was. She knows what I think of her, so now she's moved on to telling lies to you. Don't believe a word she says."

"It's not her fault," Max said. "She can't help it. No one goes crazy on purpose."

"Well," Gloria said, "now she's gone crazy at Clive's expense."

"Clive would never have been laid in his life if not for Bethany," Max said.

"I'm just giving you fair warning," Gloria said to Rachel.

"But when Bethany was in hospital," Rachel said, "Theresa told Clive that, years ago, before we moved to Canada, there was a complaint made against Dad at the University of Cape Town. She said a woman claimed that he had done something to her daughter, one of his students, but she later withdrew the complaint."

"What does that prove?" Gloria said. "Who knows what that mother and daughter were up to?"

"Planning a lawsuit would be my guess," Max said. "There may have been a settlement out of court. Settlements are not admissions of guilt."

Gloria threw her towel aside, put her sunglasses back on and lay on the deck chair again. "Wade, you should write a book about Bethany. Anorexia in Africa. Millions of people on this continent are starving. She has all the food she needs. Courtesy of Dad. And what does she do with it? She feeds it to stray dogs."

"*Because* she's anorexic," Rachel said, smacking her thigh with frustration. "It's a struggle every day. Even when she eats, she's keeping one step ahead of revulsion. I believe her when she says that no one but another anorexic understands what it's like. Getting food into you, keeping it down. For you, it's an effortless pleasure, one of many. You have all the food you need, courtesy of Max, a sugar daddy who is twice your age."

Gloria stood again, her breasts bobbing, and once more put her hands on her hips. Max was pushing burgers about on the barbecue as if he hadn't heard a word that Rachel said. Before Gloria could start in on her, Rachel began to cry.

"I'm sorry, Gloria," she said. "I just don't know what to do about Bethany. *Pregnant?* Do you think someone in her state will survive a pregnancy?"

"I don't know." Gloria picked up her bikini top and put it on. "I don't know anything when it comes to kids. Maybe Bethany thinks a kid is exactly what she needs to get her head straight. Maybe she's right. Maybe Mom's right, and it's what all four of us need. Max doesn't want kids. He thinks that my body would never be the same if I had one."

"It wouldn't," Max said. "Especially a certain part of it. My first wife was never the same."

"What do you think about kids, Rachel?" Gloria said, glancing at me.

"I think you should remind Max that his body hasn't been the same since he was thirty, which was twenty-five years ago," Rachel said.

"Touché," Max said.

"Anyway," Gloria said, "I wouldn't mind adopting, say, a six-year-old girl. I mean, I want a girl, and there's no guarantee I'll get one the old-fashioned way, and I wouldn't mind skipping all those sleepless nights and the toilet training and the diapers. I'm not sure I'd have the patience for it. And maybe Max is right. It would be my loss too."

Max stacked a plate with hamburgers.

"I'm not hungry," Gloria said.

"Me neither," Rachel said.

"Then let's pop inside for a drink," Max said. "I can reheat these later."

We went inside, and Rachel and I waited in the kitchen while Gloria and Max changed into dry clothes, Rachel silent and sullen-looking as she leaned against the countertop.

This time, it was papaya daiquiris that were thrust at us. I felt like telling Gloria that even adopting a child would send Max off in search of another woman half his age.

Three or four daiquiris later, the mood was lighter. Max and Gloria announced that they were going to bed and, before they could invite us to sleep over, Rachel said, "Wade and I are going to stay up for a bit, out there by the pool."

"Suit yourselves," Gloria said. "You know where everything is."

We went out to the pool, refreshed daiquiris in hand, and stood staring at the water. I sat in a wooden deck chair, and Rachel sat sideways on my lap and laid her head against my chest. She was soon asleep.

I tried to puzzle through what Gloria had said. Assuming she hadn't made them all up, who could have made the series of accusations against her father that Bethany had repeated to Gloria? Maybe Bethany had spoken to Gloria because Rachel was too young and because she knew that, when Carmen was stoned, she would repeat everything to Hans and Myra, if only to piss them off and get Bethany in trouble. But who was Bethany's informant? Plagiarizing his thesis, being forced to leave the University of Cape Town, which probably meant that he had been fired or had agreed to resign—and who would have told her that he had lied about taking part in the Dutch Resistance during the war?

I wished that Rachel wasn't too drunk to drive home, wished that I could just lie in my own bed and go to sleep. I shook her arm. "Let's hit the hay," I said.

She nodded but patted her shoulder bag, which was on the ground beside the chair. "You go," she said. "I've got both diaries in here." I sighed as she got off my lap. "Don't be mad, okay?" she said. I nodded.

There was no wind. There were no lights on in the house, but the pool lights were still on. "I might be back if I can't sleep," I said. When I reached the door, I stopped and turned to see if Rachel was waiting to wave good night. But she was hunched over her book, writing in the dim light as if she was trying to get down every word that the four of us had said.

From *The Ballad of the Clan van Hout*

SPECIAL LOVE (1967)

It's time we spoke of Special Love,
the greatest gift a girl can give,
a gift that I give, just like you;
remember, girls, that this is true.
How fortunate your father is—
remember well these words of his—
to have not four, but five of you;
girls give the gift, but women, too—
you know by nature what to do,
for Special Love is natural,
the greatest of all miracles,
that comes from God to you and me,
the Holiest of Mysteries.
But only certain families
are chosen for this Mystery;
God chose us for His family
but swore us all to secrecy.
Most families he doesn't choose—
that doesn't mean He loves them less;
we mustn't question what he does
for God is infinitely wise
and knows what's best for all of us.
The ones who don't have what we have
have never heard of Special Love,
so if you tell them, they'll feel bad,
and feeling bad will make them sad,
and that will make God very mad.
You mustn't make God mad with you;
you never know what God will do—
he's kind and gentle, like your dad,
but even dads can get upset.

(You haven't seen me angry yet,
and God gets angrier than that,
a million times as much, I bet,
so do what Daddy tells you to
and God will not get mad with you.)

There was a time when Love was new;
you didn't know what I'd been through
or what I went through every day
(girls, mind what I'm about to say).
You girls had never been Without—
you thought it like the Land of Hout—
but I had suffered there for years,
so lonely and unloved, my dears.
You treated me with Special Love,
the balm and salve of Special Love,
and, very quickly, I improved.
Remember that She Loved me too—
it's simply what you're meant to do;
that's why God made you as you are,
that's why you have such lovely hair,
and why you're softer than boys are,
and why some parts are not like theirs,
the special parts for Special Love
that comes to us from God above.

My girls, what's right is always "wrong";
the "wrong" has been right all along.
Keep that in mind when Rumours creep
into your heads while you're asleep.
The Gossipers of History
are out to get this family—
they're jealous of the love we have,
they hate the thought of Special Love;
they think that if they call it names,

it might go back from where it came.
They hate the thing they cannot have:
the rebel Angels turned on God,
who gave them Life and Paradise,
but that was not enough for them—
the Angels wanted to be Him.
They couldn't stand to think that One
could be a greater Thing than them—
that's where the first great war began.
Across the plains of Paradise,
archangels came to God's defence
and Lucifer has ever since
burned in the lake of fire
that feeds the flames of his desire.
He burns in hell because he tried
to overturn the rule of God,
and God continues to bestow
nothing on the souls below,
but on the souls who dwell above,
he showers down his Special Love
and bids us that we do the same,
forever do it in His name.
You are the Hens of Hans, you see,
you are what God meant you to be:
my angels, a lesser four
than those who vanquished Lucifer,
mere Cherubs but so dear to me—
you love me so, and so does She.

The beast we know as Claws von Snout,
one of Lucifer's Lieutenants,
crawled out of the lake of fire,
an archangel still entire,
who slunk into a dragon's lair
and with a dragon mated there,

two beasts by lust transmogrified
into a monster twice their size
who kept the name of Claws von Snout
and ever since has roamed about
the desecrated Land Without.
I know that you girls know him well,
his angel wings and dragon tail,
his ripping jaws and cutlass teeth,
his scalpel claws, scale-shedding feet—
we'll be devoured by von Snout
if we should stray into Without.

The more you speak of Special Love
the more unspecial it becomes—
nothing more than ordinary,
something merely momentary.
It's better not to talk about it:
we are not van Houts without it.
And if it somehow fades away—
you may not like what I must say—
the van Houts will grow faint of heart,
a great storm from Without will start,
bring down the walls of Hans van Hout,
Within will turn into Without,
Without will turn into Within,
and everything will be a sin.
Today will cease to be today,
there will just be yesterday,
and we will have no memory
of Special Love or family.
Each of us will be unknown,
forgotten, lost, each one alone,
helpless to resist von Snout,
the dragon-angel from Without
who leads the ones who disapprove

of nothing more than Special Love.
We call them the authorities;
they interfere with families.
If we break this solemn promise,
authorities will come for us—
they will take us from each other,
mother, daughter, sister, father.
They'll separate the Clan van Hout—
we won't be six when they're about.
Each one of us will be alone,
each one of us will be just one,
each one in a different place—
there won't be one familiar face.
The Land Without has many dangers,
not just von Snout but these Strangers—
they don't know us, we don't know them,
but they're in charge of everyone.
They disapprove of everything
except the rain; they hate the sun—
they even disapprove of fun.
The food they cook is terrible;
it will make you miserable.
We must not wind up in the hands
of Strangers from the other lands,
the followers of Claws von Snout
who chews girls up and spits them out.

So let's recite the Vow of Right,
the one we end with every night:
"Special Love is just for Daddy;
it isn't for just anybody.
And Daddy loves no one but us—
he'll never love us any less
than he does now with all his heart;
we just have to do our part

to lift his spirits when he's sad—
after all, he is our dad.

"I swear to God and cross my heart,
I promise I will do my part
to hold the family van Hout
above the One that lurks Without.
All we have is one another,
mother, daughter, sister, father.
We are the ones who understand
what happened in the Netherlands,
but we will never speak of it—
it will always be a secret.
The same is true of Special Love—
it's just for us and God above.

"So once again I make my vow,
I make it here, I make it now.
I pledge my loyalty to you,
my mother and my sisters, too,
but most of all I promise Dad,
I promise that I won't be bad.
I swear myself to secrecy
as part of Glormenethalee."

WADE

One afternoon, when Rachel was at her yoga class, Fritz called and invited us to visit him and Carmen at their house in Kommetjie, about an hour southeast of Cape Town, on the Cape Flats. "Come out next week," he said. "You guys should visit us at least once while you're here. I'm inviting Bethany and Clive, too."

I told him I would ask Rachel, which I did when she got home. "I suppose we have to sooner or later," she sighed.

Clive had to teach, but Bethany said she would go with us.

They lived half an hour inland because, Bethany said from the back of the car, the coast was too bourgeois for Fritz's liking.

"That means he can't afford it," Rachel said as she drove along the winding coastal road, which was even more hazardous than the road to the Twelve Apostles. She drove slowly, much to the irritation of drivers behind her, who blew their horns incessantly until they had a chance to pass, coming within inches of us as they went by on the safer side. At the slightest nudge from them, our car would have plunged off the cliff.

"This is very relaxing," Bethany said. "It's so nice to get out and see the countryside. Living to tell about it would be a bonus, but that's just splitting hairs."

Rachel glanced at her in the rear-view mirror. "If you'd like to drive, be my guest," she said.

"I wasn't criticizing your driving, sweetie," Bethany said. "After all, you'd perish *with* me and that would be punishment enough. How are you doing, Wade? Are you feeling emasculated because you're not driving the car?"

"I'd be doing better if I'd thought of putting a couple of bags of sand in the trunk for some ballast," I said.

"The baby and I will have to do," Bethany said. "All eighty pounds of us."

We made it to Fritz and Carmen's house, a square, stucco-sided bungalow with a roof of gleaming, corrugated tin. There were a goat and a pair of chickens in the yard.

"What does Fritz do with all the money he makes from selling drugs?" Bethany said. "Does he barter with the Bantu for goats and chickens?"

The front door of the bungalow flew open and Carmen, in a T-shirt, denim shorts and flip-flops, ran down the steps, waving her arms as if signalling to Rachel from half a mile away.

"We're cleansing," she shouted. "Nothing but water and green grapes for the next six days."

"Otherwise known as the poor woman's anorexia," Bethany said. Carmen seemed not to hear her. "Hi, Carmen," Bethany shouted, but Carmen did not return her greeting or look at her.

"Don't get out of the car," Carmen said. "We're all going on a road trip." She pointed at Fritz's car, a dented, rusting Saab plastered all over with peace signs and decals bearing clenched black fists and anti-apartheid slogans. "You guys follow us."

"I'm not going down that cliff road again without taking a break," Rachel said.

"No, no, don't worry, we're going the *other* way."

The front door of the house opened again and Fritz appeared. Clad in his usual white V-necked, bluebell-bordered smock, his thick black chest hair looking like an undergarment, he jumped off the side of the steps, a khaki bag, also plastered with peace signs and black fists, slung over one shoulder.

"Well, he's just a one-man salute to peace, isn't he?" Bethany said.

Fritz waved to us and made a "follow me" motion with his hand. He and Carmen jumped in the Saab, which, despite its dilapidated look, started with a roar.

It turned out that, when Carmen said we were going the other way, she meant we were going to continue south on the treacherous coast road. "We don't have to follow them to our doom, Rachel," Bethany said as Fritz turned left. "We could just go back to the city."

"If he doesn't stop in ten minutes, I'll turn around. I think I'd rather go off a cliff than be teased by Fritz for the next six months about how I couldn't keep up with him."

"I choose death by teasing rather than by a fiery crash," Bethany said, "but I might not if I was a man who didn't know how to drive a stick shift."

"You're in fine form today, Bethany," I said. "Enjoy it. Soon, your fine form will be that of three basketballs tied together."

She laughed, and so did Rachel, until Fritz began to pull away from us in a cloud of red dust.

After about five minutes, Fritz turned right onto a steep dirt road flanked by brush so thick and high it blocked our view of everything but his car—and soon, our view of that was blocked by dust. "This is like driving in a snowstorm," I said, trying not to think of the possibility that Fritz might have to stop suddenly.

The slope began to lessen. The dust cleared. Fritz was well ahead of us now. Below stretched the bluest sea I had ever seen. A beach at least a mile long extended about half that distance from the water, where it ended in a kind of breakwater of thick brush. It looked as if no one had ever set foot on the pure white sand. It was not strewn with kelp or bordered by driftwood. It was empty of everything—people most conspicuously, given that it was superior to any beach I had seen so far in South Africa. We parked at the north end, beside the Saab. We got out and, for a few seconds, the five of us stared, wonderstruck, at the sight in front of us. "It's so beautiful, Fritz," Bethany said, as if complimenting him on one of his artisanal creations.

He nodded, pulled a Nikon camera out of his shoulder bag and, dropping to one knee, took a picture of the beach. "Fritz takes the best photographs," Carmen said.

"You'd think this place would be very popular," Bethany said.

"Too far out of the way for tourists," Fritz said, winking at me.

"What's it called?" Rachel asked.

"I have no idea," Fritz said. "Nothing, I hope. Let's go for a walk."

Rachel, Bethany and Carmen took off their flip-flops and began to wade, three abreast, in the shallow waves. "Oooh, the water is so warm," Rachel said. "We must have crossed over onto the Indian Ocean side. It's not like the water at Clifton."

"No," Fritz said, "but it's not the Indian Ocean. It's just that the water here is shallow for a long way out."

"Join us, Wade," Rachel said.

"Maybe in a bit," I said, not wanting to intrude on this rare moment of sisterly togetherness.

"The three of you hold hands and look at me," Fritz said, and they did, the three of them wading through the water. "Beautiful, just beautiful," Fritz said, snapping picture after picture as he shuffled backward along the water's edge. "Too bad Gloria's not here," he said. "She would complete the picture."

"Why don't you walk in the water with us?" Rachel called to me again.

Before I could answer, Fritz said, "A man would throw off the symmetry. Besides, Wade is almost as white as the beach."

"I burn easily," I said. "I'd have worn a hat if I knew we'd be going to the beach."

"Just go with the flow, Wade," Fritz said. "Today's flow, not the flow of history. The English won the Boer War, but the Boers got the last laugh—we got the Cape, South Africa, that is. Unfortunately, we fucked it up big time, oppressing our black brothers." He snapped a picture of me. "Wade the oppressor," he said, "plundering our women. Tsk tsk tsk. There'll be no oppression and plundering in the new South Africa. The revolution is coming. God help the oppressors then. Whites like Carmen and me, the ones who helped the blacks and didn't call them "coloureds," will be welcome in that new South Africa. The rest will be in some very deep shit."

"And you," Bethany said, "you'll be the official photographer of the revolution."

"You bet your skinny patrician ass I will," Fritz said.

"Revolution is the opiate of the intellectuals," Bethany said, flipping Marx's famous dismissal of religion and quoting from a movie

I had once seen. I wished I could think of something to say, but nothing wittily dismissive came to mind. There was something about Fritz that stifled, in everyone but Bethany, verbal response of almost any kind. Perhaps it was that I knew that nothing but a good pummelling would shut him up—and I couldn't help wondering about that knife of his, though I hadn't seen it since the day I'd first met him in St. John's.

Rachel, Bethany and Carmen waded ashore as we neared the end of the beach, the three of them still holding hands, Rachel between her two older sisters—the sight made me think of the many photographs in the albums of them as children, all dressed alike.

"We're on a mission of mercy," Carmen said as she pulled her hand from Rachel's.

"A mission of mercy?" Bethany said, shading her eyes with her hand as she looked about for signs of other people. Fritz put his camera back in his shoulder bag and began to walk away from the beach over a large sand dune. He beckoned for us to follow.

"Where are we going, Fritz?" Rachel called, glancing worriedly at me. Fritz crested the sand dune and disappeared down the other side.

"Wait for me," Carmen shouted after her husband, and ran to catch up with him.

Rachel, Bethany and I plodded upslope through the sand. When we reached the top, Fritz and Carmen were waiting for us below. We followed them along a narrow path that wound through a grove of palm trees. At the end of it, we came upon a corrugated iron wall with a gap in the middle that afforded us a clear view of what might have been a long-deserted black township—there wasn't a soul in sight.

"No, no, no, no," Bethany said. "This is not a good idea."

"Believe me," Fritz said, "they already know we're here. They've seen us coming for quite a while. That's why they're all indoors or hiding somewhere. That and the heat."

"What's up, Fritz?" I said.

"What's up?" Fritz grinned at Carmen, who loudly laughed. "What's up is that, if not for me, you would have had the piss beaten out of you by now, and the girls, well, I think you know what would have happened to them."

"We should get the fuck out of here right now," Bethany said.

"Everything will be just fine as long as no one runs or cries," Fritz said, looking at me. "Did you hear me, Wade? No running, no crying."

"Fuck off, Fritz," I said, peering through the gap in the wall behind him. A small yellow dog watched us, sitting on its hind legs in the middle of the narrow road that ran between two rows of windowless tin houses.

Fritz patted his shoulder bag. "I have goodies to distribute," he said.

"Fritz is the Johnny Appleseed of the revolution," Carmen said, looking expectantly at Fritz, who didn't acknowledge her.

"No one will bother you as long as you stay put," he said. "They know me here. I come here at this time of day once, sometimes twice, a week."

He went through the gate-like gap and was gone from sight. Carmen sat on the sand and patted it with her hand to suggest that we all do the same. "No wonder there's no one on the beach," I said.

"It's fine," Carmen said. "I wait here by myself sometimes and nothing ever happens. Sit down. Time for a toke, I think." She fished in the back pocket of her jeans, withdrew a crumpled joint and lit it with a plastic cigarette lighter she took from the pocket of her top. She took a long drag, then held the joint toward us. Getting no takers, she shrugged and put the joint back in her mouth. "I'm going to get so stoned if you guys don't help me smoke this joint. Especially since I've had nothing but green grapes and water for days. Cleansing is good for you, it really is, but I'd just as soon sleep through it."

I shot Rachel a questioning look. "I think we're okay," she said. "If we turn back now, we might provoke them."

"Jesus," Carmen said. "*Provoke them?* They're not dogs. Everyone's a liberal in South Africa until they wind up in a place like this."

"I don't think everyone's a liberal in South Africa," Bethany said. "I think we might be related to a few non-liberals. And that leaves out the other ninety-nine per cent of the white population. Meanwhile, I think I'll just stroll back along the beach."

"You won't make it halfway to the cars," Carmen said. "Not by yourself. Too tempting. They leave me alone because they know that, if they don't, Fritz won't come back. No one will come back. But you—well, they don't know who you are to Fritz. They don't know you're his sister-in-law. Some of them might not care because they're wrecked enough already. I'd stay put if I were you. Sends them a message. If you don't seem to be afraid, you must be someone important to Fritz, or just important, period, someone who's used to these missions of mercy. No one sells to them for less than Fritz does. He practically gives the dagga away. So no one fucks with him."

We sat on the ground in the shade of the palm trees, waiting for Fritz to return. Every now and then, I looked through the gap in the iron fence. The township seemed like some sort of temporary workers' camp. In front of each of the metal shacks was a circle of scorched stones, makeshift fireplaces. Clotheslines from which brightly coloured clothing hung sagged almost to the ground, the clothes hanging limp because the wall blocked the ocean breeze.

A few small boys clad only in shorts eventually appeared at the opening to look at us, their wide eyes full of fear and curiosity. Rachel tentatively waved and they disappeared for a second behind the wall, reappearing one by one.

Then an old man arrived at what I had come to think of as the gate. He was barefoot, wearing slacks so smeared with dust I couldn't tell their colour. He was shirtless but wore a tattered black sports jacket and a grey stocking cap beneath a dented fedora. He looked nattily dishevelled. He smiled and raised his hat to us. Carmen waved and held up what was left of the joint. One hand in the pocket of his slacks, he gingerly made his way to her, took the joint, raised it to his mouth and drew so deeply from it he had to let it drop before it burned his fingers. "I have another one," Carmen said, standing up and reaching into the back pocket of her shorts again.

A middle-aged black woman wearing an orange head scarf, a green blouse and a light-blue sarong came out through the gate. "Get back inside, old man," she said, pointing the way she had come. The rest of us got to our feet.

"No, Seri, I will not go back inside," the man said. "I am not a child who must listen to a woman."

She turned to face us. Every word she spoke she punctuated with a chopping motion of her index finger. "Why are you sitting here and watching us like this?"

"We're waiting for Fritz," Carmen said.

"You," the woman said. "You must not give this old man drugs. He is my father. What would you think if I came to where you live and gave drugs to your father?"

Carmen laughed. "I'd think it was great."

"Do not laugh at me, madam. I warn you, do not laugh. I have seen you here before with this man called Fritz. You are making nothing but trouble, the two of you."

"Well, sorr*eeee*," Carmen said, "but I think you could use something to loosen that cork you have stuck up your ass."

"Do not disrespect me. I do not use drugs."

"Well, maybe you should."

"*Carmen*," Rachel said.

"Yes, Carmen," Bethany said, "settle down."

"The three of you are sisters. You have the same eyes. Three sisters selling drugs and giving them to old men."

"My sisters don't even use drugs unless they get them from a doctor," Carmen said. She pointed at me. "He's never smoked a cigarette, as far as I know. My sisters used to be cool—well, except for one, but she's not here—but not anymore."

The woman shook her finger at her. "The last thing we need here are drugs. They make people lazy and stupid. We stay home from work and lose our jobs. Our children fall asleep in school, *if* they go to school. No one takes care of the little ones. I would find a way to get rid of this Fritz, but, if I did, someone would get rid of me and another Fritz would soon show up." She pointed at the township. "Someone from in there would get rid of me, or someone from out here. We turn on each other because of these drugs and all of you just walk away. I was a teacher, and now I am still teaching but I get no pay. That man, Fritz, should not have brought you here, and he should not have left you alone. He is a bad man and he is a fool."

"Fuck off," Carmen said. "I've been here dozens of times and nothing has ever happened until today."

"Do not swear at me, young lady," the woman said. "I am trying to help you. Some young men who have no jobs, no wives and no children are here. Young men, not old men like my father here. They are sleeping, maybe. If they come out and speak to you, don't say a word."

"She's bullshitting," Carmen said to us.

"Shut up," Rachel said.

"If the young men come out, don't run," the woman said.

"Don't run," Carmen said in the voice of a whiny child. "Don't shout, don't cry. The big bad black men will get you. They can smell fear and will chase you if you run."

"I would like to see that one run," the old man said, pointing at Rachel. "She is very beautiful. They are all very beautiful. I would like to see them run."

"I'll run for you," Carmen said.

"You do not know what you are saying," the woman admonished her. "We are not allowed in your cities and towns and homes except to work for you for next to nothing. Now here you are in our home, but you haven't come to work for us. You have come without asking our permission. You've come without cards like the ones we must carry when we are in your neighbourhoods. I am trying to help you. I am trying to keep you out of bad trouble. You are a foolish, stupid woman."

Two young men showed in the gateway. Shirtless, they wore shorts and sneaker boots without laces. "They have nothing worth taking," the woman said to them, her tone much softer.

The old man laughed and raised three fingers in the air. "Three young white women. I think they have something worth taking."

"And you are too old to take it," the woman said. She looked at Rachel. "Go away now. Take your sisters." She looked at me. "Go away. Take these girls with you. If you provoke these boys, you will not see Fritz again. Go away, now. There is nothing here for you."

Rachel and Bethany did not look at the young men but at the ground. *I* looked at them and they stared back at me as if in disbelief at how out of place I was. They might have been in their late teens or early twenties and stood there in silence, appraising me.

"They only came out because you started shouting at us," Carmen said to the woman. She took another joint out of her pocket and held it out to the two men in the gateway. "Want some, fellas?"

Their eyes widened and they smiled. "Oh yes, miss," one of them said.

"I will take it to them," the woman said, plucking the joint from Carmen's fingers as she spat on the ground at Carmen's feet. She gave the joint to one of the young men, and the two of them went back inside. Four others soon took their place in the gap in the wall.

The woman came back to us, holding her sarong clear of the ground. "You are not from here. I can tell by your voices."

"Yes, we are," Carmen said. "Me, her, her and Fritz, we were born here." She pointed at me. "He's the visitor. But we all grew up in Canada, except for Fritz."

"So you have come to visit the continent that your elders stole from us. Your parents are from here?"

"One of them is. Lady, I get it. I'm on your side. I know you got ripped off. I know about the slave ships and all that. Who doesn't? You're lucky you didn't wind up in the States. I know that Africa was hunky-dory before the white man came. I'm just saying it's not my fault where I was born. And I'd like to make up for what's been done. I'd like to do my own little bit of reparation. I'm here to help you."

"God does not help those who help themselves to what belongs to others."

"I'm not *God. Jesus*. I'm not Jesus, either."

The woman spat on the ground again.

"Fucking cunt," Carmen said as the woman turned around and walked toward the young men, who obeyed her when she motioned them inside the gate. The old man blew Carmen a kiss and followed his daughter.

"Bitch," Carmen hissed. "Maybe I'll call the cops."

"Shut up," Rachel said. "Not another word."

Fritz came through the gap in the fence. Walking at a steady pace, he went straight past us without looking at us. "Time to roll," he said.

He sounded nervous. We followed him. "The natives are always restless when I leave. Not everyone gets what they want and some get nothing. Don't look back. And don't hurry. Hopefully, they'll just watch us until we're too close to the cars for them to catch us."

"Did something happen?" Carmen said. "Did that woman say something about us?"

"They tried to bargain me down even though I'm practically giving it away. I used the word *polisie* a lot. It was one of those days."

"I bet that woman—"

"Never mind that woman," Fritz said, picking up the pace in spite of having warned us not to.

"What the fuck did you bring us here for?" Rachel said, trying to keep up with him.

"Who else makes life easier for them?" Fritz said. "How would you like to live like that with nothing to take the edge off? No electricity, no toilets, no running water, almost no money?"

"I asked you a question, Fritz," Rachel said.

"I sell them whatever I can get my hands on," Fritz said, breathing rapidly. "It's cheap because it's grown or made right here at home. The cops know what I'm up to but they don't bother me. The more wrecked the kaffirs are the better, as far as they're concerned. As far as most whites are concerned, especially the government. But I can't change all that. I can only do so much. It's less risky than selling to the whites—though they'd pay a lot more. The government doesn't want the whites strung out. They want to keep them on their toes so they can hold all of this craziness together. Whites buying drugs is bad for the economy. Money spent on drugs is money not spent on South African goods and services, not taxed, not invested in South Africa. Lower worker productivity, less efficiency, the loosening of social ties and family ties—you can't afford that when you're going it alone in the world."

"Fritz," Rachel said, "you're on something and it isn't dagga. Cocaine? Speed?"

"I've brought other people here," Fritz said, "and nothing has ever happened. Nothing would have happened if not for that woman. She stirred up a lot of grumbling with all her shouting." He glanced over his shoulder at Carmen. "And you, you should know to keep your cool by now."

"She started it," Carmen said. "Uppity bitch."

She ran down to the ocean's edge and stepped into the water.

"No frolicking in the surf on the return trip," Fritz said. "They already took my camera."

"*Fuckers*," Carmen said.

"Just walk, okay, everyone just walk."

"*Uppity bitch*," Bethany said. "That's a nice liberal expression."

"Fuck off, Bethany," Carmen said.

"Yes, Bethany," Fritz said. "The only difference between you and them is that your drugs are paid for by your parents."

"Well, soon I'll be getting them from a chemist paid by Clive," Bethany said. "So you think you're their therapist and their chemist."

"You bet I am. If it wasn't for me, they'd be sniffing glue and drinking aftershave."

"You're a true humanitarian, Fritz," Rachel said.

"That's right, baby sister."

"The woman that you said stirred everything up *lives* here. Someone who lives here was bound to complain about you sooner or later. You should have told us where you and Carmen were going."

"If you're so concerned for that woman," Fritz said, "go back and introduce yourself. I bet you didn't think to do that, did you? We came because we thought a great writer from Canada like Wade would like to see what a township looked like. I thought you and Bethany would too. But no more reality road trips from now on for third sister, baby sister and her boyfriend."

"It will take a lot more than green grapes and water to cleanse you," Rachel said.

"Baby sister—"

"Shut your trap, Fritz," I said from just behind him. "Shut your trap and keep it shut until we reach the cars."

I didn't care if he pulled that knife of his, because I knew that, if we fought, I would win no matter at what cost to him or me. I would win because I had made up my mind to get away from this nightmare of a country as soon as I could convince Rachel that Bethany no longer needed her. I had had enough of all of it. I was overheated, thirsty and fed up with the beauty of the beach, the gentle surf, the treacherous perfection of the sea and sky, and the beguiling breeze.

We followed the Saab up the slope, Rachel wrestling with the gear-shift as the car lurched, stopped, skidded sideways in the gravel. We stalled out several times as Fritz pulled away from us, navigated around potholes and tree stumps that Rachel couldn't see until the last second in the dust Fritz's car kicked up; she had to brake so suddenly that we kept on slipping back as if we might slide all the way to the beach.

"He is definitely on *something*," Rachel said.

Fritz reached the top of the side road, turned left onto the coastal road and drove away, rear tires screeching on the pavement.

"Bastard," Rachel said. "He just took off."

"My fault," I said. "I picked the wrong time to piss him off."

She pressed the gas pedal harder as she tried to shift gears, and the engine stalled. "This would not be a good place to break down or get a flat," she said as she restarted the car.

"Fritz gets the last laugh," Bethany said, laughing.

"Very funny," Rachel said.

"Or I get the last laugh," Bethany said. "I'm laughing, right? Am I, Wade, am I laughing?" She poked my shoulder.

Rachel looked back at her. "You *didn't*," she said. "Bethany, tell me you didn't."

"I think I did, I think I did. I think I took two tabs."

"When?" Rachel said.

I turned and looked at Bethany, who doubled over, laughing, her hair obscuring her face.

"Fucking Carmen," Rachel said. "She knows you're pregnant. She knows you're on those pills."

I began to face forward again when, out of the corner of my eye, I saw what might have been the entire population of the township making its way toward us on the beach, led by a group of shirtless, barefoot young men, their running form so perfect that, under any other circumstances, I would have admired it. "Jesus," I said. "Look."

"Look, look, look," Bethany said, shaking her head from side to side. "They're giving us a royal send-off."

"Goddamn it," Rachel said, stamping the clutch and shifting into low, flooring the gas to no effect. "Please," she said.

"What's wrong?" Bethany looked out her window. "What's *that*? Something's coming. It looks like a giant spider doing somersaults." She banged her forehead against the window. "Whoops," she said. "That hurt." She laughed. "Better get out of the way, Raitchie, or that thing will run right over us."

"I'm trying," Rachel said.

The front-runners, their torsos glistening in the late-afternoon sunlight, were a couple of hundred yards away.

"It's going to run us right over," Bethany said. "I think it's a train or something, Rachel, or maybe a bus, a big black bus."

Suddenly, she was out of the car and in front of us, half running, half crawling up the road.

"Go get her," Rachel said. I struggled to open the door, wondering how Bethany had managed to open hers so quickly with the car at such an angle.

Bethany had lost both her flip-flops. By the time I got to her, there was blood on her feet and hands and on her face. She patted her halter top and denim shorts as if ants were crawling all over her. "Get off the road, Rachel!" she screamed, looking back. When she saw me, she opened her mouth wide but no sound came out.

"Bethany, come back to the car," I said. She kept crawling but I caught her, grabbing her upper arms.

"Let go, let go," she said, kicking me with her bare feet. I put one arm around her back, the other under her thighs and picked her up as she struck me in the face with her fists. "Don't leave my flip-flops. I love my flip-flops. They're so blue. See how blue they are?"

I started back toward the car. The young men, streaming sweat, wide-eyed and smiling, had made it to the bottom of the road. They stopped there, ten or so of them, and looked up at me and Bethany, then back at the others who were hurrying toward them, gesticulating, shouting.

The woman who had argued with Carmen was leading the second group. I looked at Rachel, who was in tears, still trying to get the car to move. A kind of calm came over me—a feeling of resignation or indifference—even as Bethany continued to struggle in my arms.

Rachel got out of the car and stood by the driver's door, looking down at the group of young men. Bethany stopped struggling and rested her head against my chest. "Wade's heart sounds like a gun," she said. "Bam, bam, bam."

The woman in the orange head scarf reached the bottom of the hill, put her hands on her hips, looked up at us and shook her head in seeming disbelief.

"Is the young woman hurt?" she called.

"Just cuts on her hands and feet," Bethany said meekly, but then she began to laugh uncontrollably. "There's a gun going off in there," she said, tapping my chest.

"There's no gun," I called. "She's upset."

"I know what she is," the woman said. "Among other things, she is pregnant. I saw it in her face. Put her in the car and get into the back seat with her." She pointed at Rachel. "You, get back behind the wheel. These boys will push you up the hill. You are all fools. All fools. You don't know how big a bunch of fools you are."

We did as she said. I sat in the back, holding Bethany. Rachel got behind the wheel and eased the car into gear.

"Push them, push them," the woman shouted.

Soon, surrounded on the back and the sides by the young men, all of whom were laughing, the car began to move and Rachel managed to get it started. "Thank God," she said.

We pulled away from the young men. At the top of the hill, Rachel blew the horn in appreciation but didn't slow down or stop. We drove away while some of our rescuers waved and others raised their fists in triumph.

"She's not going home to Mom and Dad like this," Rachel said.

"She needs to see a doctor anyway," I said. "Her hands and feet are cut up pretty bad from the stones and thorns on the hill. I hope there's no blood coming from anywhere else. Those tabs of acid—will they hurt the baby?"

"I don't know. Mixed with her pills, they might. I should have warned Carmen not to give her anything."

"How long will the acid last?"

"Twelve hours, maybe more if she really did take two. She's so quiet now. I've seen her on acid before. This is not how she usually acts."

"Because of the other pills?"

"*Maybe*. I don't even know what kind of drugs they are. She took one before we left and Mom gave her one to take later. I have a feeling that she took that, too. I hope she hasn't overdosed. I don't like how quiet she is."

"So we bring her to the hospital—and then what?"

"Well, she's not going home while she's still stoned on acid, even if the hospital says it's okay. When we get to Cape Town, I'll call Mom and Dad and tell them that she wants to spend the night with us. They'll buy it. Even if they don't, they'll pretend to."

By the time we got to Groote Schuur, Bethany seemed to be unconscious, but she was breathing evenly. I carried her into emergency as blood dripped from her hands and feet. The admissions nurse saw us and grabbed her phone. We were halfway to her desk when medical staff came running at us from all directions.

We waited for ten hours in the emergency waiting room, much of which I spent more or less asleep while Rachel read *Het Achterhuis* and wrote in her diary at such a frenzied pace that people stared at her as they went by. Finally, a nurse took us to Bethany's doctor, who looked not much older than me.

"What happened?" he said. As we told him what we knew, he stared at us, his hands clasped behind his head as he leaned back in his chair. "She's on lithium, antipsychotics and tranquilizers, and you give her LSD, a psychosis-inducing drug?" he said. "She's lucky to be alive, given how much LSD she took. Not two tabs. More like ten."

"We didn't give her anything," Rachel said. "Someone else did. It doesn't matter who."

"You drove the car. There are ways of getting an invalid out of the house that don't involve drug pushers and tours of black townships."

"I'm sorry," Rachel said. The doctor nodded and glared at me as if I was the person responsible.

"God knows why, but she hasn't had a miscarriage," he said. "She's been inoculated for tetanus and typhus because of the lacerations on her hands and feet. She's come down from the LSD. She's telling us what she told us before and then retracted. Making accusations. I don't believe her, but—"

"You still think she believes what she's saying?"

"I think she's still psychotic."

"Why don't you believe her?"

He shook his head. "Too complicated to go into. I didn't want to discharge her before, but I was overruled. Not this time. My older colleagues agree with me that she's likely suicidal, so she's staying here unless someone reliable comes forward into whose care we can discharge her. That clearly isn't you two. And given her accusations, it isn't her parents. It isn't her fiancé and his parents, either, because they're too close to the van Houts."

He pointed at Rachel. "She's been asking to see you. Just you. Are you up to it? You look exhausted. More so than him." He nodded at me.

"I'm fine," Rachel said. "I do want to see her. But I have to phone my parents and her fiancé and tell them *something*." He nodded.

Rachel phoned her parents and Clive and told them that Bethany had readmitted herself and that the doctors recommended that she have no visitors until she said she was ready for them. When she got off the phone, she told me that Clive had asked no questions. "In fact, he didn't say much more than hello and goodbye. And my parents—Dad said, 'Very well,' and passed the phone to Mom. And Mom said, 'I'm sure the doctors know best.'"

"Does *anything* get them upset?"

"For now, let's concentrate on Bethany. I'll come get you after I see her. I'll tell the doctor she said it was okay."

Rachel took me to her about an hour later—it was about seven in the morning. Bethany lay in the hospital bed, eyes closed. Her hands were bandaged and lay limply on the blankets. When she opened her eyes and saw me, she shrugged. "Welcome to my second home."

She sat up in bed with the help of a nurse. I told her I was sorry that the day had turned out the way it had. "Don't be sorry," she said, glancing at Rachel. "I'm the one who took the acid. I pulled the two of you into all of this. I spilled the beans on Dad and let a lot of other people clean them up. And then I changed my mind and expected everyone to understand. Well, now I'm changing it back, for good. Dad did what I said he did, and Mom not only knew all along, she helped him, shielded him, made excuses for him. She was, she is, his one-woman alibi. Anyway, I want out of their house and out of my engagement. If I marry Clive, I will die. If I don't marry him, he won't die. He'll be pretty broken up, but he won't die. I want this baby. I want out of daughterhood. So I've asked Gloria and Max if I can live in their house when I'm released, and they've said yes."

"You said before that they'd side with your mom and dad," I said.

"They *are* siding with Mom and Dad. But the doctor spoke to Gloria and convinced her that, whatever the truth is, it's better that I not be around our parents, at least for now. Once they take me in—well, I'm not leaving there until they kick me out. Maybe they won't. It might not be so bad, having my baby in the Porn Palace of the Twelve Apostles."

"How do you know all those other things you told Gloria about Dad?" Rachel asked.

"I don't blame Gloria for telling you about that," she said. "Remember, Clive and I have been corresponding since 1975. He told me things he overheard his parents say. You'd think that even Clive would have more sense than to repeat such things in a letter that Mom and Dad might intercept or find in my room, but, well, Clive was even more Clive-like back then. Peter drinks when he's at home, when it's just the three of them. Clive says he's a closet alcoholic. When he drinks, he goes on about anything and everything. I don't think Clive told anyone but me. In his letters, he tried to make out that it was funny that Dad told so many lies to get ahead. Peter said Dad was never really in the Dutch Resistance. And Dad got into trouble with some first-year student, a girl at the University of Cape Town. I never got the rights of it, but the university paid the student's family to hush things up and made a deal with Dad that, if he left without a fuss, they would recommend him to another institution in another Commonwealth country. And that, my dears, is how we all came to move to Canada. Oh, and Clive said that Dad plagiarized parts of his master's thesis. He stole them from a graduate student and bragged about it to Peter when they met up in Amsterdam one year."

I looked at Rachel, whose expression was blank, eyes downcast.

"Do you still have any of Clive's letters?" I said.

"Nooo," Bethany said. "I destroyed them lest they fall into the wrong hands. My word is not good enough for you?"

I shrugged. I suspected that she was telling us half of what Clive had told her and that he had made up or misremembered half of that.

"Anyway, Doc says he'll release me into Gloria's care the day after tomorrow—he says he likes the sound of me living with a sister who has no vices. I didn't touch that one. I am a mess, and it's going to be a while before I'm not a mess. I hate being so helpless, so needy and dependent. So melodramatic. I hated having to say to Gloria that, without her help, I'd die."

"You can't keep forcing people to do things by threatening to kill yourself, explicitly or otherwise," I said.

"I wish I was as virtuous as you think you are, Wade, or as strong as Rachel. Call it self-pity if you want, but I think I've been through a lot more than the two of you. So, here we are—I'm the one who's in the nuthouse. Gloria and Carmen and Rachel—I don't know about them. Maybe Dad did just pick on me. Easier to keep a lid on one daughter than on four? Lucky me. I don't know what will become of them, Carmen especially. No one in South Africa is free. No one thinks it matters if you tell the truth, or even if you know the truth. The truth is whatever it suits you to pretend it is, whatever you can get away with pretending it is. I know I'm the pot calling the kettle black. And yet I plan to live here for my baby's sake, because Max has money and I haven't got a cent. Isn't that heroic? Clive and Peter and Theresa won't like me much. Mom and Dad, well, it's not like I haven't accused them in the past, to no effect. I'd disown them if I could, turn my back on them forever, but nothing less than a restraining order would stop them from keeping up appearances. Going forward, I'll just have to make sure that I'm never alone with him. When we're alone, I can't say no to him. That's a fact that almost no one understands, so I don't expect you to."

I shook my head in disbelief. "How could you stand to be in his company, even with other people around?"

"Don't judge me, Wade," Bethany said. "Clean Wade, from the pure white north. Unlike you, I don't have a lot of options."

"You need to rest, Bethany," Rachel said. "We all do. You might change your mind about some things when you're feeling better."

"I want to confront them. Mom and Dad. I want to confront them."

It was mid-evening and Rachel had just finished writing in her diary. She'd sat sideways on the sofa for two hours, writing and then crossing out what she wrote until her pen tore the paper to pieces. She dropped her notebook onto the floor. "All these accusations and I've never looked Dad in the eye and asked him if they were true. Or Mom. None of us have. Bethany spoke to them on the phone. And retracted on the phone. I'll write to them, get it all down on paper, and then we'll make a date to go see them. I'll tell them about the beach and what Bethany told us when she was in hospital. I have to do this or I'll always wish I had. I'll write to them and dare them to meet me face to face. If I tried to say *everything* in person, they'd interrupt me and I'd get nothing said. Mom will tell Dad not to agree to it, but he will—I know he will. He won't want it to look like he backed down from me."

I was greatly taken with the idea of confronting the van Houts at last, of putting aside all delicacy and discretion and having it out with them.

A few days later, we met them in the house on Liesbeek Road. We knocked but there was no answer, so we let ourselves in. It was four in the afternoon. Hans and Myra were in the front room, standing side by side, dressed as if they were about to leave for some special occasion, Hans in a new-looking grey suit, white shirt and blue tie, his black shoes gleaming, Myra in a long, green, belted dress and high heels, her short, thick hair arranged just so.

"Right, then," Hans said, clapping his hands, then putting them in the pockets of his slacks. He looked at Rachel. "So. So you have something to say to me?"

"I said everything I had to say in the letter," Rachel said. "You should have something to say to me."

"This is absurd, Rachel," Myra said. "Taking LSD while she's pregnant—no wonder Bethany is making more empty accusations. She'll marry Clive and have her baby, and the three of them, with everyone's help, will do the best they can." She tilted her head and smiled as if to say she understood Rachel's misplaced loyalty to her older sister and even admired her for it, but there were limits.

"She is very ill," Hans said.

"All of your daughters are ill," Rachel said. "Look at Gloria. Married four times by the age of twenty-five. Carmen is a heroin addict. Bethany is anorexic, depressed and suicidal. I'm writing and reading myself to death."

"But, Rachel," Myra said, "those are all different things. We can't be to blame for *all* of them."

"Why not? What does it matter that they're different? What does that have to do with anything? Just because Dad might have done the same things to all of us doesn't mean we should all react the same way."

"I did nothing to you," Hans said, pointing at her. "You were a virgin until you met this fellow. You told your mother. Bethany says it started when she was a toddler. Do you think I have nothing between my legs?" He grabbed his crotch with one hand.

"You—" I started, but he shouted at me. "You have no say in this. You are not part of this family."

"There are many other things you could have done to us," Rachel said, "things that leave no mark of the physical kind."

"*Might* have done," Hans said. "*Could* have done. Ridiculous. I have no idea what sort of filth you mean. Anyone *might* have done anything. As for Gloria, Carmen and Bethany, when it comes to virginity, we know how they lost theirs, because, like you, they told their mother about it."

Myra nodded.

"You're acting like a selfish and ungrateful daughter," Hans said.

Rachel took two steps toward her father. "The Resistance," she said. "You were never in the Resistance. You were never a war hero. The university got rid of you to save its reputation. You molested that student and used portions of student papers in your thesis. You got into so much trouble that, at the age of forty-three, you had to uproot us all and take us to another country. What should I be grateful for?"

"What proof do you have of any of this?"

"Clive told her things that Peter said—"

"Third-hand gossip. I will not be held responsible for what I am accused of by mentally unstable young women and the limp-wristed son of a weekend drunkard like Peter DeVries."

"Have you lied for so long, both of you, that you don't know how to tell the truth about anything? Mom, why did you always tell us not to mention the Resistance when Dad is around because it would only bring back unbearable memories of the girls our age that he tried to save but couldn't, girls like me and Gloria and Carmen and Bethany that he risked his life for, girls like Anne Frank—"

"Anne Frank?" Hans said, forcing a laugh. "She never existed. That diary that you're obsessed with is a forgery. Propaganda. The Jews, the goddamn Jews, made her up so that people would feel as sorry for them as they feel for themselves, the gentle, peace-loving, money-grubbing Jews. Look at him, your boyfriend, *look* at him and tell him that I laid a hand on you. LOOK AT HIM AND TELL HIM WHAT I DID TO YOU, TO *YOU*."

Tears streamed down Rachel's cheeks but she didn't look at me. She stared at her father.

"There, you see? You can't tell him because there's nothing to tell. I never touched my daughters, but what if I had? You are my daughters. I can do anything I want with you."

I lunged for him but Rachel grabbed my arm. "*I* have to do this," she said. "He *wants* to provoke you. Then it will seem like you were in the wrong."

I shook free of her but stayed put.

"Mom," Rachel said. "Please tell the truth. Please. Is any of what Bethany is saying true?"

"We speak with one voice," Myra said, taking Hans by the hand.

"I could easily hide behind an excuse," Hans said. "I could say, 'What was I supposed to do? Four young women parading naked around the house.' I suppose your boyfriend thinks he wouldn't be tempted. I've seen the way he looks at Gloria. He'd be tempted. Tits and ass everywhere I looked. But I didn't lay a hand on a single one of you. No one gives you credit for crimes you might have done but didn't do." He pointed at me. "You can't stand the idea that anyone had her but you. That's what this is all about."

"Or maybe," I said, "you can't stand the idea that anyone had your daughters but *you*?"

"Your proof?" he said. When I didn't answer, he laughed. "Now look," Hans said, turning to Rachel. "I've answered all your questions. We'll forget this ever happened. So. Where are we going for dinner?"

"Dinner?" Rachel said. "Where are we going for *dinner*?"

I shook my head in disbelief.

"You have planted lies in her head," Hans said, pointing at me. "She believes everything you say. She thinks you're the only man on the planet with a penis. She wouldn't believe Bethany's lies if not for you, or put any store by what Peter says when he's drunk, or should I say, what Clive claims Peter says when he's drunk. You've poisoned her mind against us. If what Bethany says is true, why haven't Gloria or Carmen accused me of something?"

"Maybe they will," I said.

"Bethany will change her mind again," Hans said.

Myra nodded. "Time will prove us right. Bethany will come back to us and so will you. Soon, I'm sure. You both value family above all else. Clive, the poor dear, will take her back again. Her baby won't be fatherless or grow up without grandparents."

"I could have given up and died like so many others did during the war," Hans said to Rachel. "You owe your life to me. I ask again, who is Anne Frank to you? Have you ever met anyone who met Anne Frank? You spend your time writing in a language no one else can read, making up imaginary characters like her. You prefer that to the truth. Death is nothing when it happens in a book. Wait until you meet it face to face."

He pointed again at me. "I betrayed Anne Frank, boy. I phoned the Gestapo. I got sixty guilders for those Jews, seven and a half for each one. *I* did it. Do you believe me?"

"No, I don't believe you. I don't believe a word you say."

"Look at *her*. *She* believes me."

Rachel fled the house, sobbing. I ran after her, through the front door, which she had left open. She was already in the car. I just had time enough to climb in before she floored it in reverse, the rear tires spinning on the gravel, the Citroën barely missing the van Houts' front steps and the rusting Ford Cortina, which she sprayed with stones.

"Rachel, slow down," I said as she dodged the giant yellow tree fern, working the wheel as if she thought her father might come running after her at any second. She pulled out of the driveway and onto Liesbeek Road. "He was only baiting you about Anne Frank. Surely you know that."

"I guess that visit wasn't such a good idea," she said, her tone eerily flat.

"Slow *down*," I said.

She did, and also took a deep breath as if to slow her body down. "If he had even one family member who was still alive," she said. "But of course, he doesn't, except for some old aunts and an uncle who have always lived in Leiden and have no idea what he did in Amsterdam during the war."

"You don't need someone else to tell you that your father is an ineffectual accounting professor—assistant professor—who has spent his adult life trying to build himself up in the eyes of the world. It was mean and petty of him to pick on Anne Frank, but I don't think he's ever had the nerve to actually *do* anything except tattle to the dean about his colleagues."

"Maybe he tattled on the Franks."

"Please, please don't get caught up in your father's nonsense."

"What if it's not nonsense?" she whispered as if she was alone in the car. She was no longer crying but looked indescribably sad.

When we got home, she immediately immersed herself in her diary, scribbling at a frantic pace. A couple of hours later, she set it aside at last and, sitting at the kitchen table with me while I nursed a beer, began to speak as if she was picking up from where she left off writing.

"The informer had to be someone who had reason to suspect that Jews were being harboured at Prinsengracht 263."

"Rachel, it's ridiculous to think that your father—"

"Why? Why is it ridiculous? Because he's a mere man who has lived in a place as far removed from Amsterdam as Newfoundland? A couple of months ago, he told us at dinner that he collaborated with the Nazis. He took it all back, but why would he say it in the first place?"

"I've already told you what I think. He only confesses to things that he didn't do."

"The war didn't happen in the movies or on TV. It happened in places just as ordinary as St. John's to people just as ordinary as your family. You've never been to Amsterdam."

"I think it's time we went back to what *I* call home," I said.

"Yes," Rachel said. "It is."

"Thank God. I thought you'd want to stay for Bethany."

"No. I've had enough. We should go home through Amsterdam and visit the Secret Annex."

"*Jesus Christ*. Why? Do you think you can find out if your father betrayed Anne Frank by going there? Do all the secrets of the van Houts, if there even are any, lead back to Anne Frank?"

"I've never been there. I want to go there at least once."

"All right, then. Fine. I don't care what route we take or what we do along the way as long as we go home."

A week later, unable to sleep, I got up and was reading when the phone rang on the table beside my chair. I answered it as quickly as I could, hoping to keep it from waking Rachel, who, after hours spent writing in her diary, had finally gone to bed.

It was Max. His voice quavering, he said, "Wade, I'm afraid I have some very bad news."

By mid-morning, that news was all over Cape Town, in the papers and on the radio and on TV. A middle-aged couple who lived in the City Bowl neighbourhood had been murdered in their home by someone who was still at large. The killer, or killers, let themselves into the unlocked house on Liesbeek Road—their maid was asleep in the shed at the back of their garden—crept upstairs, where Myra and Hans van Hout were sleeping, and shot each of them once in the head. It did not appear to have been a botched robbery, since nothing had been stolen or disturbed.

I was still talking to Max, fighting to control my own voice, when Rachel came out of the bedroom in her nightshirt and grabbed the phone from me.

"Max, what's *happened*?" she said. A few seconds later, she dropped the receiver, which I caught before it hit the floor. She covered her face with her hands. I hung up the phone and led her to the sofa, where we sat side by side.

"It can't be true," she said, her voice muffled by her hands, her head bowed. Tears seeped between her fingers and dripped onto the floor. "It can't be true, it can't. Mom was supposed to be spending the weekend at the Star of the Sea Convent School reunion with Theresa DeVries."

"Theresa went by the house late in the afternoon to pick her up. But your mother said that Hans's ulcers had been acting up badly and it looked as if he might have to go to hospital. She said she felt she couldn't leave him alone. So Theresa went to the reunion by herself."

I tried to take Rachel in my arms but she was rigid. She dropped her hands. Lips quivering, she said, "I knew it was possible, after that argument, that I would never see them again. I almost hoped I wouldn't. But I would never wish for something like this—*never* . . ." Her voice trailed off. Tears trickled down her cheeks. "My God. A few days ago we argued and now they're *gone*? What's happening? In spite of everything he said, I thought that, someday, he might own up to the truth, whatever it was. I thought *she* might. I thought that, sooner or later, there'd be some kind of truce. I know it makes no sense, but it almost feels like they committed suicide."

"I don't know what to say," I stammered.

"How is Bethany?" Rachel said. "And Gloria? What about Carmen? Does she know?"

"Carmen knows. Max said he spoke to Fritz. Bethany . . . Max said she's in pretty rough shape. They want to take her to hospital to be assessed, but she refuses to go. Gloria . . . I don't know. He didn't mention her."

Max had told me that Nora and the van Houts' neighbours hadn't heard any shots. Nora was woken by the sound of the front door banging shut. She heard a car drive off, tires spinning in the gravel beside the tree fern—just as those of the Citroën had done when we drove away from the house the last time. Terrified, Nora stayed in her shed for half an hour. Afraid to go into the house by herself, she eventually went to one of the next-door neighbours and told them what she'd heard. The husband went to check, saw that the front door was open and called the police, who, unsure if an intruder was still inside, entered with guns drawn. After finding Myra and Hans, they went to the neighbour's house and interviewed Nora, who gave them the only family phone number she knew, Gloria's. The police used a reverse directory to find Gloria's address and drove to the house to tell them what had happened. And to interview both of them.

"They want to interview all the children and their spouses," Max had said. "We gave them your number and address. They said it's just standard procedure. They said to tell you to sit tight. They'll be there as soon as they can. "I've also called Peter and Theresa and Clive. The police are going to speak to them as well." I repeated this to Rachel.

"One thing before the police get here," Rachel said to me, wiping her eyes, which were puffy and swollen. "If they can't find out who did it, they will put the blame on Nora or her husband or God knows who, as long as they're not white."

The two inspectors arrived at our door just after eight that morning. Rachel and I had stayed up all night, me watching Rachel most of the time as she stood in silence at the window that overlooked Table Mountain as if she was staring at her own reflection. Only at sunrise did she move away from the window to sit down in an armchair, her eyes no longer leaking tears.

The inspectors were in their forties, but both were very fit, lightly muscled, blond, brush-cut and deeply tanned. They wore black suits and crisp white shirts. Detective Nap did all the talking while the other, whose name neither of them offered, scrutinized us and took notes. One of the first things Detective Nap said, after a perfunctory offer of his condolences, was, "So the two of you aren't married? You're living common-law, is that right?" It was an expression that Rachel and I hated, and she looked like she was about to say so, so I blurted out, "Yes," and Nap nodded.

We sat on the sofa while he and the other detective sat in the two armchairs opposite us. Nap did not tell us what Gloria and Max had told him, but it soon became clear that they had told him quite a lot. "Did you bear any animosity toward your parents?" he asked Rachel. As if she had long felt the urge to tell her story to someone in authority, Rachel spoke without interruption for ten minutes as Nap, from time to time, shook his head in wonderment and distaste. Finally, he interrupted her. "And you are planning to leave soon, is that right? Go back to Canada with your boyfriend here?"

"Yes," Rachel said.

"And the maid, Nora, she said the two of you argued with the van Houts for quite some time a few days ago, early in the evening. She could hear you from the shed. You must have been shouting."

"All of us except for my mother were shouting," Rachel said. As she recounted the argument for him, the other inspector stopped taking notes. Nap shook his head and sighed from time to time. At last, he interrupted her again.

"Terrible, terrible things. Or they would be if they were true," he said.

"They could be true," Rachel said.

"Now that your parents are deceased, there's no reason for you and your sister Bethany to publicize your accusations, is there? Your sister Gloria, she seems to have thought quite highly of Professor van Hout and your mother. A war hero. He made it through all that, saving others' lives as well, only to be murdered in his sleep by some animal." He shook his head. "Your other sister, Carmen . . . well, she was quite distraught one minute, and the next she was laughing. I expect you know why. High as a kite on something. You don't seem upset at all."

"I'm *very* upset," Rachel said. "I just don't like to show it." Nap nodded, approvingly it seemed.

"Anyway, Gloria and her husband say they were home all day yesterday, and all night, too, with Bethany, who was in bed for most of the time. Carmen and her husband, Fritz, also say they were at home, with friends. They gave us their names. And the DeVrieses—the wife was at the reunion in Kalk Bay, and the father and son each vouch for the whereabouts of the other. What about you two?"

"Except for the afternoon, when I went to yoga class and Wade went out running, we were here all the time," Rachel said. I nodded.

"We rarely see this kind of crime in the City Bowl," Nap said, "but when we do, we don't always find the guilty parties."

"Are they ever white?" Rachel said.

Nap frowned at her. "Don't make any trouble for your dead parents," he said. "Common human decency and all that. We've seen a few killings of this kind elsewhere in Cape Town. Money is often involved. Drug money, sometimes. The country is rampant with drugs. I'm not saying your parents had anything to do with drugs. Drug money is used for a lot of things. Loan sharking, for instance. Your poor father may have got in over his head with some very bad people. It happens. The most decent people can be drawn into situations when they're desperate. A pair of killings like this, they send a message. This is what happens if you don't pay up. We'll catch them or we won't, but I hope you won't run around telling tales about your father. You should let him and your mother rest in peace. No need to sully their good names. The coloureds bring the drugs in, you see. Anything for a few rand. Often, they're paid in drugs. It's all too much for us to keep up with. The drugs come in from the north, from Rhodesia and South West Africa, from the jungle and the Bantu. There might as well be no borders. It would be one thing if the drugs stayed in the townships, but they don't and here we are."

"You're very dogged," Rachel said. The other inspector laughed.

"*En Jy's 'n saucy 'goed koop' meisie*," Nap said and the other inspector laughed again. They left abruptly, without saying another word to either of us.

"What did he say to you at the end?" I said.

"I think he said I was a saucy slut."

Neither Gloria nor Carmen called Rachel, and she did not call them. The next day, on the radio, on the SABC television station, in the *Argus* and the *Times*, it was reported that the police were stymied. They hadn't found a murder weapon; they had no suspects. Everyone on Liesbeek Road and nearby streets had been interviewed. No one had seen anything suspicious on the night of the murders.

"It's only been a day," I said.

"In South Africa," Rachel said, "swift justice is the only kind."

"Are you still worried about Nora?"

"Maybe the police are right," Rachel said. "Maybe Dad borrowed money from someone he shouldn't have and couldn't pay it back."

"Wouldn't he have borrowed from Max if he had to?"

"Maybe. But that would have been a lot of pride for *him* to swallow."

SABC reported a day later that newly obtained eyewitness accounts suggested that an as yet unidentified "coloured or black man" had been seen in the neighbourhood on the night of the murders.

"Surprise, surprise," Rachel said.

We gathered up our nerve and drove past the house on Liesbeek Road. It was surrounded by police tape that read "*polisie halte*." The doors and windows were sealed with yellow plastic. Two police cruisers were parked outside.

That night, after spending hours with her diary, Rachel lay sleeping on her side, faced away from me, her knees drawn up to her chest, her fists clenched on the pillow. She shivered as if she was freezing, shook with jolt after jolt, but she remained asleep, flinching, twitching, wincing, faint whimpering sounds coming from her throat.

We went to see Bethany the next morning. Max and Gloria left almost as soon as we arrived. "We're off to Port Elizabeth for a couple of days," Gloria said, her eyes hidden by sunglasses. "You're staying here with *her* until we get back. Don't even think of saying no."

They hurried out the door without so much as a mention of Hans and Myra just as Bethany came downstairs to the front hall. She seemed self-possessed and untroubled. Noticing that I seemed surprised, she looked at me and said, "I have no tears left for them, Wade. Maybe I'll have a delayed reaction, but I don't think so. Have you told your parents?"

"I'll wait till I get home."

"And what about you, Rachel? You're acting kind of weird."

"Well, the last time I saw Dad, he told me he was the one who tipped off the Gestapo about Anne Frank and the others."

"Did he also tell you that he killed JFK?"

"It's not the same thing."

"Obviously not," Bethany said, "judging by the amount of ink on the side of your hand."

"I don't care who knows how much I've been writing. We're *your* minders for the next two days, remember?"

"Don't worry, I'm almost self-maintaining. Wade, I appoint you Keeper of the Happy Pills. It's not that I might take the whole bottle. I might just *forget* to take them. One every eight hours, with lots of water, please." She gave me an unopened bottle and a prescription for refills—the latter, she said, in case I lost the bottle. "Are we still on the outs with Carmen and Fritz?" she asked.

"I haven't spoken to them," Rachel said. "I barely had a chance to say hello to Gloria and Max before they lit out. I've kind of been waiting for everyone to call or drop by or something. We need to get together to make some decisions."

"The police told Gloria it will be a little while before they give us Mom and Dad," Bethany said. "That's how Gloria put it."

"Well, I'm not driving that cliff road out to Fritz's place and, after two days here, I'll be craving our apartment, no offence, so I think we should all meet there when Gloria and Max get back."

And that's what happened a few days later, after dinner. Gloria and Max and Bethany arrived first and everyone hugged awkwardly. When Carmen and Fritz arrived, Rachel warned them as they came in the door: "If one of you slips Bethany something—"

"Don't worry, baby sister," Fritz said. "I've been clean and sober and empty-handed for six days now. In case the cops come back to visit. Six very long days." Carmen, sullen, dark rings beneath her eyes, didn't say a word or look at either of us. She was clearly having a hard time dealing with being straight.

"Nice place," Max said, looking about the room. "A bit small for seven of us, but nice."

"It's bigger than the Secret Annex, where eight people hid out for two years," Rachel said.

"Mandiba is six foot two and he sleeps in a cell six feet long and four feet wide," Fritz said. "Imagine that, Rachel. And he's been there a lot longer than two years."

"If I'd known that we'd be playing Name the Martyr with the Least Leg Room, I'd have done my homework," Bethany said.

"I expect there's not much meat on Mandela," Max said. "But then again, it's what he deserves." Fritz laughed scornfully.

"Anne Frank was not a martyr," Rachel said.

"All of this squabbling," I said. "When does it stop? Does it *ever* stop?"

Fritz snickered. Rachel looked chastened but said nothing.

"Oh, I'm sorry, Wade," Bethany said. "It's just that our parents have almost never been murdered before. How would you recommend that we comport ourselves?"

Rachel put her hand on my arm before I could respond.

"Has anyone heard from the DeVrieses?" Bethany said.

"I have," Gloria said. "I don't think they're long for Cape Town. Peter told me on the phone that they may move to Stellenbosch or Pretoria. He thinks he can get a job in either place. He said the three of them need a new start."

"He means a place they're unlikely to run into me," Bethany said.

"I'm sure Clive needs a new start," I said. "Engaged, dumped, re-engaged, re-dumped, a soon to be father who will never be a dad."

"Lay off Bethany," Rachel said.

"No, no, that's all right, Rachel," Bethany said. "It was kind of fun to hear Clive's resumé recited by someone who grew up in Blissville, Newfoundland."

"I wonder how Nora is doing," Rachel said after a short silence.

"I can tell you exactly how she's doing," Fritz said. "She's unemployed and living in Langa. No one will hire her. No one white, anyway. Not the kind of conversation piece you want around the house."

"Poor Nora," Rachel said. "Maybe we should give her some money."

"Severance pay," Fritz said.

"We'll see what we can do," Gloria said. "I'm not sure how to contact her, but we'll try." She wiped a tear away. "I can't believe Mom and Dad are gone. And to go like that."

"Fast. Painless," Fritz said.

"You know what she means, Fritz," Max said.

Fritz shrugged. "They'll pin it on some coloured, but they'll never catch who did it. They were very good, whoever they were."

"And you know about things like that, Fritz?" Rachel said.

"Fritz Boonzaire," Bethany said, "expert on the underworld."

"You'd be surprised, baby sister," Fritz said as if Bethany hadn't spoken. "I know what I know."

"So, Fritz, why would someone 'very good' kill Hans and Myra van Hout?" Max said.

"Money. What else? They did it for money. I know the type. Ex-cops, retired military. Which doesn't narrow it down much in South Africa. What I wonder is, who were they working for? One thing I know:

whoever did it was white. A black man, or black men, in that neighbourhood at night—well, they wouldn't have been *able* to get into or out of that neighbourhood. Even the servants have to be in their sheds by nine o'clock."

"What did you do in the national service, Fritz?" Rachel said.

"Enough," Gloria said. "It's our parents we're talking about. Mom and Dad. Remember them?" She glared at Bethany. "Some of us are very upset."

"They *were* murdered, Gloria. Shot in their bed. Has it occurred to you that they might have died that way because he messed with the wrong guy's daughter? Or do you think someone shot them by mistake?"

"That really is enough, *everyone*," Max said. "We've got things that need to be attended to. You can scratch each other's eyes out afterward, for all I care."

Gloria wiped her nose with a Kleenex, then said, "The police and the coroner have been in touch with me because I'm the oldest. The remains have been released, though they're still in the morgue. Max and I were thinking cremation might be a good idea. We thought maybe we could scatter their ashes at the Cape of Good Hope. They used to like going there. We wouldn't go out in a *boat* or anything. We would just scatter their ashes from shore." This was met with silence, but Gloria nodded as if everyone had given their assent. She also told us she had written a joint obituary that she was going to place in the newspapers.

"Have you told your family, Wade?" Gloria asked.

"No," I said.

"I thought we should run the obit in the paper in St. John's."

"I'll write to them by first-class mail, then," I said. "I might lose it on the phone. I haven't heard their voices in months."

"They're very sweet," Rachel said. "Very normal. They won't know what to make of this."

"*We* don't know what to make of it," Bethany said.

"Maybe some neo-Nazi took them out," Fritz said, looking from face to face.

"There *are* still Nazis out there," Max said. "Lots of them. Plenty right here in South Africa. Maybe Fritz is right. Hans was a member of the Resistance. Some Nazi nutcase might have done this."

Rachel said, "It might be just as likely that a Nazi *hunter* did it, given some other things Dad claimed to have done."

"It's absurd to even think about," I said.

"Will the rest of you come with us to the Cape of Good Hope to scatter Mom's and Dad's ashes or *not*?" Gloria said.

"Will the DeVrieses be there?" Bethany said.

"Not if you are," Gloria said.

"I'll go if it's just us," Bethany said.

"Mom and Dad didn't have many friends," Rachel said. "There's no reason it can't be just us."

"We're in," Fritz said, glancing at Carmen, who was hanging her head as if she had nodded off. Gloria looked at Rachel, who looked at me. I nodded.

"Right, then," Gloria said, pushing back her chair and standing up. "The Cape of Good Hope."

RACHEL

Ten days after my parents were killed, Gloria and Max came by in their gleaming, just-washed BMW around noon. We followed them to Fritz's house, where everyone got out to stretch their legs. Max wore a black bomber jacket, white shirt, black tie and black slacks, Gloria a black anorak over a new-looking black dress. Fritz and Carmen wore T-shirts and shorts, as did Wade and I.

"We might have to hike a little bit," Fritz said, appraising Max and Gloria.

"We've been there before, Fritz," Gloria said. "We brought some walking shoes just in case. It doesn't matter that it's the Cape of Good Hope. It's still a *funeral*." Fritz shrugged.

We—Wade, Bethany and I—followed Fritz, who followed Gloria and Max along the Cape Road, a small procession of three cars.

We soon got caught up in tourist traffic, lots of cars stopping by the side of the road to buy trinkets from the coloureds, mostly women. In addition to Cape souvenirs, there were pin-on Elvis buttons, Ronald Reagan buttons, Margaret Thatcher buttons, wooden crosses, metal crucifixes, prayer beads.

"You can't get more authentically African than that," Wade said.

Soon we came to a complete standstill on the narrow, dusty road. Max got out of his car, stopped for a second to speak to Fritz, then came back to us. "We might as well get out for a bit," he said. "That's what *we're* doing, anyway."

We joined the tourists. It soon clouded over and the wind came up, gusting from the east, toppling some of the smaller items on the tables.

Coloured pennants flapped loudly overhead. Clouds of red dust swirled along the road. The hawkers looked up at the sky as if waiting for a sign. The tourists looked up as well, perplexed, amused. The corners of the tablecloths rose up, revealing flimsy Formica tables with skinny legs propped with stones.

It felt like it was going to rain. "I'm freezing," I said, wrapping my arms around myself, wishing that I'd brought a sweater. Wade rubbed my upper arms. As if the something they'd been searching the sky for had finally appeared, the hawkers—all at once, it seemed—jumped up from their chairs and began to fold the tablecloths corner to corner to make huge sacks in which they dragged their wares along the ground. Walking backward, they pulled the sacks with both hands as they inched toward the vans, whose rear doors opened as though of their own accord.

Soon, the dust was intermixed with drops of rain, large, discrete drops that stung like hail. The tourists, hands on their straw hats, headed toward their cars. There were so many hawkers and tourists on the road, I kept bumping into the person in front of me. I felt a sudden surge of panic. "It's just a bit of wind and rain, for God's sake," Fritz shouted. "We're less than a mile from the Cape of Good Hope—what do they expect?"

Max, his bomber jacket glistening, asked us what we thought we should do.

"Well," I managed to say, "it looks like everyone's clearing out, heading west. They'll be bumper to bumper for an hour. Maybe we should go the rest of the way to the cape. By the time we come back, the road might be clear."

Impelled by gusts of wind and rain, we struggled toward the Citroën. When we got in, the windows were so caked with mud that it was dark inside. But the rain drummed even louder on the roof, and the mud began to wash away as the wind rocked the Citroën from side to side. "Now this," Wade said, "is what I call a car wash."

My hand shaking, I started up the car. My hair hung in thick strands about my shoulders, red mud staining the front of my T-shirt with what looked like blood. The sight made me want to throw up, but I managed not to. We waited until most of the westbound cars had manoeuvred around us, then followed the BMW and the Saab.

The end of the road, where we parked, was about a hundred yards from the sloping shoreline of the sea, down which several paths led among the rocks to the water. The wind, unimpeded by trees now, blew harder in a series of gusts, ramming our car time after time, causing it to rise and fall as if we were in a boat at sea. The rain was so heavy, the seaward windows were a blur, the raindrops sounding like a volley of small stones against the glass. "Jesus," Bethany said. "I'm not budging from this car unless the storm lets up."

I kept the windshield wipers going, but I could barely make out the two cars in front of us. A handful of jackass penguins waddled up one of the paths, passed between our car and Fritz's and continued up the hill. The sight of them made me feel desolate. "The poor things," I said.

"I'm sure they're used to it," Bethany said, just as a baboon leaped on the car roof and, hanging upside down, its white-rimmed eyes agape, stared in through the windshield at us. I screamed and pounded the glass with my fists.

"Jesus," Wade said, grabbing hold of my arms, "you'll break your fingers." He struck the glass with the heel of his fist, but the baboon didn't move.

"Please get it off the car," I shouted.

"God, Raitch, you've seen baboons before," Bethany said.

"It's attacking us," I said.

"No, it's not, Raitch," Bethany said. "Wade, they're harmless unless you corner or provoke them. There are car windows between us and him. We're safe."

As if to prove her wrong, the car was stormed from behind by baboons that, as they galloped across it, pounded on the roof. I covered my ears and screamed, watching the baboons slither every which way down the windshield, grabbing each other for purchase, tumbling, leaping, arms and legs and tails flailing, their bright-red, ridiculous, affronting backsides gleaming in the rain.

"The weather has them all worked up," Bethany said.

I wondered if any European sailors had ever made it ashore from a sinking ship only to have a herd of baboons converge upon them. They took the path the penguins had taken, and soon I lost sight of them among the rocks and wind-stunted trees.

"We could have spread the ashes at Muizenberg Beach," I said, wiping tears from my eyes. "Mom and Dad liked going there, too. Jesus."

"Maybe I should take the wheel on the way back," Bethany said. "Right now, I'm the less crazy of the two people who can drive this car."

"Maybe," I said, gripping Wade's hand as tightly as I could lest I completely lose control.

"Maybe we should get one of my tranquilizers from Max for you," Bethany said.

"Maybe," I said again.

In a few minutes, the rain began to let up. The wind was still a gale, now blowing from the north. From time to time, the sun broke through, clouds racing past it. When at last the rain stopped altogether, we got out of the car and joined Fritz and Carmen at the trunk of Max's BMW. Max opened it and took out two purple velvet bags with drawstrings made of gold-coloured braid.

"Let's get this over with," Bethany said. "Some of us were kind of losing it back there."

Gloria took off her pumps, put them in the trunk and put on a pair of black and white sneakers.

"No photographs," I said to Fritz, who had hung his brand-new Nikon camera from his neck.

We made our way single file along one of the criss-crossing paths, which were covered in shallow mud and very slippery. Spray from the large, white-crested waves stung my eyes. I had left my sunglasses in the car.

My legs shook so that I could barely stand, and I grabbed on to Wade to keep from falling. Max, the first in line, the velvet bags hanging by their drawstrings from his hands, came to a stop on a flat rock about twenty feet from the water and declared that it would not be safe to venture closer.

He laid the bags down, undid the drawstrings and took out the bronze urns, which were smaller than I'd imagined they would be—they looked like martini shakers in his hands. Fritz snapped a photograph of them and glanced at Gloria, who merely shook her head. Max shrugged as if to say, *How should this be done?* The rest of us stood on the rock, facing the ocean that, without interruption, stretched to Antarctica, our backs turned to the freezing wind and the incessant spray that had already soaked us all to the skin. We looked around at each other.

"*Open* them," I said, surprised to hear my voice so shrill with impatience. One of the bags bore the initial *H* on the side, the other *M*. Max handed Wade the latter and they unscrewed the lids. Mom's urn contained what looked like white beach sand, but the ashes in Dad's were black—coal black. I gasped and covered my mouth. Everyone gathered around to look inside the urns. "Why are they different?" I shouted above the crashing of the waves. "Why are hers white and his black?"

Bethany scrambled down from the rock and began to make her way back up the path toward the cars, slipping and sliding every which way in the mud.

"Let's get this done," Max said.

"Just hold them up and shake them into the wind," Fritz said. "The ashes will make it to the water eventually, or they won't—what difference does it make?"

"I think we should take turns," Max said, "unless no one else wants to."

Carmen, Gloria and I stood there, arms folded, as if refusing an order. Wade took the urn from Max, and Fritz snapped a picture of him as he shook a sprinkle of ash from each of the urns that was instantly dispersed to nothing by the wind. He extended the urns to me but I shook my head. Gloria did the same when he offered them to her. Next came Carmen, her hair blowing about her face, who stood there staring at them as if she was trying to make out what they were. Then she shook her head and turned away from us, her hair whipping out behind her.

Wade gave the urns to Fritz, who, wielding them like salt and pepper shakers, dumped out what I hoped were their entire contents. Then he passed the urns to Max.

"Last chance, Gloria," Max said. She shook her head again. Mascara-tinted tears streamed down from beneath her sunglasses. "Someone should say something," Max said, but, almost in unison, the rest of us shook our heads.

"Ashes to ashes, dust to dust," Max shouted as he emptied both urns at once. Fritz took several photos, the shutter of his camera clicking rapidly.

"Don't you point that thing at me, Fritz," I said as I felt my legs regain their strength.

"Let's get the fuck out of here, then," Fritz said, grabbing Carmen by the arm and pointing her up the path.

When we reached the cars, I opened the back door of the Citroën and poked my head inside to see if Bethany was all right. She said something but I couldn't make it out above the noise of the wind. She wasn't crying and didn't seem to be sick.

We were about halfway back to Cape Town when Bethany asked, "Why weren't their ashes the same?"

"Maybe they coloured his black so they wouldn't get them mixed up or something," I said.

"I know it makes no sense," she said, "but those black ashes—I can't help feeling that he didn't die, that he's still out there. I *know* it makes no sense. It just gave me that feeling, that's all."

"I'm just glad it's over," I said.

"It will never be over," Bethany said. She was silent for a while. Then she said, "It went on for a long time, Rachel. When it started, I remember not knowing it wasn't normal. The doctors say that if a dad starts early, he'll stop by the time you're ten or twelve, most of the time. They say that others start then and stop when you're about fourteen, most of the time. And others start then and stop when you're nineteen or twenty, most of the time. Most of the time, most of the time. But some of them start when you're just out of diapers and they never stop. Opportunity is all they need. As long as they have opportunity, they never stop."

"Bethany," I said, trying not to cry, "you have to hold up for your baby, okay. Think about your baby."

"Jesus. Advice about keeping it together from my baboonaphobic, Anne Frank–freakaholic sister. Don't worry, I'll hold up. It was Clive who knocked me up. It wasn't Dad. He was careful. He was always careful."

Wade glanced at me then, and I faintly shook my head to indicate that he shouldn't say a word.

From *The Arelliad*

THE SHADOW SHE (1985)

I hear the roars of Claws von Snout—
the more he roars, the more I write.
It seems the words keep him at bay,
he hears my pen, he stays away.
He never knows what I might say,
I never know what he might do—
is that the deal between us two?
He takes the other ones, not me—
so far, at least, he's let me be—
for that's the thing with Claws von Snout:
he knows it's him I write about,
he knows I'm hurt and getting worse,
he'll separate me from the herd
when I spell out my final word.

I'm waiting for the yellow sky, for morning in Arellia—for all I know, there won't be one. That other nights have come and gone is a guarantee of nothing. Arellia's astronomy is still a mystery to me.

I gave him my sisters, betrayed the three of them the way that Dad betrayed the Franks, the van Pels and Fritz Pfeffer. Did I? Did he? No sooner do I think of them than all eight of them appear, soon joined by the van Houts, me among them. They are my blended family, fourteen in all. They smile at me expectantly. They're posing for a photograph, the girls in front, Anne Frank and I holding hands, and Bethany holding Margot's. Dad's hands are on Anne's shoulders. I want to tell him to let go of her, but I simply turn away. How can *any* of them stand his presence? How can I? How can the other me?

"He betrayed you all," I shout, but they simply go on smiling.

Arellia goes black, but soon the lighthouse light returns. Every one of them has vanished but for me. I'm standing face to face with me. I hear the roars of Claws von Snout. The other me seems not to mind, or else she doesn't hear the things I do. But then I see that she's not me. She's the Shadow She, the also-Anne whom I betrayed.

Why must it all take place again, the same dark road, the same cold wind, the scent of perfume in the car? She didn't have to travel far. She's wearing the black coat she wore that winter night, the coat that wasn't found. Soon, the snow will start. The wind is cold and she's so small. They look at me, those strange green eyes. She never blinks. If only I could turn back time—the end would come the way it came. Nothing would be different. I'd turn my back on her again, just as, moments ago, I turned my back on Anne Frank. I'd betray, again, the girl called Anne, who said, "I'm just an also-Anne." Von Snout was there but no one else to hear her shout. His was the only voice she heard. She and I are alike, but I'm not the one for whom bells toll.

She stares at me and says, "I vanished then; you'll vanish when the wind blows from the west again."

WADE

I was surprised that, not long after we told them of our plan to go through Amsterdam rather than London on our way back to Canada, the others—all of them—decided to come with us.

"I can't stand the idea of you being in Amsterdam by yourselves," Gloria said when she came by to give us the news. "The place is full of so many reminders of Dad, and even Mom—I'm sure that one or more of us have been there with them twenty times over the years. We're not about to leave Bethany in the house by herself, and Fritz says he and Carmen have business to conduct in Amsterdam. I can just imagine what he means by 'business.' The two of them will wind up in jail for life if they're ever caught bringing drugs into South Africa."

Some shopping had to be done before the seven of us left. I had promised my parents and brothers and sisters that I would bring them back souvenirs. Rachel and Bethany each wanted a neck pillow to help them sleep on the flight. Gloria and Max were in search of things to give to Max's many relatives in Amsterdam. As Max was out of town and Rachel was spending most of every day with Bethany at the Apostles house and Fritz and Carmen, who wore only used clothes, had more or less sworn an oath to never be caught dead in a mall, Gloria and I were left to do the shopping.

Gloria picked me up in Max's BMW in mid-afternoon. She didn't come in but merely blew the horn and waited for me. She shifted over to the passenger side as I came down the driveway. "It's an automatic," she said when I got in.

"I've never driven on the left side of the road," I said, but she dismissed me with a wave of her hand. "I'll guide you. It doesn't look right, a woman driving a man around."

"Rachel doesn't mind," I said. "Neither do I."

"How do you know she doesn't mind?" Gloria said. "And you *should* mind."

I was wearing a T-shirt and blue jeans and a pair of leather sandals. "Someone should teach Rachel how to dress you," Gloria said. "After someone teaches her how to dress herself." She wore a low-cut, lavender-coloured number that rode up her legs when she crossed them.

I had feared that I would have to run a gauntlet of flirtation but, except to tell me where to drive and warn me that I was drifting into oncoming traffic, she said almost nothing. We made it to the mall, which was so busy I had to park on the lowest, least-used level of the underground lot after navigating a series of sharply winding and steeply descending ramps.

I picked up some things for my family first, and then Gloria shopped in a frenzy, never bothering to tell me which way she was headed or when she was leaving one store and making for another. I felt like I was ten years old, all but chasing her to keep up lest I be left behind and have to ask directions from a grown-up.

At last, we carried our bags back to the car in the underground parking. I drove the BMW back up the winding, steep ramps. I had no sooner stopped the car at an automatic pay booth a few feet short of the exit when two men in black fatigues and toting machine guns appeared from out of nowhere, flanking the car. At the sound of a thud against the window, I turned my head and looked into the barrel of a gun.

My mind and body braced pointlessly for a bullet that would have killed me so fast I wouldn't have had time to hear the shot or the breaking of the glass. "Jesus," I heard myself shout. Gloria grabbed my hand and cried out, "Don't shoot," over and over.

The two men slowly moved around to the front of the car, their guns trained on us all the while. I put my hands up and Gloria did too. "What do they want?" I managed to say.

Gloria began to stamp her foot over and over, hissing, "That bastard Fritz, that bastard Fritz," each time she made contact with the car mat.

"What *about* Fritz?" I whispered.

"I knew he'd screw it up somehow," she said. "How could he have been so *stupid*? *Jesus*."

Abruptly, the two men lowered their guns as if some third person we couldn't see had told them to, then backed away from each other until they no longer blocked our way. With a loud bang, the metal door in front of us lurched into motion, rising, slowly opening, admitting daylight until I was blinded by the sun.

"Get us out of here," Gloria said. "Just drive. Go, go."

I drew in a deep breath and slowly released it as I managed to pull out of the parking garage and onto the ramp that led to the street. As I merged into traffic, Gloria began to sob uncontrollably.

"I have to pull over," I said. "We're both too upset, and I don't know the way. And what was that about Fritz?"

"You're not pulling over until we're out of the city. I won't have people gawking at me while I'm trying to explain myself to someone who will never understand and whose opinion of me I do not give a *shit* about. There is a place out by the house that overlooks the sea. You'll drive but you won't say a word until we get there."

She stood with her back to the water, the offshore wind turning her hair into a black pennant. I looked at the road, which wound halfway up the cliff that faced the sea, then at her house in the distance, the glass walls of its upper storey glinting in the sun.

Arms still folded, eyes on the ground, she walked in her high heels back to the car, turned and leaned back against the hood. The red dust of South Africa fanned out across the water, casting faint and fleeting shadows on the sea.

Seagulls used the offshore wind to hover above the water, rising and dipping like kites. They eyed us, hoping perhaps that we had stopped to have some food that we might share with them or leave behind.

"What *happened* back there, Gloria?" I said. "Why did you say those things about Fritz?"

"They were only mall cops," she said. "They must have mistaken us for someone else. There must have been a robbery or something. This doesn't happen to me every day, Wade." Sniffling, she wiped her nose with the back of her hand. "I was terrified. No one has ever aimed a gun at me before. And all I could think was that it could just as easily have been Fritz who was driving, because he does nothing all day but lie around that house with Carmen and get stoned. Fritz could have taken you there. If I wound up hurt or worse, it would be Fritz's fault."

"Gloria, when that gun was pointed at my face, the first thing that came to my mind was not Fritz. I don't believe he's the first thing that came to your mind. Fritz and me *shopping* together? That's almost as unlikely as *you* and Fritz shopping together."

She struck the hood of the car with the heel of her hand. "All *right*," she said. "All *right*, just give me a second."

"You didn't think they mistook us for someone else," I said. "You thought they knew exactly who we were."

She leaned on the car, eyes downcast as I moved to stand in front of her. She was waiting to see if I could guess.

"Your parents," I said. "You thought Fritz had turned on you, or slipped up. I can't believe—"

She laughed. "Fritz knows more about it than you or I will ever know."

"I can't *believe* it," I said. "*Jesus*—"

"*You* can't believe it. *You* can't believe this; *you* can't believe that. Ever since you came to South Africa, you've had a look of disbelief on your face, or a look of disapproval, or sometimes a smug look. I know what you think of me. But I'm not some vapid twit who always dreamed of being a stewardess. I left home as soon as I could, the best way I knew how. I don't *care* what you think of me, but I know. I'd rather live here than anywhere else because, if you're white, you can do almost anything and people will either pretend not to notice or explain it away. The police have no proof, though they may have suspicions, which they'll keep to themselves unless Fritz does what the sight of that gun pointed at me made me think he'd already done."

"Which was what?"

"Something like you just said. I thought he messed it up, somehow, maybe tried to keep all the money for himself, or shot off his mouth to someone while he was stoned. I'll explain it all if you give me a chance. I panicked at the mall. If I had had the time to think it through . . ."

I moved even closer to her but she turned her head away.

"Rachel . . . ," I said.

"She had absolutely nothing to do with it. Fritz and I agreed that the fewer who knew the better. She didn't, she *doesn't*, know anything about it. Bethany and Carmen don't know either, or Max. I *wouldn't* trust any of them to keep a secret like that. Fritz is the only one I needed, anyway."

"But not Rachel."

"Not your precious Rachel. Rachel . . . for a long time, I assumed that Dad had done to her what he did to Bethany and me, and maybe Carmen. Seeing you and her together, I think that, maybe, for some reason that no one will ever guess, he never laid a hand on her."

"But—"

"Listen. LISTEN. And don't interrupt until I'm finished. Don't you judge me until you *know*."

"I don't know what to say, Gloria," I said, barely able to keep from breaking into tears.

I turned away from her and took a few steps toward the sea. The tide was coming in, the waves exploding in white froth upon the rocks just as the waves below our house in Petty Harbour did when the tide was on the rise. "Come back and sit beside me," she called. I returned to the car and leaned with her against the grille of the BMW.

"For a while, I lived two lives," she said. "The two of them ran side by side, and I moved back and forth between them pretty easily. Family outings, picnics on the beach, visits to the zoo, birthday parties, school trips. We sang the South African national anthem two or three times a day. I knew it by heart and I loved every word of it, and believed every word of it. But my other life was always there, at night, mostly behind closed doors. Secrets. Promises. Warnings. 'Don't tell your mother what you did. She'll be very upset with you. You know how sad your mother gets when you misbehave. Don't tell your sisters.' I was convinced that Dad did what he did because of something *I* did. I tried to think of what it was so that I could stop doing it, but . . . Sometimes he told me to tell him I was sorry, and I did."

I couldn't credit the things she was saying. Nor could I look her in the eye, for I knew I was wearing the look of disbelief that so offended her.

"I soon had a reputation among the boys and girls at school. Especially the boys. A reputation that I earned and lived up to. Glory Hole van Hout. I didn't smoke or drink or do drugs like my sisters did. I wasn't invited to parties. But I knew things that other girls my age didn't know. Things that some of them probably still don't know.

"Then we moved to Canada." She folded her arms and tightly hugged herself. The wind blew her hair over her face but she didn't bother with it.

"The others, maybe even Carmen, thought we were going somewhere where everything would be different, where everything unpleasant would just go away. Me, I was leaving a boyfriend I knew I would never see again, a handful of friends I knew I would never see again. And I was leaving the one place on earth that, in spite of everything, was home to me. I have a lot of good childhood memories. Children can enjoy themselves in spite of almost anything. I did. The bad, as bad as it was, didn't spoil the good, not entirely, not at first, at least. But it did more and more as I got older. I knew we were not setting sail to a new life. I knew that we were bringing with us more bad than good. And I felt, believe it or not, that what we were leaving behind was more good than bad.

"I got engaged. I got married. I got divorced. A few times. I wound up back here with Max. When I heard that Dad was retiring and the two of them were moving back here . . . For so long, I had thought the most I would have to deal with was a visit every year. I thought I could handle that.

"Max loves it here. He often says that there is nowhere else that he would live, not even Amsterdam. I'm going to have children,

Wade. Girls, maybe. If Max goes on insisting he doesn't want children, he'll have to get used to not having me. And I know how this sounds but, if Dad was alive, I can't say for certain that I would be able to shield a baby girl from him, or a ten-year-old, or a teenager. I can't say for certain that I wouldn't go on pretending that everything was fine and looking the other way, that I wouldn't leave my children alone with him or them, because that's what daughters do—they leave their children with their grandparents, the last people who would ever harm them. I don't know for certain what happened to Carmen and Rachel. I should know, but I don't. Like Mom, I covered up for him because I didn't want anyone to know about *me*, because I thought I was to blame.

"The thing is . . . it never stopped, Wade. Do you know what I mean? I can't explain it. Maybe someone can, but I can't. I'm afraid that, if I tell Max any of this, he won't want me anymore, in part because I lied to him and in part because he'll be sickened by the sight of me. My father once said to me, 'A woman belongs forever to the first man who has her. And he should be the only man who has her. But even if he's not, she'll be his forever. I was the first man to have you, Gloria. You will always be mine.'"

She looked sideways at me.

"Jesus," I said.

"Since they moved back, every night that Max was away, I stood at the window that faced that road. If, by nine, Dad hadn't shown up, I knew he wasn't coming. I felt relieved, but there was always the next night to think about.

"Dad would tell Mom he couldn't sleep knowing I was out there by myself in that big house on the coast—even though the house is guarded by a man with a machine gun. And she'd say, 'Well, you know I don't sleep well in any bed but my own.' So he came out to the house by himself. It even made sense to Max. 'Dad slept over every night while you were away,' I'd tell him, and all Max would do was smile as if he was amused, or even charmed, by Dad's concern for me. Sometimes, I think that even Max was pretending not to know, especially after Bethany made her accusations.

"I didn't accuse them, disown them, tell them I never wanted to see them again. To move away from them was one thing, but to disown them was something that I simply couldn't bring myself to do. I couldn't accuse *him*. Where did doing that get Bethany? I couldn't defy him or resist him. Or her. It was easier, in a way, to pretend, to let everyone go on pretending that the van Houts were what they seemed to be.

"When I opened the door, Dad didn't push past me. He merely waited for me to step aside, as he knew I would, as I always have."

"Jesus," I said.

"I can imagine what it was like for Bethany. Mom goes out from time to time in the middle of the afternoon. I don't know where she goes and she isn't gone for long, but long enough. And then there's Carmen. I have no idea. My guess is yes, but I have no idea.

"I would have handled the whole thing myself if I could, but I had no money, so I told Max that Rachel and you were nearly broke. He never asks questions when I ask him for money. All he said was 'How much?' I told him not to mention it to either of you because you'd be embarrassed. And then I got in touch with Fritz."

"Jesus," I said.

"This was the only way I could think of to stop it. The point of all this, Wade—I say it again—is that he *never* stopped and he never would have. If there was any other way to stop him, they'd be alive today. Mom—she wasn't supposed to be there. She was supposed to be at that reunion.

"Fritz has been keeping his eyes on me ever since, looking for signs that I've told Max or someone else what we did. He's *always* watching me. But he did everything he was supposed to. I have to give him that much credit.

"Fritz and I, we did our parts. Max did his, too, though he doesn't know it. I'm begging you, don't tell him, and don't tell Fritz that you know what happened. And please, please don't tell Bethany, Carmen or Rachel. They had absolutely nothing to do with it."

"I think Rachel loves me," I said. "She says she does. I think she does. And I'm not sure I could take it if she didn't, or even if she loved me less, which she would after she found out that I'd been keeping such a secret from her. I couldn't take it if she left me again. I wish that Hans had done nothing to any of you, but I'm also sure that what happened to you and Bethany didn't happen to Rachel. I don't understand why it didn't, but I'm *sure* it didn't. I'd *feel* it, wouldn't I?"

"You should stop trying to understand a man like Dad. Tornadoes have been known to rip apart an entire town but leave one or two houses unmarked. No one is running this show called life. Anything is possible."

I felt that she was patronizing me. "Well," I said, "I can't keep something like this from Rachel. There would always be this thing between us, for however long we last."

"Telling her won't make any of it go away. You think that couples shouldn't keep secrets from each other. That might be true for some secrets, but it's not true for this one. There are no secrets like this one."

"If I don't tell her, I will lose her, if not right away, then months or years from now. Imagine our kids asking why they only have two grandparents and me thinking, *Well, there used to be four, but your aunt did away with two of them.*"

"Don't *joke* about it," she said, pointing her finger. "Don't you dare make *fun* of me. Just *listen* to me."

"I'm sorry," I said. "I shouldn't have—I'm sorry."

"It will only hurt Rachel if you tell her what I did."

I was leaning on a car in a seaside parking lot in Cape Town, South Africa, with my girlfriend's sister, who had just told me that, with the help of her brother-in-law, she had had her parents killed. I wasn't as certain as I'd let on to Gloria that Hans had kept his hands off Rachel. Only a tiny measure of certainty had been erased, and yet its erasure made me feel infinitely worse. It was as if I had been monitoring the progress of an egg whose shell had been reduced to a transparent skin, allowing me to see the shadow of the thing inside. I fought down the urge to be sick and struggled to focus on the moment's primary revelation: the van Houts had been murdered by their oldest daughter.

Murdered. Was that the right word? The police had said they were killed execution-style. *Executed*? Something about the word seemed wrong, in spite of everything I knew.

Gloria had been watching me struggle. "You don't understand and you never will," she said. "No one it hasn't happened to can understand. If Rachel really can't remember, or has nothing to remember, then she won't understand. Maybe Carmen wouldn't. I don't know what they'd do. I know almost nothing about Carmen. In a way, I was the odd one out among my sisters. I never got along with them. Half the time, we were at each other's throats. The other half, we avoided each other.

"People often say that nothing has been the same for them since this or that. For me, there *was* no before this and after that. There was always *this*. Only this. Nothing else."

"Gloria," I said, "all of this just seems insane to me."

"It is. It is insane. And now that you've been caught up in it, nothing will ever seem the same to you. The world made sense to you for twenty-something years. It has never made sense to me. Even if you broke up with Rachel now, nothing would ever seem the same."

"I'm never going to break up with Rachel," I said, but Gloria went on as if she hadn't heard me.

"Do you understand what could result from telling Rachel? Believe me, she is not sorry they are gone. None of us is. If that seems heartless, your imagination is not what you think it is. I don't know the guy that Fritz hired, what he might think he had to do if word got out about this. That's why I was so freaked out in the parking lot: I thought we were going to be killed. Don't you understand, Wade? If you tell Rachel, we could all end up as loose ends that need to be tied."

She was crying again. I looked over my shoulder to see if anyone was watching but, as far as I could tell, no one was. She gathered herself and turned to me. "I'm asking you, not as a favour to me, but as a favour to them, don't tell Rachel or Carmen or Bethany or Max. Don't tell them what I did, and don't tell them who helped me. And for God's sake, don't tell Fritz that you know what *he* did. More people could get killed. What my sisters don't know would hurt them even more than they've been hurt already. It was my responsibility to do what I did. As the oldest daughter, I owed it to Bethany, to myself, and, if all the truth were known, I suspect, to a number of others whose last names are not van Hout."

"All right, Gloria," I said, won over more by her fear of what Fritz and the man who had killed her parents might do than anything else. "But I am going to tell Rachel about the mall cops because, when she sees me, she'll know that something happened. I'm not expecting to get much sleep tonight."

"Promise me," she said. "Promise me that we'll keep this secret between us."

I looked her in the eye. "I promise," I said. And I meant it.

"Thank God." She covered her face with her hands and began to cry so hard her shoulders were heaving. I put my arm around her and she turned and put her arms around my neck and pressed her head sideways against my chest just as Rachel often did. After a few seconds, she pulled away and patted me with both hands.

"I'll drop you off at your apartment but I won't come in. Tell Rachel I said I wanted to get back home and get a swim in before dinner."

We got back in the car. She pulled the sun visor down to reveal the small mirror on the back of it. She opened her purse, took out an assortment of cosmetics and arranged them in a row on the dashboard. Then she took a brush from the glove compartment and went to work on her hair, tilting her head away from me, stroking savagely, grimacing. "I should have stayed in the car, out of the wind," she said through clenched teeth. Then she fixed her face.

Rachel had once told me that Gloria believed that the people who ran the world deserved to run it, that she trusted authority to do the right thing, the best thing, for everyone. How she could maintain such a belief given what her father had done to her, I couldn't imagine. She had made it sound as if, by arranging the murder of her parents, she had done what any sensible person would do to restore good order to its usual infallibility. But I couldn't know what Gloria actually thought. She may not have been as remorseless as she seemed. In my worst moments, I would dwell on the fact that his blood ran in her veins, as it did in Rachel's, and Carmen's and Bethany's too. Perhaps it was that portion of Gloria's blood that was his that made it possible for her to rid the world of him without letting the act destroy her.

These murders were the kinds of things that happened in potboilers and thrillers, in supermarket tabloids. I had an overwhelming sense of unreality when I thought about what must have happened on Liesbeek Road that night. Gloria and Fritz had negotiated a fee for the murder of her parents. What sum of money was involved? They must have had several conversations over a significant period of time during which one or both of them could have changed their minds but didn't. They could have stopped short of doing something that would alter them forever—assuming that, when it came to murder, Fritz was as much of a novice as Gloria. Was it as simple as him knowing a guy who knew a guy, or had he known right away who to contact? And who was that person and what did he do, and how did he live between phone calls from people like Fritz?

The killer had parked in the driveway. The door of the house had been unlocked. He knew the layout. I pictured him moving about like a handyman. He did what he was paid to do. He shot Myra and Hans in the forehead once, left the house and drove away, the spinning of his tires on gravel the only indication of urgency or panic.

I knew that, in the days that followed, every time I looked at Gloria or someone said her name, I would think of Hans and Myra lying in the darkness of their room. And every moment I spent with Rachel, I would debate telling her what happened to her parents. To keep such a thing hidden from her seemed like an unthinkable betrayal. *Gloria paid to have them killed.* I couldn't imagine the effect that sentence would have on Rachel. What if Gloria, soon or years from now, had a change of heart and admitted everything, including her confession to me? Rachel might not forgive me. Out by the Apostles, with her house in sight, Gloria had warned me about the effect of the truth on her and her sisters, and its effect on me. She had spoken as if I was one of *them* now, one of the van Houts, marred for life for a reason that no one but Gloria might ever know.

I also wondered what Gloria would be like if Hans had never laid a hand on her. Bethany had been telling the truth about Hans, about her parents, all along. What would Bethany have been like if Hans had never laid a hand on her? What would Rachel and Carmen have been like?

When I told Rachel about the close call Gloria and I had had at the shopping mall, she began to cry and hugged me fiercely. She told me how glad she was that we hadn't been hurt, how precious I was to her and how guilty she felt for having persuaded me to come to South Africa. I was so happy we were leaving, I didn't think to tell her she had no reason to feel guilty.

Two nights before our departure, I woke to find Rachel sitting on the side of the bed, her hands on the mattress on either side of her. She sounded as if she was talking in her sleep: "We have to keep away from the windows, Papa says, or someone will see us. We have to keep them closed or someone will hear us. He says that one cough could give us away. We mustn't drop things. We must walk about like mice. I can't remember all the rules. I hope we don't get caught but, if we do, I hope it's not my fault. I hope it's no one's fault."

She turned and looked at me. "I'm awake," she said. "Those were my words, not Anne Frank's. Sometimes I write what I imagine I would have written if I was in her shoes. I should write about myself instead of paraphrasing her." I turned on my side and rubbed her shoulder.

She nodded, not in appreciation but as if in agreement with some inner voice. "I hope they died in their sleep," she said. "I hope they weren't afraid."

From *The Ballad of the Clan van Hout*

MANIFESTO (1977)
(Read only to my Rachel Lee,
who still has time for poetry,
if not for other things that she
withholds, unlike the other three.)

So many people say it's wrong
(but many more just play along).
They could have caught me long ago
but they pretended not to know.
How well I know that knowing look—
they seem to read me like a book,
but then, I read them just as well:
we tell each other we won't tell.
They know the signs, I know them too,
I'll look the other way if you
will look the other way for me;
faced with the opportunity,
most men would do what I have done.
Am I supposed to be a monster
when other men have had *their* daughters?
So I have mine, they have theirs too—
these are the things that real men do.
The ones who don't, don't have the nerve,
but they're the ones who disapprove.
They can't admit how much they'd like
what they don't have the nerve to take,
so they say, "abomination,"
and predict the ruination
of the father and the daughter
(and the uncle and the brother).
They're on the outside, looking in;
they lack the stomach of most men.

The streets are full of married women
who've never come to any harm
though they were loved by their "old man."
Those who object don't know their wives
were often left unsupervised
when they were young and pretty things
who, taken underneath the wings
of older men, forgot the boys
who really didn't have a clue,
who didn't know what they should do
with girls who really wanted to.

Who says that I'm too old for them?
What's old today was young back when
the Rooster played among the Hens.
Love that happens in the shadows
was long ago the status quo,
the commonly accepted thing—
no one had to bother hiding.
The rules are endlessly revised,
hypocrisy must always thrive;
nature has to be repressed
or we'll be beasts like all the rest.
The things the Bible says are right
become forbidden overnight.
Where love's concerned, there's no right age;
I love my girls—is that depraved?
In ancient Rome, it was the norm
to sleep with boys the age of Carm.
How does what's right become what's wrong,
unless it was so all along,
in which case, nothing is allowed
by the new enlightened crowd?
A vice was virtue yesterday—
it never goes the other way.

The truth will change while you're asleep
and be a lie when you wake up.
That fellow Darwin was no fool;
he knew that nature makes the rules.
You cannot deny a notion
that survived by evolution
or by natural selection.
The survival of the fittest
should be the one and only test.
A need, a want, an urge, a drive
must never go unsatisfied
or else the race will not survive.

I know they'd say that I'm to blame
for how my girls behave today;
of course they overlook the drugs—
they are such prigs, they are so smug.
They overlook society
and all of its hypocrisies;
they overrate psychiatry:
it can't explain my Bethany
or even little Rachel Lee.
For proof, I know enough to know
that almost any proof will do
to prove the thing you want it to.
The testimony experts give
(they need their fees, they have to live)
won't hold up for very long
when each side proves the other wrong.
How much worse would my girls be
had I not loved them specially?
Did they get sick because of me,
or is it that I saved all three?
How would some expert doctor choose
if those he almost lost were his?

Who knows what causes this or that?
How can they be so sure of it?
The things my girls watch on TV,
the violence and sex they see,
the drugs they get so easily,
the lyrics of these modern songs—
no wonder girls like mine go wrong.

I lie awake in bed sometimes;
the night goes by in quarter chimes.
The house is empty but for me;
the girls are out and so is She.

The man the cops look for is me—
She tells Herself: "It cannot be;
the man who left the house tonight,
the one for whom the bright porch light
is always on above the door
can't be the one they're searching for.
He'll be Hans when he comes home;
when he comes home, the four of them
will still be them, their names the same
as yesterday, when they stayed in
and no one waited up for him.
There is this and only this;
it has to be this way for us.
It's lonely in the house these days:
I dread the night, I miss the noise,
the children playing with their toys.
I stay up late because their dad
is out there somewhere, on those roads,
or parked somewhere; he sits and broods
about the war, about the past,
about how time goes by so fast.
I'd like to keep him company

but he prefers his thoughts to me;
he misses Glormenethalee.
He won't say so but I can tell—
when it gets dark, he can't keep still.
Sometimes I think I might go mad;
I fret about the years ahead.
How will he deal with growing old
when he is forced to stay at home?
The house will seem more silent still
when he is here against his will,
avoiding me from room to room,
wide-eyed and still remembering
his boyhood years in Amsterdam,
the things they must have done to him,
the things they said they saw him do,
the things that they accused him of,
some girl, perhaps, that he once loved . . .
I'll never know what it was like
to be that boy who rode his bike
along the streets of Amsterdam
before the war made him a man."

There is nothing in creation
that defies all explanation.
You've never lived as I've had to;
you think there is a thing called You
that will not change no matter what,
your heart, your soul, inviolate.
You call it this, you call it that,
it really doesn't matter what
you call a thing you haven't got.
What is this thing that makes you You?
It doesn't matter what you do,
you'll never find it anywhere—
and yet you're certain that it's there.

You think no matter what you do,
no matter what is done to you,
it cannot change what you call You.

We're all the same when we start out,
each one of us a clean blank slate
(who was the fool who first said that?)
on which the world writes God knows what.
We share the same environment
(don't be absurd—of course we don't),
have equal opportunity
(except for things like family,
geography, intelligence,
random events, coincidence),
and even if you doubt all that
it's easy to make up for it—
just pull free will out of your hat:
free will is free, no matter what
(the one such thing on planet Earth);
free will can conquer anything
(so you're to blame for everything).
You could have used what God gave you,
you could have done what others do
whose every cell is just like yours
(except for the above, of course).
As for free will, the magic pill,
they'll go on preaching it until
they find something to take its place—
a phantom with a human face.
How can anything be free,
affected by no agency?
It's something that the church contrived
to keep belief in guilt alive
when science showed that God was dead,
the bogeyman beneath the bed

who wasn't really there at all
but seemed so big when we were small.
You only have to look about
to see the reason things turn out
the way they do, the way they must:
it's nature that determines us.

This is not a dress rehearsal—
there is this and no reversal,
no chance to do it all again;
there is, at best, "remember when,"
perhaps the game of might have been.
The world to come makes nothing right
if nothing follows day but night,
no second chance, no change of mind,
no past-perfecting afterlife,
no cure-all of eternity,
no never-ending history,
no soul but merely flesh and blood.
No kiss and make it better God,
with iodine, Mercurochrome,
is waiting for us to come Home.

From *The Arelliad*

DEAR ANNE (1985)
It may be that, one day, I'll be
the last one of the family,
the last van Hout still left alive,
the last of some forgotten tribe
whose native tongue will die with her,
untranslated—who would bother?
It could have been like that for you—
Anne Frank, the last remaining Jew.

I know every word of *The Ballad* that he recited to me, still hear the words inside my head and always will. I hear that voice of his until I close my eyes and I can see the five of us—but where is She? She must be somewhere in the house. She listens and she waits for us.

I wish we'd had our minders too, not that I envy the Franks and the others, but it would have meant so much to my sisters and me to know that we were not alone, that someone knew about us and cared enough to intervene, our personal Resistance. It may seem ridiculous that I compare us with the Jews, that I equate what four girls lost with the murder of six million, but tell me, Anne, what do you do when he who should be hiding you is he that you are hiding from and his lieutenant is your mom?

The two of us are kindred souls, for we had a common enemy, a member of my family whom no one but my mother really knew. He hated you for being famous, even though your fame came at the cost of your life and because of a book that he swore that others wrote for you.

I wish I could forget the night we put an end to her, the also-Anne. We struck a deal without ever saying so: "I'll let you go, if you pretend . . ."

We didn't use those words or any others. I gave her and my sisters up. Was there nothing else I could have done? My sisters think I got the worst of it, alone with him so many years, the only daughter in the house. I think they feel the same guilt that I feel, something I could relieve them of if I had the courage.

He told me what he did to you, how much he got for just eight Jews. He made his gloating, boasting confession. Now I'm flaying myself with new guilt because it was your blood he spilled, even though it was not my fault. Yet it seems to me that I'm to blame for his every crime, even those he committed before I was born. No one accuses me but me, and also-Anne, my Shadow She.

The yellow light is long since passed. You're here with Margot and the Shadow She. Von Snout will have his way with all of you unless I intervene. You look as if you think the same thing, stare at me as if to say there must be something I can do, the deal-making daughter whose deal with Dad saved only me and let him have the rest.

The stream of time flows but one way,
it has to carry you away,
it has to carry me away.
The trick is to remember how
you saw when you were just a child
and see that way when you are old
in spite of everything you're told.
All things are what they were again;
time is an illusionist,
a charlatan, a sorceress.
You must look forward to the past
and make the future what it was.
No one, no thing is ever lost,
no moment is the uppermost
because it seems it happened last.
Time streams in all directions;
dismiss all the contradictions.
Don't try so hard to understand—
the truth will get the upper hand.
Death is neither near nor far—
it simply isn't anywhere.

You are not gone, you never were—
just know that you are always here
and you will never know despair.
Wise words I wrote when I got better
are nothing now but rows of letters,
a mere recasting of the Curse
that's always written in reverse.

The night persists, as do all the things of night. Von Snout, who lacks the courage of a boy, must destroy the things he fears.

What I wouldn't give for one night's sleep. I'd give my gift with words to sleep and never dream again. To sleep and never wake again.

The west wind rocks my mind from side to side. Perhaps, the more often you choose it, the easier the ultimate alternative becomes.

The yellow sky may not return. The rhymes that used to scare him off, the words I used to save my life, will soon be of no use to me. He'll call my bluff and revoke our deal. Should I give in or should I fight? Fight. A euphemism for what I have in mind. I can't go back; I'd rather fight him to the death, his death or mine. I hear him pacing back and forth, weighing the odds, remembering what it was like when I was young and he would bounce me on his knee.

"She's crazier than her sisters. She's been taking me for granted for ten years, ten years I have to make up for. I've had enough of it. I'll never have enough of her. Parading around the house half-dressed in front of me since she was thirteen and we happened upon that stupid girl.

For nights on end, I lay awake,
I listened to the sounds she'd make
as she lay awake in bed,
reminding me of what we did
and what we could be doing now—
she won't say no, she won't know how.
She's back to where she used to be:
she's holding nothing over me.

One vanished then, she'll vanish when
The wind blows from the west again."

Von Snout is almost sure of me.
He paws the dust and mauls the trees
and thrashes through the underbrush
as if I might grant him his wish
if he destroys Arellia.
He's roaring with frustration now,
but he'll work up the nerve somehow.
It won't be long, he'll come for you,
for Margot, Anne and You Know Who.
It won't be long, he'll come for me,
but not tonight—for now, we're free.

RACHEL

There wasn't a trick he didn't know, such as how to find out when my sisters and I were alone, or likely to be. Gloria, Carmen, Bethany and I, we all knew what he was up to when he asked Mom to fetch something from his office at the university or get him something at the supermarket. She knew too, and never said no. No one asked what sense it made for Mom to walk to the university or the store, to spend an hour or two doing what they could have done in ten minutes if they used the car.

Even when we were sailing from Cape Town to Southampton, it continued. We had three berths on the *Edinburgh Castle*, one for Bethany and me, one for Gloria and Carmen, and one for Mom and Dad. In each of the children's berths, there were two narrow bunks.

At various points during the voyage, Dad invented ailments for all four of us—seasickness, toothaches, tummy aches, earaches—and removed one of us from our bunk and sent us to sleep in his and Mom's bed so that he could be on hand if the "sick" one needed him through the night. When he announced that one of us had told him we weren't feeling well, we didn't contradict him or even say a word. We'd been chosen and that was it. Mom said nothing.

I sometimes worked up the nerve to be mischievous. "Why can't Mom keep me company?" I asked one night during dinner in the ship's dining room after Dad announced that I had told him I had an earache that would keep me up all night.

"Your mother's too tired after all the sun she had today," he said. My mother had spent the day in the shade, as she did every day, but didn't protest.

On another occasion, also at dinner, when he announced that Gloria was seasick, I observed that the rate at which she was working her way through dinner would have been remarkable even for someone who *wasn't* sick. "Seasickness is like that," Dad said. "Food makes it better for a while, but not for long." No one challenged this absurd assertion, not even the strangers who shared our table. It was as if he couldn't be bothered to make up a convincing excuse.

As a child, I thought every house with one or more girls in it was like our house. I didn't know that other fathers didn't do what he did to us. I had nothing to compare us to. I didn't ask the few friends I had about it.

He was like a doctor, gently persuading me to submit to things that, though new to me, were old hat to him, momentarily unpleasant things that he would see me safely through, just as he had done for many others. I was so young when he started that, by the time I was ten, I knew my part as well as he knew his. He didn't have to say a word. I didn't wonder why it happened. It was how things were, just as Elsie living in a shed and eating by herself in the kitchen and going back to Langa on the weekends was how things were.

I woke to the sound of doors being eased open and closed in the middle of the night, the floor of the hallway squeaking as he padded back and forth in his bare feet. I wondered which room he was headed to, preparing for the possibility that it was mine, but hoping it wasn't, and hating myself for hoping that he would go to one of the other three, or that he would go out in the car and look for girls whose names I would never know. Once I was certain that he hadn't chosen me, I went quickly back to sleep, so normal-seeming was it to be, or not be, spared. There was Dad by day and Dad by night, the house by day, the house by night; they were entirely different. He acted like a dad in the house by day. No one ever talked about the night, as if it was only an interval of silence and darkness and dreamless sleep that separated one day from the next. There was a place in my mind for what happened in the house at night, a place that, except at night, was locked and sealed.

I thought that, if I kept absolutely still and didn't make a sound, he would go to one of the other rooms. I clung to this notion even though he sometimes came to my room no matter how quiet I was. I pulled the blankets over my head and covered my ears with my hands as if the darkness and the silence would protect me, and I went on doing this even though it didn't work. I worried that he would come to my room every night if I wasn't careful. I thought of Anne Frank, lying awake in the Secret Annex, listening for sounds from outside, footsteps in the courtyard that might be those of the Gestapo, the clumping of boots on cobblestones growing louder as they neared 263 and then receding as her prayers that they wouldn't stop were answered every night. I thought of her wondering if Dussel, in the bed so close to hers, could hear the pounding of her heart.

When I heard the door opening, I pretended to be asleep, even though I knew it would not deter him. It was my opening gesture of doomed defiance, a delaying tactic that he seemed to relish. "I know my little Rachel Lee is not asleep," he said as he closed and locked the door.

"I'll tell Mom," I said. He didn't answer. "You have to leave in five minutes," I said.

"Ten minutes," he said.

"You should go to Carmen's room," I said. "You never go to Carmen's room."

"You know that's not true," he said as he knelt beside my bed. "But your sisters would be jealous if they knew that you're my favourite girl." I shook my head. "It's much too warm in here for all these blankets," he said.

"I'm afraid of my room."

"A room can't hurt you. You know that."

"This one can."

"Don't be silly."

"Now you have eight minutes."

There had to have been a first time. It was likely Gloria that he chose first. Then it got easier for him. It must have. How long had he considered it by then? Didn't he realize that there was no going back? Once you touch your daughter, you will forever be a man who touched his daughter, even if you never do it again. If you stop just short, you will only be a man who considered it. Did he know he was about to cross an infinite divide? There are many other infinite divides. By then, he may have crossed some of them. During the war. Once you cross one, you may as well have crossed them all. Is that how it is? Is that how he saw it? You can't take a life and give it back. And once you've taken one . . .

The day after they went shopping together, Gloria came by while Wade was at the library and told me she had confessed to Wade. She was in a panic but, though I was near panicking too, I managed to calm her down.

"He believed you?" I said. "You're absolutely sure that he believed you?"

"How can I be absolutely sure?" she said. "But he *seemed* to believe me when I said that no one was involved but me and Fritz and the man he hired."

"Have you told Fritz about this?"

"*No*," she said. "I've been thinking about what to do, but I haven't done *any*thing."

"Thank God," I said. "Don't tell Fritz Wade knows. Don't tell *any*one."

"I won't," she said. "But I thought you should know in case Wade confronted you, or told you, or *something*."

I hugged her and said she had done exactly what I would have done. She touched up her makeup in the mirror and left looking more or less composed.

I had called her on a Wednesday night when Max was away in Amsterdam.

At first I was so nervous I couldn't speak. Then I managed, "I think we need to do something about Dad."

Gloria said she didn't know what I meant.

"I can't stand to say it any other way," I said.

"I don't know what you mean."

"You *do* know what I mean," I said.

I told her things I'd never told anyone else. Each of my sisters had always known that what was happening to us was happening to us all, but we'd never said a word about it to each other until Bethany's accusations. But I told Gloria. She broke down, sobbing. And then she began to tell *me* things.

"I can't stand it," she said. "When I'm alone with him, or even just speaking to him on the phone, I feel as if I'm six years old again. I become a frightened little girl who does whatever Daddy says. I believe it when he tells me I've been bad and must be punished, or when he tells me that I have to do something again tomorrow because I didn't do it right today. He calls me his 'little G.' One minute, he tells me that I'm his favourite daughter because I'm the only one who loves him, that he'd be all alone if not for me, and the next he says that he likes you and Bethany and Carmen more than me because I never do what he tells me to. I still get sad when he tells me that he's sad. I still tell him, 'Don't be sad, Papa.' I still feel guilty when he tells me that he's mad with me. Jesus, Rachel, I can't go on like this. I can't. I literally can't. I've been thinking of how easy it would be to kill myself . . . It's the only thing that makes me feel a little better.

"You were the only one of the four of us still at home with them for years. You don't have to tell me what that means. I believe you that he hasn't gone near you since they came back from Switzerland. But he will. Once he's sure of Wade's daily routine, he will. And when you and Wade settle down somewhere, they'll visit you, mark my words, announced, unannounced. He arranges his entire life to maximize his access to his girls. He's bored to death between visits. That's why he can't keep still when none of us is available. Even if the police and the courts were an option, I know I wouldn't hold up through a trial. You wouldn't, and neither would Carmen or Bethany. And what credibility would we have? We're not exactly shining examples of normalcy. They moved back to South Africa because they knew you would soon be leaving home and Carmen and I are here. If Max and I moved, they'd follow us or go to live where you or Bethany are living. Max has actually given them money so they could visit us. He'll go on doing that, and he'll give them money so they can visit you, too. *I'd* give them money if Dad asked me for it. You and Wade would. They'd visit often and stay for as long as you let them. I can't say no to them. None of us can. If we could, we'd have done it by now. That's why we have to do something else."

It was as if she had forgotten that I was the one who suggested the idea in the first place.

I told her that, once, when Carmen was stoned on something, she had admitted to me that Dad had been driving along the Cape Flats late at night to Fritz's house and waiting outside in the car with the engine running until she came out. Carmen had been telling Fritz that Dad needed someone to keep him company while he drove around when he couldn't sleep. She'd been leaving the house in the dead of night, and Dad had been taking her someplace to park and taking her home afterward. She'd been going back to sleep without a word to Fritz.

"Bethany will go back to them," I said. "I know she will, long before that baby is born, if it ever is. It will make no difference to Dad that she's pregnant. Or else it *will* make a difference to him. He'll use it against her somehow. I'm sure he already has. Even if she keeps staying at your place, he'll visit her when you and Max are out of town, or even when you're not. You have a big house and he's gotten away with everything for years in smaller ones. He doesn't want to get any of us pregnant but he's jealous of any man who does. Imagine being jealous of Clive. But he is."

"Could we really do something like this?" Gloria said.

My heart was going a mile a minute. I told her what I had in mind, but I used so many euphemisms that she had no choice but to do the same. We spoke as if we thought the line was tapped.

"Do you know someone who does things like that?" she said. "Fritz does."

"Do you think *you* could live with it, Gloria?"

"I can't live with the alternative."

A week later, I sounded out Carmen and Bethany. Max was still travelling, so we met at Gloria's house—me, Gloria, Carmen and Bethany. And Fritz—Fritz, to whom Carmen had, a few nights before, told the truth about Dad. My excuse for Wade was that Gloria could use some company because Max was away. We sat around the enormous dining room table. The view through the window of the lights along the shore of the Apostles was so distracting that Gloria drew the drapes. Or perhaps she couldn't stand the thought that we'd be seen conferring.

I sat at the head of the table, Gloria on my immediate right, Bethany beside her, Carmen on my left, her head resting on Fritz's shoulder.

"The Star Chamber," Fritz said, grinning at me. I ignored him.

"Here's what I think," I said. "If we turn him in, the police will think we cooked it all up together. Or they'd believe us but blame us. They'd say, 'If you didn't want him to do what he did, why didn't you tell someone about it?' People would rather blame anyone than blame the father. Girls who have no better sense, wives who won't put out. Anyone. People don't understand that, after it's been through enough, your own mind will turn against you. A lot of people just wouldn't swallow that this was going on for so long and we said nothing."

There was much nodding around the table, everyone looking grim-faced, even Fritz.

"But this is not going to happen unless we all agree to it, all of us," I said. "If you're against it, say so now and we'll never speak of it again."

There was a long silence until Fritz spoke at last.

"Hans drove out to the Flats just last night," he said. "We heard the car pull up and saw the lights. I went out and he took off. I'm not always there. Even when I am there, I'm sometimes so out of it I don't notice when Carmen leaves the house."

"Dad stays in the yard for hours if he has to, waiting," Carmen said. "Sometimes I go out just to get it over with."

"There's nowhere else we can go to live," Fritz said. "Our life, whatever the rest of you might think of it, is here."

"What about Mom?" I said.

"She's as bad as him," Carmen said. "Worse. He's crazy. What's her excuse?"

"This is not about revenge," Bethany said. "For me, it's about my baby."

Fritz laughed. "Not even a teeny-weeny bit of revenge, Lady MacBethany? I don't mind saying that I want payback for what he's done to Carmen."

"If we leave Mom out of it," I said, "she'll divide her time between the four of us until she dies." Carmen and Fritz snorted derisively. "The three of us, at least. And you never know, Carmen, when your marital circumstances might change. You might get tired of waiting for the revolution."

"Wishful thinking," Fritz said.

"I've imagined our lives with her still in it," I said. "Myra van Hout alone because of us. Imagine my children's lives, your lives and your children's lives if she was still around, if we had to go back to pretending, for her sake, that he never touched us, if we had to go back to pretending that one million other obviously untrue things were true. We are under her control as much as we are under his. That would continue without him. On the other hand, I can't bring myself to hurt her. I've thought about it and I can't."

"We'll hurt her by hurting Dad," Bethany said. "But she doesn't use us the way he does. We should leave her out of it."

"Hans the unknown hero of the Dutch Resistance," Carmen said.

"We don't know what he did or didn't do during the war," Gloria said.

"Oh, come *on*," Bethany said, looking to me for support. "I still wake up reciting *The Ballad of the Clan van Hout* in my head."

"Gloria's right," I said. "We don't know and we'll never know. Not for certain."

Fritz frowned and shook his head. "The guy I have in mind—I don't think he'll be in unless it's both of them. Too tricky to pull off otherwise. How you all feel about your mother is irrelevant."

"No, it's not," Bethany said. She dabbed tears from her eyes with a Kleenex. "I wish there was some other way. It seems hard to believe that there's not. Were we never a family? I remember times when I was happy."

"Children live in the moment," I said. "That's why they heal so quickly. For a while, at least." I, too, remembered times when I was happy. When I was a child, happiness could come on the heels of misery and not be tarnished by it. I saw phantoms of happiness in family photographs and heard them in *The Ballad*. I also remembered what it was like when the four of us were little girls, waiting for the sound of him getting out of bed or hearing the car in the driveway and his footsteps on the stairs, each of us wondering which room he would visit, which one of us he'd pick that night. There was no pattern. Having been chosen the night before didn't mean you wouldn't be chosen again. But I wasn't a helpless child anymore. I didn't want to die before my time. I didn't ever want to lose my mind. As things stood, both seemed definite and imminent.

"I hate this so much," Bethany said.

"So do I," Carmen said. "But not as much as I hate them."

"I don't *hate* them. I hate *this*, having to do *this*."

"You don't have to lift a finger," Fritz said.

"I have a conscience," Bethany said.

"It was implanted in your brain when you were too young to resist," Fritz said. "You know, this is how revolutions start. A handful of people, a cell meeting secretly."

"You're not a revolutionary, Fritz," Bethany said. "We're not revolutionaries. This is a conspiracy. You're not here for Carmen's sake. You're here to make money. You're here because you're the only person we know who can find someone to do this."

Fritz laughed. "Bethany, keep trying to work up the nerve to kill your*self*. This is not a country of merciful Canadians. The penalty for murder is not life in prison; it's death. My fee reflects the fact that I'm the only one who knows the name of the guy we're hiring."

"Sleep lightly," Bethany said. "You never know when your guy might decide to tie up a loose end."

"The four of you would be loose ends too. You and your consciences."

"You might keep all the money for yourself and do nothing, Fritz," I said. "What could we do about it? Or you might try to do it yourself to avoid splitting the money with this man of yours who you say will do it right. He might not even exist."

"He exists. And he'll do it right."

"Do it *right*?" Bethany said. "There's no way of doing this right."

This is how it was—bickering, threats and, threaded through it all, the gradual piecing together of a plot to kill our father, which, as the hours went by, became so detailed and plausible that the squabbling stopped and we stared blank-faced at the table like children who'd been scolded into silence.

"What we're planning," I said at last, "won't rid us of our memories of him. But there is a way to leave Mom out of this."

"Are we agreed that we should?" Gloria said. "Speak up if you're not." No one did.

I took a notepad and a pen out of my purse, opened it and placed it on the table in front of me. "I've written some things down, in Arellian, just in case. But there are still some things left to talk about. Things we know about Dad that Fritz's guy will need to know."

"I always knew that that language you invented would come in handy someday," Fritz said.

Bethany leaned across the table toward him. "She wants you to swear on your word of honour as a scumbag that you won't double-cross us."

"You'll have to trust me," Fritz said.

"This all sounds so creepy," Carmen said.

"She's right," Bethany said, shuddering. "Maybe if we didn't refer to them as Mom and Dad—"

"Make up your minds now. We do it or we don't," Gloria said.

"Okay, okay," Bethany said.

By this point, the only one in the room not crying was Fritz. I asked him to go upstairs so that the four of us could talk.

As he made for the stairs, he stopped and looked back.

"The Final Solution," he said.

"Never mind him," Gloria whispered to me.

Carmen leaned back in her chair and closed her eyes. I took her hand and joined hands with Gloria, who took Bethany's hand as she reached across for Carmen's. Carmen opened her eyes and looked around at the three of us. I tried to think of something to say.

—

I made a checklist and went over it countless times, convinced that I had overlooked something. It had to be late enough for Nora to be asleep in the shed. There was no point in trying to make it look like a botched burglary, because my parents' rundown house with the rusting Ford Cortina in the driveway looked far less promising for a thief than any other house on the street. Also, if Nora or the DeVrieses or Max noticed that something had been taken and it was later found, because it had been sold or imperfectly disposed of, it might be traced back to Fritz's man.

After Gloria gave Fritz the money, I made him promise that he would not contact us to let us know that it was done. We would simply wait to hear.

I chose the day Mom would be away attending the Star of the Sea Convent School's annual reunion and fundraiser with Theresa DeVries. She'd been looking forward to it since she'd come back to South Africa.

Early in the afternoon, Gloria and Max went by Liesbeek Road to visit Mom and Dad. Gloria told them she had to go to the bathroom. She did go to the bathroom but, on the way back to the front room, she went to the kitchen and opened the fridge. His glass of Horlicks was there as always, a saucer on top, which she quickly removed. She broke in half four of Bethany's Valium capsules, poured the powder into the Horlicks and stirred it around. Forty milligrams of Valium. We had to be sure that he was in bed, asleep, and not lying awake as usual, or walking around the house or the backyard, or out prowling in his car.

I thought often about phoning Fritz to tell him to call it off, to give the money to the man he said he'd hired, and to keep his share and forget about the rest of it. I thought about it, but I didn't do it.

From *The Ballad of the Clan van Hout*

SCAPEGOAT (1985)
I know My looked the other way.
I've known it ever since the day
I came to bed from Carmen's room,
my face so flushed, my clothes askew.
I knew that I had been found out;
at first I thought She might walk out
or turn me in or turn me out.
We made a silent pact that night:
she'd overlook what wasn't right
but we would never speak of it.
We'd go on as we had before;
I'd keep it all behind closed doors.
It binds us like no other thing,
the meaning of a wedding ring,
the sacred secret that we share,
the thing that makes us what we are.

Why was She not enough for me?
(Nor was my Glormenethalee
and others too—I doubt She knows
how many there have been of those,
or what became of most of them.)
I think of when She was so slim,
when She was young and beautiful,
not that much older than those girls.
I couldn't get enough of Her.
She tired of my flattery,
but it was not because of me,
so I went down the hall to them,
but they were not enough for me:
no number was enough, you see.
I wanted what I couldn't have;

sometimes it makes me want to laugh.
It made me want them all the more,
for She was just the appetizer,
my girls my entree for a while,
but still not quite a bellyful . . .

I read this part to Rachel Lee;
soon after, she abandoned me:
This is not the Nazi waiter;
this is something even greater,
which means it's even worse for us,
and that is why we must discuss
the accusations being made
by those Without about your dad.
I drive the streets alone at night,
get out of bed, turn off the light.
Oh how I love my nightly drives;
they let me think about the lives
of other husbands, other wives.
I like to watch the girls, of course—
by ten they're always out in force.
I see the girls in twos and threes,
the girls like you girls used to be,
and like the ones I used to see
back home in the Land of Hout
on sleepless nights when I went out
and sometimes came home furtively,
so worried that I would wake My
or wake you girls that I would stay
downstairs till you began the day.
I know I needn't spell it out;
you know your father drives about
because his ulcers keep him up—
he hardly gets a minute's sleep.
It's better that I leave the house

than creep around it like a mouse
and keep the two of you awake—
a family of insomniacs!
No movies play around the clock;
you go to bars, you have to drink.
The strongest thing I drink is milk—
sometimes the Horlicks makes me sick!
So out I go into the night—
there's not another soul in sight.
The bad man must be Hans van Hout
because the bad are always bald
and most are fifty-four-year-old
university professors:
the jails are full of lecturers,
and vicious intellectuals.
The worst are the accounting profs
who scramble up onto the roofs
and jump on young girls passing by.
(The ones with gowns know how to fly.)
Because some crimes have gone unsolved,
and someone must have been involved,
they've got it narrowed down to this:
it's either me or someone else.
It seems my car is everywhere—
they saw it here while it was there,
or going east while headed west—
almost enough for an arrest.
It seems I own a magic car
that goes so fast it disappears.
It seems that I'm behind the wheel
of every single vehicle
on every single city street
at every moment every night
and every car looks just like mine.
It's all the fault of the police,

this witch hunt that will never cease.
They can't seem to investigate
the number of a licence plate.
I never drive it very far
but they're obsessed with van Hout's car.
More often home than it is not,
it sits there in the very spot
I park it in night after night:
the driveway of the van Hout house—
you can't get more conspicuous!
They still suspect me of those crimes:
I wish I knew how many times
they've parked across from 44
and stared and stared at our door
and stared and stared at that front step
till they deduced the sun was up.
While criminals just roam about,
they wait in vain for Hans van Hout!
They seem to think they have their man
and yet the crimes go on and on;
they took me in for questioning
and then they let me go again.
I'm not ashamed to say that My
is glad to be my alibi—
"Where did you go three months ago,
the night that there was so much snow?"
Who has that kind of memory?
She told them, "He was home with me."

Beware of what you hear out there;
my enemies are everywhere.
Their daughters went to school with you
and gossip like their parents do.
They'll seem so nice, it's just pretend—
they'll play a game called "let's be friends"

to try to worm it out of you:
they'll say they know it isn't true,
it isn't true what people say,
but still they'll say it every day,
and they'll closely watch your face
in case you show some hint, some clue—
and if you don't, they'll turn on you.
When they do, you must be ready—
no one else will vouch for Daddy.

Who are these girls that disappear?
It's in the winter of the year
that girls go missing everywhere.
They're not the ones from proper homes;
they run away from home in droves—
you don't run from a place that's safe
to strike out for another life.
They have one thing to bargain with,
the ones that are so slim and lithe—
they get more than they bargain for
the second they step out the door.
The evil man who lurks about
is not Professor Hans van Hout.
The safe place is the House Within;
let's both say those words again.
The way they dress, they freeze to death:
they don't grow up, they don't grow old,
they catch their deaths out in the cold;
their deaths catch them is what I mean—
their epitaphs are "when last seen."
No one has taught them wrong from right;
they stand beneath street lights at night,
alone, half-dressed, on drugs, drinking—
what on earth are parents thinking?
All of it is self-expression—

an odd way to express yourself,
to dress so as to bait the wolf.
Not until they've been undressed
do girls these days feel self-expressed.

Cops can't admit they got it wrong;
they must invent a bogeyman
who steals their precious girls away—
they have to make some stranger pay:
"Some man was seen the other day—
he's not from here, it must be him.
We can't blame us, we can't blame them,
we'll blame the high-and-mighty man,
the foreign-sounding also-ran;
it's obvious where he went wrong—
he simply cannot get along."

It seems your father, Hans van Hout,
has been chosen as the scapegoat,
a role that he was born to play,
Professor Hout, from Bantry Bay,
who drives about the streets at night
and parks his car in vacant lots
and other such suspicious spots
and listens to the radio
and thinks of things from long ago
that his accusers do not know,
the war, the fall of Amsterdam,
the ones who fought, the ones who ran,
the memories that forbid sleep,
the secrets I have had to keep.

It all starts in the House Within;
that's where the best and worst begin.
You have to bring a girl up right

(make sure her jeans are not too tight).
Don't let her stay out after ten.
The House Within, the House Within—
that's where the tale begins again.
I must go back to chapter one;
I have to get it right this time:
the lines must scan, the words must rhyme.

Throw out the drafts, erase the past;
I know this chance will be my last
to re-right what they did to me,
to rewrite what they wrote of me.
I must create the world anew;
it's what the greatest writers do.
There were no other families—
I must invent the memories:
in order to perfect the world
I'll have to raise four perfect girls.
You let me down, my Rachel Lee,
but I still have the other three.

From *The Arelliad*

MYRA (1985)

He comes home late most every night—
I go to bed, leave on the light
above the door, but I don't sleep:
there is a watch I have to keep.

He thinks that I'm protecting Him
(unless he only thinks of Them
and never thinks of me at all).
What those who take Him for a fool
take me to be is plain to see
(to Him, perhaps, a mystery).

The truth is I'm protecting me. It's far too late for Myra van Hout to be a prison inmate's loyal and faithful wife. Hans would never leave me for anyone except those four. I've taken my share of the blame for Him, and I've done my best for Them.

They think that they have had it bad, but I grew up without a dad. I didn't throw myself at every pair of pants or starve myself. I didn't self-lobotomize with drugs and booze. I never tried to run away inside some book like someone half-demented, pretending that she wrote in a language she invented while idolizing long-dead Jews.

The four of Them are women now, and still He has his way with Them. They won't, or can't, say no. It seems He needs all four of Them but has no need of me—we last kissed when I was forty.

It's no big deal what they've been through. Others have come through it none the worse. I suppose I cleared the way for Him: He wrote for Them, He read to Them—my Husband was *my* gift to Them, as were my girls my gift to Him. The five of them have special love, but I have none at all—though, in my way, I still have Him.

If He was caught, they'd let me go. I'd be the wife who lived in blissful ignorance, so blinded was she by her love for Him and Them.

Or else I'd be regarded as stupid and gullible, or even callous, the woman who knew but looked the other way.

You'd be surprised what women do
to make the fairy tale seem true,
the perfect spouse, the wedding dance,
the perfect house, the picket fence,
the perfect kids in Perfect School,
the backyard with the perfect pool—
and what was she? A perfect fool.

Years ago, I thought of nothing but the worst. How would it look if people knew? Where would we go? How would we get by? "The hero of the underground." He had to spread all that around. For all I know, it might be true, but saying it made Him look like such a craven fool, as much in need of a pat on the head as some attention-seeking child. He said things first, then thought them through.

What He does when He goes out is something I don't think about. I know what He's guilty of, but He's not guilty of *everything*. I think I know the man I love better than others do. I'm not some twit who wouldn't see a monster right in front of me. They're barking up the same wrong tree that others barked up long ago. Hans van Hout, the bald professor, is not the man they're looking for—it's just that He can't help saying and doing things that make Him look suspicious. He's not their man, no, He is mine. They need someone to blame it on, someone to frame for it. They can't just come out and admit that, although young girls in St. John's go missing more and more, they don't know why. To cover their incompetence, they'll try to force Him to confess to something that He didn't do, and I doubt that He could stand up to the kind of methods they would use. It's not a crime to drive at night. He always has because of his insomnia. But they hope that His inconsequence can cover their incompetence. We have to get out of here.

It may not be too late to start again
back there in the Land Within,
back there in the Land of Hout,
back there where we started out,
back where *The Ballad* first began
and Hans was still a strong young man
and I was young and beautiful
and everything seemed possible.
It's not too late to turn back time—
the lines still scan, the words still rhyme.

RACHEL

I suspected that Fritz and the others were worried about our plan to go home through Amsterdam, where, at the sight of Anne Frank's house, I might fall apart and tell Wade everything. I was surprised that Gloria hadn't tried to convince me to take a different route back to Canada. I confronted her about it on the phone. "So the whole gang's coming," I said. "Are you and Carmen and Bethany as worried as Fritz must be about what I might do in Amsterdam?"

"It's Fritz we want to keep an eye on, not you. When he said he and Carmen were going with you, I convinced Max that, given how fragile you are, we should go too, and there was no question about leaving Bethany on her own, so . . . But, your first visit to Anne Frank's house, coming so soon after—I don't think some sisterly support would hurt, do you?"

"I suppose not," I said, and left it at that.

Sisterly support. I didn't doubt that the prospect of Wade and I being watched over by no one but Fritz and Carmen made Gloria and Bethany uneasy, but I was a problem for them because I was not only in love, but in love with honest, earnest, idealistic, truth-seeking Wade. They saw Wade as the foremost of my many weaknesses. And so, I must admit, did I.

I called a professor at Leiden University whom I had frequently corresponded with about Anne Frank when I was doing my honours paper, a woman who didn't know about my breakdowns and thought I was still working on it. I asked her if she might know of anywhere we could stay in Amsterdam for a few days. The woman told me that my timing was perfect. She visited Amsterdam so often to do research and give lectures and papers that she had rented a small flat there, and she would not be using it for a while. She said we could stay there at no cost and told me to think of it as one scholar doing a favour for another. She seemed so sweet, I felt bad for having tricked her into lending us her flat, which was on Prinsengracht, just a few bridges away from Anne Frank's house, and one canal and a few bridges away from the house in which Dad had grown up.

At the airport, I hoped I didn't look as nervous as I felt. I worried that the authorities would find it suspicious that *all* of us were leaving South Africa just weeks after the murder of the van Houts. It might seem, even to the apathetic police, that we were on the run. What if the man Fritz had hired had given himself away by spending too much money, or boasted of his exploits to a friend while he was drunk?

I imagined all of us being taken into custody, if not now, then at Schiphol in Amsterdam, or Wade and I being detained in Halifax, where we had to touch down before the final leg of our journey home.

At the check-in counter, we sisters were recognized by name by a ticket agent who, as she was handing Bethany her boarding pass, burst into tears. All the ticket agents, young women like us, gathered around. Soon, they were crying over the tragic deaths of our parents, which set Bethany off, which prompted Carmen and I to begin to cry as well.

"I'm so sorry," the ticket agents kept saying, almost in unison.

The knot of weeping women attracted the attention of everyone within sight, people staring, craning their necks. "Who is it?" "What's happened?" "Is something wrong?"

To my great relief, the ticket agents eventually returned to their stations and we made it through security without incident, in spite of the sullen scrutiny of the ever-present military men in military fatigues.

For the first time, it occurred to me that my parents' secrets were now safe. We were free to reinvent them; in death, Hans could be the man who risked his life to save the lives of girls like us, and Myra, his loving wife and the mother of their perfect girls. The family charade could be maintained in its entirety for relatives and friends forever. The only flaw in the whole thing was Wade. Gloria must have been cursing the fluke of her confession. I wondered if she was cursing Wade, the one person who might try to wreck it all. *I* still wondered if he could withstand the pressure of his conscience or the chastening presence of me in his life. For days, he had watched me as, worn out from writing in the diary, I lay sleepless in bed. At any point during those hours of darkness, without having to look me in the eye, he could have told me what had happened at the shopping mall and what Gloria had confessed to by the sea below her house. But, somehow, he hadn't.

WADE

I wondered if the share of the money Gloria had given Fritz to arrange the murder was on his person or in his luggage. I couldn't imagine him leaving it in his house out on the Cape Flats while he was in Amsterdam, because, the Cape Flats being what they were, he couldn't even be reasonably sure that his house would still be standing when he got back. But Fritz seemed relaxed, gazing about in his black beret, sunglasses, tie-dyed shirt, bell-bottoms and sandals. He all but whistled as the security agents rummaged through his khaki shoulder bag, the one plastered all over with peace symbols and decals bearing images of clenched black fists. If some other security agents went through his checked baggage with as much zeal as these were going through his carry-on bag, they would surely find something incriminating—even trace amounts of drugs. If Fritz was detained or taken into custody, would Gloria be next, and if so, what might lie in store for Rachel and me?

But we boarded the plane without incident. Max and Gloria sat in first class, dressed in their SAA uniforms, with Bethany, Rachel and I seated three abreast in coach, Fritz and Carmen several rows behind us.

As we taxied down the runway, I remembered Rachel telling me how she had felt during the Soweto riots in '76 when she waited for her plane to lift off from the airport in Johannesburg. It seemed entirely possible to me that our plane would be stopped and boarded by police come to arrest Gloria and Fritz, and to detain the rest of us for questioning or worse.

After takeoff, I kept waiting for the pilot to say that we were returning to the airport, kept waiting for the plane to bank in a series of turns that would point us back the way we came. Even when I felt certain that South Africa no longer lay beneath us, it occurred to me that all of Africa and the Middle East lay between us and the relative safety of Holland—relative because there was nowhere in the world, now, that we could go and be absolutely certain that we were out of reach of the South African police, or Interpol or any other number of agencies, or the man Fritz had hired.

"Hey," Bethany said from her window seat, "Remember the *Edinburgh Castle*?"

Rachel nodded and smiled.

"I remember looking at all the other kids who got on board in Cape Town and wondering how many of them were leaving home for good like us," Bethany said.

"I bet that almost none of them were," Rachel said. "I bet that most of them came back and grew up in South Africa. We must have looked out of place in first class, all six of us, I mean."

"Maybe that's why Mom and Dad aren't in any of the photographs from the boat."

"Maybe," Rachel said. "Whenever I've left South Africa, it's been with them. It seems strange, leaving without them. I wonder if I'll ever come back."

"Of course you will," Bethany said. "You'll come back to visit us."

"I suppose," Rachel said. "But don't you plan to get out of there as soon as you get the chance?"

"I can't think that far ahead. I can't imagine having choices."

Later, Bethany moved to the empty row behind us, stretched across the three seats and went to sleep. As I was wondering, yet again, what she and Rachel would think if they knew what Gloria had told me, Bethany rose up and stuck her face between our headrests. "Raitch," she said, "I read *The Diary of Anne Frank* last night. I'd forgotten most of it, no offence. God. For almost two years, she slept in a tiny room with that dentist, Fritz Pfeffer. Don't you think he sounds kind of creepy? Maybe it's just because his first name was Fritz. No wonder she didn't like him very much. And he ate far more than his share of the food. I bet he was dashing in a chubby, disgusting sort of way." Bethany laughed but Rachel didn't. "Sorry. I shouldn't make jokes about the sacred book. Prinsengracht 263. One of the most famous addresses in the world. I can't believe Otto Frank died only a few years ago. He lived a long life even though he lost his wife and his two daughters. No one thinks about Margot. The forgotten sister. He survived Auschwitz, somehow, and then he lived for another thirty-five years. He lost everything, but he never gave up. He must have been very tough."

"He was a great man," Rachel said. "A great father. At least, I hope he was."

"The four of us have been to Amsterdam so many times, but we've never been to Anne Frank's house. Don't you think that's strange?"

"Not at all," Rachel said. "We didn't go because I went nuts about Anne Frank. That and the fact that Mom didn't want Dad finding out that we'd been there. This might be my last chance to see the *Achterhuis*. I feel like I *have* to see it."

"Well, *I* have to say that I don't think you visiting her house is a good idea."

"I don't either," I said.

"I *feel* like it is," Rachel said to Bethany. "Just like you *feel* that you're fat."

"Ouch. Oh well, I'm penniless, pregnant and stark raving mad. What do I know? Who knows when *I'll* get back to Amsterdam again? And, by the way, a pregnant woman gets fatter the more pregnant she gets. It's not her imagination. I'll finally be able to convince other people that I *am* getting fatter. I'm starting to think that Gloria is the most normal one of us all. Scary thought."

Bethany went on like that as if she might keep it up all the way to Amsterdam, but she eventually went back to sleep.

As was the case on the flight to South Africa, the passenger announcements from the captain and flight crew were made in English, Dutch, German, French and Afrikaans. I was tired of being surrounded by people who seemed to be able to get by in any language.

Half the time over the past few months, I hadn't understood what *anyone* was saying. Dutch, German, French, Spanish, Afrikaans, Xhosa, Zulu, Swahili—I couldn't speak any of them.

And there was one language whose very existence affronted me—Arellian. Written by no one but Rachel. Comprehensible to no one but her. Never spoken except, rarely, by her. I had never heard it. A non-existent language? I again wondered. Over the past few days, every time she'd said the word *Arellian*, I'd felt like screaming at her that there was no such thing.

What went through Rachel's mind while she was "writing," I couldn't begin to guess, even after months of living with her. Nothing, perhaps. Surely the most obsessive, the most delusional thoughts, would be better than nothing. I wondered if she would ever get back to writing in the diary for only an hour a day, let alone rid herself of Anne Frank and the book. I knew what would become of her, and of *us*, if she got worse.

I was glad I had given in to Gloria's plea that I keep her secret. What chance of a return to even near-normalcy would Rachel have if she knew what Gloria had done?

As if my unspoken question had triggered her, Rachel took a large notepad from her seat pocket and began to write at a furious pace, hunched over her serving tray, her hair hanging like a tent around the page.

AMSTERDAM

(1985)

WADE

Six months ago, the sight of Amsterdam would have exhilarated and confounded me: the bewildering network of canals spanned by innumerable bridges, the slick, polished-by-time cobblestones, the criss-crossing streams of old-fashioned bicycles with baskets on their handlebars—bicycles as likely to be ridden by nuns and men in three-piece suits as by students. However, aside from the fact that I felt more at home in the chilly early summer of Western Europe than I had in the heat of South Africa, my main impression of Amsterdam was that it was not Cape Town. Gone were the "*Blanke*" and "*Nie-Blanke*" signs and all the other racist trappings of Cape Town, the ever-lowered eyes of the coloureds and the blacks who moved about among the whites as unobtrusively as if they were invisible.

Gone, too, of course, were the blacks and the coloureds, for the city was full of whites paler than those of Newfoundland.

After finding our flat and dropping our bags, Rachel and I walked two and a half miles to Merwedeplein, the apartment building in Amsterdam South, where, after fleeing Germany, the Franks had lived on the second floor from 1933 to 1942. I tried to imagine Amsterdam after its occupation by the Germans in May of 1940, those who had been identified as Jews walking about the cobblestone streets, the conspicuous yellow Star of David enclosing the word *Jood* stitched onto the front of their clothing, the Jews still seemingly free but soon not to be.

Rachel pointed at the window of the Franks' flat. "The only film that exists of Anne Frank is of her leaning out that window to watch the wedding of some family friends. It lasts about three seconds. She laughs and smiles. She was happy here. They all were, for a while."

By 1942, Jews were not allowed to use the trams, so, the day they went into hiding, the Franks had carried all their movable possessions with them for two and a half miles through the rain to Prinsengracht. "People sometimes forget that the Franks were Germans," Rachel said. "Anne's father fought on the side of the Germans in World War I. It's said that he was proud to have served his country with such honour. Anti-Semites try to make Otto Frank out to be a bit of a shady character. The business he co-owned with his non-Jewish friend made food preservatives. When he and his family went into hiding, he signed the company over to the friend and it operated throughout the war. People say that he made money from helping to keep the Germans in rations, the very Germans who killed his wife and daughters. But that's not true. He was so poor by the end of the war that he had to live with friends for the next seven years.

"Fritz once said to me, 'Have you ever wondered how he survived Auschwitz? He did it by informing on the other prisoners, that's my guess. He was once a German soldier. That would have impressed the Nazis.' But none of the others who survived Auschwitz accused him of being an informer. None of them accused him of anything."

On the way back, we walked by the house in which Hans grew up, one of a row of high, attached houses that opened onto a canal-facing street, all of it unchanged since the war, just as the *Achterhuis* and the buildings around it remained unchanged.

"He was a child once, in that house," Rachel said, her eyes welling with tears. I put my arm around her waist and pulled her to me. "I wonder what happened in there. Nothing, maybe. Or did he do what he did to Bethany, and maybe to me and my other sisters, because someone in that house did the same to him? Or did something even worse happen to him? It's just a house. But it was just a house in the 1930s and '40s, too. Our houses were never just houses. Each of them seemed like the entire world. Maybe this house was never just a house to him."

"Things will get better," I said, hugging her hard. "They will when we're back home."

I looked again at Hans's childhood home. In Amsterdam, many collaborated in the hope of saving their lives or improving their lot. From what I now knew about Hans, I suspected he wanted to be accepted by the Nazis because he had never been accepted by any group before. In his adult life, he was excluded by every group in which he sought membership because he repeatedly curried favour with his superiors by informing on those he believed to have been unfairly promoted at his expense. He was certain that he had been held back by favouritism, nepotism or inexplicably bad judgment. He may even have believed that what the Nazis sought to create was a pure meritocracy in which the strong would advance and the weak be left behind, a society, a world, in which there would be no advantage in being high-born, and in which those who accrued wealth by usury, dishonesty and greed would be relieved of it and thereafter relieved of life itself. I imagined Hans having been made a kind of honorary Nazi by the men whom he amused by his presumptuous eagerness to be one of them. If I was right, it was a wonder one of them hadn't shot him dead on a whim.

It struck me that Rachel had been right when she said that history happened not in some nebulous, exceptional elsewhere, but in ordinary concrete places, to commonplace people. My world shrank to this pair of unexceptional streets, to Hans and his family, to Anne Frank and hers. History, the war, the fate of the Franks, were personal, local, terrifyingly actual and immediate. I imagined Hans as a teenager looking out of one of the windows of the house, his hands pressed to the glass as the Nazis marched past, their boots clumping on the cobblestones, row after row of bluff and bravado and menace without purpose, a lethal behemoth composed of men just like the ones who ran South Africa and those who supported them, greater only in number, driven to savagery by a group of men whose madness they need not have fallen for but did for reasons that flattered none of humankind.

More than forty years ago, when my father was less than half his present age, these things had happened *here*. One street away, the two teenage daughters of a man who, ostensibly, was not unlike Hans van Hout were dragged from their hiding place along with six other people and, for no reason but that they were Jews, were sent to concentration camps. Westerbork, Auschwitz-Birkenau, Bergen-Belsen—in chronological order, the series of camps to which Anne Frank and her family were sent and where they stayed until they died, places that, before the war, were no more sinister-sounding than St. John's or Halifax.

RACHEL

I didn't sleep a minute during our first two nights in Amsterdam. I sat up in bed beside Wade, writing in a frenzy in the diary.

"Two days now and we haven't gone to Anne Frank's house," he said. "You've barely budged from this apartment, from this *bed*. This is how you told me it was when you were sick."

"Not even close. I mean it. I'm not shipshape but I'm a far cry from being at my worst."

"You write and write, but you never seem to stop to think about a single word. You write as if you're writing the same thing over and over."

"I'm not. And I'm not ready to go, but I will be soon."

"You're writing so hard, the bed is shaking and the springs are creaking. There are better ways to make a bed do those things."

"I'm sorry," I said. "Things will get back to normal. *We* will. But right now, here in Amsterdam, it feels as if she's everywhere. I can't think about anything else."

That night, I left Wade sleeping and I went to stand on the canal bridge closest to *Het Achterhuis*. I leaned on the rail, facing the water. Every man who crossed the bridge slowed down to appraise me. None of them spoke, but I sensed them wondering, hoping. What is a woman doing on a bridge by herself this late at night?

I thought of what might happen if I told Wade the truth about my involvement. I was afraid that it would drive him away, but also afraid that it would destroy him, whether he stayed with me or not.

He loved me. There was not enough left of me to love him as much as he loved me. I would lose him if I told him. I might lose him if I didn't. It seemed that dead ends lay in all directions.

I had my first copy of *Het Achterhuis*, mummified by various kinds of tape, hidden beneath my coat. I tried to work up the nerve to let it slide from my hands into the water as if by accident. I wasn't sure that it would sink, and wished that I had tested it in the tub in our flat. If it floated away, I might follow it as I would a person who was in need of rescuing. I might follow it until I lost sight of it. I wouldn't have minded if someone rescued it, ripped the tape open and found the forbidden book and somehow preserved it. *Look what I found, floating in the canal. There must be a story behind it. What do you think it could be?* It would be nice if it inspired speculation, stories—another myth, another legend, yet more lore about Anne Frank, of which I was secretly the origin. Perhaps the mummy would make it all the way to the Amstel River and never be found. Eventually, the tape would loosen, decay and release the book, which, upon contact with the water, would dissolve.

I could just jump in when there was no one on the bridge but me, leaving the book and Wade and the world behind. Another abandonment of Wade, possibly his destruction. I decided that I would not jump, or drop the book. I needed to go back to him because *he* needed me.

From *The Arelliad*

HOLOCAUST (1975)
Beware, my friends, because the past
Becomes the present very fast.

I move among them every day as if some invisible spy has infiltrated their hiding place and has no fear of being caught, an eavesdropping, trespassing voyeur. In Anne's book, the observations are the same; their life-prolonging self-confinement drags by through a tedium of days that seem identical, nothing to distinguish one from another but the food their minders cook for them on the free side of the bookcase. Just the length of the breezeway away is a world that was once theirs, but whose very air is forbidden to them now.

It isn't with her liberation
that her words reach their conclusion,
or with her words that her book ends.
It ends: "Anne's diary ends here,"
the words of her first editor—
that's where it ends; the book ends there.
The diary must end too soon,
or, rather, it must never end,
only seem to be abandoned,
put aside because of boredom,
cast aside because of freedom.
In time of war, in time of peace,
the record of events must cease—
the writer is outlived by time
and time outlives the writer's name,
for time continues just the same.

The last entry of *Het Achterhuis*, ten days before the raid took place, does mark a kind of ending, though—she must have sensed, the story goes, that they were about to be caught. She wishes that she was the last person left on earth, that there was no one left alive but her, Anne Frank, living in a world of absolute freedom and solitude, a respite at last from the suffocating confines of those tiny rooms.

The sunrays move around the walls. The dark is coming much too soon. It's summer, but the light is that of a winter afternoon, the afterlight of a sun that set before the day was done.

Might she have known the end was near and not have been surprised by the breaking down of the lower door, the sound of footsteps on the stairs, the loudest sound she'd heard in years, the thundering Gestapo boots, her mother screaming, "Please don't shoot." So long confined to one small space, so long accustomed to the faces and voices of the others and their minders, she must have known this was the end. How strange the strangers must have seemed as more and more Gestapo streamed through the secret passageway as if into the hiding place of the only eight Jews they'd been searching for since the war began. They stormed and stomped about that secret tiny space where, for years, only whispering had been allowed, where three children, three men and two women had been hiding out but now were caught, each of them soon accused of being born a Jew and refusing to sacrifice themselves to murder. Her father, shamefaced, looked about as if he thought he should have found a better place for them to hide. His daughters froze while Edith fell to the floor.

All eight were sent to Westerbork, a transit camp at which they worked until the Franks were moved again, this time to Auschwitz on a train.

I'm travelling with them in a windowless boxcar whose destination is known to all, though no one dares to say its name. All of us are crammed together, with no choice but to use each other to keep from falling to the floor as the speeding train sways wildly back and forth.

"It's barely possible to breathe."

"I think I might just sweat to death."

"It won't be like some people are saying. There'll be a place for us to stay. Why else would they let us take so much with us, clothing, linen, pots and pans. I'm not expecting first-class accommodations, but all this talk of coming misery is nonsense, if you're asking me."

> I see the Frank family. I have no doubt that it is Them.
> I speak, but in Arellian.
> They cannot hear me, anyway—
> the youngest of Them looks my way.
> I have no doubt that it is Her,
> the very picture of her picture,
> the famous one that Otto took,
> the cover of her famous book.
> Her face takes on a different look,
> no longer Anne of Anne Frank's book:
> she stares at things but doesn't see,
> nor does she see them inwardly;
> her mind's a blank, it's not like mine
> that must be thinking all the time—
> or so it seems, perhaps she spies
> the look that I cannot disguise;
> she understands it, in which case
> Anne Frank has recognized her Fate.

Crammed into a corner of the car, Otto, with his back against a wooden bar that is nailed across two doors, his arms around his wife and daughters, can think of nothing but mere words. I hear him tell them that this will be the hardest day, so they should try to think of the better ones that lie ahead. Margot, resting her head sideways on his chest as if to hear his heart, closes her eyes but gives a jolt like someone waking from a dream.

Anne smiles to reassure the other two, but Edith cries and faintly shakes her head. She looks at me as Anne did, as if she's able to tell by my expression that all hope is lost.

I fall in with the family and listen as Otto tells them that, at Auschwitz, men and women will be separated. Edith interrupts him: "Stop exaggerating. They wouldn't do that. Some sort of arrangements have been made. There might be underground shelters. The Germans are renowned . . ."

I hear these words in Otto's head: *What if, when all of them are dead, I think of things I should have said that might have saved their lives? The girls are younger, but they're stronger than Edith.*

So he tells them, in a whisper: "There won't be time to say goodbye and there are things that you should know . . .

> Do what you're told, my darling girls,
> don't laugh or smile or say a word.
> Don't dare look up, don't look around,
> look straight ahead or at the ground.
> Curiosity is impudence,
> to look at them is insolence.
> But there are things that you must do—
> remember what I'm telling you.
> You must care for one another,
> never, never leave your mother,
> never, never leave each other.
> If you are sick, no matter what,
> you have to make them think you're not.
> Remember, I'm not far away,
> I'll think about you every day;
> remember, I'm just over there.
> They won't let you see or hear me;
> remind yourselves that you are near me;
> write letters to me in your head . . .
> Remember all those books you read,
> the ones about young girls like you,
> remember things you know are true
> no matter what the Nazis do . . .
> The Allies will be coming soon . . ."

The whispering goes on and on. The Frank girls, wide-eyed, nod and nod, looking more and more solemn. The hours left are far too few, the things they must and mustn't do far too many, a litany that is the measure of his dread and only makes them more afraid.

I can't just leave them here like this. A final scene of family togetherness would be a better way to end, the suffering to come redeemed for me, at least, if not for them. I should do something, turn tragedy into romance, *something.*

I'll stay with them until the end, unable to change anything, able only to imagine what they think and feel. For a while, I attempt to finish Anne's diary, write what she would have written if she'd been allowed to take it with her and still had the strength to write . . .

For so long confined to one small space, we are now confined to another, but we can ***feel*** *that we are moving, heading unimpeded from one place to another. This feeling is cruelly exhilarating and makes some of us, especially the children, faintly hopeful of one day being free. There is little water and no food. Even those of us who know about the camps, who know what lies in store for us, feel relieved when we arrive, as if we have made it through the first of a series of ordeals that will lead to our salvation.*

Mama, Margot and I stay together as Papa told us we should do. We sleep as near to one another as possible, though we are often crammed into bunks with strangers. Each morning, we stand side by side at roll call and sometimes dare to hold each other's hands. At night, for as long as we still have the strength, we make ourselves heard to one another among the many mothers and daughters contending to be heard. By day, when we are overseen by the guards, no one cries. At night, many do, some comforted, some not . . .

I tell Anne that the commandant, the Monster of the Land Without, lives with his family nearby. "His house is over there behind a hedge of cypress trees. We see the smoke that streams from his chimney, and he sees the smoke that ours makes. Very often he complains about the ash that it contains: when the wind blows from the west, his children have to play inside."

I tell her I'm afraid to die. I tell her that I've never seen anything worse than oblivion, which I've come face to face with more than once.

I know so much she doesn't know; I know that she is soon to go to another camp called Bergen-Belsen with Margot, but Edith will be left behind and, losing them, will lose her mind.

Now comes the quickening of time. In seconds, days and weeks go by. The girls no longer notice me. Unlike them, I'm never cold or hungry. They have no hair, but I have all of mine. I'm wearing clothes; they're wearing none. There are no numbers on my arm, just blue ink on the heel of my left hand. I've never been of any use to them. Is there nothing I can do but shadow them from place to place? Their fate won't be altered if I stay. They won't survive or suffer less if I'm among the witnesses. But then, it's not for them I'm here but for me. I could pretend the Franks are in the heaven of what might have been, but what would be the point? I won't let myself off so easily as to turn back now.

War has been declared on women; that's how it seems. The only men are those who guard them with their guns and with their black Alsatians that snarl when they are told to snarl, and heel when they are told to heel. The dogs are what they were made to be: they lick the faces of the guards, then sit and wait for their rewards.

He appears, the commandant, Claws von Snout himself, though there are many clones of him about, men with faces just like his, whose purpose is to repeat the orders that he issues, which are the same day after day. The women know them but are too tired and too sick to obey, which inspires von Snout to say that they are typical Jews, weak and faint of heart.

"This camp is run by a precise system that I invented, but its success doesn't just depend on me. There are so many Jews you'd think that we were running out of Zyklon B. I didn't overestimate the efficiency of the ovens. It's as if the Jews are multiplying every day by mitosis. The more I kill, the more that come, more trains arriving all the time. I go to bed just after nine, but what's the point? There's too much noise to sleep. The older Jews go on about what they could possibly have done to deserve extermination. 'Who judges us, what is his name? Why does he think we are to blame for all the wrongs of history?'"

Edith thinks that I might be
a portent of insanity.
She has two girls but there are three,
the third a girl her daughters see,
or seem to, as she cannot tell
if that's some kind of trick as well.
"All this might be my frame of mind.
I may have left the world behind.
I wish that one would go away,
but there she is, all night, all day,
as if she's taken Otto's place.
I hate to look her in the face
for there is something in her eyes
that she's unable to disguise,
that makes me wonder if she might
have the gift of second sight.
What can that look of pity mean?
What does she know; what has she seen?"

The end of October. There is not much heat left in the sun, which sets early in the afternoon. The time that I foresaw has come, when Margot and Anne will be parted from their mother and leave Auschwitz, which is rife with rumours that the Allies are not far away. Von Snout has been ordered to accelerate the Holocaust, silence the last of the Jews, the witnesses to what's been done, dispose of them or relocate them, for they are evidence that will be used against the Nazis if the war is lost. The healthiest ones are chosen to be sent to Bergen-Belsen, the camp in Germany. Von Snout is glad to see them go. "They're someone else's problem now," he says, "but still a million more remain."

Edith, told her girls are gone, begins to push her food aside, convinced that what she doesn't eat will wind up on her daughters' plates. She believes that she is saving them and still believes it when she dies.

Margot and Anne are on the last train that will ever leave Auschwitz, which arrives on All Hallows' Eve at Bergen-Belsen. I ride with them and so does she, the one in black who shadows me.

Bergen-Belsen, March 22, 1945. Margot and Anne are still alive.

It is winter in Germany, the camp so far past full capacity that there is no room to lie down at night. The luckiest sit with their knees drawn up to their chins, while the rest must stand, propped up by each other as they drift in and out of sleep. Remembering what their father said, the girls stay together, holding hands when they are able, Anne doing most of the talking. They must not lose hope like the rest.

The morning roll call never ends. The number who are still alive plus those who did not last the night must add up to the number who were still alive the day before. If they do not, Margot and Anne and the others stand in line, naked, their bare feet freezing in the snow, until someone or something shows the cause of the discrepancy and all the Jews are accounted for.

Now comes the quickening of lines
that almost overthrows my mind.
The end for most is almost here,
the dead and near-dead everywhere.
Fed by the bodies of the dead
and those that are as good as dead,
the fires burn throughout the night
like giant haystacks set alight.
The prisoners can see the light
reflected on the cloud of ash.
"They're only burning piles of trash,"
they tell the youngest of the girls,
who know the truth but like the words.
Ash mixes with the falling snow
and gathers on the ground below.
The ash falls too upon the Jews,
who have no hats, no clothes, no shoes.

Some soldiers won't go near the Jews lest they, too, come down with typhus, the lice-borne plague, the Jew disease, and are charged with insubordination. They say that the best solution would be to set fire to the entire camp and simply walk away, every bit of Bergen-Belsen gone in one great conflagration.

The commandant won't allow it. "So many Jews are not yet dead; they'd flee into the countryside and spread the typhus everywhere."

Would anyone presume to guess how even war could come to this? The dying console the dying, who need to know that they are loved, if not by God then by someone who, like them, He has forsaken. A few try to pray but only manage to mumble a few words before they trail off into silence.

I stay with the girls throughout the night. Margot regards me as Anne and Edith did, sees in my eyes the look of pity that can only mean one thing. I don't feel what the sisters feel. I don't feel anything at all. I'm like some derelict guardian angel who doesn't watch over them but merely watches as they fall. Their time is near; they have that look. They speak about their mother, who they hope is still alive, and about their father, the way he whispered to them on the train.

> The time has come to turn back time,
> to somehow *beat* it back in rhyme,
> to slow it down, give Them a chance—
> I cannot alter circumstance.

On and on my left hand goes, faster than ever, as if to defy me and spare the sisters what it can. The girls hold hands as they did before the war in Margot's bed on summer nights when they were hoping for a storm that would clear the air.

As Margot pulls her hand away, Anne thinks she hears a woman say, "I think this one will go today." Anne doesn't know which one of them she means. She drifts off and, when she wakes, Margot isn't there.

The woman says, "Your name is Anne," as if she is so near death she needs to be reminded of her name. "You fell asleep."

It's almost like a reprimand for letting go of Margot's hand, as if the sisters made a pact that Anne betrayed by coming back. Anne didn't feel her sister's death, though Margot died beside her—her time had come and she complied.

Anne has never been compliant. She thinks about her diary, no doubt long since disposed of. She thinks it wasn't much good, nowhere near as good as she wanted it to be. She's no longer the girl who wrote it; she'll never be that girl again.

They named her Annelies Marie.

In August 1942, they went into hiding. How long ago was that?

She hears Margot's voice: "In Frankfurt, all the boys asked me, 'How can a blond girl be a Jew?' They were too shy to talk to you."

Now she is back in her bed at the Secret Annex. The day is done. The time has come for her to write.

I'm going crazy in this house. I wish the moon was like the sun, but it's so cold, just looking down. What use is it to anyone?

Her pen in hand, her writing album on her lap, Pfeffer asleep in the bed beside hers, she looks at me.

I have to get some writing done, but that girl stands there so silently, watching, waiting.

I can't pretend I don't know why—
she's waiting there for me to die.
Have pity, Angel, pass me by.
I stand before you, but fifteen,
so many things I haven't seen.
So much remains for me to do—
must I commend myself to you?
At last the world is giving way;
how nice it feels, how warm today.

I didn't leave her, not like I left the other Anne. I didn't save her, but at least I didn't run away. I stayed with her till the end.

——

The Shadow She. The gaze of those unblinking eyes. It seems my Shadow She can see nothing at all, nothing but me. She stares at me and shakes her head. Why won't she speak? She spoke a lot when she still could—perhaps she's waiting for me.

"I can't make up for what I did, for what I let Him do. There's nothing that will bring you back. The blood of more than three will be on my hands if I tell the truth." She nods but doesn't look away.

From *The Arelliad*

THE NIGHT SONG OF THE COMMANDANT (1985)

The gypsies from the countryside
play music for them every night,
and peasants volunteer as servants—
they love to help the commandant.

"We're the lucky ones," his wife says. "We're not in Berlin; it's safer here." They have bodyguards, sometimes more than one, though all of them look the same and never say a word. They stand at attention at the end of the driveway, rifles at the ready. His children are not sure what it is they guard them from. They're schooled at home, for there's no school nearby. They rarely leave the yard and often ask about the sounds that come from beyond the cypress trees, but his wife tells them not to nag their papa, because it only makes his headaches worse. His migraines get so bad she makes him lie down and puts a cold compress on his forehead, but it does him little good.

From the windows of their bedrooms, his children can see the crematorium. They don't know what is burnt there. Sometimes the smoke blows their way and gets so thick the children have to play inside, though even inside they can smell it.

At times, he can't see a thing from the kitchen windows, not even the sentries, who might as well be out there in a blizzard. When the wind changes, the smoke clears, but still he asks the children to stay indoors until the servants rake the grass, and leaves it to the guards to say when it's safe to go outside.

"We live beside a factory that's busy making history." That's his favourite joke, a riddle he tells his daughter Birgitte about the smoke that billows from the yellow stack. She asks him what the factory really makes, but he only laughs and says that she's not old enough to keep a secret.

He laughs again and strokes her hair
and says that, when they win the war,

when all the missions are complete,
the world is rid of every rat
that interferes with purity,
the enemies of clarity,
the flaws within the molecule
that have been with them since the Fall;
the cleansing of the universe,
the confounding of the Curse,
the raising of the Nazi Cross,
its shadow over every land—
when all of this has come to pass,
his little girl will understand.

They never leave the grounds without an escort. The guards go with them everywhere, a car in front, a car behind, a soldier on the running board, four motorcycles with sidecars. The Poles who stand along the roads salute him and the children, and they salute them back.

In bed, at night, he hears the ceaseless din of the camp. He tells himself there is still a chance that they will win the war.

The factory goes on and on, the sound seeming to bore into his very brain. Listening to music helps him get to sleep. He likes to be sung to. The last song in the house at night, the night song of the commandant, is something like a lullaby. *Ofoozyb*. He prefers a voice that's strong and clear, the kind his family can hear as they, too, are drifting off to sleep. All day he looks forward to it. The singer who stands beside his bed must not get it wrong.

The song's the same night after night; the singer, too, if he sang well the night before.

But if, throughout the song, the master stays awake, someone else will take the singer's place, another gypsy who will know that he sings to save his life.

The commandant lies beside his wife, who seems to be unbothered by the noises from the factory.

The gypsy waits until his master's eyes are closed—he knows, he knows, how easy it would be, he knows. But he goes on singing till he's sure that he's not needed anymore. But if the commandant's wife should stir or cough, the commandant will wake again and ask him for a second song, a better one, so he must stand there all night long, beside the bed, beside the bed, rehearsing music in his head.

The ghost assassins of von Snout
are silent as they move about.
They can't be seen, they can't be heard;
they never have to say a word.
The business of the camp goes on
and will continue when he's gone.

Von Snout awakes and soon sits up. He simply cannot stay asleep, such is the clamour in his head. There is no singer by the bed, no one waiting for him to name another song.

The ghost assassins don't have much time before daybreak—the guards and Jews will soon be adding to the noise.

Smoke billows from the yellow stack. When the wind gusts, the assassins can see the sparks, frenzied swarms of red mosquitoes that go out as they are carried east toward von Snout.

He can smell the smoke—three times, tonight, one of the children came to his room, coughing so hard he thought they'd choke.

How She can sleep, God only knows. He started out with such high hopes—how can it all have come to this?

The ghost assassins need no weapons. They think a thing and then it's done. There'll be no noise; they won't be caught. The small von Snouts, asleep downstairs, will hear the death word in their heads. She'll have to tell them Papa's gone: a peaceful end; he felt nothing. Auschwitz won't see his like again.

Arellia is overcast.
The commandant's asleep at last;
we think the worst of it has passed.
The House Within, the House Without
hold out no hope for Claws von Snout.

Glore, Carm, Bethany and I
think Snout has had it for the night,
but soon his sighs say otherwise:
"Just one night's sleep before I die.
To sleep and never dream again,
to die in peace like other men . . ."

He complains about his ulcers, growls about the snores he hears from Her side of the bed.

"I should have built a second house, one for the girls and me. The seven of you must sing tonight, though seven hundred would not drown out the noise of Mrs. Claws von Snout."

The four of us, we think he means, four voices chanting in the gloom, but three more meet us in the room as if he summoned them.

The commandant will soon be dead:
the seven girls surround his bed—
we think the song, no words are sung—
a song I learned when I was young.
We sing for him, all seven do,
we sing because he told us to,
the van Hout girls, the other three,
seven singing beautifully,
the siren sisters of the night,
the night song of the commandant.
He makes a cross upon his chest,
preparing for his final rest,
the last dreams of his lonely life.

We sing the nocturne while, Without,
the factory that never sleeps
ignores the watch the sirens keep.
We sing him to his final rest,
the monster of insomnia,
the Master of Arellia.

We sing till he gives up the ghost—
the seven sirens, voices lost,
see him give it up at last,
or should I say it gives him up?
It leaves him when his body stops,
the ghost, the soul of Claws von Snout,
floats in the air above the bed
and drops the ashes of the dead
upon the body and the head
of Claws von Snout, the commandant
of Auschwitz and of Birkenau.
Who were the three who joined us there?
The three unsummoned sirens were
the one in black, my Shadow She,
the Frank sisters, who, passing by,
heard him when he chose to die.
We sang to him his final song,
"The Mystery of Right and Wrong."

WADE

On our fourth morning in Amsterdam, I asked Rachel if we were ever going to the Secret Annex.

"I still don't think I'm ready," she said.

"You know, you don't ever have to go if you don't want to," I said. I hoped she wouldn't. "We could just go home."

"I've been thinking I want to see another place first," she said. "The one where Anne Frank died—Bergen-Belsen. I want to go there. I want to see it. It's only six hours by train from Amsterdam. I'm going. *We're* going, right?"

"The place where she died? Is that such a good idea?"

"You and the others don't have to come. I know I can't undo anything by putting flowers on a grave. But not being able to fix everything is no excuse for fixing nothing, is it?"

"What are you trying to fix?"

"Maybe that's the wrong word."

"Your father didn't inform on the Franks. Even if he did, nothing you could do could change it, but he *didn't*."

"This is not about that. Look. I'm going whether you come with me or not. I just want to *see* the place."

I couldn't let her go without me.

We met up with the others for breakfast at a café, where the seven of us sat at a large table near the front window. "I've already eaten," Bethany said. "Toast and jam. Gloria saw me."

Gloria was staring at Rachel, who'd just announced her plan. "Going to Bergen-Belsen might be one step too far, and I know you know what I mean, Rachel," she said.

"She's right," Bethany said. "God, I just said that Gloria was right. Someone note the date and time."

"I'll understand if you don't come," Rachel said, but tears began to run down her face.

"Your sisters might be right," I said, taking her hand. "You're already so upset."

"Has she had a wink of sleep since we got here?" Bethany said to me. "She doesn't look like it. Raitch, those dark circles under your eyes will soon be down to your chin, and the blue ink is halfway up your arm."

Rachel looked beseechingly at me. "Maybe, if I go there, I won't have to go to her house?" She drew a deep breath and let it out, shakily.

"Forget breakfast. Let's go outside," Gloria said, glancing around at the people at the other tables, who were staring at us.

"Fifty thousand people died at Bergen-Belsen," Rachel said loudly, as if she was trying desperately to convince us of the truth. "There were no gas chambers there. The camp was so overcrowded, people had to sleep with their knees drawn up to their chins. There was no sanitation, only night pots like Elsie and Nora had to use."

"Calm down, sweetie," Gloria said, turning for help to Max, who was looking mortified by the scene that Rachel was causing.

"Let's go outside and get some air," I said. I grabbed Rachel by the arm and all but dragged her to the door.

"I'm not spending my short time at home reliving the war at a concentration camp in *Germany*," Max said. He wrapped his scarf around his neck. "I have people to visit. Ones that are still alive." He left without a glance at Gloria.

"I have business associates waiting for *me*," Fritz said. "So count me out."

"Well, she's not going there alone," Bethany said. "And no one can keep her from going, so I'm willing."

"I'm going too," I said. Gloria and Carmen agreed to come as well, and the five of us headed on foot to the train station.

I had the window seat. I tried to focus on the passing countryside, but Rachel was speaking non-stop to Bethany, who was sitting across the aisle from her. "Bergen-Belsen was liberated April 15, 1945. By the British. Too late for Anne and Margot. A couple of months too late, that's all. It's not like Auschwitz or Birkenau. The British bulldozed everything, even the bodies, and there were thousands of them—they bulldozed it to keep typhus from spreading to nearby villages. That's what Anne and Margot died of, *typhus*."

"Shhhh," Bethany said.

"Most days," Rachel went on, her voice no lower than before, "the only thing the prisoners were given to eat was a square inch of bread and a few ounces of rancid turnip soup. They were sent to Westerbork first, a transit camp where the conditions were not so bad. If they had been allowed to stay there, they would have survived. But they were sent on to Auschwitz, and then Margot and Anne were sent down to Bergen-Belsen without their mother. I've seen pictures of Bergen-Belsen as it is now. If you didn't know what happened there, you would walk straight past it."

"That's what I'd *like* to do," Bethany said.

"Dad had to have a reason for saying that he's the one who informed on the Franks to the Gestapo," Rachel said.

"You're not going to repeat that to the authorities, whoever they are, *are* you?" Bethany said. "You're going to go on being the sanest of the van Hout sisters. You have a lot to lose. You have a reputation to uphold and a boyfriend that you're closer to scaring away than you might think."

Rachel took my hand but continued to talk to Bethany, staring straight ahead. "It's just as likely that Dad turned them in as it is that any one of thousands of others did. He's the only one who has claimed credit for it, as far as I know."

"Didn't you tell me once that there were about a dozen people who were worth investigating, people who worked at night in the warehouse below the Secret Annex?" Bethany said.

"I told you that before Dad confessed—"

"He didn't *confess*," I interrupted. "He was only taunting you. He knew that you worshipped Anne Frank. There's no mystery here."

"I don't *worship* her. She's *not* my patron saint. I'm not trying to model myself after her. Dad wasn't with the Resistance. He didn't do anything to help the Jews. We all know who he sided with."

"All I know for certain is what he did to me," Bethany said. "I'm sure you haven't forgotten that, for years, he told everyone he almost *saved* Anne Frank. He said he warned his contacts in the Resistance that there would soon be a raid on 263 Prinsengracht but, for some reason, nothing was done."

"He betrayed them; he tried to save them," I said. "What next? What else? It's ridiculous."

"You have no idea," Bethany said. " 'The man who almost saved Anne Frank / was mocked by men of lesser rank.' "

"We just don't know the truth," Rachel said. "Most people don't."

"I *wish* I knew why we're on a train headed for Bergen-Belsen," Bethany said. "I wish *you* knew."

"I do know," Rachel said. She looked past me out the window.

"It never stops," Bethany said. "The two of them are gone and they're still setting the four of us against each other. We could never stand to be around each other, but the two of them got along just fine. I don't think they ever argued."

Rachel did not respond. In the row behind us, Gloria and Carmen said nothing. I looked back between the seats. Carmen, eyes closed, may have been asleep, or she may have been signalling that she had heard all that she could stand to hear from Bethany and Rachel. Gloria looked aloof, wearily reflective, as if she was pondering something altogether unrelated to our destination, Anne Frank, the Holocaust, her sisters and even the deaths of her parents.

RACHEL

The latest volume of my diary was in my shoulder bag. I had convinced myself that I wouldn't write in it, that I was taking it with me as a talisman to protect me from what I might see or hear. But I longed to take it out. I could go to the bathroom and write there, pretend not to hear when someone tried the door. Or I could write in front of Wade and my sisters, defiantly unconcerned with what they thought. But I did neither. Instead, I took out *Het Achterhuis* and read it, indulged in my familiar, allowable obsession, what Carmen had once called my maintenance dose. I stared at the pages, not so much reading as silently reciting.

The Franks, in windowless freight cars, saw nothing of the lush green countryside we passed on the way to Bergen-Belsen. The only prisoners to survive the concentration camps were those who arrived at them not long before they were liberated. But even most of those did not survive. Some died a month, a week, a day or even just hours before the Allies happened upon them. The average survival time of a girl of Anne Frank's age who was in good health when she arrived at Bergen-Belsen was six weeks.

In the diary, Anne writes everything in such detail—but then, abruptly, the writing stops, and by the time it does, you have been fooled into expecting it to go on forever. How could this voice go silent when so much is still to happen? How could this journey be abandoned when you haven't even guessed its destination?

—

We took a bus from the train station to the camp. The road was unpaved, a wide swath of graded gravel that wound its way through a forest of white birch. A light drizzle had begun to fall.

Bergen-Belsen. It looked like any other long-abandoned place, grown over with trees, bushes, high grass and wildflowers. The ruins of structures built for some forgotten purpose showed through here and there, the shells of concrete basements dripping in the rain. The sites of the mass graves, the deep, wide pits into which the bodies of the Frank sisters were thrown, along with thousands of others, were now berms of bright green grass.

Winding among the mass graves were roped-off paths that you were not allowed to stray from lest you step on someone's grave. There were tokens of remembrance, marble stones and tilting wooden crosses scattered randomly across the fields.

Many of the visitors, Jews and non-Jews, were dressed in black. No one objected out loud, but some looked askance at us or faintly shook their heads when they saw our anoraks of various colours, and blue jeans and sneaker boots and sandals.

Everyone had come to visit Anne Frank's grave but hadn't reckoned on the grim enormity of Bergen-Belsen. The camp was hushed, the visitors muted by the many who had died here, not just Anne.

I tried to imagine what went through the mind of a soldier stationed here for the war. "This is what we're doing instead of all the other things we could be doing. We do this from day to day with an end in mind that makes sense to us. This is pre-eminent and purposeful. This is rational and sensible, and best done as efficiently and conscientiously as possible. Each day is like the one before and the one to come. We know what to expect. We are orderly people, orderly performing orderly, uncomplicated tasks. We go to sleep in the evening and wake up in the morning knowing what the day will bring. This is what we do because this is what we *have* been doing. We are borne along by the impetus of habit and routine."

Gloria bought flowers in the Documentation Centre and gave some to each of us. Following the map given to us by one of the guides, we made our way to Anne Frank's stone. There was a long line of visitors waiting to pay their respects, some holding flowers, others votive candles or photographs of Anne. One woman held a teddy bear, others merely cameras, while many carried stones they planned to leave behind.

"I'm freaking freezing," Carmen said, teeth chattering, arms folded, eyes blurred with tears. The white birch trees bowed and creaked with every gust of wind. We were soaked with mist so fine that I could barely see it.

The marble headstone of Margot and Anne Frank was surrounded by wreaths and bouquets of flowers, as well as photographs of Anne on which people had written messages, tributes and condolences in many languages. The obelisk and memorial wall raised by the British liberators lay directly behind the headstone, half a mile away. Almost immediately behind the stone was a grassy berm that had grown over the mass grave in which, it was believed, Margot and Anne were buried. The headstone had been installed and unveiled in 1977. "Thirty-two years after 1945," I said. "For thirty-two years, she and her sister lay here in an unmarked mass grave with fifty thousand others."

No one stood in line to visit the other stones and crosses. "It doesn't seem right," Bethany said. "They look so lonely." She left the queue and followed the network of pathways to the other stones, flowers bunched in one hand. A few other people followed her lead.

By the time Bethany came back and took her place in line with us, I knew I couldn't bear to stand eye to eye with Anne and Margot. The closer I got to their stone, to the mass grave in which they lay among the other dead, I realized that I would die if I let go of Anne, or she let go of me.

We were perhaps ten minutes from taking our turn at the stone when I said, "I'll wait for you at the end of the line. The rest of you keep going if you like." Before Wade could ask me why, Gloria grabbed my arm and said, "What are you doing, Rachel? You're the reason we're here. You asked us to come with you. Carmen is freezing and Bethany has been putting flowers on the graves of strangers just to pass the time, and Wade is completely—"

"Not graves," I said. "Memorial stones. She should be putting flowers on those grass-covered mounds of earth. We all should."

"Hold it together, okay?" Gloria whispered, arching her eyebrows as if to add: *not just for your sake.*

An elderly woman in front of Carmen, her head covered in a black shawl, turned around and said, "No one is allowed to set foot on the mass graves. It is strictly forbidden."

"Mind your own business," Carmen said.

"You women should at least cover your heads. This is not an amusement park."

Carmen all but poked her in the face with her index finger. "Listen—" she began, but Gloria took her by the arm and turned her around the other way. The woman faced the stone again.

"I'll wait for you at the end of the line," I said again, but the four of them broke free and followed me as we again took up our places at the end of the line.

"What are you doing, Rachel?" Wade said, his voice quavering.

"I don't want to stand face to face with that memorial stone," I said. "I've seen photographs of it before today, and I thought that I should come here and see it for myself and pay my respects in person, but I can't do it. The rest of you can stay in line if you like, but I can't. The Hebrew inscription on the stone means 'The spirit of man is the candle of the Lord.' Does anyone really feel that in this awful place? The inscription on the wall built by the British liberators of the camp reads, 'Earth conceal not the blood shed on thee.' But that is exactly what the earth is doing. No number of memorial stones and memorial walls can make people remember what happened. The testimonies of survivors are merely sad stories to everyone but fellow survivors. People read them or watch them on TV, and they cry and think about them for a while. And then they forget and move on unchanged. The world has carried on unchanged since 1945, just as the van Hout sisters never change. We are not survivors, but the walking wounded whose wounds will never heal. And, as Bethany said, the four of us have so much in common, but we can't even get along with one another."

I rummaged in my shoulder bag and withdrew from it the tape-wrapped copy of *Het Achterhuis* that I had shown to Wade in Cape Town.

"What in God's name is *that*?" Bethany said. "It looks like something you pulled out of the garbage."

"It's a copy of *Het Achterhuis*. My first one ever. It was given to me by a friend when I was thirteen. A birthday present. I was planning to make a grand gesture. I was going to leave this at the base of the stone with all the other offerings. My oh so unique tribute to the memory of Anne and the others, a ceremonial and final parting with my past. But I can't leave without it. I thought I could, but I can't."

Wade sighed and surveyed Bergen-Belsen. I kissed his cheek. "I'm sorry I dragged you here on this phony pilgrimage."

I had to get out of here now, had to leave her here with her sister. I felt the pull of the dark that I was half in love with. I couldn't imagine the place *after* dark. Among the people who maintained it, there must have been some who would have to spend the night, patrolling the grounds, the museum, what ruins still remained, ensuring that the dead were never left alone. I must have read her book ten thousand times, but I wondered if I'd ever really read it.

The words I had planned to say to the stone came out of my mouth: "I am sorry about what was done to you and the others, Anne. Margot, I'm glad that you had Anne until the very end. Anne, I'm glad the end came quickly for you after Margot died. I'm glad that all three of my sisters are alive."

"She's talking to ghosts," Bethany said. "We'd better go before we offend them, too."

WADE

"I won't be much company on the ride back," Rachel said when we were once more on the train. "I have a new Dutch copy of the book in my bag and I'm going to read it, but not for long because I'm so tired."

She did read the book for a while and fell asleep as she said she would. I decided to move to another seat so as not to wake her. There were empty seats near the back of the train. I sat in the last one on the other side of the aisle, from which there was a better view, one not blocked by the never-ending stand of blazing white birch trees.

A few minutes later, Bethany made her way down the aisle and sat beside me. "So how are you doing, buddy boy?"

"Fine," I said.

"Really? You seemed kind of out of it back there."

"Concentration camps have that effect on me."

She looked at me for longer than she ever had, her eyes searching.

"What's up?" I said.

"Can't a girl chat with her sister's boyfriend? That was a strange odyssey, wasn't it?"

"Relatively speaking? Not really."

"Try to hang in there. She might not be as far gone as she seems." She gently rubbed her belly. "I, on the other hand, am exactly as far along as I seem. I've been giving you a hard time since we met. Truce?"

"Truce," I said.

"I guess Rachel is just as screwed up in her own way as we are, but she's not selfish. All of this Anne Frank stuff, I don't understand it. It's as if she thinks the death of a girl before she was born is somehow her fault. Maybe she thinks the whole bloody Holocaust was her fault. All that reading, rereading, and all that writing—it's as if she thinks she is to blame for everything and has to find a way to make it right, or explain it, or keep it from happening again."

"She used the word *fix* this morning. She feels like there's something that she has to fix."

Bethany shrugged.

"I don't get it, Bethany—"

"Shhh, not so loud," she said. I looked up and saw several people staring back at us, including Gloria, who, I was not surprised to see, looked especially concerned. Bethany waved to her and she turned around.

"Bibliomania can happen to anyone, right?" I said. "You don't have to have been traumatized. If you're genetically predisposed—"

"You're never going to know for certain, Wade. You have to decide if you can live with that. You take this whole life thing very seriously, don't you?"

"Yes. So do you."

"You're right. I do. But you think those green eyes of yours can see right through everything, and they can't. Some things just are, period. Not what a writer wants to hear, I guess."

"I'm not a writer. A writer *writes*. I'm starting to think I'll be a would-be writer the day I die."

"Like I said, hang in there." She rubbed her belly again. "I called it my bundle of boy, trying to convince myself that it *was* a boy. Over and over I prayed, 'Please God, don't let this baby be a girl.' Now that Dad's gone, I won't mind if it's a girl. I'll mind that she's his granddaughter. That's how he would have thought of her, as *his*, even though he wasn't the father. When I found out I was pregnant and went back to Clive and Mom and Dad—well, I was thinking of the baby then, too. I had this notion that a baby would fix everything, make up for everything, almost undo it. A new start for everyone, the baby with four doting grandparents, all of us oozing domestic bliss in pastoral Cape Town. Did you know that after she moved back to South Africa,

Gloria wrote to Mom and Dad in St. John's every day? Every day for seven years. That's about 2,500 letters."

"Is *everyone* in this family a writer?"

She sniffed. "The van Houts' beautiful, dutiful daughters. When I was in Halifax, I wrote to them every week and they called every Sunday, and I took their calls and we made small talk for four or five minutes. I was a faithful correspondent last summer. Now we are all beyond his reach. I need to keep reminding myself of that. I have never been in love. Before you, Wade, Rachel had never been in love. Gloria and Carmen have never been in love. But Rachel is in love with you. She seems just plain better than the rest of us in some way that she might deserve no credit for. It may be that she has some innate gift that God withheld from her sisters.

"I can never become clean again. How do you wipe away that stain? When doctors tell you not to blame yourself for what was done to you against your will, they still sound as if *they're* blaming you for something, as if they're convinced that, at some level, you wanted to be defiled, that you enticed him in some way, that *he* was helpless to fend off *your* advances. When people find out what your father did, it's you they point to for having no better sense than to let him do it, or for giving in to some primal urge that other girls and women can resist.

"The few times that I slept with Clive, thinking of England wasn't enough to distract me from what he was doing. The only thing that worked was imagining what it would be like to live on Madagascar. Poor Clive. I wanted a baby. I'm not sure what he wanted."

She folded her arms and closed her eyes. A tear ran down one cheek. She opened her eyes and stared at the back of the seat in front of her. "So." The word was one long sigh.

"I'm sorry, Bethany," I said. "For what it's worth, I do believe you. About your father, I mean."

Another tear ran down her cheek. "Have you noticed that I'm eating? Not voraciously, but it's a start. Bethany van Hout, eating for two—that's ironic, isn't it? But I'll never get married unless there's a greater demand for knocked-up crackpots than I think there is. Anne O'Rexia, a lovely Irish lass. I wonder what kind of mother I'll make.

I know where the smart money is right now, but that could change. Everyone rolls their eyes when they think of a newborn depending on me. Gloria's agreed that I can stay with her and Max, not just for now but for as long as I like after the baby is born."

"That's good," I said. "One less thing to worry about."

She nodded. "Hug?" she said. I held out my arms and she wrapped hers around my chest and laid her head sideways on my shoulder. "Be nice to Rachel," she said. She broke our embrace, got up and gingerly went back to her seat.

It was late when we got back. I went for a quick run through the streets of Amsterdam, hoping to clear my head of the sight of the camp, the marble stone that bore the names of Anne and Margot Frank. I returned from the run, opened the door and saw that Rachel was standing at the front window, arms folded, looking out at the canal. She didn't turn around.

"Gloria called," she said.

"What did she want?" I said, trying to sound casual.

"She said that you and I should leave for home tomorrow."

"I'm all for that," I said, but she shook her head.

"I want to do what we came here for," Rachel said. "I want to visit her house. I want to go there with you and with my sisters."

"What's the point, Rachel? Look at what happened at that concentration camp."

"I'll go there by myself if I have to."

From *The Arelliad*

THE NIGHT BEFORE (1985)

Tomorrow I will see Anne's house—
already, I can hear her voice:
"I didn't die to change the world.
I was an ordinary girl
with ordinary girl concerns.
I represent the Holocaust—
if I had lived, what would be lost?
Had I grown up, what would I be
without a place in history?
I would still be ordinary,
and someone else's diary,
a better book, one overlooked
because of mine, would be The Book,
some other girl the heroine;
some other girl would be The One—
how many others might have been?
Had I grown up, what would I be—
an obscure writer, probably,
if I was any kind at all,
but everything seems possible—
the heaven of what might have been
is where you do it all again.
If there had never been a raid,
the eight of us would have been freed
when the West was liberated.
The two years in *Het Achterhuis*
would have been a mere hiatus
from the life I took for granted—
could I have just returned to it?

"I envy you your real life:
what will you be, perhaps a wife—

a mother, too? What you will be
would be of no concern to me
if I were not a part of you
that must do what you tell me to.

"I have no wisdom to dispense,
no words to say in your defence—
likewise none of condemnation,
absolution, accusation.
I have not come back from the dead
to judge you for the things you did.
I would forgive you if I could;
I wonder if you think I should.
I have to wear this yellow star;
the star reminds me who you are—
that is, it tells me I was caught,
the thing I was that you were not.
You want to know what I would do
if you were me and I were you.
I may as well just say it straight:
it's you that you interrogate."

Her lips move as she speaks to me,
but my voice is the one that she
seems unsurprised to find that we
are using interchangeably,
the voice of Rachel in her mouth
and mine. She always told the truth;
I wish that I could do the same—
dissenting voices with one name.

"You're older than I ever was;
I was the happy one of us.
You had to hide inside your head;
I chose my diary instead,

although I wrote it long before
the declaration of your war.
You chose it too, you made it yours—
we disappeared at age thirteen;
I survived until fifteen,
two years of self-imprisonment.
Things could have been so different;
I still exist inside the books,
yours and mine, the one you took
to mean things that I didn't mean—
the real Anne is what might have been.
I'd like it if you set me free
but I am you and you are me
and so, it seems, we'll always be."

RACHEL

We went to *het Achterhuis* in the afternoon the next day, Wade, Gloria, Carmen, Bethany, Fritz and I. Max had been there before and said he didn't want to go again. Fritz said that we were horror tourists like the ones who visited Dealey Plaza, voyeurs of suffering who got a thrill out of going to places where bad things had happened. "Her house is the Disneyland of bleeding hearts. Non-Jews go there to reassure themselves that they would be incapable under any circumstances of doing what the Nazis did. They cry. They kneel down and pray. But where were their parents and grandparents when everyone in North America and Europe knew what was happening to the Jews? Laying low, that's what they were doing. Looking the other way."

"I'm so glad you feel that way," Bethany said. "I cherish the times when you're not around."

"I didn't say I'm not coming," Fritz said. "I want to witness baby sister's first visit to her heroine's house. Baby sister returns to the scene of the crime."

"Shut up, Fritz," Wade said. Fritz, raising his hands to shoulder height as if to fend him off, backed up a few steps.

In the queue, it was cold enough to see your breath and a light drizzle was falling. There were many schoolchildren of Anne Frank's age. Their teachers did their best to impress upon them the solemnity of this field trip, but as they waited, the children laughed and skylarked and passed cigarettes back and forth.

"I could use one of those cigarettes," I said, my hands in the pockets of my jacket. Wade put an arm around my shoulders, which were shaking.

The stairs that led to the Secret Annex were very steep and narrow. Visitors ascended and descended at the same time in two never-ending streams, crushing each other against the walls amid protests, apologies and laughter. "It's nothing but a bunch of empty rooms," someone said as he hurried down the stairs.

"Pregnant lady coming through," Bethany shouted. "I might not look like it, but I am. Don't squish the fish."

People made way for her as best they could.

"It's a good thing they didn't have to walk up and down these stairs every day," I said to Wade. "I already feel like I'm suffocating."

The second I passed the bookcase that had hidden the secret entrance, and crossed over the breezeway into the bare and empty house, I wobbled unsteadily and would have fallen had Wade not grabbed hold of me.

"Nice catch, big guy," Bethany said. "Wade is going to carry you out of here if you do that again. You're as white as a sheet."

I wondered what, in the circumstances of me and my sisters, the all-forgiving fifteen-year-old of the Secret Annex would have done with Hans van Hout. Had Anne Frank still believed in the basic goodness of people when, though it was winter, she could no longer stand to wear her lice-infested clothes?

Fritz tagged along with each of us in turn, holding Carmen's hand, standing with Bethany and whispering something that made her roll her eyes and slowly shake her head in disbelief. He walked in silence with Gloria, who seemed not to notice him. He moved among the crowd like a pickpocket. He stood beside Wade and me as we looked out the rear window of the Secret Annex onto the quadrangle across which free people had walked every day during the Franks' confinement. By day, scores of people had walked beneath the window; by night, only a few. The window was supposedly one of the back windows of the working warehouse they hid above, so a sound coming from the window at night would have been more startling than one by day.

"Isn't it all so fascinating?" Fritz said. "Empty rooms, bare walls." He all but shadowed me for a while, staring at me as *I* stared at the meagre contents of one of the world's most famous houses. There were pictures of Anne's drawings on the walls of the bedroom she had shared with Pfeffer.

"What do you want, Fritz?" Wade said.

Fritz shrugged and went away just as I began to cry. The visitors stared as if I was part of the exhibit. "We should go," Wade said, but I shook my head and told him I was fine.

"I just need some time," I said. He frowned but let me move away from him.

I'd seen photographs of reconstructions of *Het Achterhuis*. I stared, with my mind's eye, at Anne's little bed, a cot pushed against one wall, and Pfeffer's pushed against the other, three feet of space between.

They trusted Anne with Pfeffer, Anne, who was thirteen, not Margot, who was seventeen. What a choice to have to make. A flimsy curtain hung between the rooms. Pretend you didn't hear. Pretend you didn't see. Pretend you don't know. If everyone did this for long enough, they'd forget they were pretending, and pretense would become the truth.

Each of them, forever in fear of being caught, forced into silence most of the time, looked at the same seven faces day after day, dreamt of freedom and fresh air, heard the drumming of boots on cobblestone streets. Anne lasted for six months after she was caught, far less time than she spent in the Secret Annex, which would otherwise have been the worst time of her life.

Eight people had lived here for more than two years in secrecy and safety and deprivation until someone whose identity is still unknown betrayed them in a phone call that lasted thirty seconds.

I wanted to shout, *I know who betrayed them. I know who it was. It was my father.*

My heart pounded. Sweat trickled down my face.

I felt a hand on my shoulder, shook it off and turned about to see a long-bearded man wearing a yarmulke, his black hat pressed to the heart of his white shirt. He nodded, bowed slightly and smiled. "You are Jewish," he said. A statement, not a question. I shook my head, feeling guilty for having somehow made him think I was a Jew, or perhaps for not being one. "A friend of the Jews, then," he said. I managed to nod. He smiled, gently patted my shoulders and moved away.

I examined the marks on the door jamb where Otto Frank recorded Anne's and Margot's heights every six months during their two years in the annex. The taller, Margot, had been several inches shorter than me. Anne was half a foot shorter. Perhaps she would have grown another inch or two.

As Bethany suddenly appeared beside me, I thought of Anne and Margot dying from typhus, naked in the winter cold. My sisters and I were older than they ever were. Bethany had four times attempted suicide, which, some fools might have thought, should have made her feel ashamed in a place like this, where people had tried so hard to stay alive.

Before I went into the hospital for the second time, I believed that Otto Frank had done to his daughters what Dad had done to us. I believed that, at night, in the cramped space of the Secret Annex, he visited his daughters' beds, and that the others, the van Pels and Pfeffer, didn't know or pretended not to. I believed that, just as Anne Frank's father had survived Auschwitz, mine would survive no matter what and that nothing but my death would free me from him. I read *Het Achterhuis* as if it was a coded indictment of two fathers, Anne's and mine, each of them the only man in a family of women.

I thought of my father, not Pfeffer, lying on that bed so close to hers. He could have reached out and touched her while she slept without budging from his bed.

WADE

Hans had a part in this, I thought. He helped do this. Even though he wasn't the one who made the phone call to the Gestapo, he helped do this. So many Jews had gone into hiding, in part because of men like him. Maybe he did what he did to his daughters because of what the Nazis made *him* do, if they made him do anything. I wasn't sure which of the things he had said were true and which weren't. There were plenty of willing collaborators, people who hated Jews, people who offered to help the Nazis because they were afraid of what would happen if they didn't. Any one of them could have been inspired to make that anonymous call by nothing more than a lucky guess that there were Jews hiding out at 263 Prinsengracht.

I wished I could be certain that he'd been driven crazy by the war. I wished I could be certain that he hadn't been. I wanted to be certain of *something*. I wished I knew without a doubt that he wasn't crazy before the war and that, after the war, he *chose* to do the things he did and wasn't predisposed to do them by some combination of illness and circumstance. But I wasn't sure that anyone chose to live the way he did. If he did not—as Rachel had speculated—it absolved him of blame. Similarly, the Nazis. Blameless, innocent Nazis, victimized by nature and happenstance, compelled by ineluctable forces to commit history's worst crime—the notion seemed heretical. But Christianity offered absolution to the sincerely contrite without exception, and followed that absolution with the promise of an eternity of perfect happiness. Other religions did much the same. Row after row of contrite Nazis, forgiven by priests, by popes, by God, marching in formation past a welcoming St. Peter through the gates of heaven.

While Anne and the others were in here, caged like animals, was Rachel's father out there, posing as a freedom fighter, kneeling on the cobblestones to tie his laces, to leave the messages that led the Nazis to other girls in other hiding places, to intercept entire families just one step from escape and freedom?

"Christ," Fritz said, startling me by grabbing my arm, "Rachel is looking at that diary as if it's the original Bible. You know, the truth about most people is in the fine print. No one knows what really went on in here. Nothing as noble and courageous as Rachel likes to think."

The diary lay open, under a glass case, on a gossip bench–like table. There was a queue of people waiting to examine it, getting longer and longer because Rachel just kept staring at the open book. "Please, miss, there are others who would like to view the diary," a young staffer called from just inside the doorway to the annex. Rachel stepped aside, withdrew a copy of *Het Achterhuis* from her shoulder bag, opened it and held it in front of her. Head bowed, eyes fixed on the book, she completed a slow circuit of the room, her eyes and lips moving. Not looking up to see where she was going, she started to walk randomly throughout the annex, forcing people to get out of her way, sometimes bumping into them but seeming not to notice. Occasionally, she wiped a tear away.

I went to her. "Maybe we should leave," I whispered. "You seem to be getting more and more upset." She moved away from me without a word and I followed her.

"They lived here, forty years ago," she said, as if reading the sentence from her book. "This is not King Tut's tomb or Mount Calvary. Peter van Pels was young. Where is the statue of him in Amsterdam? Where is the statue of Margot Frank? Where are the statues of the millions of children who also died in the concentration camps? People have said that, after D-Day, June 6, 1944, the occupants of the Secret Annex were so certain that the liberation of Amsterdam by the Allies was imminent that they became careless, leaving windows open, talking loudly, shouting and dropping things. There's nothing else to blame them for, so people blame them for being caught."

Rachel was sweating now. She put her hand over her mouth and mumbled something.

"Do you need to leave, Rachel?" I whispered.

She shook her head. "They were just girls," she said. "This is the last place they were free, but it's like a prison. Still, their parents loved them and other people risked their lives for them. In a way, they were lucky. For a while, they were. Whoever betrayed them was not the father of any of them. It wasn't their mother. I keep wondering if, when Anne died, she still thought that, deep down, people are basically good. Everyone wonders that, don't they? I hope she was right, even if, near the end, she changed her mind. I think she was—Wade, don't you?"

"I'm not sure that everyone is good," I said, "no matter how deep down you go."

RACHEL

It was as if I had stepped inside the book, knowing what happened outside the book and with no way to warn them. All eight were gathered around me and it would soon be too late to escape. A young man who would go on to commit other crimes was about to commit his worst, and there was nothing I could do. A young man was calling the Gestapo even as the eight of them were milling around, planning their futures, for they knew how close the Allies were, how close freedom was. And there it was, the diary of which I had hundreds of copies, preserved under bulletproof glass, under seal as it was when she wrote it.

I got back in line and waited until my turn came again, but I still couldn't make out what was written on the pages to which it was open. I wished I could visit the house when it was empty. I wished I could spend the night here, have it all to myself and hear the outside world much as she had heard it. I fancied that, while alone in this empty house at night, I might be able to reconcile myself to the mystery of absolute betrayal.

There, in front of me again, was the diary, hermetically sealed in glass as if it was meant to be a symbol of her—pent up, gaped at, suffocating.

WADE

She grabbed hold of the glass case and tried to lift it. It must have been fastened to the table, which must have been fastened to the floor, for neither budged. I grabbed her from behind, pinning her arms with mine. As she struggled, writhing and kicking, her head struck me hard in the mouth. I loosened my grip and she broke away from me. She made for the exit, fighting her way through the other visitors as if her life depended on it.

By the time I got outside, she was kneeling on the cobblestones, doubled over and gasping for breath, surrounded by her sisters. There was no sign of Fritz. Bethany was rubbing her back in slow, soothing circles. "It's okay, Raitch," she said, looking nervously about. Some of the visitors had followed us outside and were watching from a distance.

"A panic attack," Gloria snapped at me as if she thought I had told Rachel the truth about their parents.

Rachel sat upright, drew a deep breath and slowly let it out.

"There you go," Bethany said.

"I bet he saluted the Germans in their tanks as they rolled into Amsterdam," Rachel said. "Lots of people did. I've seen photographs."

"This is probably not the best place to talk about that," Bethany said. "You need to get back to your flat and then you'll be all right."

Rachel nodded in a way that, though it seemed to satisfy Bethany, did not convince me that she was back from wherever she had been. But she managed to stand.

"Maybe we should take you to a doctor," I said.

"No," Rachel said. She drew another deep breath and slowly let it out. "I should never have come here," she said. "I lost my book and shoulder bag."

"I've got them," Carmen said, handing them to her.

"A lot has happened in the past month," Bethany said. "You just need some time. We all do."

My arm around her, we walked in silence back to the flat, where Rachel pulled away from me and ran up the steps. When I reached the top of the stairs, the door was open and Rachel was on her hands and knees, rummaging for something in the closet. "Don't say a word," she said. "Just let me say what I have to say and then, if you still want to, we can talk." She stood and turned away from the closet, holding in both hands the book she had shown me in Cape Town, the one she had taken to Bergen-Belsen, her first copy of *Het Achterhuis*, a bizarre-looking bundle of tape of various kinds. She set it down on the bed as gingerly as if it was a bomb. I sat in an armchair, my back to the window that overlooked the street.

She pointed at the book. "The truth is in there and in all my other copies of *Het Achterhuis*. I wrote the truth right in front of you and many others. In this book. It's indecipherable, even to me, but it's in there. I'll unwrap the book so that you can see it." She went to the kitchen, came back with a pair of scissors, carefully cut one end of the package, reached in and withdrew a small stationery box with thick elastic bands around the middle, its two halves sealed with Scotch tape. "It's been ten years since anyone but me has seen it." She looked at it as if it was some ancient artifact. "I know it's morbid of me to regard something that almost killed me with such reverence. But I still think of it as it was when Anne Wilansky first gave it to me. That book still exists in my mind. So does she, as innocent, sweet, funny, sad and, no doubt, petulant, gossipy and vindictive as Anne Frank. *A typical teenager preserved inviolate in the desecrated heart of history's worst century.* That last phrase is from my uncompleted master's thesis. Kneel down beside me."

"Rachel, you're—"

"Please, *please* just kneel down."

So I knelt with her at the foot of the bed as she gingerly tore off the strips of tape and removed the lid of the box. There was Anne Frank's ever-smiling face on the cover, Anne Frank looking up, pen in hand, from something she was writing, perhaps a part of the diary itself.

"Look," Rachel said as she opened the cover with as much care as she had the box, holding it still with her index finger. There was an inscription that read: "This book was written by the heroic girl whom you are named after. Her father gave her the famous diary when she turned thirteen. May God give you her courage and her strength, and may he confer upon you many blessings all your life. Happy Birthday, Anne, from Mom and Dad, March 19, 1970."

"I wouldn't have accepted it if she hadn't insisted. She gave me the birthday present that her parents gave her. Such a strange thing to do."

"Who gave you this? Who is Anne Wilansky?"

"A friend of mine."

"I don't understand."

"The book seemed important when I was sick. Everything did. Not anymore. I mean, it's strange to give away your own birthday present, right? She gave it to me. I was *sick*. Never mind. I can't think. I don't know what I'm saying."

She got up and grabbed the book from the bed and strode about the flat as if she was searching for a way out of it. I tried, several times, to put my hands on her shoulders, but she flailed at me with the book, from which pages fell and fluttered to the floor. She grabbed them up, randomly replaced them, then went on darting about, changing direction every few steps as if someone only she could see was blocking her way, daring her again and again to try to get past. She stopped and stamped her foot with frustration.

"When Anne gave me her book, there was almost no blank space left in it because she had made so many notes. So I wrote over *her* notes in Arellian until hers were illegible, as are mine, even to me. The truth is in this book. Anne Frank's, mine, even hers. It's in here somewhere."

"What are you telling me?"

She dropped to her knees and gathered the pages together and put them back into the book, which she threw into the closet. I felt a great gulf opening between Rachel and me. Something had happened to her that I would never understand.

"I don't know what I'm saying," she said. "I don't. I'm just so tired and upset."

As she had done in front of the entrance to the annex after running down the stairs, she sat back on her heels and doubled over, her arms folded across her stomach as if someone had kicked her. I knelt beside her and rubbed her back as Bethany had done. She looked as if she was fighting to draw what might be her final breath. Finally, she fell against me, her forehead on my chest, gasping like someone who had surfaced from the dark just short of death.

"If you're going to leave me, you should do it now," she said. "Don't put it off. The longer you stay with me, the harder it will be for me to lose you. There may be no going back for you, now that I've dragged you into this. But it's different when the innocent are pulled across a great divide, isn't it? I hope it is. A few months ago, you knew nothing about me and the rest of the van Houts. I knew what I was dragging you into, but I did it anyway. I made you one of us. Maybe you can undo that. It might not be too late."

I pulled her to me with one arm. I kissed the side of her neck. "I will never leave you," I said. "Never. Unless you send me packing with a sweater in my suitcase."

She managed a faint smile and turned her face to me. I kissed her lips.

"We'll go home," I said.

"Home?" she said. "Where is it? I don't belong anywhere."

"With me."

"With you? Do you believe that I belong with you? Do you still believe it, after everything that has happened and everything I've done?"

"Yes."

"So we'll be home when we're together, no matter where we are."

"Yes."

"That would be nice."

"It will be."

"Let's just fall asleep here," she said, pulling me down beside her. "Here, on the floor. Let's just fall asleep. I hope we don't wake up."

ST. JOHN'S

RACHEL

At the start of grade ten, I was informed by my school principal that I had been made a member of the junior high school ice hockey cheerleading squad at the request of my mother, who thought cheerleading would make me more outgoing. I went through the motions, blank-faced, a cheerleader who didn't know the cheers, or the rules of ice hockey, rarely spoke to the others and *never* spoke to the players, not even the one who escorted me home after the first game because, he said, the principal had told him to.

In mid-December, during the Christmas break, when it was dark by four thirty, my father was late picking me up after a game. I was the last person waiting at the rink. The players and cheerleaders and supporters of both teams had left. The concession hut was closed. I stood at the window of one of the doors, looking out at the empty parking lot. As he swept the floor between the rows of seats, the janitor, an old man in a parka, kept his eye on me.

"Don't go out unless you have a ride," he said when he reached my end of the rink. "That wind will cut you in two." I heard the wind and saw the occasional cloud of snow drift across the pavement. I was wearing nothing under my coat but my cheerleader outfit. I stamped my feet in a vain attempt to keep them warm. My legs, bare but for nylons, shook uncontrollably.

Finally, Dad drove up. I could tell he hadn't been in the car long because frost was still melting from the windows and I could see my breath when I closed the door. When I complained, he said, "If I had waited for it to warm up, you would still be in there."

There was almost no traffic. "No one wants to venture out in this," Dad said. "Wouldn't it be nice if we were in Cape Town? It's summer there now. Summer. I picked a place where summer never comes."

As we drove home, we spotted a girl hitchhiking on a street that was mostly lined by schools and churches. I saw her beneath a street lamp, the thumb of one bare hand stuck out, the other hand pressed to her ear. She wore a short black coat that had no hood, and she hunched beneath the weight of a heavy-looking knapsack.

"That's one of my students," Dad said, and began to pull over.

"Dad!" I protested, but he ignored me.

"Professor van Hout!" the girl said, leaning in when, at Dad's instruction, I rolled down my window. She was pretty, petite, with short black hair.

"Anne, isn't it?" he said.

"What a good memory," she said. I rolled my eyes.

"Climb in," he said, and she opened the back door, got in and slammed it shut behind her.

"It's *so* cold out there," she said, blowing on her hands.

She said that, after leaving work, she had missed the bus that went by her house, so she decided to walk. She hadn't realized that a cold wave had set in while she was at work. She told us she'd used her hands to warm her ears until she could no longer stand the pain in her fingers—then she put her hands in the pockets of her coat until her ears hurt so much she covered them with her hands again. She'd been about to stop at a stranger's house to ask if she could call a cab and wait indoors until it came, when we pulled up beside her.

"Where are you headed?" he said. She gave an address that I was afraid would take us out of our way, though I wasn't sure where it was.

"My daughter Rachel," Dad said, and the girl behind me said, "Hi."

I said nothing. I pictured the three of us in the car outside her house, my father spouting small talk to his captive audience. It occurred to me that it was likely he would suggest that he and I go in with her for a surprise visit. He would barge into the house with me in tow, the professor and his daughter dropping in on Anne's unsuspecting family for no reason but that he had magnanimously picked her up because she'd missed her bus. He might linger there an hour while the girl's bemused and nervous parents fussed over him.

"Dad, drop me off first," I said in as pouty a tone as I could manage.

When my father said something about me being frantic that I would miss a minute of a TV show I liked, Anne laughed and said that she had been like that at my age.

"I'm thirteen," I said, "not six," and the two of them laughed together.

She was chewing gum, probably the only habit that my parents disapproved of that my sisters and I had never picked up. I had a low opinion of those of my classmates who chewed gum. I couldn't stand the sound when they talked and chewed at the same time. She worked at a convenience store and was still, she said, wearing her uniform beneath her coat. I fancied that she would quit university as soon as her parents let her, which would be very soon. She would become a beautician or a secretary, get married and have three kids by the time she was twenty-five, and would still be chewing gum.

My father looked at his watch. "That television program of yours is over," he said to me. "Why don't you just come along for the drive? You can talk to your new friend, and you can keep me company on the way back."

"It's not that far to her house, is it?" I said.

I knew he was trying to annoy me for talking back to him in front of the girl he likely had as low an opinion of as I did.

"It's fine if she doesn't want to," the girl said. "I mean, it's fine by me to drop her home."

It was true that the TV show was over. If I hadn't been so full of spite, I probably would have stayed in the car. She gripped the seat with one hand, trying to get a look at me. She wore two large plastic rings shaped like butterflies on her right thumb, one green and one yellow. She saw me looking at the rings.

"Prizes from boxes of Cracker Jack," she said. "I wear them as a joke, but not everybody gets it."

I kept acting as if she wasn't there.

"What grade are you in, grade eight?"

"Grade ten," Dad said.

"Ten? Most people are fifteen in grade ten."

"She was promoted two grades," Dad said. "She's very bright. Like you. Highest mark in my class."

"In high school," Anne said, "people think that if you get one hundred in everything, you're weird. They think that all you do is study. It's a bit better now. I have a few friends. And I'll soon be far away from here, anyway."

"Rachel gets one hundred in everything too."

"Dad!" I said.

The girl laughed. "Wow," she said. "That's amazing."

"It was Rachel's birthday, yesterday," Dad said.

"Happy birthday!" the girl said. I only sighed. "Oh, you're so pretty," the girl said. "If I wore my hair as long as yours, it would look like a mop."

She asked me if I'd ever heard of Anne Frank.

"We're doing the book in school next term," I said. "I've already read it a dozen times."

"Then you'll have a jump on all the others," she said, sounding not at all offended. "My favourite book is *To Kill a Mockingbird*. I *love* Scout. But I like *The Diary of Anne Frank* too. When you're a Jewish girl, it's supposed to be your favourite. But it's so sad."

"It's not sad," I said. "What happened to her after she stopped writing it is sad, but the diary is not sad."

"That's true. I've got a copy with me. I always do."

I heard her opening her knapsack. She said she liked the book so much when she *first* read it that she had underlined almost every word. She held the book over the seat so that I could see it. My curiosity got the better of me, and I took the book from her. I was determined not to look at her, but she leaned over the seat so that she could see my face. Her expression was so impish I couldn't help but smile. I leafed through the book. As she said, she had underlined a lot of passages or highlighted them with yellow marker. And she had written things in the margins and in between the lines.

"Not much resale value in *that* book," she said. "I mark up all my books, but that one is the worst. My parents think the world of Anne Frank."

"Why do you carry it around if it's not your favourite?" I said.

"It was a birthday present. And I still read it a bit. Once something gets into my knapsack, it tends to stay there."

I was now in the strange position of wanting to stay in the car while he drove her home, but not wanting to admit that to my father. So I didn't.

"My parents, they gave it to me on *my* thirteenth birthday. See, there's an inscription."

I read it: "This book was written by the heroic girl whom you are named after. Her father gave her the famous diary when she turned thirteen. May God give you her courage and her strength, and may he confer upon you many blessings all your life. Happy Birthday, Anne, from Mom and Dad, March 19, 1970."

"That's nice," I said.

"I want to be a writer," she said. "I'm taking accounting because my parents want me to. No offence, Professor van Hout."

"None taken," my father said. "But it might come in handy someday when you get rich from writing."

She laughed and looked at me again. "A Jewish girl named Anne who wants to be a writer. What a cliché. There may be thousands of us, but, still, it's what I want."

I told her that Dad grew up close to the Secret Annex.

"Oh my God, Professor van Hout, that's amazing," she said.

"I don't like to talk about Anne Frank," he said, and adjusted the rear-view mirror so that he could see her. "Where are you from?"

"Here," she said. "I was born here. But my parents came here from Halifax in 1950. My mother's side of the family is from Hungary and my father's is from Poland. All four of my grandparents came to Canada just after the First World War."

"Good timing," my father said.

"Yes. Mom says that, if my grandparents had been more successful, I might never have been born."

"She's right," my father said.

"I know you're not Jewish, because my parents would have met you if you were," she said. "Not many Jews in St. John's."

"No. We are not Jews. We would not be here if we were Jews. Alive, I mean. What's your last name? I'm sorry, but I've forgotten it." He looked at her in the rear-view again.

"Wilansky."

"The dry cleaners on Water Street."

"Yes," she said. "People think that if you're Jewish and your name is on a sign, you must be rich. My parents barely manage to get by."

"I suppose that depends on what you mean by getting by."

"I suppose."

"I am from Amsterdam, originally. I was there when the war broke out. I was there throughout the war. I was about your age when it started."

"Oh my God. It must have been terrible."

"It was."

"Dad was in the Dutch Resistance," I said.

"Really? Oh my God, really? You must have been so brave. I would have been too scared. My parents will want to meet you when I tell them. They'll think the world of you."

"No. No. I don't like to talk about the war, or to be reminded of it. Rachel knows that."

"I understand," Anne said.

The three of us were quiet for a while.

"Rachel was born in South Africa," my father finally said. "Her three sisters were as well."

Anne said, "I don't know anyone who wasn't born in Newfoundland besides my parents."

"Well, now you've met two more and know of four others."

"I don't know anything about South Africa," she said. "I mean, absolutely nothing."

"Really?" Dad said. "You've never heard of apartheid, then?"

"No," she said. "What is it?"

He didn't answer, instead saying, "I bet there are more Jews than South Africans in St. John's. Jews are everywhere. Everywhere I've ever been, there have been Jews."

"The diaspora."

"Yes. You should give Anne our number, Rachel."

I thought about making up a number—I don't know why I didn't, since I didn't want to talk to anyone about my father or Anne Frank. Instead, I tore a piece of paper from my school scribbler and wrote our number on it and handed it to her over the seat.

She smiled. "I'll call you," she said. "We don't have to talk about Anne Frank. We can talk about anything."

When Dad stopped outside our house, I got out in a hurry. She got out as well so that she could sit in the front. "You seem so nice," she said. "I hope we meet again."

"Nice meeting you," I said, but my words were lost in a gust of wind.

"Don't worry, I won't call you," she said, and winked at me. It was so cold that her bright green eyes were blurred with tears. So were mine. I jammed my hands into the pockets of my coat. She tucked the piece of paper with my number on it into one of my pockets. "We might meet again, someday when a few years difference in age is no big deal." She pried my arm from my side just enough to wedge her copy of *The Diary* beneath my armpit. "Here," she said. "Happy birthday. I want you to have this. Your dad was her neighbour."

"But it was a birthday present from your parents," I said.

"And now it's your birthday present," she said. She gave me a little hug. "Get indoors before you freeze to death."

And it was such a relief to get inside, where it was warm.

HANS

December 14, 1974

"It's so cold out there," she said as she got back in and slammed the door. "As soon as I can afford it, I'm going to buy a car."

He hadn't been able to smell her perfume when she was in the back, but he smelled it now. It was as if she had doused herself with it, sickly sweet, cheap, mint-scented perfume.

"You'll have to get your driver's licence," he said as he pulled out into the street.

"Oh, I have my licence," she said. "Dad taught me how to drive, but he never lets me use the car. What sense does that make?"

"None at all," he said. "One of my daughters, Gloria, has her licence. She's in Quebec at university, learning to speak French, which I could have taught her right here at home. What sense does *that* make?"

They drove in silence for a while. "It's quiet without Rachel," the girl said, her voice quavering a touch with nervousness. He wondered how long he'd been lost in thought.

"Gloria got married just recently. She was nineteen," he said.

"That's really young," she said. "I'm almost eighteen and—"

"And you won't be married by this time next year, *will* you?"

"Who knows?" she said, laughing and throwing up her arms as if to say there was no telling what might happen to her in a world in which there were men such as him who could not control their daughters.

Pellets of road salt and grains of sand pinged against the windows and the doors. "I'll probably forget how to drive before Dad lets me use the car," she said.

"What does he think you'll do if you go out in his car?"

"He doesn't give reasons. He just says what he says and that's that." She sat there with her knapsack on her lap, her arms folded on top of it, her chin resting on her arms in a pose of reflectiveness. She was pretty for a Jew, petite, delicate, but her personality didn't match her looks. How could it? The first time she'd opened her mouth, he'd seen that she was like all the Jews he'd ever known, in love with the sound of her own voice, irritatingly argumentative, deaf to the difference between eloquence and cant, and completely self-absorbed.

"You can drive *this* car if you like," he said.

"Really? But we're only about five minutes from my house."

"That's true. Not much of a chance to brush up on your driving skills."

"It was very nice of you to offer, though."

"I wasn't thinking. Your parents must be expecting you."

"I'm the baby of the family, and they *treat* me like a baby even though I'm as good as eighteen. They didn't even want me to get a job."

"But you got one. You put your foot down. Good for you. Rachel's the baby of our family and, as you saw, she has me wrapped around her finger."

The girl fell silent.

"No one was watching at the window for *me*," he said. "I have them well trained. They know that I hate to be tied down, that I like to get out of the house. I often drive around the city at night just to be by myself. Sometimes I can't sleep. Too many memories."

"Of the war?"

"Yes," he said. "It was not a nice time. I think that, after I drop you off, I'll drive around for a while. If I go straight home, I'll only wind up going out again after midnight when it's even colder."

"Where will you go?" she said, sounding sorry for him.

"Oh, I usually just drive around, see where I end up and then drive somewhere else."

"You really wouldn't mind if I drove your car?"

"Not at all. You have given me your word that you are licensed to drive. I won't ask for proof."

She laughed. "It's a deal!"

"It's a deal," he said, pulling over to the side of the street. She giggled and opened her door, which was caught by the wind and pulled her from the car so that she wound up on her backside on the sidewalk.

"Are you all right?" he called.

She laughed loudly as she struggled onto her feet. He held tight to his door as he opened it and stepped out onto the street. When he saw that she was coming around the front of the car, he went around the back, one hand on his fur hat lest he lose it in the wind.

He got in the car on the passenger side. Sitting behind the wheel, she tugged her door with both hands but lost hold of it as the wind kicked up. She reached out and grabbed the door again but couldn't close it. He leaned across her lap, his left elbow on her thigh and clutched the handle of the door with his left hand, which enclosed both of hers. Together, they barely managed to shut the door. They shared a laugh as he shifted back to his side of the seat. The cold, the smell of her minty perfume, the feel of her hands beneath his, her hair brushing his cheek, their conquest of the screeching wind exhilarated him.

"We did it," he said. She laughed and shuddered at the same time, hugging herself as her lips quivered.

"Oh my God, it's cold out there," she said, blowing on her hands. He nodded and rapidly clapped his hands together to warm them, but she mistook it for applause and joined in. "We did do it, Professor van Hout," she said, laughing as if he was a child to whom nothing mattered more than her praise and approval.

"Where to next?" she said.

"You're the driver," he said. "You decide."

"Well," she said, "first we have to move the seat forward." He reached beneath the seat, took hold of the lever, dug his heels into the floor mat and shifted forward, causing the seat to lurch ahead until his knees were just inches from the glove compartment. "Perfect," she said, "for me at least. You're kind of squished up."

"I'm just fine, Anne. Let's see how well you drive."

"I'm serious. Where to next?"

"The driver chooses where the car goes and by what route it gets there."

"Is that the van Hout rule? Is that what you tell Mrs. van Hout?"

"My wife was raised to think it's unladylike to drive a car," he said, resenting the girl for having mentioned Myra.

"Really?" She laughed as if they were sharing a joke about a woman who had tricked him into marriage, the sort of woman other men would have known should be avoided.

"Yes," he said, "really. It's not that odd. Many people in South Africa thought that way back then."

"I shouldn't have laughed. It just sounded a bit old-fashioned. But maybe it was like that in St. John's, too."

"I doubt it. Ladylike women are rare in this place, present company excepted, of course. But Myra enjoys being a fish out of water. She says it makes her feel as if she's a rebel among a crowd of conformists."

"She sounds interesting."

He felt like asking her why she insisted on talking about his wife. Instead, he said, "Very well, then, let's get this Malibu Classic on the road."

She eased the gearshift into drive and pulled out into the street. "I still can't help feeling that it's magic," she said, "the way a car just *goes* when I want it to. It gives me such a feeling of power."

"Yes, it does, doesn't it?"

Why did he say things he didn't mean? What was he doing, letting this impudent, gum-chomping Jewess drive his car? Everything she'd said since he stopped to pick her up had been at his expense or that of his wife or one of his daughters. "Can you even see over the dashboard?" he said. "I think this may be too much car for you."

"Do you want me to pull over? I bet I made a mistake, didn't I?"

"I was just having fun with you, Anne," he said. "I am just a passenger. The wheel is yours. You're a very good driver."

"You're so *nice*."

The pavement was bare and dry and bore large stains of salt. It hadn't snowed in a week, after a storm that had changed to heavy rain had left nothing on the ground but wind-polished ice. "Would it be okay if I drove over to the Brow and out to Cape Spear? Otherwise, I'll be stopping every ten seconds for a stop sign or a traffic light. I'd love to just *drive*."

"Of course," he said, "that would be fine. There's something about just driving, isn't there, getting away from all the things that slow you down or stop you in your tracks? There's freedom in it."

"Definitely."

"I often go out to Cape Spear when I drive around at night. You should get a car of your own as soon as you can."

They crossed the bridge that spanned the small stream that divided the city in two. She really was a good driver, confident, relaxed. As if she had done it a thousand times before, she shifted gears as they climbed the steep hill to the crest from which the road dropped off to the sea in a series of winding curves that led to the unmanned lighthouse at Cape Spear. There were no houses now, and the street lamps were so far apart that, between them, there was nothing visible but the stretch of road revealed by the headlights. "It's really dark," she said, "but I know this road like the back of my hand. I like hiking in these woods with my brothers and our dogs, even in the winter. We have snowshoes. I'm a tomboy, I suppose."

"I've never gone hiking in my life," he said. Everywhere he'd lived, but here especially, he'd assumed that the woods were even more boring than the parks he'd sometimes been obliged to stroll through.

"Because you've lived in big cities."

"I suppose."

"What's Amsterdam like?"

"There aren't as many Jews there as there used to be. Some that survived went to Israel. But many didn't survive."

"I'm sure that you and the others in the Resistance saved a lot of people," she said, glancing at him. "You shouldn't blame yourself."

"I don't like to think about it."

"I shouldn't have mentioned it again. It's just . . . I remember the first time I read *The Diary of Anne Frank*. Until I read it, I thought that no one stood up for the Jews. And it's so sad because, by the end of the diary, she knows that the Allies are so close, and she's convinced that she and the others will be rescued, but—"

"But the Allies were delayed because they fell short of taking an important bridge. I remember that very well. Too well."

"You must have been so disappointed when you heard they had to stop."

"I shouldn't be talking about it."

"So many people died trying to help Jews get out of Europe."

"Yes, they did. I was there. I didn't die. I hope you don't hold it against me."

"Oh no, I'm not saying that. I'm so nervous that I'm saying all the wrong things."

"Why are you so nervous?"

"You're my *professor*!" She giggled.

"Do you speak Hebrew, Anne?"

Yet another laugh. "Mom and Dad speak a little bit. But 'hello' and 'goodbye' are about as much as I can manage. My brothers were taught it, but I wasn't."

"I speak five languages fluently: English, Dutch, German, French and Afrikaans, the official language of South Africa. And I can get by in Spanish and Italian."

"Wow. Five, almost seven. I'm taking French."

"You need to live where the languages are spoken."

"I'll do French immersion—"

"In Canada. Yes. My eldest, Gloria, did that a few years back. But French isn't spoken properly in Canada." He thought of the trip he would soon take to see Gloria in Quebec.

"Almost seven languages and you were in the Dutch Resistance. Everyone in Accounting 214—well, if they only knew."

"Why? How am I regarded by everyone in Accounting 214?"

"No, it's not that. I just meant—"

"You meant that, if they only knew, they would think even more highly of me than they do already."

"Exactly," she said, sounding relieved that he didn't mind that his students laughed at him behind his back, didn't mind hearing that he was the butt of a universal joke.

She pointed out the windshield. "There it is," she said. He saw the flashing light atop the barrens of Cape Spear. "We're nearly there," she said. "I drove all the way. You should drive back, Professor van Hout. I don't want to push my luck."

"Whatever you like," he said as she pulled into the small parking lot at the end of the road. The lighthouse and its ever blinking light were just a hundred yards away, behind and above them.

"Let's just stop here for a few moments," he said. "This has been a refreshing change for me. I should hire you to drive me around when I can't sleep." She laughed. Did she do nothing but talk and laugh? Every time she had laughed since she got into the car, he had smelled the gum that she was chewing.

"It's so windy," she said. "It's so loud I can't even hear the ocean."

She put the car in park and turned off the headlights. "You can usually hear it. It sounds nice at night when you can't see it."

"Do you often come out here to listen to the ocean when it's too dark to see it?"

Another laugh, a loud one, another waft of the gum that she was grinding with her teeth.

"What's so funny?" he said.

"Couples come out here to park. I came out here with my boyfriend once or twice before we broke up."

"Aha, a boyfriend. I might have known, a pretty girl like you."

"Yes, but not anymore." No flirtatiousness, no guardedness. The boyfriend was history, whoever he was, water under the bridge. He hadn't known it, but that was all she had ever meant him to be.

"What's the expression? You washed him right out of your hair."

"Yes," she said, vigorously nodding her head and smiling, "that's exactly what I did."

"How did *he* take it?"

"He'll live."

He'll live. "The war wasn't just about the Jews, you know," he said.

"Oh, I know . . . I know there were many other factors."

"*Factors*? Factors. Yes, there were many other factors. You'd be surprised how many other factors there were. The kind that people never hear about."

She nodded solemnly, trying to look chastened, indulging an old man's memories of things that were still important to no one but him. He could just make her out, looking straight ahead as if she could see the ocean. "I should just zip up my mouth," she said.

He eased apart the fasteners of his winter coat, each one popping loudly. "So cold out there, so warm in here," he said. "Ten or fifteen minutes out there and we'd be done for."

The wind slammed the car so hard that it rocked slightly from side to side. From time to time, the foghorn sounded. The light from the lighthouse came and went, super-illuminating their surroundings for fractions of a second. "I wish we could see the waves," she said. "But you couldn't pay me enough to get out of this car."

"Imagine if the car stalled and wouldn't start," he said. "We'd freeze to death. You shouldn't have suggested that we come all the way out here on such a night."

"Oh, I'm sorry," she said. "You're right, you're right, what was I thinking? We should head back right now in case something does go wrong."

"You can make it up to me," he said.

"What do you mean?"

"Just like a girl to ask a question that she knows the answer to. My daughters do it. Rachel does. You know what I mean, Anne. It won't leave a mark on you or me."

He unzipped his fly. "Be a good girl," he said.

"You've got to be *kidding*." She stared at him in wide-eyed disbelief. He saw it all in the look she gave him, the scorn, the revulsion, the outrage and amusement. Another Jewess had once looked at him like that. "You picked the wrong girl, mister. We're getting out of here."

He grabbed her hair with his left hand just as she was shifting the car into reverse.

It might have been over in a minute. Or an hour. All he wanted her to do was what she had done many times with boys she didn't even like, such as the one she'd come out here with until she'd decided she would rather come out here with a different one. She had done it here in this very spot, in the front seat of her boyfriend's car. In car after car. Why not in the front seat of his? He had been kind to her. He had indulged her far beyond the point at which other men would have lost all patience with her, and had asked for nothing in return but what she had goaded him into asking for. She wouldn't do something to him, so he was left with no choice but to do something to her.

So he did it. It was done.

He had got on top of her. He hadn't been ready for a fight of any kind, let alone a fight like that. All women had to do was announce their availability and men came running. They could get it whenever they wanted it, but not men. Men had to play by *their* rules. Men had to play *their* stupid games. He had only done to her what she wanted him to do, except that he ignored her rules and games. It was absurd of her to think she had to play so hard to get. He was used to the dark and silent rooms of his own house, and ever-available daughters who complied and followed his instructions and liked what he did, and didn't make a sound as he crept back to his room. But this had been fury and anger and vicious desperation, the first fight of his life. She had said things that made him want to shut her up, but that was not his fault. She should not have spoken of Anne Frank or the other Jews whose deaths she thought he was haunted by. She should not have spoken of the girls she thought were still alive because of him. Every word she'd said since she got in the car had been an insult in disguise. He could have let it all pass and driven her home and swallowed his pride as he had done so many times before. But there comes a point when you *have* to act.

It seemed to him that his life had led inexorably to this very time and place. He'd invited Rachel to *stay* in the car. He hadn't stopped for this girl with anything in mind but giving her a lift. And here he was with a woman who was not his daughter or his wife. She had left him with no time to consider the risks of doing what she drove him to. A Jew who so loathed the idea of doing what he asked of her that she couldn't hide it, or didn't bother trying to, but *laughed* at him.

What sort of man would accept such an insult from a Jewess who, thirty years ago, would have been his for the taking if not for the Nazis, who kept such women for themselves and were amused when he tried to convince them that he didn't mind because he had women of his own and no need of theirs? How could he have looked at himself in the mirror again if he'd let her deny him?

He'd heard her fingernails breaking as she tried to get a grip on the back of his coat. She punched the windows until there was no skin left on her knuckles.

When he was done with her, he looked in the rear-view. There was blood on his face, which he wiped clean with his sleeve. Her blood. There wasn't a mark on him except for a scratch on his left earlobe, on which a drop of blood had formed. A girl who fought and screamed like that would never cease to fight and scream until she brought him down. He couldn't let her go. So. He crossed the only infinite divide that was left for him to cross. He took another life with his bare hands. He put both hands around her neck and squeezed until all the things that need not have happened stopped and silence took the place of all the things he need not have heard. During the war, others had taken the lives of people he betrayed, but he had managed to keep death at a distance so that, when the war was over, the winners thought his hands were clean.

He had been about to drag her from the car and leave her when he remembered that Rachel had written their phone number on a piece of paper that she had handed to the girl. What had she done with it? He checked the pockets of her coat and uniform. He pulled inside out the pockets of the jeans that he had tossed into the back seat. Nothing but Kleenex and a few coins. He took off her boots and socks. Nothing. She must have put the note in her knapsack. Aside from having innumerable pockets, the thing was crammed with textbooks, into any one of which she might have slipped the piece of paper that, if it were found, would lead the police straight to his front door.

He realized he couldn't take the time to check the books, and he knew he might have missed the note when he rifled through her clothes. He had to get rid of everything. He stripped her naked and stuffed her clothes in the knapsack, along with her boots and socks. He tried to refasten the straps but couldn't.

He got out of the car, walked around the front, opened the driver's door and lifted her until he was able to push her onto the passenger side. He backed the car up and turned it around. Leaving the parking lot, he pulled onto the road with no thought in his mind but that he would submerge her, her clothing and her knapsack in one of the lakes or ponds out here that were so numerous they had no names. But then he remembered that every stream and pond and lake was frozen over. He would freeze to death looking for a place to safely conceal her.

He stopped in the road, putting the car in park but leaving the headlights on and the engine running. He got out and went around to the passenger side. He opened the door and carried her from the car to the gravel margin. He tried to throw her into the ditch, but she merely tumbled from his arms onto the ground at his feet, lying on her side, facing the road. He crouched and positioned her arm and her leg so as to cover her private parts.

He got back in the car and drove at a steady pace toward the city. A strange calm came over him, almost a sense of peace. He believed he would be caught. He was resigned to it, not because of Rachel, who, he knew, wouldn't say a word, but because of whatever it was that would catch up with him this time, backfire on him as something had always done no matter how carefully he thought things through, no matter how sure he had been that he had made allowances for everything. He drove down into the city, his ears popping on the steepest hill. He went past his house five, ten, fifteen times, until, at last, there were no lights on but the one above the door.

He felt contempt for those he thought had wilfully misunderstood him, and those who would condemn him even though, dealt the same cards, they'd have played them just the same, or even worse, than he had. He began to laugh in scorn of his hypocritical accusers, because he had done what they had stopped short of doing simply because they lacked the nerve.

He pulled into the driveway and turned off the headlights but left the engine running. He looked at the bulging knapsack resting against the back of the seat beside him like some odd-looking passenger. "Be a good girl," he'd said to her, as he so often had to his daughters, and to other girls who never saw his face because he wore a ski mask that, even now, was in the glove compartment. She'd decided she would rather be dead than good. Her intransigence would cost him everything.

He turned off the car, grabbed the knapsack, got out and walked to the door with it, swinging it back and forth as if he was coming home after a long but pleasant walk, even as the wind again forced him to grab hold of his fur hat. He opened the front door and went inside, closing the door loudly behind him, then doing the same with the door that led into the vestibule, where, after turning on the light, he took off his hat and coat and boots and threw them on the floor.

In the living room, he drew an armchair close to the fireplace, put the knapsack in the chair, picked up the coal scuttle, which was almost full, and emptied its contents into the hearth. He made no effort to minimize the noise, for he knew that, unless he called out to Myra, she would not come down to see what he was doing. He doused the coal with lighter fluid from the can beside the scuttle. He picked up the knapsack, sat down in its place and settled it on his lap. He lit a match and threw it on the pile of coal, which erupted into flame with a loud whoosh.

He waited for the coals to reach white heat, then began to burn the contents of the knapsack, feeding the fire with her flimsy coat, her jeans, her green store uniform, her underwear. He poked the clothing into the coals and watched it turn to ash. Next he burned her leather boots, which sent up clouds of thick black smoke until nothing but the heels remained, hard, square, wooden heels that he thought would never catch—but, once they did, they quickly vanished. Last, he burned her books, all of them hardcover, tucked into one of which, he was convinced, was the note on which his telephone number and Rachel's name were written. He placed book after book on the fire, splayed open, covers facing up. He saved until the very end the accounting textbook he had written and self-published and prescribed as a mandatory text in his courses. He didn't notice that *The Diary of Anne Frank* was missing.

He watched his textbook burn, certain that everyone in the house was awake and listening. In the extreme unlikelihood that one or more of them came downstairs and caught him in the act of burning clothes and books, they would simply go back to bed and forget about it if he told them to. A roaring fire at one in the morning. Finally, he burned the knapsack.

He found a small Band-Aid in the downstairs bathroom and put it on his ear.

He went to the kitchen, opened the fridge, took out his glass of Horlicks and gulped it down.

No one was more surprised than him that he got away with it, that the knock on the door never came.

He spent the night after he came home from killing Anne Wilansky lying on top of the blankets of the bed in the spare room, his hands behind his head as he stared up at the ceiling through the glasses he thought it would be pointless to remove because of the imminence of his arrest, which he planned to meet without remorse or cowardice.

A memory came to him. The worst row in the history of the family had erupted over Gloria's decision to leave home when she was just eighteen. That August, she'd announced that she was engaged and had been accepted at Laval University in Quebec starting in September.

"And how are you going to pay for it?" he'd said.

"Stephen's father is paying for us both," she said. "Tuition fees, residence, everything." She'd met Stephen on a trip to Halifax, had become engaged after five days and had been flying back and forth between St. John's and Halifax ever since, courtesy of Stephen's wealthy father. Eighteen and flying back and forth for liaisons with her fiancé.

He'd become enraged. "I won't have another man paying my daughter's way," he'd said. "Don't you see that he is buying you for his son to play with?"

"I love Stephen and he loves me. Stephen's father knows that. I want to learn to speak French and Dutch and German so that I can be a flight attendant and move back to South Africa."

"Why don't you just become a stripper?" he said. "There's not much difference."

"They don't teach French properly here," she said. "They don't teach anything properly here. Not even accounting."

"I speak French," he said. "The European kind that is spoken by those who visit South Africa. I could teach you."

She said she was sure he wouldn't let anything cut into the time he spent dropping in unannounced on total strangers or driving around the city at all hours of the night.

"No daughter of mine is going to leave home before she has the sense to keep her legs closed," he shouted at her. She ran upstairs to her room in tears. He sat for hours on the back deck by himself until Myra came out and sat with him in silence.

Until Gloria's departure for Quebec, he acted as if the argument had never happened. So did the rest of them. How he'd hated that a mere boy had won her away from him, got the better of him with the help of his rich father. As she was leaving the house to get in a cab to go to the airport, he whispered in her ear, "Until we meet again." It was a promise that he'd made good on when he and Myra flew to Quebec six months later and dropped in unannounced on his daughter and her all-but-adolescent husband. There'd be no more surprise visits to Quebec now, all because of that *girl*.

And so it went, night after night, other memories of other times whose like he would never see again. The unfairness of it made him feel such spite that his stomach churned. A night came when he *wished* the police would come for him, and another when he considered turning himself in just so that he'd never again have to wait for the knock on the door. But, just as that knock had never come during the war as he lay awake, waiting for it, it did not come now. Eventually, he realized that he was not even a suspect, that he had got away with murder and could resume his life in freedom and impunity.

He often said to himself, while eating, driving, standing in front of a classroom, lying in bed with Myra: *Of all the people alive, I am the only one who knows what happened in the car after Rachel went inside the house.*

There were others after her. Each time, he told himself that this one was the last.

From *The Ballad of the Clan van Hout*

VAN DOBBEN (1980)
Perhaps I shouldn't write this down—
I think of it when I'm alone,
what happened in that place that night;
no one but me, if I am right,
no one remembers anymore,
though most of us survived the war.
I dream about it all the time;
I may go mad and dream in rhyme
the way my youngest daughter does.
(Am I the only one who knows?
I've heard her rhyming in her sleep,
translating from that book she keeps,
repeating lines she heard from me
and memorized indelibly,
the ballad of the family,
but also lines that Rachel wrote,
a rush of rhymes but none of note.)

In a back room at Van Dobben,
the Germans slept with girls and women,
the wives and daughters of the men
who brought their food and drinks to them;
others, too—some were regulars—
the favourites were teenagers
who did what they were told to do
to stay alive, the chosen few,
for those who didn't please the men
were not brought back or seen again.
The *techtelmechtel* Night Salon
that never closed till after dawn:
no Dutchmen went into the room
but those who cleaned up after them,

kitchen workers, older waiters,
sullen, bitter Nazi haters
who never said a word out loud,
not even to young Hans van Hout.
(The Luftwaffe left by the back,
the women, too, half-dressed and drunk.)
My fellow Dutchmen wined and dined
on what the Germans left behind,
the glasses of champagne and beer
that were abandoned everywhere—
they drank them all, flat though they were;
on hands and knees they searched the floor.
They ate the smallest scraps of food,
the crumbs of cake and crusts of bread.
As well-fed as the German men,
I sat and watched, ashamed of them.
I locked up after all were gone
and walked home in the morning sun.
I slept until late afternoon
and rose when it was dark again
for the night shift at Van Dobben.

My birthday came, they sang to me,
pretending I was twenty-three:
Zum geburtstag liebe van Hout;
they said I was *männliche Jungfrau*,
too old to be a virgin now.
"We'll take you to the Night Salon,
where virgins go, but not for long:
hanky-panky, *techtelmechtel*,
give some *frau* your pumpernickel;
a strapping lad like Hans van Hout,
make sure you put it in her mouth."
I claimed I was not a virgin,
I had slept with many women,

some who were almost twice my age,
so famous was I for my sausage.
"I doubt you've even kissed your mother,"
one of them said, at which the others
threw back their heads, mouths open wide,
and laughed as if to split their sides.
"You're going to the Night Salon—
you've been a virgin far too long
for one with one that is so long."
I played the fool to lesser men
(I swore I never would again).
They sang their songs, I played along,
as if I thought nothing was wrong—
but then they sat me in a chair
and stripped me to my underwear.
They hoisted the chair from the floor
and raised it high into the air.
Above my subjects, looking down,
I sat as if upon a throne
that rose and fell upon the sea
of soldiers who served under me.
"King van Hout must not be late—
his queen longs for her potentate."
They chaired me round the restaurant:
"Three cheers for Hans, the sycophant."
And then they chaired me to the room,
the *techtelmechtel* Night Salon—
and then, at last, they put me down.

Before the war, the Dutch elite
had gone there late at night to eat,
to mix with others of their kind—
for this the room had been designed:
leather and lace from wall to wall,
elegant booths and private stalls.

To see and to be seen they came,
the upper crust of Amsterdam.
The middle class, the mere riff-raff
who hoped to glimpse the other half,
always went home disappointed—
they were kept from the anointed.
Now the room was but a brothel:
the whores had once been clientele,
the women who had dined so well,
their husbands the celebrities
the lesser lights had hoped to see.

Despite the half-lit chandeliers,
I couldn't see the officers,
so acrid was the drifting smoke,
so thick it almost made me choke.
I heard the snickers and the jeers:
"That's quite a uniform he wears."
"I think the boy's a fusilier,
but he forgot his bayonet
or else he hasn't grown one yet."
"Well, I can see no sign of it.
It may be in his underwear,
assuming that it's anywhere."
"Great oaks from little acorns grow."
"Well, this boy's wood has yet to show."
"He's got a pair of acorns, though,
to come like that into this room."
"Good thing for him the light's so dim."
"Good thing for us, I think you mean."

My eyes adjusted to the light—
there was a table on my right:
four men were sitting side by side,
none even bothering to hide

that they wore even less than me—
nothing at all that I could see
but what I guessed were pillow slips
that lay like napkins on their laps;
the crazy images of dreams,
for nothing there was what it seemed,
the smoke so dense I couldn't see
if they were looking back at me,
those faces conjured from thin air,
or even noticed I was there
or realized that I could hear.

The men who chaired me in were gone.
In many booths along the walls,
some things were taking place, my girls,
that I had never seen before,
and so I couldn't help but stare:
women with women, men with men—
some Germans stood round watching them.
Their togas had been tablecloths;
their laurel crowns were made of wreaths
from which the flowers had been picked.
The smell of something made me sick
but I did not give in to it.
A woman with a painted face
who wore a tablecloth of lace
came up to me and took my hand—
the woman may have been a man.
In that place it was hard to tell
what wasn't there and what was real.
She led me through the smoky room—
my underwear was *my* costume,
a pair of shorts, an undershirt
that I had not removed since birth,
or so it seemed, for they were grey,

their colour long since washed away,
threadbare and frayed and full of holes,
my only set of underclothes.
She turned around and spoke to me—
her voice seemed so unwomanly—
"There was a raid this afternoon,
eight Jews crammed into tiny rooms
like rats that live between the walls
of houses on the cold canals.
Two girls have been our guests tonight,
two virgin Jews still full of fight.
I think they look much better now
than they will look at Birkenau.
Two virgins, just the right reward
for Hans van Hout, who is the third.
Who better, Hans, to lose yours to,
than such a pair of sister Jews?
They're yours to do with what you will,
they're yours until you've had your fill,
until they are brimful with you,
two untouched girls, two nubile Jews.
They fight like cats when we come near,
they bite and scratch and pull their hair.
We were saving them for later—
I think Hans, the Nazi waiter,
could make a meal of both of them:
I'd rather watch than touch the scum,
so you can have the Jewesses.
What would *der Führer* think of us?
We can use the inspiration
and avoid miscegenation."
"It's not as if he has a choice—
a boy that age could do both twice
and still have room left for dessert;
it's time he had a piece of skirt."

The voices came from in my head,
or so it seemed, from what they said:
"They'll need some taming, I'm afraid,
before they're well and truly laid.
They're locked in cloakroom number one:
we'll let them loose and have some fun.
They're here, just here, behind this door,
bound, gagged and naked on the floor."
Then, as if of its own accord,
the door swung open and I heard—
nothing at all, not one small sound.
The German men all gathered round.
"They seem to be much more subdued—
you'd think they were already screwed.
There's not much left for Hans to do—
he might not have to force them to."

The two girls lay upon the floor,
bound back to back, beyond the door,
heads bowed as tears ran down their cheeks—
one bit her lip and crossed her feet.
Their hair was wet with tears and sweat;
I couldn't see their faces yet.
They slumped to hide their breasts from me;
I saw more than I'd ever seen,
one blond, the other raven-haired—
I didn't care that they were scared.
It was not as if I could refuse
this gift of virgin sister Jews.
I'd never touched a girl before—
they soon lay naked on the floor
in front of me, their legs splayed wide,
two sisters lying side by side,
afraid to move lest they be shot.
"It's time to show us what you've got.

Are you a man or are you not?"
They made one get up on all fours:
"Show her that massive thing of yours—
it's time, young Hans, to drop your drawers."

I wanted them so much it showed—
it showed too much—"Oh look, good God,
the Cock of Doodle Do has crowed.
We thought you were the Prince of Males.
Prince Hans has crowed before two girls."
"He saw a bit of Jewish tit
and off his gun went, just like that."
They went on with their gleeful rhymes,
their stupid jokes, their stupid games—
and then began to shoot their guns.
They shot the pictures on the walls,
they shot the leather booths and stalls,
they even shot the ceiling fans.
I covered my ears with my hands,
for they were ringing from the noise,
and tears ran freely from my eyes,
so heavy was the smoke by then—
the popping of spent Luger shells,
the dust as chunks of plaster fell . . .

I grit my teeth and shut my eyes—
I was convinced that I would die
when all at once the shooting stopped
as if someone had spoken up.
"Good Lord, young Hans just came again."
"His gun goes off so easily."
"It doesn't look like that to me.
I think young Hans just took a pee."
And so I had, unknowingly.
Despite them I continued to—

you know what's coming next, don't you?
"Let's leave him here with his two Jews."
The German soldiers laughed and roared:
"He really put them to the sword.
He'll never be much of a suitor,
judging by that small pee-shooter."

How could a man feel more absurd?
I shouldn't write another word.
I might forget but for that girl,
the one still on her hands and knees,
the one still staring at the floor,
the younger of the Jewish whores—
the raven-head looked up at me
(the coldest eyes I'd ever seen;
brown eyes with little flecks of green),
her face a mask of plaster dust:
she might have been some sort of ghost.
She wiped her mouth with one small hand
and, whispering, said, "*Ik ben Anne.*"

That's all she ever said to me.
I can't be sure; I can't, you see,
for Anne is such a common name
and girls that age all look the same.
And she was all but in disguise,
except, of course, for those cold eyes
that looked at me so scornfully,
so gleeful was her mockery . . .
"It's easier for you," I said.
"You only have to lie in bed.
The slightest touch and you get wet—
you only have to wait for it."
At least that's what I should have said,
but all I did was turn my head.

I can't be sure; I can't, you see—
unsure is all I'll ever be.
Eight Jews, black hair, the greenest eyes . . .
I'm almost sure I recognized
her later when I found that book:
I think I recognized that look.
"*Ik ben Anne*" I heard again—
I've heard it many times since then.
That smirking face keeps me awake;
I see it often at daybreak.
I hear her say, to me, a man:
"You can't deny that I am Anne."

RACHEL

I was in bed when I heard him come home, hours later. In the morning, I was not surprised when he told Mom that he had paid some friends of theirs an impromptu visit the night before. Nor did she seem to be, no more than she had been when I came through the door and told her he was driving home a hitchhiker we had picked up.

That day, at school, I heard about a university student who was missing. Because of the cold wave, a search had been started when she didn't get back from work, though it was dark. She had been found dead near the side of the road in a wooded area called Maddox Cove, near Cape Spear, just after sunrise. She was naked. She had been raped and strangled. The police said that, as yet, they had no suspects.

In the evening, I happened to glance at the newspaper that lay on the coffee table in the front room, still folded in half because no one had read it yet. There was a story about the missing girl, as well as a photograph of her. I recognized her instantly. I turned the paper over so that her picture was face down and ran upstairs. I told myself it was possible that she was abducted after my father dropped her off at her house, while she was walking to her door.

In the following days, accounts of her all-too-short life began to appear in the papers: she had graduated at the top of her class every year from kindergarten to the end of high school. She had thought she might become a doctor, but she loved books and hoped she might write books of her own someday. She was also, at her father's insistence, taking courses in accounting in case she had to abandon her more ambitious plans. She was saving to go to university on the mainland and that was why she had a part-time job.

Anne Wilansky's mother told a reporter that, when her daughter was late, they thought at first that she was working overtime. She often did and didn't always call to let them know. But when her father phoned the store at eight o'clock and was told that she'd left for home on foot at five, they called the police.

Mrs. Wilansky said, "It was a long night. The police looked and other people with cars looked for her. Our car was in the garage for repairs. My husband went out with a friend in *his* car, but I stayed at home so that there'd be someone in the house if she came back. I guess I didn't have to wait as long as the families of other girls have had to wait. A lot of them are still waiting. Some of them will wait forever."

No one had seen us stop to pick her up, so the police didn't even know what kind of vehicle to look for. They said she might have been killed in someone's house after being dragged into it and raped, then carried to a car and driven to the outskirts of the city.

She was frozen to the ground when they found her. Several people had seen her but had driven by, mistaking her, they said, for a store mannequin that someone had thrown away.

She lay on her right side, facing the road. Her left arm was draped across her chest and her legs were crossed. I wondered if he had posed her that way out of some vestigial sense of decency. I had to believe that she was dead when he left her, that she didn't feel that brutal cold, that she went to heaven the second she died, that it was just her body that was dumped there in the dark. She didn't care about the cars that didn't stop or about being found with no clothes on when the sun came up.

I wondered about her clothes. That thin coat of hers, her store uniform, her underwear and socks, her boots, her books, her knapsack—where could he have hidden all those things? Then I remembered that I'd smelled smoke from the fireplace after he came home. He had burned everything, I guessed, even as I lay in bed upstairs. Did he notice that Anne's copy of the diary was missing? Perhaps he had, but it hadn't occurred to him that she might have given it to me.

Weeks after the murder, it was leaked that the killer had left a bite mark on the girl's right breast, which was going to be compared to other bite marks found on the right breasts of girls in the city who had been raped while gagged and blindfolded, and then released. The whole city was talking about the involvement in the case of an odontologist from Montreal. Bite marks had never been used in evidence in Newfoundland before.

A few days later, when I came home from school, my mother met me at the door. "He's sitting in front of the fire," she said. "He's in a lot of pain."

"What's wrong?" I said. "Is it his ulcers?"

"Well," Mom said. She flashed me an odd-seeming smile. "Well, dear, your father had all his teeth removed today. Every last one of them. He didn't tell me he was going to do it. It was a big surprise to me when he got home."

"What? Why?"

"He's getting dentures."

"Were his teeth that bad? I don't remember his teeth being bad at all."

"Well, you're right, they weren't, but he says he got tired of going to the dentist for fillings and cleanings."

"I don't remember Dad ever going to the dentist."

Mom carried on as if I hadn't said a word. "And the expense, well, he didn't think his teeth were worth it. It's not as unusual as you think, not for people of our generation."

"Are you planning to do it?" She tilted her head and frowned as if to say that I knew better. "So it's normal for him, but out of the question for you?" I said. Mom turned the palms of her hands outwards and pressed her lips together in a kind of smile.

I went inside and, as she said, Dad was sitting in an armchair in front of the coal fire, which was roaring. If Dad heard us, he gave no sign, but simply went on staring at the fire. Mom placed her hand on his shoulder. "Have you taken what the dentist gave you for the pain?" He nodded and placed his hand on hers. "He can't speak," she said to me. "His mouth is too swollen. He's been writing notes to me all day.

I asked him if he would rather watch TV, but he shook his head. He hasn't had anything but broth since he came home." Dad nodded again.

Mom and I sat on the sofa. It was almost comical, the two of us staring in silence at Dad, who had come home toothless to his wife, who had no idea what was wrong with him until he told her in a note.

Months of police investigation turned up nothing. During March Break, Dad drove his car to the mainland and sold it there, somewhere, and came back in another one. His excuse was that it was much cheaper to buy a car on the mainland and drive it back than it was to buy one in St. John's. He made the trip alone and none of us ever asked him why. Had he done it because of bloodstains I never noticed, or pretended not to, or because he knew the car bore hundreds of her fingerprints? He may have worried about someone coming forward after all to say they saw a car stop to pick her up. Or did he get rid of the car because it reminded him of her, because he could no longer bring himself to drive it, no longer stand to use it as the *family* car.

I said nothing to anyone. In the months before he sold it, I often rode in the back seat of the car. Given what a cold night it had been, it was likely that everything had happened in the car, probably in the back seat, the very one that I was sitting on. I knew that, but . . . but I didn't know it.

I could have made sure that justice was done for her. I could have given her family some measure of peace, the relief, at least, of knowing who did it and how she came to be in his car. But I was afraid that nothing would happen to him if I went to the police, or informed on him to anyone, especially my mother. Even though I had the book, I believed that it could be explained away by *them*. I didn't know how my parents would explain how I'd come to have the book, but I was certain they would find a way. Perhaps I had come across it lying on the sidewalk, dropped there by her by accident as she hurried home from work that night or some other one. By the time she died, it might have been days since she lost the book. Or the book might have come out of her knapsack during a struggle as her murderer forced her into his car. The police would only have had my word on it that Dad had stopped to offer her a ride. My word. And when my accusations were explained away, I would still be living in his house. Carmen was still there too, technically, but she often didn't come home for days and nights on end and I had a feeling that she'd soon be moving out. We weren't close anymore. I would soon be the only one of Dad's daughters still at home. He had killed a girl and might kill others, or might already have done so, but there was nothing I could do. These—the thoughts of a thirteen-year-old who had always feared the House by Night—may be forgivable.

But there was also this: I was to blame for her death. I didn't want people to think—or to know?—it was as much my fault as his.

I had given her the silent treatment. That didn't put her off. I made it plain that she was an inconvenience, but she went on talking to me. I warmed up to her a bit when Dad agreed to drop me off first, and she acted as if I'd been nice to her all along. I gave her my phone number as if I was doing her a favour, and she gave it back to me. I'd had no childhood. She'd had one. But that's all she had. When I got out of the car, she gave me a quick hug as if we were close friends, as if she thought I needed a hug or knew that we would never meet again.

I couldn't think it through. I tried but I couldn't. I knew what he had done to me, so I should have known that he might do the same to her. Was that right? I knew what he had done to my sisters. Why didn't it occur to me that she was in danger? Maybe it had. Had it? Why didn't I stay in the car? He'd never have the nerve to hurt her, because I was a witness to the fact that he had picked her up, because I had spoken to her and because she'd told us her name. Was that how I'd thought it through? I couldn't remember having thought it through. Mine was probably the last voice she heard except for his. It's such a small thing, a normal thing for a girl that age, to want to get home in time to see her favourite TV show, and to be upset with her father, even to be spiteful, when she misses it because of him. And so, for spite, I made him drop me off and thereby served her up to him. And what of my sisters? If I had spoken up to him, or threatened to tell someone, could I have freed all four of us from him? I convinced myself that I couldn't, no more than I could have protected Elsie or

Nora or all the other maids who lived in the shed at the back of the garden. Who knows what he was up to the nights that, unable to sleep, in St. John's and in Cape Town, he went out walking, or driving in his car? Who knows how many girls and women he hurt over the years? Who knows how many times Mom provided him with an alibi?

I may have served up countless women to him, not just my sisters and Anne Wilansky. Was there no going back for me? He was accused of being an informer. Should I have been one?

Anne Wilansky wasn't one of his daughters. She wasn't me. He wasn't used to women fighting back. Anne Wilansky fought in fury and vicious desperation. Her fingernails were broken. There was no skin left on her knuckles. Her hair was soaked with her own blood. This might have been the first fight of his life, his first encounter with such terrifying fury. A woman. She was more than he had bargained for, more than he was able to imagine. So he crossed the only infinite divide that was left for him to cross. He took another life with his bare hands.

I tried to shut out the thought that I had killed her as surely as he had, but I couldn't and he knew it. He was so sure of me, he didn't even bother to tell me to keep my mouth shut. He knew I wouldn't speak up. Without saying a word about it to me, he held it over my head for years. I saw it in his eyes every time he looked at me. He saw it in mine.

He stopped coming to my room after the night we picked up Anne Wilansky. He left me alone for six months. He never laid a hand on me. It was as if we had struck a kind of truce. He would spare me from now on if I kept my mouth shut. I didn't think of it that way, but that's how it felt. Maybe he left me alone because he didn't want to push his luck. Or is that just a different way of saying that we struck a truce?

Six months after Anne. The door was closed but not locked. Anne's book was on my bed. He walked in without knocking. I was getting undressed and had removed everything but my underpants. I don't remember if he closed the door behind him or if the lights were on or off. I froze. Neither of us said a word. He walked up to me and put his hands beneath my breasts, which he moved up and down as if assessing their weight. "You're getting to be a big girl," he said. I wasn't angry or afraid. I wouldn't have resisted.

I grabbed the book from the bed.

"What's that you're reading?" he said as if he'd never seen a copy of *that* book in my hands before. He took it from me, gently tugging when I put up a token resistance. I was terrified that he would see the inscription to Anne Wilansky on the inside of the cover. "Ah, *Het Achterhuis*," he said. I wasn't sure if he knew, or suspected, that Anne had given it to me. He closed it and tossed it aside with enough force to send it spinning across the floor until it hit the wall.

"Filthy Jewess," he said. "She got what was coming to her. I made sure of that." I wondered which filthy Jewess he was talking about.

"She died in a concentration camp with her sister, Margot," I said.

"Yes, but you don't know why. What if I told you that I was the one who tipped off the Gestapo about that secret annex of Anne Frank's? What then, ha, what then? Do you think Anne Frank's hiding place was given away by someone of prominence? It's not as if the Germans were *looking* for her and the others. The Germans knew where thousands of Jews were hiding, but by 1944, they were too busy to bother with them. Amsterdam fell to the Germans in 1940. But the Germans didn't put a bounty on the Jews until 1942. I saw the Franks walking through the streets. Many people did. We all knew what was up. I saw the whole family trudging through the rain like refugees, on their way from Merwedeplein to Prinsengracht. I followed them. I watched them going in and out, moving in with their belongings in broad daylight. How stupid.

"I didn't know what to do. I knew men who worked with the Colonne Henneicke, Dutch men who made their living by finding Jews for the Germans. I could have told them to call the Gestapo right away. *Zi waren brutale mannen*. I didn't want to make them mad with me. Those Jews might have gone right out the other side of Prinsengracht, for all I knew. They were very tricky. What then? Thousands of them were in hiding like rats. No one liked the Jews. It's the same today, here, in Holland, in Canada. Everywhere. They are the scourge of humankind. I kept my eye on 263 and 265. I saw things. Heard things."

I told him to prove it was true. He told me to prove it wasn't. "I lived two streets away from Anne Frank's house," he said. "I saw a lot of comings and goings, put two and two together, or rather four and four together, for there were eight of them, eight filthy Jews crammed into a couple of rooms. Eventually, I called the Gestapo. It was as simple as that. Yes. I'm the one. Eight Jews. Eight and they're still trying to hunt down who did it."

"Seven Jews," I said, tears streaming down my cheeks. "Otto Frank survived."

"Yes," he said. "Just like a Jew to let his wife and daughters die so that he could live. But I got seven and a half guilders for each one of the Jews. Sixty guilders. Do you think I'm lying?"

"Maybe you're joking," I said.

"I'm not. There is only one way to deal with Jews."

He sighed as if he wished it wasn't true. He sounded tired, disheartened, as if he had recently suffered some great and final disappointment. "I wasn't a collaborator. I served with the Resistance. The ones who weren't there don't know what happened in the war. I helped the Jew-hunting Nazis, but that didn't make me hate the Nazis any less. I helped to save my share of Jews, but that didn't make me hate *them* any less. It wasn't just this side or that side. There were many sides. I worked for them all, against them all. I was only a few years older than you. On my own in occupied Amsterdam. Can you imagine that? An unaligned young man of little consequence. I'd rather have been one of no consequence at all—but I survived. You should be proud of me, my little Rachel. I've read the version of that Jew's diary with all the dirty parts left in. Disgusting. But she's worshipped by so many, you're not allowed to talk about that. We're supposed to believe that she was a saint, but you should read the things her father cut out of that book. Anyway, a fat lot of good her diary did her in the end. Typhus was too good for her."

He got up abruptly and left. I never stopped wondering when he would come to my room again, but he never did.

From *The Arelliad*

MRS. WILANSKY (1985)

Now comes the quickening of time
that happens when I start to rhyme.
It's like a spell of vertigo;
I know what's next, or should by now—
just when I think it never will,
the spinning stops, the world stands still.

There she is, the green-eyed Anne—she beckons me to follow her. The foghorn sounds, warning of sunken wrecks, unmindful ships. She stops and turns to look at me. "I'd rather not go there alone," she says. "Will you go with me?" Somehow I know she means her home, the house where she grew up. I'd rather not go there, and almost say so, until I realize that this is the first time she has spoken without accusing me. "I'll go with you," I say.

We're side by side and holding hands, standing on a city street in front of a bungalow I take to be her house. We go inside, where she leads me to a small dining room—and there they are, her parents, having dinner at a table set for three. "They always set a place for me," she says. "I guess it's kind of corny, but I think it's nice."

Mrs. Wilansky looks up from her plate and says, as if she is thinking out loud: "I'm glad I don't know who he is, his face, his name. I'd think about him even more than I do now. Sometimes I dream that she's out there on the cape, alive but lost. There's not much light left in the sky and no one knows she's missing. No one is looking for her. In the dream, she's lost because I let her down somehow. I feel such guilt. You see, it must be someone's fault, or else each of us could die because we missed a bus. In the absence of the killer, the mother is the murderer, the negligent creator who let her stray too far from me.

"I stay awake to ward off dreams, but even so, he sits beside my bed at night on a chair, his back to me like a prisoner I'm interrogating. He listens while I ask him where he went after he left her there, and how he got her in the car in the first place. She was smart; she would have run. She must have known and trusted him. The ever-silent, unseen Man. What sort of divine plan required her to die like that? To Whom was it necessary that she should die instead of me? What appetite is satisfied by the murder of a child? I pose these questions to his back, this Man who sits there in the dark but never speaks or moves.

"When she got in, where did they go? He wouldn't have parked beside that road—he must have taken her to some other place. I fancy it would give me peace to know exactly where she died. It might have happened miles from Cape Spear, where the wrecks of long-abandoned cars lie everywhere among the trees. Why leave her, then, where all could see, my little girl, my Anne Marie? Where are her books; where are her clothes? What could that Man have done with those? I'd like to have them. I hope he didn't keep them. I can't stand to think that he still has them hidden in his house or somewhere else, that he looks at them or takes them out from time to time . . .

"I lie awake for hours while the night goes by in quarter chimes. Usually, I fall asleep just after dawn and wake to find nothing but an empty chair beside the bed.

"Who was the someone that she knew and trusted? Had we had him in our house or had we been to visit his? A family friend?

"We don't go out anymore, and it's been ages since anyone stopped by. There's no man that I don't suspect. We gave up our dry cleaning business. I couldn't stand the thought that he might have been a customer. Anne worked on weekends at the store—he might have got to know her there. I'd see a man coming in and think of her inside his car. Every man whose clothes I cleaned might be the man who murdered Anne. I might have cleaned the very clothes he wore that night in Maddox Cove. Would anyone be so cold, so shameless as to chat with someone whose child he killed? In my worst dreams, such things make sense—the sons and husbands of the world conspiring against my girl.

"I stay at home because, out there, her killer might be anyone. The man who politely holds the door for me, the man in front of me in the checkout line at the grocery store. In a cinema, he might be in the audience, in the same row as me, this man who never has to hide. I don't know him but he knows me. My picture has been in the paper. I've been on TV, the mother whose resemblance to Anne is unmistakable.

"He preferred winter, the police said, the early dark, no one about, the bitter cold. He cruised around for girls in cars that wouldn't start or that broke down on side roads. Girls in danger of freezing to death must have been so relieved when they saw his lights. Some were found and some were not. The searchers stop when winter comes and then a rosary of storms keeps them going until spring."

The house spins around and, when it stops, I am sitting on the chair beside her bed—*I* am her prisoner now.

> It's hard to eulogize the young,
> list all the things they might have done,
> the things they wanted to become.
> These are the things they liked to do,
> the countries they'd have travelled to.
> You plan to read, if time allows,
> what others say about them now
> but never thought to say before.
> "Do you remember what she wore
> the last time you laid eyes on her?"

"You collaborated to save yourself, just as he did. You saw your chance. He taught you well. You gave her to him. 'If you touch me again, I'll tell them what you did to Anne.' You'd never had the proof before, just his 'confessions,' but now you had the perfect trap. Anne, the innocent bystander, was caught between the two of you. She would never have guessed that such families existed. But then . . .

"You didn't know your name sometimes. You lay in bed, the diarist of 44, self-imprisoned in your room, writing, hinting at the truth in such a way as to hold the interest of your non-existent audience. You were a thirteen-year-old girl who had had ten years of Him. How much of 'you' was still alive after all that he had done? How treacherous and conniving could you have been when you could barely frame a thought? If you had spoken up, or threatened to, would he have stopped? Or would you be among the dead, and helpless to prevent all the things that he went on to do?

"In the heaven of what might have been, anything can be forgiven: a single act of treachery, a century of butchery."

So this is what I must live with. In spite of what was done to me, what little was still left of me, could I have chosen to be brave? Could I have chosen anything but what I chose because of him? Anne's crimes, it seems, were two. She was a girl, and she was a Jew.

I spent the night in my warm bed;
I heard the screeching of the wind
protesting that a girl was dead.
The wind came gusting through the walls,
a million slantwise waterfalls;
an avalanche destroyed my soul
because I let her go with him.
I drew the elements within,
I tried to scream above the wind,
the torrent and the roaring flame,
but I was trapped inside my room,
which turned the colour of my mind
because I left your girl behind.

There is a roll not often called;
its names are not engraved on walls
or on the war memorials.
I promise I will not forget
the ones who cannot answer it.
They are the missing and the dead,
the women and the girls who said,
"We vanished then, we'll come back when
the wind blows from the west again."

The wind is rising from the west.
They come from the unwritten past,

each one alone, each one at last:
the murdered and the missing girls,
the stolen women of the world.
Each holds a candle in her hand
and each one holds another's hand;
they hold this vigil for each other—
mothers, wives, sisters, daughters.
They march for no cause but their own;
this regiment that died alone
is numberless and has no name,
no anthem, flag or uniform.
The lights are on above the doors,
as they will be throughout the years,
for days and nights that never end:
the rest of us must make amends.
All hope is lost, yet hope endures
if someone waits for their return:
they live as long as candles burn—
not long unless they pass them on,
from wick to wick, from flame to flame—
a different kind of light brigade;
the flames burn out, the names remain.
The roll begins and ends with one
as long as we remember them.

There is a roll not often called
(some names are never called at all).
I promise I will not forget
one girl who cannot answer it.
I know a name that few recall;
I wish that I could tell it all.
Her story must begin somewhere:
It was the winter of the year
that girls went missing everywhere.

WADE

We flew from Amsterdam to St. John's, connecting through Halifax. It was mid-afternoon when we arrived, weary from the flight, though we had slept through most of it. As the plane made its approach to the airport over Cape Spear and Signal Hill, I cast back to our departure from Schiphol, where we'd bade goodbye to Rachel's sisters just outside security.

"This is goodbye," Gloria said. "We've never been much of a foursome, but it breaks my heart to have to say that I doubt the four of us will ever be together again. I have a going-away present for you, Rachel."

"We'll meet again," Rachel said, but her tone was so perfunctory that a surge of sadness for her filled my throat.

Gloria drew three white envelopes out of her purse, each of them inscribed with one of her sisters' names. "I was going to give one of these to Carmen and Bethany when we got back to Cape Town, but it seems like the right thing to hand them out all at once. One wedding band and one engagement ring for each of you. I don't want you to ever wear them. They are mementoes of my three ex-husbands, and they are worth quite a lot of money. I didn't look for, or accept, a penny from any of those men when I left them. I preferred to start over without any baggage. Starting over is my specialty. But I didn't want to give them their rings back or sell them. I haven't been able to decide what to do with them until now."

She stood directly in front of Carmen and handed an envelope to her, then did the same with Bethany and Rachel. "I love you all," she said. "You might not believe it, but I do."

"What a weird present," Carmen said as she stared at the envelope in her hands.

Gloria smiled fondly at her, her eyes welling up with tears. "Carmen, we used to hold hands when we walked home from school in Rondebosch. I bet you don't remember that."

Carmen shook her head and looked again at the envelope, as if it might help her remember.

"Bethany," Gloria said, "maybe those rings will come in handy when the baby's born." Bethany smiled at her.

Gloria turned to Rachel. "Please, please remember me, baby sister, and please don't judge me too severely."

"I *love* you," Rachel said. "And I think you're wrong. The four of us will meet again. Why wouldn't we?"

Gloria wiped tears away with the heels of both hands. "You may be the closest thing to a baby that I ever have, baby sister. I hope not, but who knows?"

They huddled together in a hug, and I couldn't help feeling like an intruder. I wasn't one of the van Hout sisters. I wasn't a woman. A terrible thing had happened to Rachel when I had yet to meet her. What happened to Rachel happened to no one but Rachel. What happened to Gloria and Bethany and Carmen happened to them, to each of them, alone. Their sisterhood conferred commonality upon them in everything but this. They were not sister victims or any other kind of foursome. Each of them was absolute, entire unto herself. The same crime committed countless times does not become a single crime. Each of the sisters had her own story, much of which was unknowable to the others. And to me.

Word of the murders of the van Houts reached home before we did. The house was empty but for Mom when we got there. I told her everything I knew, except for the part that Gloria had played in her parents' deaths. Mom could tell there was more to the story. My eyes gave me away. Hers gave her away. But it was Rachel she hugged first.

Then we told her of our plans to move to the mainland, and she said she had long known that I wouldn't stay in Newfoundland. "We're spoiling your perfect record of keeping your children near, Jennie," Rachel said.

"Rachel," Mom said, "you'll get over the loss of your parents somehow. With Wade's help and God's, not that I'm making comparisons. The two of you will visit us just as often as you would have if none of it had ever happened, and we'll visit you if we can. You're going to the mainland, not to the moon. My son is in love with you, and he's never been in love before. You're in love with him, and you've never been in love before. So keep at it. You'll never get it right. No one ever has. But there it is."

I knew that, after we were gone, after my father and sisters had come home and gone to bed, she would sit at the kitchen table, smoking cigarettes, nursing a glass of rye and ginger. And then she would go out on the front steps with her cigarettes, her ashtray and her glass, and look up at the stars until she couldn't see them anymore.

My brothers and I had often come home hours after midnight to find her there, waiting for whichever one of us was out so late she couldn't sleep, waiting for Dad's car or a taxicab or the police to pull into the driveway at the bottom of the hill.

By the time we'd got inside, she'd be in bed, too fed up with us to say good night. But she would be the first one in the kitchen in the morning, making breakfast for the early risers, who would have been astonished if she wasn't there, and she would still be there when we, who had come home late, finally got up, and she would make us breakfast too and never say a word about the night before.

Until we left for Toronto, we stayed with my parents, sleeping in separate bedrooms that had been my older brothers'. We borrowed Dad's car when we could and drove to St. John's. We avoided Freshwater Road, Rachel saying she never wanted to set eyes on 44 again. We went to the university campus and had lunch at the picnic table where we'd spent so many summer nights. Spring had come early but there was not yet much heat in the sun, so we huddled together over a Thermos of coffee and some sandwiches my mother made.

"In June, it will be two years since we met," I said.

"It seems a lot longer," Rachel said as she surveyed the distant hills of Petty Harbour. "Let's never get married. Let's live in sin forever."

It was the most that ever passed between us by way of a proposal. I accepted.

From *The Arelliad*

DEAR WADE (1985)

These lines of verse, *The Ballad* kind,
are still those of an anguished mind—
or so it seems, I can't be sure;
they read unlike they read before,
and I don't feel as I once did
while writing *The Arelliad*.
I write for me now, and for Them:
He taught me to—but I'm not Him.

I hope you don't regret the day
you saw me and I looked away
when we were in the library,
or wish that I had not looked back
the second night among the stacks,
or that, when I broke up with you,
I did just what you hoped I'd do—
when you were starting to move on,
I turned up in your life again.
It isn't often words I lack
(sometimes they come by sneak attack)
but I was stuck for words that night
and needed time to get them right.

Will you cast back in fifty years
and wish I'd never climbed those stairs
to the garret that September?
Will you be sad when you remember
and wonder how things would have been
if I had not come back again?
Will you resent me, Wade, come then,
and think of things that might have been?

—

Sometimes my words are all I have—
more often they have me, my love.
There's nothing that I wouldn't give
to give them up and simply live.
I know that that will never be . . .
you know and yet you still love me.

But there are things you mustn't know
(what happens when the west wind blows),
the scars I hope will never show,
the smudge of blue on my left hand
that you will never understand:
the scars of little Rachel Lee,
the things I cannot let you see,
the crime of Glormenethalee.
I couldn't stand to see you go;
you know the pain, I know you do.
I wouldn't hold up like you did;
I'd go back to the yellow wood
and give myself to Claws von Snout
and never, never come back out . . .
You think the things I say are true—
it isn't fair, I know, I do.

The lens through which I've seen my life—
a restoration of belief
would be difficult enough,
but to begin at twenty-three,
feel happy to be Rachel Lee—
I have to try but not just yet.
I know that not all men are bad;
I think that some are like your dad.
Your mother trusted me with you—
it might destroy her if she knew.
I mustn't sentimentalize:

a heart of gold and, oh, so wise—
but she saw more than you could see
the first time she locked eyes with me.
I'll do my best, it might take years
to read some book that isn't Hers,
or write uninfluenced by Him.
The words come when I summon them
but don't do what I tell them to;
someday they will, I promise you.
I shouldn't promise anything:
I still fear what the night will bring.

There's so much that I haven't done;
I lost the knack of having fun.
I think I had it way back when,
but maybe not, not even then.
I don't feel like remembering.

The future, then, let's think of that . . .
but then again, I'd rather not;
I'd rather count the things we've got.
We have each other, first of all,
the shadows on the bedroom wall . . .
the sounds that came from the canal,
the children running on the bridge,
the humming of the garret fridge.
It isn't hard to find the good—
let's look for it, I think we should.
The casement curtains rise and fall;
there's hardly any breeze at all.
In Newfoundland there is no war,
no midnight knocks on neighbours' doors,
no fear that, next, they'll knock on yours—
not that the past has been undone,
but this is now and that was then.

—

But this is now, it's all we have:
how good it is to be alive
when you are only twenty-five;
how wonderful to be in love
at any age in any time;
the lines still scan, the words still rhyme.
Ten years of yellow have gone by
but now, perhaps, another sky
is showing through the yellow cloud
(dishonesty is not allowed).
I don't know what more I can do
than dedicate my life to you,
and dedicate my life to Them,
my literary heroines.

There is a watch I have to keep
with you beside me, sound asleep.
There is a pledge I have to make:
I'll be the one who stays awake,
the one who's ever vigilant
(this is what your mother meant).
I looked away once, not again:
I'll guard you with my soul and then
I'll guard you with it when I'm gone.

WADE

She still reads only *Het Achterhuis*. She writes in her diary, in Arellian, for one hour every day, a copy of *Het Achterhuis* beside her. Sometimes she's alone. More often, I sit with her, reading while she writes, as we did in Cape Town. I ask her what she's writing, knowing that she'll answer "Nothing new."

I sometimes ask myself: Does the truth never matter where the van Houts are concerned? Never? Is it only the consequences of telling the truth that are important? Is the truth not important for its own sake? What if the Holocaust had somehow been concealed? What if the disappearance of six million Jews was a mystery to everyone but you? Would you keep the solution to yourself forever lest the truth do you more harm than good? Rachel is not a Nazi, but she is the daughter of one.

There is nothing left of the van Houts. Rachel's sisters have taken their husbands' names, and their children bear those names. Rachel and I do not have children yet. Perhaps we never will. Small wonder that Gloria was right that they were soon to separate for good, for none of them needed to start anew more than she did. They don't keep in touch and they live far apart. Rachel says she doesn't miss them, because she sees no point in dwelling on things that might have been. The longer I keep her sister's secret, the more unthinkable it becomes to reveal to her the truth about the deaths of her parents.

The books I hoped to write remain unwritten, because, as I came to realize in the wake of all that happened to me and to the van Houts, especially to Rachel, there is a great difference between wanting to be a writer and being meant to be one. I am not a writer, just a reader. Just. Merely. No, I'm a great one, I think. There may be as few of us great readers as there are great writers. It torments me not at all. To be a great reader is its own reward. To my relief, I no longer bear the burden of a counterfeit vocation. To read, and to teach others to read with hard-won discrimination, is what, if anything, I was *meant* to do.

Rachel is a writer. I think she knew from the moment I told her that I meant to become one that I never would. Rachel is a writer who needs no readers, no one's admiration or approval. She writes neither for the moment, nor for the ages, but *merely*, irresistibly, for herself. Rachel is a true writer, the kind who has no choice but to be one, just as she had no choice but to be Rachel van Hout.

She'd like to be as normal as she thinks I am. But I fell in love with a greater, more tormented mind than mine. I had underrated normalcy, the preciousness of an ordinary life. Still, it was not her exoticism, but her pathology that drew me to her, her courage in the face of it, her insistence on confronting it no matter what it cost her. She will always be miles ahead of me, but I can't keep from wanting to catch up, because I need her as much as she needs me. Each of us was what the other was in search of when we met, though neither of us knew it. She is my elusive masterpiece and I am her one handhold on the real and solid world.

Home is the place we visit, and away is where we live. It's had to be that way for Rachel's sake, though she doesn't think of home the way I do.

As for the real Newfoundland, I miss it more and more. My parents, my brothers and sisters, the many friends I've made there since I moved away. It isn't true of everyone that they can't go home again. Almost any path but the one I stumbled onto when I was twenty-five might have led me back to Newfoundland.

Still, my mind and my house are at peace more often than not. Only those who have paid it understand the price of peace.

From *The Arelliad*

THE HEAVEN OF WHAT MIGHT HAVE BEEN (1985)

The slightest tweak of circumstance would have saved Anne Wilansky's life. If one thing had been otherwise, if he had shown up at the rink early or on time or even later than he did . . . he turns left from the parking lot instead of right, and it's me he takes out to the Cape instead of her. He did before . . . But everything happened as it had to in order to ensure her death, including much I'll never know. *As it had to*. It makes it sound as if her death was meant to be.

What happens when she gets back in the car? I followed the Frank sisters to Auschwitz, and to their deaths at Bergen-Belsen, but I cannot bear to follow her to hers. When I write about it, it always ends there on the sidewalk in front of our house. "You seem so nice. I hope we meet . . ." But it should end beside that road in Maddox Cove. I think of no one more than her, the two of us standing there beside the car in which her life is soon to end. Small for her age, as tall as she will ever be, she puts her hands on my shoulders as if she's been my friend for years. I think of those green eyes of hers, the wind so cold they fill with tears. She sees something in *my* eyes, a need that she can think of no way of fulfilling but by giving me her book.

"Some have had it worse but didn't do what you have done. You seem to expect perfection from everyone except yourself." So says the nagging voice of guilt:

"Thou shalt not kill. Though shalt not kill,
you must submit to those who will.
Be brave and turn the other cheek,
forgive the ones that stalk the weak.

"What could have been so bad that it led four girls to patricide? Why did their mother have to die for what their father did? Who knows what was done to him when he was just a child, what happened in that house of theirs? His father fled the very year his mother died and left him on his own, a boy who had no one when Amsterdam was overrun—who knows what he was like by then?

"The tanks of the master race come rolling into Amsterdam. One day it seems some things make sense, the next it seems that nothing does. So begins four years of madness: he sees the inconceivable day after day, and it begins to seem possible that life will always be like this. He is among the lucky ones, who are only witnesses to everyday atrocities, not the victims of them. All around him, people die but, somehow, he survives. Is that a crime? Whose fault is it that he goes mad? Who knows for certain that he does? What is the law, what are the rules throughout the reign of savagery? Surely some allowances can be made for those who come back from the dead."

Was it the sum of his experience that made my father what he was, or some mechanism in his brain, some defect in his DNA? Perhaps it was the chain that he descended from, his parents, grandparents . . .

There are no pictures of him from his childhood, so I try to think of him on Elandsstraat, where he grew up, a boy at play, perhaps alone. He comes to mind, that little boy, who didn't know that he'd grow old, never having heard of time—his life would always be the same, a simple, sweet, unending game. Was he a child such as I never was, because of him?

I imagine him as innocent, though it may be that he never was. It's hard to say what "evil" is, hard to say if it exists. Is it a thing you freely choose, or is it that it chooses you? Perhaps it's just a word meant to account for the unaccountable.

I think there is hope. Not every child must live in fear of the House by Night. Our children will be happier than us, their children happier than them. So goes the endless dream of time, the consolation of the future.

In the heaven of what might have been,
where no one dies, not even Him,
there's laughter in the Land of Hout
and nothing to complain about.

We do not fear the Land Without,
which seems just like the Land Within:
we never have to keep Them out;
we never have to be kept in.

We think of Them as Mom and Dad. We know they did the best they could. How companionable they seem, as do we all, an ordinary family. We reminisce, as families do. We think about the good times and tend to overlook the bad. We've never heard of Special Love. We never really speak of love, even though we love each other. Typical, unremarkable, we muddle through like all the rest.

I see four sisters, hand in hand,
the sister ghosts of van Hout Land
who never were but might have been:
this elegy must speak for them,
four lives that never quite began—
I see them playing in the sand
or trying to outrun the waves
as if they're running for their lives.
The water catches them sometimes;
sometimes they win and raise their arms.

The sisters grow to womanhood;
they still believe what children should—
that some are bad, but more are good.
The four untroubled sister ghosts
must vanish in the morning mists—
the search for them goes on and on,
though some would say, "What's done is done,
what never was cannot be gone;
these are the girls that never were
that you insist on searching for."
Sisters, daughters, mothers, wives—
the search is what keeps us alive.

My two Annes. I never think of one without thinking of the other. I still can't help believing that he killed them both. It's to both of them I write when I write the words "Dear Anne" in *The Arelliad*, and it's both of them I picture when I say their name.

My sisters and Wade don't know that Anne Wilansky is the key to me. They take me to be the exceptional sister, the one who, relative to them, emerged unscathed from the Land of Hout, somehow able to love and be loved.

No one but Gloria and I know what *she* confessed to Wade the afternoon they came so close to death. He has never said a word to me about it. Sometimes, it's hard to remember who knows this or who believes that, so I no longer think about that kind of truth.

I remember when they found Anne's body. The police closed the road and put a khaki tent around her, as much to shield them from the cold as to preserve the evidence and her privacy. Some people managed to get close enough to see the tent, which almost came unmoored, so hard was the wind still howling from the west. It was sunny but so cold that, unless you wore a ski mask, you had to use your hands to shield your face. What a strange sight it must have been, all those people peering through the fingers of their gloves as if they couldn't bear more than a glimpse of what lay inside the tent. She'd been out there for twelve hours, her body frozen to the core and to the ground. I don't know how they got her free or how long it took, or how, later, others went about doing the things they had to do.

The memorial that marks the place where Anne Wilansky was found still stands beside what looks like it will always be an empty stretch of road. I find time to visit it whenever we go to what we still call home. I leave flowers or small stones or other tokens of remembrance at the base of the memorial, as do many people who never knew Anne Wilansky and will never know who killed her.

RACHEL

Once, alone as always, I drove in a rented car to the place she was discovered on the morning of December 15, 1974. I parked the car so that it blocked me from the view of passersby.

Her family and friends had erected the roadside memorial to her about twenty feet from the woods, a few feet from the pavement—not a memorial like those you see at the sites of fatal traffic accidents, not a wooden cross and plastic flowers and, perhaps, a graduation photograph. Facing the road, on the edge of the woods on the far side of the ditch, is a black marble gravestone like the one erected at Bergen-Belsen for Anne Frank and Margot Frank. It has a rounded top, below which is etched in white the Star of David, the name Anne Wilansky, and the dates of her birth and death.

As with Bergen-Belsen, the place seemed too ordinary to have been the site of anything exceptional, let alone what it was famous for. The stunted spruce had been cut back to make room for hydro poles, whose hum was constant, almost soothing. On the other side of the road, you could just make out the ocean in the gap between two hills. Perhaps, on a cloudy night, you could see the faint glow of the city in the sky.

It was a typical early morning in May, sunny but cold, the dew frost not yet melting from the trees and grass. There was no reason for the foghorn at Cape Spear to blow, and yet it did, just once, perhaps by accident.

Dressed in jeans and a peacoat like the one she wore, I knelt on the ground and sat back on my heels. I moved one hand over the letters of her name as if they were written in Braille.

Every word I said came out as a puff of breath.

"Anne, I've been writing to you and your namesake for so long I feel as if I know you, but I don't know you at all and I don't know her and I don't know what to say. I feel the way I did when we lined up with all the others to visit Anne Frank's stone. It's just me today and the sky is clear, not grey like it was at Bergen-Belsen. They found you here on a morning much like this one, just as sunny but much colder. He must have thought you were a fluke, an opportunity that dropped into his lap, until it hit him that you knew him and he couldn't let you go. I think of you every day. I remember your voice, the smell of your hair when we hugged outside the car. They're such small, normal things, aren't they, to get into a car, to get out of it, to get back in. They all seem so momentous now, so laden with foreboding, so obviously leading to something that need not have happened. I'm so sorry I didn't stay in the car. I'm so sorry."

Beside the stone, encased in glass, there was a plaque that bore this verse:

THIS STONE MARKS THE PLACE
WHERE ANNE MARIE WAS THROWN,
SURROUNDED BY THE WOODS SHE LOVED
BUT OTHERWISE ALONE.
SHE IS FREE, AS WE SHALL BE,
FREE FROM ALL CONCERNS,
FREE FROM DARKNESS AND DESPAIR
WHEN THE LIGHT RETURNS.

Author's Note

I was a young writer, in my late twenties, writing my second novel in the wake of a very successful first one, which had made its way into the hands of Annie Dillard, Robert Finch and many other writers who summered on Cape Cod. Annie and Robert had written to me, asking if they could come visit me in Newfoundland. I told them I'd be delighted to meet them and show them around, as I was a fan of their books. This is what my life would be like, I fancied. I would write books that were admired by famous writers, who would come to visit me in Newfoundland. I would myself soon achieve such fame as they had, even though I was just out of the gate. A greener, more naive, more parochial young man may not have existed in life or literature.

It was mid-afternoon in the fall of 1987, and I was home alone. I had a sense of where I was in my personal life, too, and where that life was headed. I was living with a beautiful South African–born young woman named Rose Langhout, the daughter of an accounting professor who had taught for twenty years at the University of Cape Town, then uprooted his family to move to Newfoundland, where he'd been offered a new position. If not for that inexplicable decision, I would never have met Rose, in whose life, it seemed, nothing had ever gone wrong.

Fate came calling, not, as it does at the start of Beethoven's Fifth, with four ominous raps on a bedroom ceiling, but with the mundane ringing of a doorbell. When I answered it, I found myself face to face with a man my age. I'd never met him, but as it turned out, he was Rose's new brother-in-law, who had recently, out-of-the-blue and with little ceremony, married Barbara, one of Rose's three sisters. He was crying uncontrollably and asked to be let in. As I began to open the door, he pushed past me and ran up the stairs to my apartment. Bemused but still suspecting nothing from him that had to do with me, I followed him.

We sat opposite each other in my living room, Rose's brother-in-law chain-smoking and still crying as he told me things that Barbara had told him in the wake of an attempt to take her own life—a host of accusations that she had made against her father, Jan. Over the next couple of hours, he told me what Barbara said Jan had done to girls in Cape Town, was still doing to girls in St. John's, and was still doing to her and those of her sisters he was able to find excuses to see alone. He looked at me as if to say, "Don't you get what I'm saying about *your* girlfriend?" I did. Before he left, I knew that my life had been divided into before his visit and after his visit. There, exactly there, my life was changed.

When Rose came home, I asked her if what her sister's husband had told me was true.

She simply didn't answer. No denials, no maybes, no supporting accusations, nothing offered in defense of her father, only silence, as if my question was composed of words she didn't understand

"Does your father still—with you, I mean?"

Still no answer. Only a poker face and folded arms.

Was this her way of telling me that, unless I dropped the matter, we were through? I was afraid to ask. Was this how people who were more sophisticated, better educated than me and my parents and the people I grew up among, pushed aside something too indecorous to talk about or otherwise acknowledge?

Rose, despite her own silence, asked her sisters the same questions I had asked her, asked them in person, on the phone or in letters, and reported to me that they, too, except for Barbara, simply refused to answer.

I fancied I could fix Rose and her sisters. I fancied that they had never happened on a sympathetic ear before, nor anyone as familiar with and articulate about the landscape of the human heart and mind as I believed my prodigious reading had made me. I told Rose she could talk to me—her sisters could talk to me. They didn't. It seemed that, but for Barbara, they could live without confronting the matter. They had done so all their lives.

If I couldn't live with Rose unless she confronted it, it might be best if I moved on. Was that the meaning of her silence, the meaning of the look in her eyes when I tried to coax her into speaking of the unspeakable?

Then came the next inexplicable development: not long after her release from hospital, Barbara also fell silent about the accusations she had made to her husband while on the psychiatric ward. She didn't retract them. She merely refused to repeat them or otherwise acknowledge she had made them. Had the accusations all been born of the delusions of psychosis? I was mystified, a state of mind to which I would soon become accustomed and was eventually humbled by.

After my umpteenth insistence that we do so, Rose and I confronted her parents in a cheap motel room that we rented for the purpose—cheap, but barely affordable by us. Nothing came of the meeting but denials from her father and mother, both of whom started out implacable, almost serene, until Rose's father lost his temper and said that he had never laid a hand on her, but so what if he had, for she, like her sisters, was his daughter and he could do whatever he liked with her.

After that motel meeting, Rose relented. Yes, she told me, the accusations that Barbara had made were true, though she thought it possible that Barbara would never speak of them again. And, Rose stressed, she would never speak to me of the details of what her father had done to her and I was not to ask. I didn't.

I *knew* I didn't need to know the details of what he had done to Rose. I *didn't* ask for them and tried not to imagine them.

We told Rose's sisters about the hotel meeting, and in its wake, every member of the Langhout family fled—Rose's parents to South Africa, her sisters to parts unknown. We didn't hear from them for many years. They were, by necessity, experts at concealment. It wasn't as easy then as it is now to find out where someone lives. At times, Rose and I weren't certain if all of her sisters were still alive. We wondered especially about Carol, who, when we last saw her, was drug-addicted and living by whatever means she could on East Hastings in Vancouver at the height of the AIDS epidemic. But we didn't try very hard to find them. Now and then, we made a token effort, but we didn't want the tumult and upheaval that we knew would come just from knowing what their circumstances were.

I didn't tell anyone else about the Langhout family, especially not my parents. I could not even imagine having such a conversation with them—telling them that the father of the woman I was living with did what Rose told me he had done to her and her sisters, or that he was wildly anti-Semitic, as I had discovered at the motel meeting when he noticed I had brought a biography of Albert Einstein with me. Pointing at the book, he shouted, "You're reading about that filthy Jew?" I didn't even tell them that we were estranged from Rose's parents. When we were asked how Rose's parents were doing, we told *everyone* that they lived so far away we rarely heard from them.

But then came the most exasperating development of all. We were informed, in a letter from Barbara, that Rose's sisters had renewed contact with their parents and had travelled to South Africa to stay with them, that they had invited their parents to visit them in Canada, and that they had come.

Rose broke off all communication with her entire family.

Rose and I somehow clung to each other despite the many, many times that to go on doing so seemed impossible.

The final major revelation about Jan Langhout came from, of all people, my mother, whose job involved frequent contact with the Newfoundland police. In the summer of 1998, she told me that she had heard from them that Rose's father had been, and still was, a person of interest in the unsolved murder of a local teenager. So that my father wouldn't hear us, she confided this to me in the basement of their house in St. John's. I replied by telling her everything about the Langhouts that I had been keeping secret. It was a scene that I will not even attempt to describe. This girl, raped and strangled and left naked by the roadside on a windy and brutally cold night, is the inspiration for the character in the book named Anne Wilansky. It is still not known for certain who killed her.

Rose and I did not tell her sisters. Perhaps they already knew, we thought, but even if they didn't, at that point we were certain it would not have changed their way of dealing with their parents.

Rose continued to confide in me. She told me of the stories that her father would tell her and her sisters at bedtime in Cape Town, the four of them gathered around him on the bed in the guest room. He was either a mythomaniac or was able to assume the guise of one when it suited his purposes, which included projecting himself as a hero in a manner that would play on the credulity and capture the imagination of his little girls, each of whose minds was already a tortuous welter of emotions—wholly unjustified guilt, irreversible confusion, pity for him, protectiveness of him and their mother, images of what had been done to them and speculation about what had been done to him before and after they were born. For all of them, this was the mystery of right and wrong.

He told them tales of his heroism as a member of the Dutch Resistance. Then, seconds later, he told them that he was the one who had alerted the Gestapo that Jews, among them Anne Frank and her family, were hiding out in a house on the Prinsengracht canal near where he lived. It was he, he said, who had turned in the Franks, the van Pels and Fritz Pfeffer, he who had been paid a bounty for each captured Jew. They believed him, but they also believed him when he told them that the opposite was true. In the many times the family visited Amsterdam, they avoided going to Anne Frank's house and no mention of Anne Frank was ever made.

Just after my notions of the world and its workings were overthrown by that visit from Rose's brother-in-law, I decided to put aside the book I was working on and write the one that he had dumped the rough first draft of into my lap. However, aside from a few notes, I was unable to make a beginning. For years, I was lost for a way to give fictional form to all the revelations that, month by month, year by year, came my way. At the same time, I was trying to sort out what was obviously true from what might be true but could never be confirmed.

I've spent half my life attempting to solve the mystery of right and wrong. During that time, I wrote many other books into which surfaced parts of *the* book I hoped to write someday, shadows, voices, small experiments and musings, seeming non sequiturs from the book that I fancied would, when I was long silent or gone, be seen as the inspiration for all the books I had ever written.

But I kept having to put that one foundational book aside because further, even more profoundly disturbing things kept coming to light that rendered what I'd written more or less obsolete. It was like peeling an onion, peeling off layer after layer of flesh, only to find that the onion wasn't getting any smaller. If anything, it was getting bigger. Real life was revising itself faster than I could write. As what lay beneath each layer of the onion was revealed, my notion of what the book would be was altered. My father-in-law had done *that*? And that? Was suspected of doing that? All but confessed to doing that to his four girls? Boasted of it? Bragged about it? That the chronic rape and psychological abuse of his children were, in a way, the least of his crimes will give you some sense of who Jan Langhout and his wife, Mary, were, and the kind of family I had happened into when I was barely out of university.

It wasn't until my wife's parents died a few years ago that I came to know as much as I ever will about the truth of their family, the parents and the Langhout sisters, and especially my wife. It was then that I began in earnest to write *The Mystery of Right and Wrong*. I am, almost literally, a character in the book. Those who know me and my life—or thought they did—will be shocked by what they read. Most of the novel's major scenes, the main narrative and thematic threads, and the major and even minor characters are drawn pretty much directly from my own life. I could have tried to write it as non-fiction, but I felt I could somehow get closer to the truth with a novel, which let me imagine my way into areas I couldn't possibly "prove" as fact.

Even so, *The Mystery of Right and Wrong* might have remained forever unbegun, let alone completed. Certainly, I could not have written and published it while my wife's parents were alive. How to try to convey it all without overwhelming the reader or me, the writer, or most importantly, the survivors—the answer did not come to me until after my in-laws died.

Was Rose keeping from me only the devil in the details of what had happened to her, which she had assured me I was better off not knowing and made me promise not to ask her about, or was there something more? What was the cost on her psyche of holding everything together?

The physical toll was obvious and seemingly benign. Always supremely fit, she had, after her brother-in-law's visit, thrown herself into becoming even fitter. She became an elite marathoner and triathlete.

Thirty years after I first thought of writing this book, I drew on my own sometimes gift and sometimes curse to answer, not the riddle of Rose's mind, but the riddle of Rachel van Hout's, my wife's fictional counterpart. Rachel, whose obsession is not fitness and running, but reading and writing. I asked of Rachel the same question that I had often asked of myself: Is she reading and writing her way into madness, or reading and writing her way out of it?

I suppose that this is *my* coming out.

Since my early teens, I have been dealing with what, in my early twenties, were diagnosed as severe hypergraphia and hyperlexia—obsessive writing and reading—somewhat rare symptoms of obsessive-compulsive disorder. There were other symptoms as well, too many to spell out here.

Most people think of OCD as what you "have" if you wash your hands too frequently or are more than usually careful about keeping your house neat and tidy and avoiding germs. Most people, in other words, have no clue as to what OCD is. It manifests itself in a seemingly infinite number of ways and, if left untreated, often becomes more and more debilitating to the point where the afflicted self-destruct. Hyperlexia and hypergraphia are often mistaken as the romantic illnesses of great, tortured artists who lead turbulent lives, such as Thomas Wolfe, Fyodor Dostoevsky and many others. I can assure you that there is nothing romantic about them.

Hypergraphia. Hyperlexia. Two of my many secret demons. Hypergraphia is a mania that some writers might assume would be the greatest gift, but that others, me included, recognize as the greatest curse—to be a writer who, literally, cannot stop writing. I have written dozens of times as many pages as make up all of my published books combined. Almost no one is aware of this. It has been my secret, as precious and sacred to me as the contents of Anne Frank's diary were to her.

Relatively speaking, OCD has only newly been recognized as a mental illness, in part because its symptoms so often mimic those of phobias and bipolar disorder. In ten years, from age thirteen to twenty-three, I wrote almost as many books as I read. Had behaviour such as mine been seen as pathological decades earlier, I would surely have read about it, for my reading, in my early OCD period, comprised the entire canon of Western literature, philosophy and science and, most importantly, psychoanalysis and psychotherapy. But I found no mention, in all those Western civilization–spanning tomes, of OCD.

Small wonder that, when I first began to show OCD symptoms at age thirteen, I had no idea that was what they were. Nor did anyone else who knew about them. All of us presumed them to be the products of extreme bookishness, signs that I would likely go on to be ineffectual, of no consequence in the real world because of my fascination with the one that existed nowhere but in the imaginations of the sort of people who wrote the books that I was forever reading.

When I began, in what I hoped was total secrecy, to read and write almost incessantly, I was dismissed as irredeemably odd because of the amount of time I spent holed up in my room, destined to become a lifelong loner living in near-hermetic solitude. I destroyed most of what I wrote—a formless, meandering diary of reflections, observations, events and even the weather—to purge the world of evidence of my oddness. I did not pause to find the right words or structure. That was not the point.

The point—I didn't know why and still don't—was simply to write and keep on writing. But after four years of university, which I spent skipping classes to indulge my ever-worsening obsession, I began to keep some of what I wrote, to revise and shape it into essays and short stories and even big, baggy but meandering novels. With the help of a friend, I got a job as a newspaper reporter and managed partly to channel my obsessions into something that others regarded as having a practical purpose. I may have thereby saved myself from madness or worse—I don't know where the road I had been on would ultimately have taken me.

But I carried on at night—all night, usually—pursuing what I had come to think of as my gift. And, somehow, I wrote things other than newspaper stories that some people, the editors of literary journals, seemed to think were worth reading. I became, in a public, unhidden sense, a published writer, who, though painfully shy and introverted, was taken seriously.

My hyperlexia and hypergraphia did not abate. I found in Rose someone who, because of her own secrets, thought better of asking me to explain myself, though I had no way of knowing this at the time we met. In our own unique way, we hit it off and let lie the sleeping dogs of each other's personalities and habits.

It was not until ten years after the onset of my symptoms that I came to think of them as symptoms and my illness was assigned a name. In 1983, Rose and I moved to Ottawa so that she could pursue her master's thesis (and, as I now know, escape the reminders of her father that were everywhere in St. John's). My illness worsened. Still green enough to think that whatever was wrong with me was entirely unprecedented and therefore incurable and certain to result in me ending my life, I suffered a breakdown. My desperation, my utter sense of hopelessness, my absolute despair led to an end that proved to be a beginning: a hospital emergency room where I collapsed on the floor after four days of reading and writing without stop, my mind and heart racing. Someone helped me to a bed. Many others helped me to survival and recovery.

My obsessions and compulsions ultimately became the answer to the question I mentioned above, which Wade, the narrator who is based on me in *The Mystery of Right and Wrong*, poses to himself: What toll had Rachel's childhood taken on *her* psyche?

Hypergraphia, hyperlexia, these were things about which I could write with hard-won authority. Rachel's would be the kind of unquiet mind I knew all too well. It would be the fictional proxy of the mind behind the "Rosa Lisa" smile, as I called it, of the woman I was living with, a mind that Rose thought both of us would be better off leaving unexplored and unexplained.

Rachel would be, as I was, hypergraphic and hyperlexic, at times unable to stop writing or reading until she reached the point of mental breakdown and physical exhaustion.

I also would have to invent a way to set some sections of the book apart from Wade's. *This* mystery was solvable. I could do it by admitting poetry into the prose. Poetry, the near companion of madness—and near, therefore, to the truth, or the closest thing to it that I, in my prosaic but obsessive sanity, could manage.

The Mystery of Right and Wrong is mostly prose, but the recurring sections, one called "The Ballad of the Clan Van Hout," written by Rachel's father, and the other, written by Rachel, called "The Arelliad," are, respectively, entirely poetry and partly poetry.

"The Ballad" is, ostensibly, a fanciful family history written in verse and read by Hans van Hout every night to his daughters. In fact, it is a vehicle of indoctrination, almost an ongoing form of hypnosis, as well as a tract of self-justification, an elaborate sleight-of-word played on the girls and, to a degree that lessens as the novel proceeds, on the reader. I thought it was crucial that Hans's personal propaganda be rendered in a way that both set it apart from the dominant prose sections and joined them in telling what I believed I could only tell in a highly dramatic and propulsive way.

As for "The Arelliad," I thought it just as crucial that, when Rachel fell into psychosis, there would be a kind of colour change in the language that was analogous to the illusory world of her mind. It also seemed natural and inevitable that, after twenty years of indoctrination by her father's verse, she would sometimes write poetry in what was essentially her diary. At the same time, however, as Rachel was fighting for her sanity—and gradually winning that fight—I thought it necessary that in her diary she would only "lapse" into poetry—meaning deeper into madness—from time to time, especially when she was most distraught and her grip on reality most tenuous. Even when she wrote poetry, however, she would not entirely mimic her father, as her poetry would be quite lyrical and honestly self-searching.

I set out writing the novel in the kind of frenzy in which Rachel, and I, were secretly accustomed to writing. In two and a half years of exhausting exhilaration—the kind of exhilaration that comes from at last addressing a long-silenced truth—I wrote a meditation on the mystery of right and wrong. Not a solution, for that eludes me still.

I owe a debt to two books by the psychologist Kay Redfield Jamison, without which I could not have written the character of Rachel van Hout: *An Unquiet Mind: A Memoir of Moods and Madness* and *Touched with Fire: Manic-Depressive Illness and the Artistic Temperament.* It was from Rachel's unquiet mind and fire-touched heart, and my own, that the poetry emerged.

Rachel van Hout is a writer by nature who, because of the trauma of chronic sexual and mental abuse, slips in and out of psychosis when she reads and writes. During a psychotic break from reality, a person sees and hears and experiences things that aren't real. For some reason that psychiatrists and psychologists cannot explain, the worlds into which psychotics descend are often monochromatic, everything tinged with the same colour. The colour of Arellia, the alternate world into which Rachel is transported while writing, is yellow. Another famous woman, Joan of Arc, who is now widely believed to have been schizophrenic, saw her psychotic world in lurid red, and sometimes in a brilliant cerulean blue.

Rachel, like Rose, is also an historian. For very similar reasons, both are fascinated by, even obsessed with, Anne Frank. I have read the books written most recently about Anne Frank, which tend to focus on the question of who it was that betrayed the Frank family and the other Jews who were hiding out from the Nazis. That question has never been authoritatively resolved, although new answers seem to crop up at an average of more than one a year. Because of Rachel's own profound experience of betrayal and her belief that she committed an act of treachery that led to a young girl's murder by her father, Rachel's life and mind become intertwined with those of Anne Frank, who went into hiding at age thirteen—the same age at which Rachel's mind and body turned against her (and Rose's, too, as I have newly discovered). The same age that mine turned against me.

Mainly for the sake of others, but also, I thought, for my own sake, I have kept a lot of things secret from everyone but the succession of therapists I have been fortunate to find. Some things about my illness and the consequences of it I couldn't bear to tell even them. Perhaps I never will. I don't mind saying that I've often pretended to be unfazed by what, even for the unafflicted, is one of the most exacting professions. The secrets I kept took a great toll on me and on others who, in one way or another, were affected by them.

I think that readers of my other books will now see in them the reasons for the recurrence of certain themes: the secrecy that underlies and often undermines family history; the mercurial, unfixed and unfixable nature of history; the idea, which now seems self-evident to me but often comes as a great surprise to others, that history is something quite different from the past. Histories are merely records of the past and are always, to one degree or another, inaccurate because of the innate biases of their writers, because of inadvertent misinterpretation, because of censorship, self-imposed and otherwise . . . and because none of us are as virtuous as we would like to think.

Eventually, all three of Rose's sisters broke off all contact with their parents. One by one, they wrote to Rose and, though euphemistically, in the same decorous manner I had come to expect of them, they admitted that all of the accusations Barbara had made years ago, all the things her ex-husband had told me the afternoon he appeared out of nowhere, were true.

Jan and Mary Langhout died within nine days of each other in the summer of 2014 in Cape Town, both in their nineties. Consequently, my wife reconciled with her three sisters, from whom she had so long been estranged. Soon after, I began to write *The Mystery of Right and Wrong*. I completed it in April of 2020, at the start of a period of near-hermetic confinement that, though nothing like the one the Franks endured, loaned me some appreciation of it.

People are shocked on a more or less daily basis by revelations about heretofore revered public, usually, male, figures. Since that day now more than thirty years ago when that distraught young man came to visit me, I have not been shocked by anything of which *anyone* has been accused or to which they have confessed.

My book's theme of indoctrination by systematic manipulation of language and mistruth is frequently found in the news of the day—propaganda of the Orwellian kind, though few of those who invoke his name seem to have read Orwell. Indoctrination of that kind is something that happens not only within society but within society's most crucial unit, the family. Every family has a culture of its own, and in certain families, that culture is pathological.

The Mystery of Right and Wrong is not, in its ultimate form, a dark book, but one that sheds light—a lot of light—on things that, once illuminated, once brought to consciousness, lose their power to distort the truth. It is also a memorialization of the lost, the missing girls and women of the world.

As for me, I have never been able to recollect in tranquility the true events that inspired me to write this book. Only in fiction have I been able to sublimate the story of my wife and her sisters into something that I think is truly beautiful.

When the book is published, I'll be able to elaborate publicly on some of these things, in some cases sparingly, but in some cases not at all because of the still-living survivors of the crimes Jan is suspected of committing and their families.

The Mystery of Right and Wrong reaches no answers to the questions that it poses. It concerns itself with the enigma of survival in a time when to survive requires that you do things to your persecutors that, to some, may seem as unforgivable as what they have done to you. What the van Hout sisters do in the novel doesn't seem unforgivable to me, but that may be the cause of considerable debate and controversy.

Rose's sisters have not yet read the book, but they know of it and have given this fictional rendering of their fight for survival their full support. The Langhout daughters *have* survived, all uniquely marred. Perhaps they are not such women as, under other circumstances, they might have become. But they endured and, almost immediately after the deaths of their parents, they reconciled and reunited. They are, in my mind, all four of them, unutterably beautiful and heroic. *The Mystery of Right and Wrong* is my attempt to do justice to their beauty and their strength. It is a wonderful, terrible miracle of womanhood that there are millions more like them.

Acknowledgements

Patience and brilliance do not often go hand in hand, but my editor, Anne Collins, is gifted with both. I owe to her an unrepayable debt that grows with every book I write. My deepest thanks to her, this book's first reader, and the first person to whom I told the true story that inspired it. Thank you, as well, to my agent, Jackie Kaiser, who, after hours one wet November afternoon, unlocked the door and let me in, and to my long-time friends at Penguin Random House Canada, who never *knew* until they read, because I could not bring myself to tell them face to face: Kristin Cochrane, Marion Garner, Scott Sellers, Louise Dennys, Diane Martin and the late Ellen Seligman. Many others, too numerous to record, loaned me their own memories and knowledge of Cape Town, Amsterdam and St. John's. I am not an expert on any of those places, only on what happened in them to me and to the scores of women whose lives and deaths inspired this book.

WAYNE JOHNSTON was born and raised in Goulds, Newfoundland. Widely acclaimed for his magical weaving of fact and fiction, his masterful plotting, and his gift for both description and character, his #1 nationally bestselling novels include *The Divine Ryans, A World Elsewhere, The Custodian of Paradise, The Navigator of New York*, and *The Colony of Unrequited Dreams.* His first book, *The Story of Bobby O'Malley*, published when he was just twenty-six years old, won the WH Smith/Books in Canada First Novel Award. *Baltimore's Mansion*, a memoir about his father and grandfather, won the inaugural Charles Taylor Prize for Literary Non-Fiction. *The Colony of Unrequited Dreams*, published in 1998, was nominated for sixteen national and international awards including the Scotiabank Giller Prize and the Governor General's Literary Award for Fiction, and was a Canada Reads finalist defended by Justin Trudeau. A theatrical adaptation of the novel recently toured Canada. Johnston's recent novels, *First Snow, Last Light* and *The Mystery of Right and Wrong*, were both national bestsellers.

www.waynejohnston.ca